KATE THOMPSON

That Gallagher Girl

AVON

AVON

A division of HarperCollins*Publishers*
77–85 Fulham Palace Road,
London W6 8JB

www.harpercollins.co.uk

1

Copyright © Kate Thompson 2010

Kate Thompson asserts the moral right to
be identified as the author of this work

A catalogue record for this book is
available from the British Library

ISBN-13: 978-1-84756-216-6

Set in Minion by Palimpsest Book Production Limited,
Falkirk, Stirlingshire

Printed and bound in Great Britain by
Clays Ltd, St Ives plc

Mixed Sources

Product group from well-managed
forests and other controlled sources
www.fsc.org Cert no. SW-COC-001806
© 1996 Forest Stewardship Council

FSC is a non-profit international organisation established
to promote the responsible management of the world's forests.
Products carrying the FSC label are independently certified
to assure consumers that they come from forests that are managed
to meet the social, economic and ecological needs
of present and future generations.

Find out more about HarperCollins and the environment at
www.harpercollins.co.uk/green

THAT GALLAGHER GIRL

Kate Thompson is an award-winning former actress. She is happily married with one daughter, and divides her time between Dublin and the West of Ireland, where she swims off some of the most beautiful beaches in the world.

For more information about Kate, please go to www.kate-thompson.com.

By the same author
The Kinsella Sisters
The O'Hara Affair

For Malcolm and Clara

I am not a friend, and I am not a servant. I am the Cat who walks by herself, and I wish to come into your house.
                                    After Rudyard Kipling

Prologue

On the morning of her seventeenth birthday, Cat Gallagher learned how to break into a house. It was fourth on the list of ten things she wanted to accomplish before she was twenty-one. The first three things she had already achieved. She had learned how to sail single-handed, how to play a winning hand at poker, and how to paint with a seagull's feather. She had also learned to conquer fear – although that particular lesson wasn't itemised on Cat's list of things to learn, for she had always been fearless. Apart, that is, from her fear of needles.

The house in question was a showcase that had never been lived in. It was the product of a former economy, a ghost house boasting brickwork so symmetrical and a roof so streamlined it appeared incongruous next to the unfinished structures that surrounded it, their foundations mapping what was to have been an exclusive development of half-a-dozen luxury dwellings. Those houses would never be finished now. The showhouse stood alone and resplendent on a building site that was being reclaimed by bindweed, buddleia and feral cats.

Cat and her half-brother Raoul were sitting on a low wall, sharing a bottle of wine. It had a posh French name and a picture of a French château on the label, but Cat hadn't paid for it. She'd nicked it from her dad's collection of vintage Burgundy, along with a second bottle from his collection of vintage Bordeaux.

'Cheers,' said Raoul, touching his paper cup to hers. 'Happy birthday, Cat.'

'Cheers.'

'I hope you didn't expect a present.'

'Are you mad? You're as broke as I am,' said Cat. 'Anyway, isn't teaching me the art of breaking and entering more valuable than any old giftwrapped crap? Passing on skills is the new birthday present.'

Raoul was ten years older than Cat. He was a student of architecture at Galway University, and had always indulged his little sister. He had been responsible for teaching her to row a boat and fix a bike chain and skip stones, and now he was mentoring her in the art of housebreaking. Their father, Hugo, had never mentored her in anything much, apart from how to tell the difference between a Burgundy and a Bordeaux.

Cat and Raoul both took after their father in looks. It was said that the Gallaghers were descended from shipwrecked survivors of the Armada, and that they had Spanish blood. Both Cat and Raoul were dark-haired and olive-skinned, with patrician noses and cheekbones like razor shells. Today, Cat's vaguely piratical appearance was enhanced by the fact that she sported a bandana, and a small gold hoop in one ear. Her eyes were heavily rimmed with black kohl, but that was her only concession to cosmetics. Cat had never used lipstick in her life, nor had she ever painted her nails or GHD'd her mane of black hair.

'I wonder what Hugo would say if he knew you were teaching me how to break into houses,' Cat remarked as Raoul upended the bottle into their paper cups before sticking it in his backpack.

4

'Being a champagne socialist, he'd applaud the fact that I'm encouraging you in the redistribution of wealth.'

'I told you, Raoul – I'm not doing this to steal stuff. I just need to know how to get into places.'

'Why, exactly?'

'I have a feeling in my bones that it's going to be useful some time. My bones tell me loads of things, and they're usually right.'

'When you become a fugitive from justice, you mean?'

'When I become a fugitive from our father, more like.'

'You'll let me know, won't you, when you decide to run away? I'll worry if you don't keep in touch.'

'You'll be the only person I'll tell,' she told him, kissing his cheek. 'You'll be the only person who'll worry.'

Cat drained her cup, then got up from the wall and stumbled sideways as her foot clipped the edge of a pothole and the earth crumbled beneath her boot. 'Yikes! Look at the size of that pothole. I wouldn't like to be negotiating this place at night.'

'Better get used to it. Good cat burglars – excuse the pun – need extrasensory night vision.'

'Let me say it again – I ain't in the business of burgling, Raoul.'

'Never say never.' Raoul took Cat's cup and drained his own before stowing them and the bottle in his backpack. 'Let's go recce,' he said.

Together they made their way along the path that led to the front door of the unoccupied house. It was fashioned from solid oak, and had an impenetrable air.

'Open, Sesame!' cried Cat. 'Bring on the breaking-and-entering master class, Raoul.'

Raoul gave the façade of the house the once-over. 'Okay. Your first challenge is to find out if a joint is wired for alarm.

5

You're safe with a place like this, because the security system has never been activated. You'd be amazed at how few holiday home owners on the west coast bother to set alarms while they're away.'

'Why don't they bother?'

'Too much hassle if they're activated by stormy weather. There are only so many times you can prevail upon your local neighbouring farmer to reset your alarm. A lot of those boxes are dummies, by the way.'

'So which houses are the most likely candidates?'

'Ones that haven't been lived in for a while.'

'How can you tell if they haven't been lived in?'

'Jemmy the mail box and have a look at the postmarks on the envelopes. The dates will tell you. If you find bills it's a bonus, because they're unlikely to have been paid. Unpaid Eircom Phone Watch bills mean that the joint's no longer being monitored.'

'Isn't there a battery backup on those systems?'

'If the bills haven't been paid, the Phone Watch people are under no obligation to let the home owner know that their batteries need replacing.'

Cat moved along the side of the house, and set her palms against a picture window, pressing her face close so that she could peer through. With the sun bouncing off the glass, it proved difficult, but she could make out an expanse of timber floor and walls painted in a bland shade of cappuccino.

'Why are people so careless about protecting their properties, Raoul?'

'It's a sign of the times. A decade ago people were reckless when they bought their second homes. All that money being thrown at them by the banks made them buy into an unsustainable lifestyle, and now they can't sell it on.' Raoul shaded his eyes with a hand, and squinted up at the roof, where a seagull was eyeing him suspiciously. 'The tax on second homes was a disaster for the property market on the west coast. The owners resent every penny they're obliged to spend on a place they can't afford to maintain, so they just don't bother their arses. They're not going to throw good money after bad – look at the state of this place.' He indicated the garden with an expansive gesture. 'Once upon a time the lawn would have been mowed every month to keep up the showhouse façade. It hasn't been done for a year, by the look of it.'

Cat turned and surveyed the quarter acre of garden. The grass was thigh-high, the flowerbeds thick with weeds. Dandelions were pushing their way up through the golden gravel that covered the path to the front door, and to judge by the wasp activity immediately overhead, a nest was being constructed in the eaves.

'Keep an eye out for unkempt gardens and "For Sale" signs,' Raoul told her. 'The properties that have been on the market for more than a year are the ones you want to target.'

'How can I tell how long they've been on the market?'

'Go to Daft.ie and see how much the price has dropped. The bigger the bargain, the more desperate the seller, and the further down the listing, the more obvious it is that nobody's been interested enough to view. These are generally the babies that have been languishing with no TLC.' Raoul gave her a shrewd look. 'Now, tell me. How do you think you're going to get in here?'

'Not through the front door, that's for sure.'

'Top marks. And not through the front window, neither. Let's have a look around the back.'

They made their way to the rear of the house, where the door to a utility room was located. A look through a small window to the left of the door told Cat that there was access to the kitchen from there. Pulling a pair of latex gloves from her pocket, she slid them on. 'Do I smash it?' she asked Raoul.

'Tch tch, Cat! How inelegant. Think again.'

'Cut the pane with a glass cutter?'

'No, darling. You'd need suction pads, you could cut yourself, and you don't want to leave samples of your DNA splashed around. Take a closer look.'

Cat ran a finger over the edge of the window. It was beaded with varnished teak, in which plugs of matching hardwood were dotted at regular intervals.

'What's underneath those?' she asked. 'They're camouflaging something, aren't they?'

'You could be right, Kitty Cat,' said Raoul. 'What do you think they might be camouflaging?'

Cat turned and gave him a speculative look. 'Nails?'

'Have a gander.'

Raoul reached into his backpack and handed her a narrow-bladed chisel. Inserting it into the fissure between the plug and the main body of the wood, Cat found purchase and prised out the fragment of teak. Underneath was the slotted crosshead of a screw. Setting to, she methodically removed each knot of wood, then set down the chisel.

'I guess I need a screwdriver now,' she said, pushing an unruly strand of hair behind her ear. 'But a regular one won't do the job. The screws are too close to the glass.'

'That,' said Raoul, 'is why I have one of these.' Reaching into his backpack again, he produced a Z-shaped tool and handed it to Cat.

'A right-angled screwdriver?'

'Go to the top of the class. I'm not going to help you, by the way. You're going to have to learn how to do this on your own.'

'Why did they fit the screws on the outside of the window?' she asked, taking the screwdriver from Raoul and inserting the bit in the crosshead of the first screw. 'It would make a lot more sense to fit them inside.'

'You're inviting serious problems if you fit them on the inside. The rain streams in.'

Cat smiled. 'This is so simple, it's stupid.' She started to unscrew the beading from the glass panel, frowning a little in concentration as she manipulated the bit. Once she got to the final couple of screws, she held the window in place by leaning her shoulder against it. Then she prised away the strip of wood, dropped the screwdriver, and went to lift the glass from its frame.

'Wait,' said Raoul. 'You'll need proper gloves for this. Here.'

Taking care not to let the glass fall, Cat slipped her hands into first the right, then the left glove, and turned back to her task.

'Voilà!' she said, as the double-glazed panel came away. 'Access all areas!'

With great care, she leaned the pane against the exterior wall before setting her palms on the sill and hoisting herself up.

'Wait!' said Raoul. 'Take your boots off. You don't want to leave footprints.'

Cat undid the laces on her boots, pulled them off and dropped them on the muddy ground below the window. Then she twisted around, slid her legs through the empty frame, and eeled herself into the house.

'How easy was that!' she crowed, and her words came back to her, bouncing off the smooth plaster walls of the house that would never be sold, never be lived in. 'Come and have a look, Raoul.'

He followed her through.

Both utility room and kitchen were equipped with state-of-the-art white goods. The kitchen floor was marble, the work surfaces polished granite. The adjacent sitting room boasted a gas fire and a panelled alcove in which to house a plasma screen. Beyond the sitting room, beyond doorways that accessed study, den and conservatory, carpeted stairs led from the light-filled lobby to bedrooms and bathrooms above. Upstairs, the walk-in wardrobe in the master bedroom was nearly as big as Cat's room in Hugo's house.

She wondered what it must be like to live in a house like this. Would you live a life here, or a lifestyle? Would you curl your feet up on a suede upholstered sofa while aiming a remote at your entertainment suite? Would you microwave a ready meal from a top end outlet while uncorking a chilled bottle of Sauvignon Blanc? Would you cuff an infant lovingly when he or she trotted mud onto your marble tiles before reaching for your eco-friendly floor wipes?

Hugo's house was so very different. Hugo's house stood all alone in the middle of a forest, and was like something out of a Grimm's fairytale. It was dark and tumbledown with a cruck frame and exposed beams and a roof that slumped in the middle. Having settled comfortably into its foundations over the course of three hundred years, Hugo's house listed to starboard, and had crooked windows and wonky stairs and worn flagstones. Hugo had refused to compromise the character of his house by introducing twenty-first century fixtures and fittings: his fridge was clad in elm planks, he cooked (when he could be bothered to) on an ancient Rayburn. There was no television, no broadband and no power shower. People described Hugo's house as 'quaint'. But they didn't have to live there. Cat had never been able to call Hugo's house home.

She had returned there when she was fourteen, after her

mother – Hugo's second wife – had died of uterine cancer. Paloma had left Hugo and the Crooked House some years previously, taking Cat with her to Dublin, where they had lived until Paloma's untimely death. Back on the west coast, the teenage Cat, bereaved and isolated, had found it impossible to make friends. Her accent singled her out as being different – that and the fact that her eccentric father was now living with his third wife.

Cat hated school. Hugo had tried the boarding option, but she just kept absconding, and running away to Raoul's bedsit in Galway. When she was expelled from boarding school, she mitched from the local secondary so often that Hugo made a pledge to the authorities to home-school his daughter. But Cat shrugged off his half-hearted attempts. How could you have faith in a teacher who sloshed brandy into his morning coffee and smoked roll-ups while he recited Shakespeare and Seamus Heaney in maudlin tones? The answer was – in Cat's case – you didn't. You gave him the finger, and went off in search of boats to sail, or cloudscapes to paint, or – the very activity she was presently engaged in – houses to break into.

And neither the authorities nor her father seemed to give a shit.

Cat strolled across the pristine oatmeal carpet of the showhome's master bedroom to a big dormer window that looked out over the building site. How many houses like this might there be all over Ireland languishing unfinished, waiting for someone to occupy them? She reckoned she could have her pick of thousands. To the east, inland, ribbon developments straggled Dublin-ward along the sides of the roads. To the south, the landscape was dotted with unoccupied holiday homes. To the west, an expanse of ocean glittered diamantine.

'Look, Raoul!' she said, turning to him as he followed her through the door. 'You can see the cemetery on Inishcaillín from here.'

Inishcaillín was where Cat's mother, Paloma, had been buried. The cemetry was on the summit of a drowned drumlin, and Cat would occasionally take a boat out to spend a day on the island, talking to her mother, undisturbed by anyone since the island was uninhabited now. Paloma's grave was surrounded by dozens of graves of victims of the Irish famine, all with their headstones facing west towards the Atlantic, that they might see in the setting sun the ghosts of all those loved ones who had fled Ireland for America a century and a half ago. It was a desolate place, whipped by raging gales that came in from the ocean, but it had been a place that Paloma had loved like no other, and that was why Cat had insisted she be buried there. When she was a little girl, she and her mother used to take picnics over to the island, and swim in the more sheltered of the easterly coves. They'd explored the abandoned village, too, making up stories about the people who used to live there, and had once even pitched a tent and stayed overnight in one of the roofless cottages.

'Do you miss her still?' asked Raoul.

Cat turned to him. 'Of course I do. But I hate her too, in a way, for leaving me alone with that bastard and his whore.' She saw Raoul raise an eyebrow. 'What's up?' she demanded. 'You know how I feel about them.'

'Cat, Cat, you drama queen,' he chided. 'Sometimes you talk like something out of Shakespeare.'

'That bastard and his ho, then,' she returned, pettishly. 'Let's open the other bottle. I feel like getting drunk.'

Cat had never been able to call her stepmother by her given name. Although Ophelia had been Mrs Gallagher for five years, Cat refused to acknowledge her and had gleefully shortened her name to 'Oaf'. Stepmother and stepdaughter were barely civil to each other now.

Raoul took the second bottle of wine from his backpack, and started to strip away the foil from the neck. 'You're seventeen now, Cat,' he pointed out. 'Legally speaking, you could leave home, with our father's permission.'

'Sure, he'd give it in a heartbeat.' Cat leaned against the wall, and slid down until she was sitting on the carpet.

'Well, then?'

'Don't think I haven't thought about it. But where would I go – and *don't* tell me I can move in with you because there's no way I'm gonna cramp your style with the ladies.' Raoul inserted the corkscrew and pulled the cork, and Cat smiled up at him. 'I'll never forget how pissed off your girlfriends used to look every time I escaped from the boarding school of doom and landed on your doorstep.'

Raoul laughed. 'It *was* a little bizarre. Remember the night you sleepwalked your way into bed with me and . . . what was her name? It was some hippy-dippy thing.'

'Windsong. I could never keep my face straight when I talked to her. Windsong *hated* me.'

Raoul poured wine, then handed Cat a cup and sat down beside her. 'So let's have a serious think about this. You can't move in with me, and you can't afford to rent anywhere.'

'You're right. There's no way I could afford to live on my allowance. And I can't live without it. It's a catch-22. I may despise our dad, but he doles out the dosh.'

'And he's not going to cut you off, kid. If you do move out, get him to lodge money in your bank account.'

'I don't have a bank account.'

'Not even a savings account?'

'No, and I can't open a current account until I'm eighteen.'

'Get him to send you postal orders.'

13

Cat gave him a sceptical look. 'To where? Cat Gallagher, no fixed abode?'

'It's dead simple. I used to do it all the time when I was travelling. You set up a poste restante in the local post office, and pick up your mail there.'

Cat made a face. 'Maybe I should get a job.'

'Maybe you should.'

'Ha! Let's face it, Raoul – I'm unemployable.'

'Don't be defeatist, sweetheart. And, hang on . . . I think . . . I *think* . . .'

'Share. I hate enigmatic pauses.' Cat took a hit of her wine.

'I think I might be having a very good idea.' Raoul gave her a speculative look. 'How would you feel about living on a houseboat, Kitty Cat?'

'A houseboat! Wicked! Tell me about it.'

'I have a friend who has one in Coolnamara. He could do with someone to caretake it for him.'

'Are you serious?'

'Yes. His wife's in a wheelchair, and they can't live on a boat any more. Can't sell it, either. And he doesn't want it to rot away on the water.'

'Where is it?'

'It's on a stretch of canal near Lissamore, the one that goes from nowhere to nowhere.'

'Nowhere to nowhere?'

'It was one of those pointless famine relief projects, designed to give the starving locals the wherewithal to buy a few grains of Indian corn back in the 1840s. As far as I know, it was never used for anything. But my mate Aidan had his houseboat transported and plonked down in a safe berth. He hasn't visited it for over a year now, and he'd love it to be given some TLC. He couldn't pay you, but I'm pretty sure he'd let you live there rent-free.'

'Oh, Raoul! I'd love to live on a houseboat!'

'I'll see what I can do.' Raoul picked up the wine bottle. 'Here. Have some more Château Whatever.'

Raoul was as good as his word. Straightaway, he put in a call to his mate Aidan, and sorted Cat out with her brand new home from the place she couldn't call home. And by the time they'd finished the bottle and left the house the way they'd come in and hit the main road, Cat was feeling buoyant and full of hope.

'Bye, Raoul,' she said, as the twice-weekly bus to Galway appeared over the brow of the hill, and drew up by the turn-off to Hugo's house. 'You are my fairy half-brother.'

'Less of the fairy, thanks. I'll be in touch.'

Cat hugged Raoul the way she never hugged anybody else, and watched him board the bus.

'Here,' he said, taking something from his backpack and tossing it to her. 'You may need this.' He gave her a final salute, then the bus door slid shut and he was gone.

In her hand, Cat was clutching the screwdriver she'd used to gain access to the showhouse. She smiled, and turned towards the path that would take her to the house in the forest, the house that she hoped soon to leave. As she passed through the gate and rounded the first bend, a voice from behind her hissed: 'Cat! Cat! Here, Kitty Cat!'

She swung round as they emerged from the trees. There were three of them. They were wearing stocking masks and stupid grins. One said, 'A little bird told me it was your birthday, Kitty Cat. Come here to us now, like a good girl, and let us give you your birthday present.'

Without pausing for thought, Cat aimed the first kick.

Chapter One

Río Kinsella thought that she had never seen an uglier building. Constructed from precast concrete, it was veined with fissures and topped with a corrugated roof of some leprous-looking material. The grey steel shutters clamped over the doors and windows lent it a hostile expression. On the forecourt, dandelions clumped, and amorphous masses of machinery lay rusting. The place would make an ideal location for one of those murky Scandinavian thrillers.

Reaching into the pocket of her jacket, she extracted an email printout.

Río – finally found what I've been looking for! It's a working oyster farm – OK, I know that hardly fits my boyhood dream of becoming a fisherman, but it's the next best thing! Might you have a gander at it for me? It's a mile or so along the beach from the Villa Felicity – or whatever the place is called now – you probably know it? The guy who sold it to me is from Kerry, and inherited it from his uncle. There's a cottage with it – he said he'd leave the key in O'Toole's so you could check it out. (I've a feeling it might be in need of

your interior design skills!) I'm very excited by this
– it's come up at just the right time!
Your friend, Adair.
PS: Will be bringing you back a present from
Dubai – can't say I'll be sorry to leave!

Oh, God. There was something so boyish, so affecting about all those exclamation marks!

Río folded the printout and slid it back into her pocket, then turned in the direction of the path that would take her from the packing shed to the cottage. It wasn't a cottage by definition, she knew – more a bog-standard bungalow. But hey – any single-storey dwelling on the west coast of Ireland called itself a cottage these days. The word 'cottage' had cosier connotations than 'bungalow', and stood a better chance of attracting the attention of potential buyers. The fact that this property came with an oyster farm attached, however, meant that offers were unlikely to be forthcoming. Who would be crazy enough to buy an oyster farm in the current economic climate? She wondered how much Adair had paid for it. She wondered if he had been suckered.

Adair Bolger was a shrewd businessman – there was no doubt about that. Or he had been. During the reign of the rampant Celtic Tiger he had bought and sold and prospered with the most pugnacious of Ireland's property barons. He had made headlines in the finance sections of the broadsheets, and in the gossip columns of the glossies. But when it came to his personal affairs, Adair was purblind. He had spent millions building a holiday home for his (now ex-) wife Felicity during the boom years, but sold it for a bargain-basement price when the market imploded. He had acquired a pair of penthouses in Dublin's docklands as *pieds-à-terre* for himself and his daughter (plus a couple more as

17

investments), but these castles in the air were now languishing unoccupied and unsellable. He had escaped to Dubai to regroup just as the tentacles of economic malaise had started to besmirch the gleaming canopy of the world's construction capital. Like hundreds of other Irish Icaruses, Adair Bolger had flown too high, had his wings scorched, and plummeted back down to earth. As he would put it himself, he was bollixed.

And now Adair wanted Río to help him realise his dream of downshifting, and living off the fat of the land or – to be more accurate – the fruits of the sea. An oyster farm, for feck's sake! Did he have a clue what oyster farming involved? Did he know that it was backbreaking, knucklegrazing work, work that had to be carried out in all seasons and in all weather conditions – mostly inclement because of the 'R' in the month thing? Did he know that demand for oysters had plummeted since recession had struck? Or that oyster farms on the coasts of all four provinces of Ireland were foreclosing, their owners emigrating? Río pictured the lucky Kerryman who'd sold Adair the property chortling up his sleeve like a pantomime villain, and rubbing his hands with glee as he cashed Adair's cheque.

The cottage and its outbuildings were hidden away in a quiet estuary of Coolnamara Bay. The man who had owned the farm had been a loner known as Madser, who had stock-piled junk and bred fighting dogs. On the rare occasions he sallied forth into Lissamore village, it was astride the ancient Massey Ferguson that he used to tow his shellfish to his packing shed, exhaust fumes spewing into the clean Coolnamara air and settling on the produce heaped on the trailer behind him. Locals used to joke that Madser's were the only diesel-smoked oysters in the world.

Today was the first time that Río had ventured beyond

18

the sign that read 'Trespasers Prosecuted' since the days when, as a child, she had routinely flouted Madser's misspelt warning. In those days, the local kids scored points for bravado every time they crawled under the barbed-wire fence that surrounded the property, daring one another to venture further and further up the lane until the barking of Madser's dogs became so frenzied that even the bravest of them had turned tail and fled. The dogs – or the descendants of those dogs – had been put down, Río had learned, when their master died.

Their legacy lived on in the form of the denuded meat bones that strewed the backyard of the house. Sweet Jesus, this was a cheerless place! Surely Adair had seen photographs of it online and read the implausible sales blurb? No amount of Photoshopping could disguise its intrinsic ugliness, no estate agent's spiel convince that this property didn't come with a big 'BUYER BEWARE!' sticker on it. Río wondered for the umpteenth time what had possessed him to buy it.

Skirting a pile of rusty bicycle parts, she negotiated the mud track that led to the back door, glad that she was wearing her wellies. She didn't need the key, she realised, as she went to insert it in the lock: the door was ajar. Oh, God. This was the bit in the horror film, the bit where you peek through your fingers and tell the stupid girl not to go in there, the bit where you get ready to jump.

Río nudged the door with her foot. It swung open with a spooky sound-effect creak.

But once she stepped through the porch into the living space, she breathed easy. There were no *Silence of the Lambs* sewing machines lined up to greet her, no Texas chainsaws caked in gore. Instead, she found herself in a room with a view.

Adair had told her once that, in his fantasy life as a

fisherman, he didn't care where he lived as long as the house in question had a view. Beyond the grimy picture window that stretched the length of the ground floor, this place had a vista to die for. The sea was just yards away from the front doorstep: all that separated the house from the wavelets lapping against the shingle was a swatch of overgrown lawn. Beyond the grassy incline, a jetty projected into the estuary, a red and blue rowing boat hitched to one of its stone bollards. As Río watched, a gull perched on the furthermost bollard lifted itself into the air and wheeled away towards Inishclare island, over which the vestiges of a double rainbow glimmered. Squalling seagulls and turbulence in the water to the west spoke of mackerel activity; a trail of bubbles told her an otter was on its way. Presiding over all, like a benefi-cent deity enthroned upon the horizon, a purple mountain slumbered, swathed in a shawl of cobwebby cloud.

Río drew her phone from the pocket of her jacket and accessed her list of contacts. *Looks like you got yourself a crib with a view – but not a lot else, mr bolger*, she texted, then paused as, from somewhere further along the estuary, came the aggrieved squawk of a heron. She turned and saw it flap past the east-facing window on the far side of the room – a bog-standard timber-framed casement. The glass was broken, Río noticed as she moved towards it, and the sill littered with dead bluebottles. Brushing them to the floor with the corner of a filthy net half-curtain, she leaned her elbows on the ledge. No wonder this window had been obscured with net, she thought, as she surveyed the dismal aspect. If the view were a drawing and she had an eraser handy, she'd have rubbed it out, for Madser's junkyard was emphatically not the stuff of picture postcards – unless you were a Britart aficionado.

Turning back towards the main room, Rio decided that the junkyard inside the house was nearly as bad. The floor was littered with detritus: bottles, cans, cigarette butts, plastic bags, cardboard cartons, old newspapers. The head-line of a yellowed *National Enquirer* screamed up at her, and she remembered with a smile how she had once made it into the pages of the *Enquirer*, whose gushing prose had described her as a 'flame-haired Irish colleen and erstwhile lover of Hollywood heart-throb Shane Byrne'. Her relation-ship with Shane had been bigged up as a 'tempestuous affair'; their son, Finn, had become a 'love child', and it was hinted that the only reason Shane had never married was because he was still 'smitten' with the 'first and only true love of his life.'

How funny to think that people reading it may have imagined some *uber*-romantic *Wuthering Heights* scenario with the pair of them pining in perpetuity for each other, when in reality Shane and Río Skyped at least once a week, swapped photographs of Finn on a regular basis, and were forever sending each other links to daft stuff on YouTube.

She was on her way across the room towards the staircase when her phone sounded. Adair.

'Hey, Río!' came his cheerful voice through her earpiece. 'What do you think?'

'I think you're mad,' said Río. 'It's like something out of *Slumdog Millionaire*, except you're not even a millionaire any more. Are you seriously thinking of living here?'

'I'm not thinking, Río. It's a done deal.'

'Jesus, Adair. The place is a mess.'

'What do I care? I've got my view, I've got my oyster beds.'

'You've got rats.' In her peripheral vision, Río registered a furry something scurrying along the skirting board.

'I'll get a cat.'

'You've got birds, too,' she said, looking up. 'There's a swallows' nest in the stairwell. That's meant to be lucky.'

21

'Then I won't get a cat.'

'You'll have to get used to living with bird shit, so.'

'Beats living with bullshit. There's been too much of that in my life lately.'

As Río laid a hand on the white-spattered banister, a feather spiralled from the ceiling. She guessed the birds had found a way in under the eaves. Gaping eaves, broken windows, unlocked doors – the place might as well have been flying a welcome banner for a come-all-ye. 'Shall I give you a guided tour, Mr Bolger?' she asked.

'You're there now?'

'Yes.'

'Thanks, Río. It's good of you to check the joint out for me.'

'I'm curious. This was the bogeyman's house when I was a kid. I've never been down this way before.'

'You might send me some pictures. I'm not sure the ones on the internet do it justice. What's that noise?'

'A cider can. I just kicked it out of the way.'

Río felt another flash of unease as the can clattered down the staircase. Who might have been here before her? Might she have company, apart from Ratty and his feathered friends? She was glad that Adair had phoned, glad his voice was in her ear. She tightened her grip on her Nokia as she climbed up to the first floor, avoiding any dodgy-looking steps. She didn't want to end up stuck here on her own with a broken ankle.

'I'm upstairs, now,' she told him, looking around. Above her, a mouldering raffia lampshade dangled from an empty Bakelite socket, to her right a beaded curtain obscured the entrance to what she guessed was the bathroom. Across the landing, a door hung off its hinges. She passed through into a long, low-ceilinged room that smelled of damp. 'I suppose this is the master bedroom.'

'It's the only bedroom.'

'The only one, Adair? What'll you do when Izzy comes to stay?'

'I'll put her in the mobile home.'

'What mobile home?'

'I'm not hanging around waiting for the boys in the planning department to sneer at any ideas I might come up with for a refurbishment project, Río. I'm not going to give them the satisfaction of binning my applications, or giving me the runaround. I don't need planning permission for a mobile, so I'm going to put one out back, and live there while I work on the place.'

'You're going to do the graft yourself?'

'I am. Didn't I start my career as a builder? A bloody crack one, too. I'm the only person I could trust to get the job done properly.'

Río guessed he was right. She had no problem picturing Adair getting his hands dirty, navvying by day and dossing down in a mobile home by night. But the notion of Princess Isabella – his beloved only child – slumming it in a caravan made her want to laugh out loud.

'Won't you feel claustrophobic, Adair, cooped up in a mobile home after all those years living in villas and penthouses and hotel suites and what-have-yous?'

'Sure, it'll only be for a short time. Tell us, what's the view from the bedroom window like?'

'Um. There isn't one.'

'What do you mean? The blurb said there was a view from upstairs, too.'

'The roof slopes down too far. There's no space for a picture window to the front.'

'There's no window at all?'

'Well, yeah. There's a kind of dwarf-sized dormer . . .'

23

'And that's *it?*' Adair sounded incandescent with indignation.

'Well, no. There's a bigger one in the gable end wall. Hang on a sec.'

Río moved to the other side of the room. Like its counterpart downstairs, this casement would overlook the junkyard: the view would be crap. Unless, that is, her eyes were deceiving her . . .

Instead of a junkyard, what she saw was a marine-blue inlet all a-glimmer in the low-slung sun. Fringed by a stretch of footprint-free sand, this was Coolnamara Bay *au naturel*, before man had left his mark on the shoreline. But it wasn't real. The view that lay before her was an imaginary one. It had been painted by a visionary's hand directly on to a canvas nailed to the window frame.

She let out a low whistle. 'Well. I didn't know that Madser had talent in the art department.' Taking a step forward, Río narrowed her eyes and gave the painting the once-over. In the bottom left-hand corner, a girl was depicted crouching by a rock pool, gazing intently at a red-spotted flatfish that lay half-buried in the sand. The girl was naked, striped all over like a brindled cat, and her lips were pulled back to show feral, pointed teeth. In the bottom right-hand corner was a tiny, barely recognisable signature. She made out just three letters: 'C A T'.

'No,' she murmured. 'Not Madser. Not a man. A woman was responsible for this.'

'What are you on about, Río?' asked Adair.

'Someone's left you a painting.'

'A painting?'

'Yeah. It's not bad. In fact, I think I might be jealous.' Río took another squint. 'It's better than any of the stuff I've done recently.'

'Nonsense. Your paintings are wonderful,' returned Adair, loyally.

'I'll take a picture of it, shall I? Send you the evidence.' Río checked the battery level on her phone.

'Is there a signature?'

'Yeah. Banksy. Joke.' Río leaned a little closer, wishing the light was better: the texture of the paint told her it was acrylic. 'Talking of paintings, did I see that your Paul Henry seascape was up for sale?'

'How did you know that?'

'There was a description of a Paul Henry in the *Irish Times* auction preview a couple of weeks ago: it sounded a lot like yours.'

'It is – was – mine.'

'D'you mind me asking what you got for it?' Río traced the raw edge of the canvas with a forefinger. It came away dust-free.

'I got many thousand euros less than it was worth, Río *a grá*.'

'Why did you sell it?'

'Why do you think? I need a roof over my head more than I need a picture by a famous dead bloke.'

'Did it cover the cost of your mobile home?' she asked, taking a step backward, and putting her head on one side. How long had this painting been here?

'No. The le Brocquy portrait did that. The Paul Henry went towards Izzy's wedding fund.'

'Izzy's getting married?' Río was astonished.

'No, no. She's no plans to get married. But she will one day, and I'm damned if my girl won't get the most lavish wedding money can buy. The fact that her dad's on his uppers isn't going to get in the way of that. Oh – hang on a sec, Río – I just gotta sign something here . . .'

A deferential murmuring could be heard in the background. Río turned away from the painting and strolled across the room to where the minuscule dormer window afforded a peek of the butt-end of Inishclare island. She imagined Adair in Dubai surrounded by flunkeys, signing documents with a Montblanc pen. Hunkering down, she thought about what he had just said. On his uppers . . . How weird! Just a couple of years ago Río would never have dreamed that Adair Bolger would wind up broke. He'd been a ringmaster at the Celtic Tiger circus, a major beneficiary of the boom. Back in those days his weekend retreat, the Villa Felicity, had been an ostentatious pleasure palace for his gold-plated trophy wife, who had swanned about the joint as if it were her very own Petit Trianon. She remembered the guided tour Adair had given her of the swimming pool and the entertainment suite and the hideous yoga pavilion, and how she had curled her lip at the unseemly extravagance of it all. She remembered how he had hoped to indulge his daughter's dreams of renaming the joint *An Ghorm Mhór* – The Big Blue – and turning it into a five-star PADI scuba-dive resort; how he had held on tight to that dream for Izzy's sake, even when he could no longer afford to. But he hadn't been able to hold on for long. Now this monument to the excesses of the Celtic Tiger era was lying empty a mile down the shoreline, waiting for its new owner to claim it. The new owner – whoever he or she might be – was clearly in no hurry. The shutters of the Villa Felicity had not been raised in over two years.

Río got to her feet and stretched. Then she reached into her backpack and rummaged for her cosmetics purse. Her nose had got sunburned yesterday and was peeling. Peering into the cracked mirror on the flap of the purse, she rubbed a little Vitamin E cream on her nose, and then on her lips.

Her freckles were worse than ever this year – although you couldn't really see them in the fractured glass. Maybe she should use this mirror more often? If she couldn't see her freckles, that meant that she wouldn't be able to see the fine lines around her eyes, the strands of silver creeping into her mass of tawny hair, the brows that needed shaping, the occasional blemish that needed concealing, the . . .

'There, done and dusted,' said Adair, back on the phone to her. 'I've just signed away my condo in the Burj Khalifa.'

Something told Río that, despite the jocularity of his tone, he wasn't being facetious. 'Are you really on your uppers, Adair?' she asked.

'Pretty well,' he acknowledged, cheerfully.

'You don't sound too put out about it.'

'You know me, Río. As long as my girl's happy, I'm happy. And she's doing OK.'

'What's Izzy up to?'

'She's got herself a grand job in marketing. How's Finn?'

'His father got him work as a stunt double on his latest blockbuster.'

'Cool.'

'I guess. But LA doesn't suit him. He's making noises about going travelling again.'

Travelling solo, Río supposed, since – as far as she knew – her son had not had a significant other in his life since he and Adair's daughter had gone their separate ways. When Finn and Izzy had first become an item, their Facebook albums had featured the kind of pictures that had made Río smile every time she browsed through them. Most of them showed the dynamic duo at work and at play as they back-packed around the world: Finn at the helm of a RIB, Izzy hosing down scuba gear; Finn signing logbooks, Izzy poring over dive plans. The pair of them together, swimming with manta rays, dancing on beaches, perched on barstools and swinging off bungee cords. The loveliest one of all (Río had printed it out) showed them lounging in a hammock, wrapped in each other's arms.

And then, once Izzy had made the decision to embark upon a real-life career, her Facebook albums had reflected this U-turn. The backgrounds of sand, sea and sky had been replaced by vistas of gleaming steel and glass edifices in front of which a well-heeled Izzy posed with the élan of Condoleezza Rice, briefcase in one hand, iPhone in the other. Finn's pictures, by contrast, continued to show him coasting in his own groove – surfing the shallows, skimming the reefs and diving the depths off islands from Bali to Bora Bora.

There was a silence, during which, Río knew, Adair did not want to talk about Izzy and Finn any more than she did. It was like a bittersweet romcom, she guessed, or an Alan Ayckbourn play. It was – well . . . complicated.

'How's my old gaff doing?' Adair asked, finally. 'Is there anyone living there?'

'No.'

'Still no idea who bought it?'

'Not a clue. If somebody doesn't lay claim to it soon it'll go feral, like this place. It's already overgrown with creeper.'

'You once told me that if you trained creeper up the walls of a house it gave it a loved look.'

'There's a difference between cultivating creeper and allowing weed to grow rampant, Adair.'

Adair sighed, then gave an unexpected, robust laugh. 'What a fucking colossal waste of money that house was! It's funny to think that I'll be living just a mile down the shore from that great white elephant, Río, isn't it? That stupid feckin' albatross of a Taj Mahal that—' A blip came over the line, and, before Río could remark on his mixed metaphors:

'Shite and onions!' he growled. 'Incoming call, Río, from a man I have to see about a dog. Thanks for the recce.'

'I'll send pictures. I hope they put you off.'

'Nothing's going to put me off, Ms Kinsella. Bring on that wheelbarrow.'

'Wheelbarrow?'

'For my cockles and mussels, alive alive-o.'

'*Slán*, Adair.'

Río looked thoughtful as she ended the call. Adair was making a huge mistake – sure, didn't the dogs in the street know that? But there was no talking to him because he simply wouldn't listen. She had quizzed Seamus Moynihan, a local boatman, about the pros and cons of oyster farming, and asked him to put his thoughts in an email to her so that she could pass them on to Adair. The bulk of the email outlined the cons. As far as Seamus was concerned there were fuck all pros: in his opinion the phrase 'the world's your oyster' was more of a curse than a compliment. Upon forwarding the email, Río had received a typically sanguine response. Adair was like Tom Hanks in *Forrest Gump*, she decided, fixated on his Bubba Gump Shrimp Company . . . except farming oysters on the wild West coast of Ireland had to be a hell of a lot more challenging than shrimp fishing in the southern United States.

What the hell. Mr Bolger was a grown man – he could do as he pleased and suffer the consequences. Río stuffed her phone back in her pocket, and resumed her inspection of the canvas nailed over the window.

It was a naughty little siren of a painting. It had a naïve, dreamlike quality that reminded her of one of Rousseau's jungle fantasies – especially when the eye wandered to that small, unexpected feral creature in the bottom left-hand corner. A ray of sun filtering through the glass set it aglow suddenly, lending it the jewel-like appearance of a mosaic. Río wanted it. Picking up a shard of slate from the floor, she used it to prise away the nails fixing the painting to the window frame. Then she rolled up the canvas and tucked it inside her jacket. She wasn't stealing, she told herself. She was safeguarding the painting for Adair. If she left it where it was, it would soon be destroyed by the damp sea air that seeped in through the bockety casement.

The damp was infiltrating her bones, now – she wanted to get back outside to where the sun was pushing its way through raggedy cloud, dispersing rainbows. She made a last, quick tour of the house upstairs and down, snapping a dozen or so photographs that she could attach to an email and send to Adair as evidence of his idiocy. In the kitchen, she even took a couple of shots of the empty whiskey bottles littering the room – proof of how old Madser had been driven to drink, and a premonition of the fate that might befall the new owner. But as she went to leave by the back door, she looked over her shoulder at the picture window beyond which the light bounced straight off the sea into the living space, and she knew that Adair Bolger – whose glass was always half-full – would somehow find a way to be happy in this house.

Chapter Two

Cat was lying in a sun trap on the flat roof of the house. She'd soaked every single item of clothing she possessed in the oversized bath, she'd soaped herself from head to toe in the blue marble wet room before towelling herself dry with her scrap of microfibre towel, and now – damp hair spread out around her like a nimbus – she was allowing the midday sun to do the rest of the work. Above her, gulls were wheeling in a hypnotic spiral, reminding her of the whirligig seeds that used to drop from the branches of the sycamore tree her mother had planted in the garden of the Crooked House, her childhood home. How different two houses could be! This house was all steel and glass and acute angles: the Crooked House was all ramshackle and bockety and – well – crooked.

Slap-bang in the middle of a forest, overlooking a lake, the Crooked House could have been a magical place for a child to grow up. Cat remembered children coming to visit, the sons and daughters of her parents' friends all bubbling with excitement as they explored the secret rooms and winding passageways within its walls, the bosky tunnels and hidey-holes without. The jewel in the crown – the treat that Cat liked to delay showing off to new friends until the very end of her guided tour – was the treehouse.

Cat's mum Paloma had built the house in an ancient cypress tree, when Cat was seven. It had been a surprise for her birthday that year, and Cat had never had a better birthday present, before or since. The flat-pack playhouses and designer dens of other children seemed mundane in comparison.

The floor of Cat's eyrie was a wooden platform, the walls constructed from something her mother told her was called 'osier', a type of bendy willow used in wickerwork. With the help of Raoul, Paloma had woven the osier into a beehive shape, then covered it in waterproof camouflage material and tacked on masses of branches and foliage. There was a rope ladder that could be drawn up against intruders, and a basket on a pulley that could be lowered and filled with provisions. There was a window with a raffia blind from which vantage point Cat could spy on the coming and goings of foxes and badgers, and a cupboard for her books and art materials. The house was practically invisible, especially when the tree was in leaf: she and her mum had christened it the Heron's Nest because, if you spotted it from below, you really might think it was one.

The Heron's Nest was Cat's refuge from the real world, her cocoon for dreaming, her very own private property. She had hung 'Keep Out' signs at the entrance, but of course she hadn't been able to resist showing off the place to all comers because she was so proud of it. She was even more proud of the fact that her beyond-brilliant mum had made it. Sometimes they had slept there, Paloma and Cat, snug and cosied up in duvets. Sometimes Cat's dad would come looking for them, blundering through the undergrowth and muttering and cursing when he fell, which was frequently. Paloma would plug them both into headphones then, and Cat would fall asleep to the sound of her mother's recorded voice telling her stories, and wake to boisterous birdsong.

Cat no longer enjoyed the luxury of falling asleep to stories or music. She kept her wits about her now at all times: even while she slept. The last time she'd been stupid enough to let her guard down she'd woken to the shrilling of a smoke alarm, and the greedy sound of flames lapping against canvas. Under cover of night, someone had boarded her houseboat. They'd crapped on the companionway, jemmied the hatch under which she stowed her paintings, slung turpentine over them, and set them alight before scarpering. That had been a month ago. The following day Cat had posted the keys of the houseboat back to the guy who owned it. After two years of living on the canal, after two years of enduring the kind of persecution that mavericks and vagabonds the world over are subject to, she had decided it was time to move on.

She'd hitched a ride on a rig, and ended up here in Lissamore. She knew the village – she'd worked as a scenic artist on a film, *The O'Hara Affair*, that had been made in the vicinity, when she'd been put up in one of the numerous B&Bs requisitioned by the film makers. But Cat couldn't afford a B&B now. Nor would she want to stay in one. Landladies were inquisitive sorts, prone to asking questions and making the kind of observations that Cat would not care to elucidate on. *Is it a Donegal Gallagher you are? It's hard to place you by your accent. Are you travelling on your own? You want to be careful, so. You're paying by cash? That's unusual, these days. Is that all the luggage you have? You're sure? Fill in the register, if you'd be so kind. Signature and ID, please.*

Cat hated registers, as she hated all manner of form-filling. She couldn't get her head round the bureaucracy, any more than she could understand why she had to divulge all kinds of personal stuff to the faceless penpushers who processed the info. Who wanted to know this stuff about her? Why did they want to know it? What was in it for them, and why did they have to make life so unnecessarily, so infuriatingly complicated?

Raoul had offered to help her complete an application form once, for a mobile phone contract, but when she got a load of the stuff you'd need to get one – ID, utility bills, bank account details – she had despaired, and opted for a pay-as-you-go instead.

That pay-as-you-go sounded now, alerting her to a text. She knew who the sender was without having to consult the display. Raoul was the only person in the world who knew her number.

Where are you, Catkin? she read.

In a gud place, she texted back.

Be more specific.

On a roof in lisamor.

I should have guessed. Tin?

No but it is hot.

I like it. Keep your phone turned on. I have news for you.

OK.

News. Good. She hoped it had to do with the house-sitting gig he'd told her about.

A couple of academics, friends of Raoul's in Galway, were taking a year's sabbatical in New Mexico, and they needed someone to dust their books and water their marijuana plants and play with their dog while they were away. The house in question was near the village of Kilrowan, and came complete with river views and a light-filled conservatory that Cat could use as a studio. It was ideal, Raoul had told her and – more importantly – it was timely, for since Cat had become a person of no fixed abode, money had become a problem.

34

She had phoned her father to tell him to stop sending her allowance to the houseboat and that she'd alert him to her new address as soon as she knew it herself. She was chancing her arm, she knew: she was nineteen now, and past the age when she could expect any kind of parental support. But, hey: she was Hugo's only daughter, she'd been motherless from the age of fourteen, and since the only affection she had ever received from her father had been of that maudlin variety that alcoholics bestow capriciously and indiscriminately, the very least he could do was cough up a few bob to keep her off the streets. It wasn't as if he couldn't afford it.

Her phone rang.

'Raoul! You punk! It's been ages since you called.'

'I could say the same thing about you, little sister.'

'I can't afford to make calls. You know that. How are you? How's your new lady? Tell me everything.'

Her questions went unanswered. 'I've bad news, Cat.'

'Shit.' Cat furled herself into a sitting position and reached for her sarong. 'What's up?'

'Your house-sitting gig's gone to a more deserving cause.'

'A more deserving cause! Is that some kind of joke? Whose cause could be more deserving than mine? I'm homeless and broke.'

'I'm sorry, Cat. Their nephew's volunteered to do it. He's just been made redundant.'

Cat looked up at the sky, narrowing her eyes against the sun, and watched a tern plummet seaward. 'Bummer,' she said. 'I kinda liked the idea of living in a house with a conservatory.'

'Where are you now?'

'On a roof in Lissamore. I told you in my text.'

'Whose roof?'

35

'I dunno whose roof it is. It belongs to one of those great big holiday villas that were being built all over the place when we Irish thought we were millionaires.'

'Posh?'

'Yeah. But it looks like no one's been near it for yonks, so I decided to breathe a little life into the joint.'

'How long have you been there?'

Cat considered. 'A week. Maybe longer. What day is it?'

'Friday. How did you get in?'

'How do you think? That right-angled screwdriver you gave me has proved mighty handy, Raoul.'

She heard him sigh in her ear. 'OK, sweetheart. You've had your fun. Don't you think it's time you went home and did some thinking about your future?'

'Home? Where's that?'

'The Crooked House.'

'Don't make me laugh, Raoul. That ain't my home any more than it's yours.'

'Then come to Galway.'

'I'm not moving in with you, bro.'

'Then what the hell are you going to do? You said it yourself – you're homeless and broke.'

Cat got to her feet, yawned and stretched. 'I guess I'll have to do that poste restante thing,' she said, strolling to the parapet and looking down, 'and get Dad to send cash to the post office here until I find myself some kind of fixed abode.'

'Cash? Hugo sends you cash? I thought it was cheques?'

'No. It's always been cash. Sure, what would I do with a cheque when I've no bank account?'

'Nobody deals in cash nowadays, Cat! How does he send it?'

'Like the way you would to a kid on their birthday. In a

card. He even managed to find a Hallmark one once that had "To a Special Daughter" on it. That made me fall about.'

On the other end of the phone, she heard Raoul sigh again. He must be thinking – he always sighed when he was thinking hard.

'Has he upped it?'

'Upped what?'

'The money he sends you?'

'No. It's still a hundred a week.'

'And that's all you've been living off?'

Cat shrugged. 'It's plenty. Sure, I had no rent to pay on the houseboat, and what would I spend money on apart from food and art materials?'

'Most nineteen-year-olds would have an answer to that.'

'Maybe. I don't know any nineteen-year-olds, so I don't know how they spend their money.'

'They spend it on clothes. Music. Games.'

'Clothes.' Cat looked down at the sarong wrapped around her nakedness. 'Hm. Maybe I *could* use a few new clothes. My boots are in bits, and some fucker stole my jacket.'

'What fucker?'

'The fucker who set fire to my paintings. He probably thought there was stuff in the pockets.'

'Did he get anything?'

'A little cash. Twenty euro, maybe.'

'No cards? No ID?'

'I don't have any cards. Or ID. Apart from that fake student one.'

'You've still no passport?'

'I've never needed one, Raoul.'

'We'll have to remedy that, Catkin. You gotta see some of the world.'

'Right now, this corner of the world suits me fine.'

Beyond the parapet, the dark blue line of the horizon stretched from east to west, dividing sea from sky and trailing a cluster of cabochon emerald islands in its wake. Cat had been painting variations on this view for the past six days, including, as she always did, a little self-portrait. Her minxy self – Catgirl – diving off a pier, or dancing down a sand dune, or shimmying up a drumlin. Having run out of canvas, and with no money to buy more, she'd taken to cutting old rolls of wallpaper into twelve-by-eighteen-inch rectangles.

'Anyway, seeing the world costs money, bro,' she resumed. 'And that brings us nicely to where we came in. I'm going to have to phone Hugo and beg.'

'Have you spoken to him recently?' Raoul asked.

'Dad? Are you mad? No.'

'He's not well, Cat.'

'Of course he's not well. He's a raving alcoholic.'

'It's worse than that. He's not painting.'

'He's blocked?'

'Either that, or he's burnt out.'

'Oo-er. That *is* bad news.'

Cat leaned on the parapet and watched the progress of a tiny spider crawling along a fissure in the concrete. A money spider! Maybe if she turned her hand over, it would cross her palm and bring her luck? She crooked a forefinger, to coax it in the right direction.

'How's Ophelia coping?' she asked.

'She's covering up quite well. I have to say I've a grudging admiration for her. She even managed to drag Hugo out to some dinner that was being given in his honour last week. The pics were all over the papers.'

'Well, it's in her interest to cover things up, isn't it? What'll become of her status as muse and keeper of the votive flame when Dad finally burns out? Our Oaf loves the limelight.

She won't like being a nobody.' The spider emerged from the crack and started to scale Cat's hand. Yes!

'She'll find some way around it. She's a survivor. And she's no eejit.'

That was true. When it came to finding her spotlight, Raoul and Cat's stepmother was exceptionally clever. She'd been an actress in a former life, and – conscious that she was approaching her best before date – she'd been glad to fill the vacancy left when Paloma wearied of her role as Hugo Gallagher's muse and ran away from the Crooked House, taking their only daughter with her. There was a lot of arty-farty crap talked about being a muse, Cat had learned. It was a thankless job really – a bit like being an unpaid minder to a grown-up baby. It wasn't about lolling around on divans eating grapes and quaffing champagne: it was about cooking and cleaning and nagging and making sure that money was coming in to pay the bills. Cat remembered her mother locking Hugo into his studio for hours on end, not letting him out until he had something concrete to send to his gallery. Then, when payment finally came through, Paloma would spend a day feverishly scribbling cheques to all their creditors and writing thank-you letters to those local tradesmen who had been patient with her – the butcher and the plumber and the market gardener (all of whom were, Cat suspected, a little in love with her mother). She remembered how, on the day electricity was reconnected after three weeks of suppers cooked on a Primus stove and homework done by candlelight, she and her mother had celebrated by making buckets of popcorn, turning on lights all over the house and playing Madonna at full blast. Hugo had celebrated by going off on a pub crawl that had lasted three days.

But things had changed since then. In Paloma's time,

Hugo had been on the cusp of success: now he was feted as one of Ireland's greatest living painters. Paloma's successor, the lovely Ophelia, could afford to hire someone to do the cooking and cleaning. She could shop till she dropped online (now that broadband had finally infiltrated the Crooked House), have all her bills paid by direct debit, and not be obliged to dream up outlandish excuses for creditors.

'How did Dad look, in the pictures?' she asked Raoul.

'Distinguished as ever, according to the caption. You wouldn't think he was burnt out.'

'What about her?'

'She looked great.'

Cat didn't want to hear this. She would have loved it if Raoul had told her instead that Ophelia had looked awful, playing up to the camera like the WAG she was at heart. But her stepmother had modified her look since she and Hugo had first met. In the early days, Oaf had traded on an overt sex appeal that turned heads – and pages in the tabloids. Once she had Hugo in her sights she had toned things down, knowing that her wannabe image was inappropriate for a gal who was auditioning for the role of real-life muse to a national treasure. Now she was more country girl than siren – softer, earthier, even a little curvier. The last magazine spread Cat had chanced upon had featured Oaf in full-on bucolic mode, waxing lyrical about life in the Crooked House and her role as homemaker and devoted wife to Hugo Gallagher. Clad in dungarees and wellies, hair artfully dishevelled, she'd been pictured scattering corn for her hens and feeding her pretty little goats.

'She's bringing out a book, by the way,' remarked Raoul.

'What? Oaf is? But she has the imagination of a flea!'

'You don't need to have an imagination to write a book any more. You just need to be a celebrity. And/or photogenic.

40

Ophelia will milk her celebrity for what it's worth. Like I said, she's a survivor.'

Cat's lip curled. 'It won't be much longer before she's unmasked.'

'What makes you say that?'

'She's a liar, and not a very good one. It takes one to know one, Raoul, and I've had her number for ages.'

'I'm sorry to say that I quite like her.'

'Ah, but you're not a liar, Raoul. You don't understand the way our minds work. She knows how to push your buttons, just like she knows how to push Hugo's.'

'But she can't push yours?'

'No. And that's why she hates me.'

'Aren't you being just a little OTT, Catkin?'

'No. My instinct is right on this one. It's that feeling I told you about – the one I get in my bones. Trust me.'

'But you've just admitted to being a liar. How can I trust you?'

She could hear the smile in his voice, and she smiled back. 'Blood ties, Raoul. We're family.'

The spider that had been travelling across Cat's palm began to lower itself effortlessly over the parapet on a lanyard of silk.

'Oh!' she said, gazing downward. 'Whaddayaknow! I got company.'

'What?' Raoul's voice on the phone sounded alarmed.

'No worries. It's just some local ICA types. They've descended on the next-door allotment.'

'ICA?'

'Irish Countrywomen's Association. There's a market-garden-type place right next to this house – very convenient, I have to say, for poor starving me. I've been feasting on organic produce all week.'

41

'You've been robbing an allotment, Cat? You're going to get yourself into trouble.'

Cat affected an injured tone. 'What else is a gal to do, bro, when her daddy done gone and left her broke?' From below came the sound of women's laughter. They were unpacking a picnic hamper, Cat saw, and laying out rugs and cushions under the apple trees. They were clearly going to be there for some time. 'They'd make a great subject for a painting,' she remarked. 'I could put one of them in the nude, like Manet's *Déjeuner sur l'Herbe*.'

'Cat?'

'Yes.'

There was a pause. 'Nothing.'

'Nothing will come of nothing. That's Shakespeare, ain't it? Better go, bro.'

Cat pressed 'end call', and stood staring at the display on her phone for some moments. She knew what Raoul had been going to say. He was going to tell her to get her ass back to school, get some qualifications, and get a job. He was going to tell her that she couldn't carry on living the way she had for the past couple of years, and that it was time for her to wise up. He was going to tell her to get real, to get a life. But Cat had a life. She had a life that suited her. And she didn't want to get real. Not just yet.

Another laugh drifted up from the allotment. It really would make a great subject for a painting. *Fête Champêtre*, Irish style. A bunch of middle-aged country women gossiping over ham sandwiches and flasks of tea, swapping recipes and showing off pictures of their grandchildren. Very *petit genre*, as her art teacher would have said! Cat pulled a scrunchy off her wrist, scraped up her mass of damp hair and wound it into a knot on the top of her head.

Then she flexed her fingers. It was time to go cut some wallpaper.

Río emerged from the water and shook salt droplets from her hair. A swim was the only surefire way to clear a gal's head after knocking back quantities of iced Cointreau and gin in the afternoon. Above her on the terraced slopes her sister Dervla was strolling between raspberry canes and strawberry beds, sampling produce; while under the shade of a parasol, recumbent on cushions, Fleur was leafing through a magazine and murmuring love songs to her baby. The words of some French nursery rhyme came floating down to the shore – *Alouette, gentille alouette, alouette, je te plumerai . . .*

This was the third picnic they'd enjoyed this summer. The first had been organised by Río, whose orchard it was. She had provided cold Spanish omelette, red wine and Rice Krispie buns. Picnic number two had featured champagne, finger sandwiches and exquisite miniature pastries, courtesy of Fleur. Today, Dervla had brought along a cocktail shaker (she mixed a mean White Lady) and canapés requisitioned from the eightieth birthday celebration she'd hosted the night before.

So far, the picnics had been a great success. They'd been lucky with the weather, they'd been able to synchronise time off work; they'd even solved the drink/drive problem by organising transport. Today, because all his regular drivers were otherwise employed, the owner of the local hackney company had dropped them off at Río's orchard himself – in a Merc, no less. In an hour's time he would pick them up and deliver them back to their respective addresses. Dervla would be dropped off at the mews behind the Old Rectory, the state-of-the-art retirement home she ran with her husband Christian; Fleur would return to her duplex above Fleurissima, the bijou boutique that had been her pride and joy until the arrival of baby Marguerite; and Río would climb the stairs to the apartment that boasted a grand view of Lissamore harbour and its fishing boats, where she lived on her own.

The view was what she loved most about her apartment. She had never read E.M. Forster's *A Room With a View*, but she didn't need to. The title said it all. How could anyone live in a room that *didn't* have a view? For Río, that was unthinkable.

Río's balcony presented her with a different picture of the village every day, according to the vagaries of the weather. On a fine day, the village was carnival-coloured: a riot of hanging baskets and brightly painted hulls bobbing on the water and all manner of summer accessories outside the corner shop – beach balls and shrimping nets and sun hats and display stands of pretty postcards. This was the view inhabited by tourists, who wandered the main street of the village, licking ice-cream cones and taking pictures with their camera phones. Río preferred the view in the winter months, when the street was deserted and the mountains on the horizon wore an icing-sugar dusting of snow and the skies were so big and breathtakingly blue that you felt no picture could do them justice.

However, Lissamore and its environs simply begged to be photographed. On occasion, Río had come across tourists who had wandered off the beaten track, and strayed into her orchard with their BlackBerries and iPhones. They would apologise, say that they hoped they were not trespassing, and Río would say '*Arra*, divil a bit' in her best brogue, and offer them samples of whatever was in season – blueberries or goosegogs or apples. And then she was delighted when these visitors contacted her via Facebook and posted photographs of her orchard on their walls and exhorted all their friends to visit Lissamore and buy Río's produce from her stall at the weekly Sunday market.

The three women had hit upon the orchard as the rendezvous for their summer junkets because no one could bother them there. None of them ever had windows for so-called 'me' time, so they'd opted for 'us' time instead, and the picnics were designated stress-free events. In the orchard, Fleur couldn't 'just run downstairs' to deal with a delivery or a fussy customer, and Dervla couldn't 'just nip next door' to check on how a new resident was settling in. And while they were there, Río wasn't allowed to fret over greenfly or weevils or mealy bugs. Río's orchard was their very own Garden of Eden, their private piece of paradise.

Reaching for her towel, Río glanced up at the Villa Felicity, the house that had once belonged to Adair. Since he had sold it, it was rumoured to have changed hands a couple of times, and it now wore the look of an unwanted frock in a second-hand shop. Or that's how Fleur – with her penchant for sartorial imagery – had put it. Río liked that the place was empty. She liked to be able to skinny-dip here unseen, she liked to be able to work in her garden unobserved, she liked to be able to lounge in the hammock she had strung up between two apple trees, knowing that she had this corner of Coolnamara all to herself. No one in the world could reach her here, except . . .

From above, came the sound of her phone – the ringtone that announced that Finn was calling.

. . . except Finn.

Río was off the starter's blocks, wrapping her towel around her, and sprinting up the beach towards the orchard gate.

'Your phone, Río!' called Fleur. 'Shall I answer it for you?'

'Please!' The ringtone stopped, and Río heard Fleur's low laugh. 'No, Finn! It's your godmother here! Hang on two seconds, she's on her way. Here she comes, tearing up the path like Roadrunner.'

Breathless, Río joined Fleur on the rug, and held out a hand for the phone. 'Finn!' she said into the mouthpiece. 'What's up?'

'Hey, Ma,' came her son's laconic greeting.

'Why are you phoning the mobile? What has you so *flathu-lach*? Why not wait to Skype later?'

'I'm a bit all over the place, today.'

Río did some quick mental arithmetic. 'It must be eight o'clock in the morning in LA. What has you up so early?'

'The clock says four p.m. where I am.'

'So you're not in LA? What's going on?'

'Are you heading home soon, Ma?'

'In about an hour. Why?'

'Then I can tell you the good news in person.'

'What do you mean, in person?'

'I'll be in Lissamore in a couple of hours, unless Galway airport's closed again. I'm in Heathrow now.'

'You brat! You never told me you were coming home! Holy moly, Finn – that's fantastic news!'

'Glad you think so, Ma. But there's more.'

'More good news? What?'

There was a smile in Finn's voice when he replied.

'It's a surprise,' he said.

Chapter Three

From: ed@sundayinsignia.ie
To: Keeley Considine
Subject: Re: Extended break
Hi, Keeley.
So you've got yourself a cottage in Lissamore?
Nice. Pity about the tax on second homes though,
ain't it ;b
Enjoy your 'extended break', but please note that
I'm holding you to your contract, which has a
further three weeks to run. (Not having broadband
is no excuse. I Googled the joint: there's an
internet café in the village.)
Yours (I mean it),
Leo
PS: Click here. You interviewed him once, years
ago, didn't you? How about nailing her?

Keeley allowed herself a reflective moment, then refilled her coffee mug and clicked on the next email in her inbox. It was from her grandmother's solicitor, to tell her that the keys to the cottage were ready to be picked up from his office, and reminding her that – as well as inheritance tax – she would now be eligible for the new tax on second homes.

On the radio, some pundit was talking about property prices. 'The reality is that prices have plummeted by fifty per cent in the Galway region. This includes holiday residences, which have been flying on to the market since the introduction of the tax on second homes . . .' Keeley pressed the 'off' switch. She didn't want to be reminded for the third time that morning about the new tax on second homes. The third email she clicked on was from her accountant, alerting her to the fact that she would now be eligible to pay . . .

Click! The email went shooting off back into her mailbox.

There would be more unpalatable stuff, she knew, waiting for her at her work address. She steeled herself before setting sail for mail2web. In keeley.c@sundayinsignia.ie there was the usual assortment of mail to do with the previous Sunday's interviewee. The subject had been an up-and-coming young model who also happened to be the daughter of a major theatrical agent, and among the acidic responses provoked were: 'She only got where she is because of who she is.' 'My daughter could do a million times better! See attached pic.' 'Who did she blow to get her face on the cover?' Delete, delete, delete. Keeley found the rancour of some of the email feedback she was subjected to truly dispiriting. Since she'd returned to Ireland from the States, she had come to realise that there might be some truth in the old adage about the Irish being a nation of begrudgers.

Keeley Considine's brief each week was to conduct an in-depth interview with an Irish celebrity-du-jour. So far, she'd included among her interviewees a singer/songwriter suffering from early onset Alzheimer's; a fashion designer who had been abused as a child; an ex-priest who was now living as a woman; and a gay government minister who had walked out on her husband and children (she was now an *ex*-government minister). What connected all Keeley's subjects was a moment of life-changing insight – an epiphany – which was why her Sunday column was called (ta-ra!) 'Epiphanies'. Since being approached by the *Insignia* the previous year, she'd conducted fifty-one interviews. Fifty-one weeks as confidante to strangers, and forty-one weeks as mistress to the newspaper's editor had left Keeley feeling burned out.

She could, she thought ruefully, have been a candidate for one of her own interviews. Attractive Ex-pat Journalist (AEJ) returns to Ireland seeking employment after a decade in New York, during which period she'd served time on a major Sunday newspaper, both as rising star features writer, and as mistress to the editor. Until his wife found out. And whaddayouknow – within three months of arriving back on her home turf, AEJ makes the very same mistake. Except this time, AEJ was in grave danger of falling in love.

Keeley's epiphany had occurred when she got the news that her grandmother had left her a cottage in the village of Lissamore in the west of Ireland. Her initial reaction had been one of bemusement. What to do with the joint? Her grandmother had moved out years ago (Keeley had child-hood memories of pootling around waterlogged beaches in the so-called summer months), and since then the cottage had languished as a holiday rental on the books of a letting agency called Coolnamara Hideaways. Keeley's dad was always moaning about the fact that it cost more to maintain than it ever brought in, but he had never managed to persuade his mother to sell. She was, for some reason, adamant that the cottage should go to her only grand-daughter on her death. And now Gran had died, and Keeley had come into her inheritance, and was liable for the property tax on second homes.

Thanks, Gran, she had thought the day after the funeral,

staring morosely at the images of her bequest on the Coolnamara Hideaways website. Curlew Cottage was all whitewashed charm outside, all bog-standard pine inside, and – altogether – most un-Keeley Considine. But then she had looked around at her Ikea-furnished apartment with its Bang & Olufsen HD TV and its Bose sound system and the Nespresso machine she rarely used because she usually bought her coffee from Starbucks, and she'd had the most surprisingly unoriginal thought she'd had in a very long time. She, Keeley Considine, with her BA in creative writing and her diploma in journalism and her award for excellence in celebrity profiles – had thought 'A change is as good as a rest'. And then she had taken Curlew Cottage off Coolnamara Hideaways' books and composed the email to Leo, telling him that she wanted a break.

It would come as no surprise to him. Their relationship had taken a hiding since his wife had happened upon them having dinner *à deux* in the Trocadero. Keeley was convinced she'd been set up. The memory of that evening had the power to make her break into a cold sweat every time she thought about it . . .

'What are you wearing under that plain – but clearly very chic – little black dress?' Leo had asked conversationally, as he refilled her wineglass. 'Anything interesting?'

'Yes, actually,' replied Keeley, taking a sip of wine. 'I'm wearing that very pretty Stella McCartney bra and panties set you bought for me in Agent Provocateur.'

'The black lace ones?'

'Yes.'

'Suspenders or hold-ups?'

'Hold-ups.'

'Lace topped?'

'But of course.'

Leo gave her a debonair smile. 'I have another present for you, Ms Considine.'

'How kind! It's not even my birthday!'

'It's your un-birthday, as per Lewis Carroll's neologism. Many happy returns.'

Leaning down, Leo had produced a small giftwrapped box from his attaché case. Keeley recognised the wrapping paper immediately. The gift was from Coco de Mer in Covent Garden, the sexiest shop in the world.

She looked down at it as he placed it on the table, then looked back at him and raised an eyebrow. 'Dare I open it in a public place?' she asked.

'You may. The box is very discreet.'

Unloosening the ribbon, Keeley peeled away the giftwrap and folded it carefully: Coco de Mer giftwrap was far too pretty to waste. Beneath was an elegant black box, that was – as Keeley saw when she raised the lid – lined with silk. Nestling in the silk were two perfectly smooth egg-shaped stones, one of jade, one of obsidian.

'Love eggs?' she said.

'Well deduced. Concubines used them in ancient China.'

'What a very, *very* thoughtful present,' said Keeley, slanting Leo a smile. 'My pelvic floor muscles could do with a thorough workout.'

'Why not give them a go?'

'Now?'

'Yes. Isn't it time you powdered your nose?'

'You're absolutely right. I'm all aglow.'

Sending Leo another oblique smile, Keeley unfurled herself from the banquette and slid the box into her handbag.

'One moment, sweetheart.' The skin on her forearm where he touched her sang.

'Yes?'

His voice was so low, she had to stoop a little to hear him.

'Leave your panties off.'

'That goes without saying, *chéri*.'

And Keeley turned and sashayed in the direction of the loo, knowing that Leo's eyes were following her every step of the way. In the cubicle, she stripped off her panties, slipped them into her handbag, took the love eggs from their satin-lined box, and inserted them. One. Oh! Two. *Oh!* The jade and obsidian felt delicious, cool and smooth against her warm flesh, and Keeley felt anticipation surge through her when she thought of the treat in store for her later. And for Leo, too. She'd bought him a silver cock ring last time she was in London.

In the boudoir of the ladies room, she reapplied her lipstick and spritzed herself with a little scent. Her reflection regarded her from the mirror, a half smile playing around her lips, the pupils of her eyes dilated, a flush high on her cheeks that was not courtesy of Clinique. Dear *God*, she was horny! There would be no dessert this evening, that was for sure. Not in the restaurant, anyway. She had Häagen Dazs Dulce de Leche at home, and fresh Egyptian cotton sheets just begging to be laundered again tomorrow. Keeley squirted Neal's Yard Lime and Lemongrass onto her tongue, tousled her hair a little, and left the ladies room, Chanel No. 5 wafting in her wake, walking tall and working her hips; the way the promise of excellent sex makes a real lady walk.

'Everything in place?' asked Leo, as she resumed her seat at the table.

'You betcha,' said Keeley, cool as you like. 'Perhaps you should think about settling up.'

Leo raised a hand to summon the waiter, and Keeley broke a crust of the remains of the baguette on her side plate, just for something to toy with while waiting for the bill to be sorted. And as she did so, a woman whom she recognised as Leo's wife came into the restaurant, and made straight for the maître d'.

'I thought you said Rachel was in Cork?' she said.

'She is.'

'No she's not. She's behind you, Leo, and she's headed our way. Oh, fuck, oh, *fuck* – this is just . . . Oh fuck.'

It was like watching a car crash in slow motion. The maître d' had indicated their whereabouts, and Rachel was moving towards them now, dazzling Colgate smile fixed in place.

'Good evening!' she fluted, as she slid next to Leo on the banquette opposite Keeley. 'Don't worry about another place setting. I've already asked the maître d' to sort that out. I know I'm a little late, but I'm sure you won't mind if I have something? An *hors d'oeuvre* is all I require, since I had a late lunch. Oh, good. I see they're still doing Baba Ganoush – I haven't eaten here in ages, and I thought the menu might have changed. And I'm so sorry, I haven't introduced myself. We met at an *Insignia* event some time ago, but you may not remember me, Keeley. I'm Rachel, Leo's wife. How nice to see you again. You haven't changed a bit. That's the same dress you were wearing last time I met you. Zara, yes?'

'Yes.'

'How brave!'

It went on, and it went on. Rachel was relentless. She ordered her Baba Ganoush and another bottle of wine, and she sat and chatted about the *Insignia* and her husband and her children and the fact that she had been obliged to give up her very successful career as a pharmacist in order to rear Leo's family but she didn't resent a single minute of the time spent with the children since they were all prodigies just like her mother-in-law told her Leo had been, and wasn't the weather stunning, and wasn't it simply wonderful that Keeley had inherited a little cottage in the west of

Ireland that she could visit when the stresses and strains of urban living became too hard for her to handle. And good heavens! Was that the time? They really ought to be making tracks – Leo had the school run to contend with in the morning, and Rachel had a parent-teacher meeting and thanks so much, Keeley, for taking care of the bill.

And all the time Keeley had sat there with the jade and obsidian eggs inside her, not feeling loved up at all, but rather like a constipated hen. And after Leo and Rachel had left the restaurant, she had ordered a large brandy and sat nursing it on her own, pretending to do important stuff on her iPhone and all the time flexing her pelvic muscles – two, three, four! – because she was fearful that when she stood up the jade and obsidian eggs might fall to the floor and be pounced upon by the punctilious maître d' . . .

Yours (I mean it) . . .

Keeley returned to Leo's email, re-read it, then clicked on the link he had sent. It took her to the website of a publishing trade magazine, and a headline that read 'Gallagher Muse to Pen Children's Book'.

Top literary agent Tony Baines has negotiated a high six-figure deal for a first-time author with children's publishing giant Pandora. 'Pussy Willow and the Pleasure Palace of Peachy Stuff', written by Ophelia Gallagher, is aimed at seven- to ten-year-olds. A former actress, Ophelia Gallagher is wife and muse of the internationally renowned Irish painter Hugo Gallagher. Ms Gallagher was inspired to write the book after visiting Sans Souci, the summer palace in Potsdam built by Frederick the Great of Prussia.

Hugo Gallagher. She didn't know he'd married again. Keeley had conducted one of her very first interviews with Gallagher about ten years earlier, when she was fresh out of college. It had been at the opening of an exhibition of his paintings in the Demeter Gallery in Dublin – his breakthrough exhibition, as it had turned out. At that time Hugo Gallagher's star had been in the ascendant. After years as a struggling artist, he had emerged from obscurity to take his place centre stage in the Irish art world with a series of astonishing abstracts. She remembered being introduced to a saturnine man, loose-limbed and sexy – a man who exuded a lethal charm. She remembered his then-wife, a woman called . . . Paloma; and a child: a tousle-haired gypsy with angular limbs and intense dark eyes. She remembered how the mother had exuded an anxious air, and how her anxiety had escalated in proportion to the copious amounts of wine consumed by her husband. The child, she recalled, had hunkered on the floor in a corner of the gallery, oblivious to the brouhaha around her, drawing with a leaky biro on the back of a price list.

Keeley wished she could remember the price a Gallagher painting would have fetched back then. Ha'penny place in comparison to today's reckoning, she suspected, because by the end of that evening's feeding frenzy, every single canvas on the pristine gallery walls had been sold. Thereafter Hugo Gallagher had been able to double, treble, quadruple and, finally, simply name his price. Was he still coining it in? Keeley was curious as to how the artist's career had fared in the intervening decade. She'd read somewhere that Paloma had left him several years ago, making way for the current Mrs Gallagher.

Returning her attention to the screen, Keeley studied the photograph that accompanied the blurb. Ophelia was a beautiful woman – petite and peachy-skinned, with huge, limpid, indigo blue eyes and an irresistible smile. She was dressed down in dungarees and bare feet, lustrous hair tumbling artlessly around her shoulders; she had a tiny tattoo of a daisy in the hollow of her collarbone and a fetching gap between her front teeth. She came across as fun, youthful, and with a sense of mischief – yet there was something of the earth mother about her too. Had she used the little Gallagher girl – her stepdaughter – as a sounding board for her book, Keeley wondered. But rudimentary arithmetic told her that Caitlín would have been way too old for children's stories by the time Ophelia and Hugo finally got married.

Google beckoned.

Wikipedia told her nothing she didn't already know about Hugo Gallagher's early life. The poverty, the drinking, the acquisition of the famous Crooked House (which he claimed to have won in an all-night poker game), the failed marriages to his first wife and subsequently to Paloma. Also listed were the offspring of those marriages: the son Raoul, an architect; the daughter Caitlín. Documented, too, was the meteoric rise to fame that followed that sell-out exhibition in the Demeter Gallery, and the stupendous prices his work had fetched in the rampant Celtic Tiger era. Lately, however, information pertaining to the Great Artist seemed a little more hazy. There had been no output for the past couple of years, although he was rumoured to be working on an important new series. Reading between the lines, it wasn't difficult to deduce that drink was to blame. Hugo Gallagher was following in the footsteps of those legendary wild men of art – Pollock, Rothko, Basquiat – destined to burn out and leave a priceless legacy behind him. The problem was that once he died, although his paintings would soar in value, it would be of no benefit to his family because – unless he really was working on a new series – all his paintings had already been sold and were now hanging in public and private collections all over the world.

The Wikipedia link to Gallagher's current wife – former actress Ophelia Spence – told Keeley that she had appeared in major theatre venues all over the world. Roles undertaken included the maid in Chekhov's *Three Sisters*, the maid in *Phaedra* and the maid in *Private Lives*. Three little maids in a row hardly constituted an illustrious stage career, concluded Keeley. Ophelia, she learned, had met Hugo Gallagher at a charity fundraiser in Dublin at the height of his fame, and assumed the mantle of his muse and mistress within a month. They had no children. *Pussy Willow and the Pleasure Palace of Peachy Stuff* was her first book.

Oh, yawn! Keeley had heard, seen and read it all before. The shelves of her local charity shop were groaning with unread copies (many of them hardbacks intended for review and donated by Keeley) of novels, cookbooks and memoirs by former actresses, models, columnists and TV personalities, all desperate to take advantage of their waning celebrity status and make a few bucks before they sank without trace beneath the public radar. Once they dipped below number ten in the search engine's ranking, they were bollixed. Something told Keeley that, since Ophelia Gallagher's main claim to fame was her illustrious surname, the former actress's season in the Google sun was a particularly limited one. Why bother extending the poor creature's shelf life by wasting a precious 'Epiphany' on her and her children's book, when there were hundreds of more worthy wannabes queuing up to be interviewed?

And yet, and yet . . . something about Ophelia Gallagher intrigued Keeley. Why had she written a children's book when she had no children? Why hadn't she written a novel or a cookbook or an autobiography? Why hadn't she divorced the drunken husband and penned a kiss-and-tell, warts-and-all memoir? Why hadn't she designed a clothing line, or launched a signature scent?

Keeley picked up her phone and dialled the publishing house. Within minutes she had been put through to the publicity department, and secured an 'at home' interview with Ms Gallagher, which she arranged to dovetail neatly into her westward itinerary. The Crooked House was just off the N6, on the way to Lissamore.

'Wouldn't it be more convenient for you to meet in a hotel?' the publicist had asked. 'No,' said Keeley. 'It's always more interesting to talk to someone on their home ground.'

It was true. Interviewees were always more relaxed in their home surroundings. A relaxed Ophelia would be an Ophelia with her defences down. And that was just how Keeley wanted her.

Chapter Four

Cat sat bolt upright. Since the night of the fire on the house-boat, she had trained herself to be vigilant against the tiniest sound. The brush of a moth's wing against glass, the plash of an otter in the bay below, the scarcely audible whine of a mosquito was sufficient to wake her now.

Someone was in the house. Staring into the darkness, Cat tried to locate where, exactly. Downstairs. Footsteps were crossing the cavernous expanse of the hall. She listened harder, alert as a leopardess. The creak of that unoiled hinge told her the intruder was in the kitchen; the echoing drumbeat of her heart was signalling fight or flight. Sliding herself from the cocoon of her sleeping bag, Cat reached for her sarong and wound it tightly around her. Then she moved on silent feet to the top of the stairs. A light moved in the darkness below . . . a torch? No. By the greenish tinge to the illumination, Cat could tell that it belonged to a mobile phone.

'Dad?' said a male voice. 'About fucking time. I've been trying to get through for ages. Yeah . . . I'm in Lissamore. No – it was too late to call in on her. I'm in Coral Mansion. I can't tell . . . there's no electricity: I'll have to wait until morning to do a recce. But I've a feeling you've had visitors. Squatters . . . yeah.'

On the landing, Cat froze. Then she lightly retraced her

steps back to the room in which she had set up camp and reached for the Swiss Army penknife that she always kept by her while she slept, cursing her stupidity when she realised she'd left it below in the kitchen. Grabbing her phone instead – her lifeline to Raoul – she moved out onto the balcony. A flight of steps took her down to the garden. Here, by the disused pool on the patio, she hunkered behind an overgrown shrub, and sucked in a couple of deep breaths.

Stupid, stupid Cat! Why hadn't she had her things packed and ready for a quick getaway, the way she usually did? Why had she left her laundry strung up on towel rails in the bathroom? She was normally so careful about being on the ball. Now here she was in a garden at midnight, half dressed and horribly vulnerable. And Cat *hated* feeling vulnerable! She wished she hadn't left her Swiss Army knife in the kitchen. Her Swiss Army knife felt good in her hand: even if she had no intention of using it, it lent her an air of bravado she did not necessarily feel.

Through the big picture window overlooking the patio, she saw that the trespasser had moved into the sitting room, and was starting to light candles. He must have found the supply she'd left in the kitchen. The kitchen and the room where she slept were the only rooms in the house in which Cat ever lit candles, since those windows could not be seen from the road. She'd learned to negotiate her way through the house in the dark, like a feral creature. The sitting room, however, was her daytime lair: she used it as a studio, and the paintings she'd made were taped to the walls.

Cat watched as the figure moved around the room, planting candles on mantelpiece and window ledges. She was freezing now: the wind was up, and it had started to rain. Perhaps she could slip back to the bedroom, quickly help herself to some clothes and her sleeping bag and leg it out of there? But leg it where, exactly? To Raoul's place in Galway? To the Crooked House? To that hellish gaff she'd spent a night in last week – the one with the junkyard out back, and the rats?

She would feel at home in none of these places: there was nowhere in the world that was home for Cat. She felt a rush of helpless rage as she stood there in the chill night air, watching through a window as this . . . this *interloper* took possession of her space.

But hey! There was something familiar about the inter-loper, now that she saw him by the light of half-a-dozen candles. The last time she'd seen him, hadn't he been all bathed in the golden glimmer of candlelight? It had been at the wrap party of that film she'd worked on – *The O'Hara Affair*. He'd had a gig as a stunt double and, that night at the party, Cat had decided on the spur of the moment that she'd wanted to get to know him. His name was Finn, she remembered. They'd shared a dance or two, then a bottle of wine and a laugh and a drunken snog. Later, they'd swapped phone numbers . . . and had never seen each other again because the number Cat had given him was bogus. Cat was careful about letting *anyone* have her number.

And yet, and yet . . . he was cool, Finn Byrne, wasn't he? He'd be cool about the fact that she'd been squatting in his house – she knew he would. He was a scuba diver, and divers were laidback individuals. Maybe he'd even allow her to stay on until she got herself sorted with money and somewhere else to live? What the hell – she hadn't much choice. She had *no* choice. She looked at the phone in her hand, then scrolled through the menu until she found Finn's number. Clicking on the cursor in the text message box, she thought for a moment or two, then smiled. Help! she entered in the blank space.

Beyond the glass, she saw Finn take his phone from his pocket, and consult the screen with a perplexed expression. Seconds later, she received the following message.

Who is dis?

I am an orfan of da storm i need ur help luk oot ur windo.

It took ages for her to compose the text, but it was worth the effort. If Cat hadn't been so cold, the look on Finn's face might have made her laugh. Approaching the big window that overlooked the bay, he placed the palms of his hands against it and squinted through cautiously.

Rong window, texted Cat. **Try da other 1.**

He turned and looked over his shoulder, out over the black expanse of the patio and the derelict swimming pool.

Ur gettin warmer but im not its freezin out here.

Finn looked really spooked now. Feeling sorry for him, Cat pressed 'Call'.

'Who the hell is this?' he said, picking up.

'I am the Cat who walks by herself,' Cat told him in her growliest voice, 'and I wish to come into your house.'

'Look, I don't know what you're playing at, but—'

'Oh, Finn! Let me in!' she wailed. 'It's me – it's Catty! I've come ho-ome. Please let me in.'

'You are fucking barking, whoever you are.'

'No, no – I'm mewling, piteously. Come . . . come to the window.' She watched as Finn moved slowly in the direction of the window through which she was spying on him. 'That's right. See? Here I am!' Cat emerged from the overgrown rose bush behind which she'd been concealing herself, stretched out her arms to him and smiled.

Lunging backwards, Finn let out a yell, and this time she did laugh. 'Who the fuck are you?' he demanded.

'I told you. It's Cat. Cat Gallagher. Remember me? We met

at *The O'Hara Affair* wrap party. Won't you please let me come in? I'm awful cold.'

'What are you doing out there?'

Moving right up against the plate glass, Cat pressed her face against it. 'Let me in, and I'll tell you,' she said.

Finn gave her a wary look, hesitated, then tugged at the handle. 'I can't open it. It's locked. Come round the front, and I'll let you in there.'

'No. I can find my own way. Give me a moment.'

Pressing 'End Call', Cat danced away from the window, and back up the balcony steps. In the bedroom, she grabbed her sleeping bag, unzipped it, and wrapped it around herself, shawl-fashion. Then she pattered down the stair-case, through the massive entrance hall and into the sitting room. Finn had moved into the centre of the floor, and was standing lobbing his phone from hand to hand, looking rattled.

'How did you manage that?'

Cat gave him a Giaconda smile. 'I flew in through my bedroom window.'

'Sorry . . . *your* bedroom window?'

'Yes. I'm squatting here.'

'You . . . but this is my dad's house!'

'Maybe. But it's been lying empty for far too long, and it suits me perfectly.'

'Is that right? Well, good for you, Catgirl, but your time as house sitter's up. You can get lost now.'

'Finn! Don't be so heartless. You should be glad that it's me and not some skanky gang of vagrants that's been living here.' She pulled her sleeping bag tighter around herself and gave him a look of appraisal. 'So. Your dad must be the Mystery Buyer?'

'What?'

'Word in the village is that this place has been bought by a Mystery Buyer.'

'A Mystery Buyer?'

'Yes.'

Finn laughed. 'That's a bit cloak and dagger, ain't it? There's no mystery about it, really. Dad just wanted to keep it quiet.'

'Why?'

'Ever heard of press intrusion? My dad likes to keep his private life exactly that – private. And anyway, what are you doing sticking your nose in? It's none of your damn business.'

Cat shrugged. 'Well, it kinda is my business, since I've laid claim to the joint.'

'Don't be so stupid,' scoffed Finn. 'You can't lay claim to a house just because you've been living in it.'

'All property is theft, squatters have rights, and possession is nine-tenths of the law.'

'That's crap. Now go away. I've just flown in from LA and I'm jetlagged and not in the mood for Marxist trivia.'

Cat gave him an aggrieved look. 'You should be grateful to me for taking care of the joint. It badly needed TLC.'

'And what kind of TLC have you been giving it?'

'Um . . . I've sprayed it with Febreze. Smell!'

Finn sniffed the air tentatively, and Cat laughed. 'It's roses. Wild roses.'

'Febreze wild roses?'

'No. Real roses. I brought masses of them in – they're growing like crazy in the garden. You really think I'm the kind of gal who'd go around polluting the atmosphere with air freshener?'

'I don't know what you're capable of. I hardly know you.'

She slanted him a smile. 'But I intrigue you, don't I?'

'It would be hard not to be intrigued by a girl who arrives out of the blue in the middle of the night wearing nothing but a sarong and a sleeping bag.' Finn started lobbing his phone from hand to hand again. 'You could be like something out of *Wallander*. For all I know you're planning to slit my throat. That Swiss Army knife I saw in the kitchen *is* yours, isn't it? Not some nefarious accomplice's?'

'Yes, it's mine.' Cat looked towards the door. 'Can I have something to eat? I saw your boxes in the hall, all piled with grub.'

There was a beat, then Finn gave a nod of assent. 'Sure,' he said.

'Thanks. I'm starving. The kitchen's this way.'

'I know where the kitchen is. I've been here before. How long have you been living here?'

'A week,' she threw back at him. 'You're very welcome to my abode. It beats the hell out of the last joint I broke into. That was a tip. This is like the Ritz Carlton in comparison.'

Following her through into the hall, Finn paused to pick up one of the boxes, then moved into the kitchen where more candles were burning. 'How have you managed without electricity?'

'I have a Primus.'

'What about water?'

'I'm a hardy creature. As long as I'm connected to a supply, it doesn't matter if it's hot or cold.'

'You wouldn't be so complacent if it was winter,' he remarked, setting the box on a countertop.

Cat shrugged. 'I managed to get through last winter on a houseboat.'

'No shit.' Finn gave her an admiring look.

'It was no big deal,' she told him, carelessly.

'So you really are a vagabond?'

'Yeah.'

'Cool!'

Cat's nonchalance was entirely affected. Privately, she rather liked the idea of Finn thinking she was a vagabond. There was something boho and romantic about it. He didn't need to know that the houseboat had all mod cons, and that the only reason she was living rough now was because her next house-sitting gig had fallen through. He didn't need to know that she was, in effect, a Trustafarian, living on an allowance from her daddy. Well, *waiting* for an allowance from her daddy. Until that came through, she guessed she really *was* a vagabond.

Humming a little tune, she set about ransacking the box of groceries. 'Let's see what you've got here. Bread, cheese, salami, tomatoes. Wine! Excellent. A very acceptable Bordeaux. You have good taste.'

'You know about wine?'

'I'm spoofing,' she lied. He didn't need to know that she knew the difference between Bordeaux and Burgundy. He didn't need to know anything about her. She could be an enigma! An enigmatic vagabond. She liked the idea of that. Passing him her Swiss Army knife, she watched as he started to uncork the bottle. 'Tell me about you. What are you doing here?'

'I've come to kick this house into shape.'

'That'll take some doing. Bits of it are falling down. What made your dad buy a crumbling mansion like this?'

'He can afford it. What made you decide to break in?'

'I was looking for somewhere to live –' Cat broke off a hunk of bread and helped herself to salami '– and I found out about this place from the barman in O'Toole's. Barmen are the most clued-in blokes in the world. They know every-thing there is to know about everything.'

66

Finn leaned up against the counter and gave her a look of assessment. 'So what did you find out?'

'I found that it was built by a millionaire who went bust, and that you'd once dated the millionaire's daughter. I found out that you and the daughter were planning to run a scuba-dive outfit here, before the recession happened and things went pear-shaped. I found out that it used to be called "The Villa Felicity" after the millionaire's ex-wife, but that everybody around here calls it "Coral Mansion". So . . . I'm guessing that your dad bought it so you can go ahead and set up your dive business?'

Finn's face closed over. 'I dunno why he bought it.'

'Yes you do. Tell me.'

'You're awful nosy, Cat Gallagher.'

She spread her hands. 'I'm just curious. And being curious hasn't killed me.'

'Yet.' Finn returned his attention to the wine bottle, and drew out the cork. He was clearly not going to be forthcoming. 'Are there glasses?' he asked.

'Yes.' Cat moved to a cupboard and fetched a couple of glasses from the shelf. There was one more thing she wanted to know. Turning back to him, she said, 'What happened to the millionaire's daughter?'

'Last time I checked she was living in Dubai.'

'With her millionaire daddy?'

'Yes.'

'What's her name?'

'Izzy.'

'Izzy. Were you in love with her?'

That closed look came over Finn's face again. 'What's with the third degree, Cat?'

Cat set down the glasses and hopped up on a high stool. 'Sorry. I find it hard to shut up once I get started. You should take it as a compliment. I don't talk much to people I don't like.'

'I remember that from working on the film with you. You used to prefer talking to horses.'

'Horses talk more sense than most people I've met.'

Picking up one of the wineglasses, Finn squinted at the ostentatious logo before pouring the wine. 'Designer glasses! Holy shit. I knew this house was sold fully furnished, but I wonder why they left stuff like this behind?'

'What else would they do with it? I guess Izzy and her daddy have all the designer crystal they need in Dubai.' Cat took the glass from Finn and sipped. 'There's designer stuff all over the gaff – Philippe Starck fittings in the bathrooms and all. Don't worry, I've taken good care of it. It's been like playing house living here. I'll give you a guided tour if you like, once I've had something to eat. Cheers.'

'Cheers.' They chinked glasses, and then Cat broke off another hunk of bread, prised out the blade from her penknife and cut into the cheese. 'I guess I'll have to find somewhere else to live, now that the Mystery Buyer's son's showed up.'

'I guess you will.'

'Let's hope I can find somewhere locally. I like Lissamore.' She let a silence fall, and looked at him expectantly. Stupid Finn! He wasn't picking up on his cues. 'When's your dad due?'

'Once I've got the place up and running. It could take a while. He wants me to fix the pool, paint and decorate – that sort of thing. I'm going to need to hire some help.'

'I could help you. I wield a mean paintbrush. I used to be a scenic artist, remember?'

'I remember. But are you any good? Someone told me you got kicked off that film.'

Cat gave him an indignant look. 'I got kicked off for not being legit, not for being crap at my job. They got all po-faced when they found out I'd no social insurance number.'

'You really are a floater, then?'

Cat nodded. 'Will work for food.'

'And bed?'

'That depends on where the bed is. As I said, I like Lissamore.'

They looked at each other warily. Then Finn said: 'All right. You can stay on here.'

'Thank you. That's very decent of you.'

'Just till my dad rolls up. How did you get in, by the way?'

Cat tapped a finger to her nose. 'Not telling. I can get into most places, if I want to. Did you never read the *Just So Stories*?'

'No. What are they?'

'They're meant for little children, but they've become cult classics. My mother used to read them to me. The one about the cat was the one I loved most. Once a cat decides she wants to come into your house, you can't keep her out, you know.'

'I'd noticed.' He smiled, then turned and went out into the hall.

Cat narrowed her eyes at his retreating back. He had a great smile, she decided, once he let his guard down. She remembered the night at the wrap party, and the kiss they'd shared. How many girls had he kissed since then? Plenty, probably. Plenty of lovely LA girls with lissom golden limbs and luscious golden hair, and pearly American teeth. She must be a complete culture shock after what he was used to. Like something out of *Wallander*, he'd said. Hell – at least she'd washed today. Her biodegradable travel soap may not

69

have had the sweetest scent in the world, but she guessed that was compensated for by the wild-rose-smelling house.

Back Finn came, lugging another box. He dumped it on the counter, and together they pulled out more provender. Coco Pops, chocolate HobNobs, apples. A bumper pack of popcorn, a six-pack of beer, a copy of *Empire* magazine, an iPod with a docking station.

'Oh, look – you have music!' she said, biting into her bread and cheese and taking a swig from her wineglass. 'Put something on, and let me show you around.'

'Any requests?'

'Surprise me.' Sliding down from her high stool, Cat helped herself to an apple. Her sleeping bag was starting to come adrift from around her shoulders, so she looped it over her forearms and let the ends trail behind her as she moved towards the door. 'Will you bring a candle?'

'I have a torch in here somewhere. You should be careful – you're a walking fire hazard in that sleeping bag.'

Cat froze, and the sleeping bag slid to the floor as the first strains of Springsteen's *Born to Run* oozed through the speakers.

'What's up?' asked Finn.

'Just what you said. About being a . . . a fire hazard. It gave me the shivers. That's why I had to leave the houseboat, you see. It was . . . someone tried to burn it down.' She gave a shaky laugh, retrieved the sleeping bag and reinstated it around her shoulders. 'Sounds stupid, doesn't it? Imagine trying to set fire to a house built on water. Anyway, I shouldn't worry about this sleeping bag. It's Millets' finest fireproof stock.'

'Shit.' Even by the light of the candles, Cat could make out the concerned furrow between Finn's brows. 'You mean, someone tried to burn you out?'

She nodded.

70

'What did the Guards have to say?'

'They said,' she told him, 'that I should have been more security conscious.'

'Did they find out who did it?'

'No. But I know who did it.'

'Who?'

'A bloke who thought I was up for it, and who got cross when he realised I wasn't.'

'Did you report him?'

'No.'

'Why not?'

'He was a Guard.'

'Bastard! It must have been terrifying.'

'Yes, it was. I don't scare easily, but that fire was no foolin' around. I was out of there like a cat out of hell.'

'Did you lose a lot of stuff?'

'I don't really do "stuff". I grabbed my backpack in time, and my paintbox. I'd have been fit to be tied if my paintbox had gone up in smoke. It'd cost a fortune to replace.'

'I saw paintings, hanging on the wall in the sitting room. Are they yours?'

'Yes.'

'Mind if I take a look?'

'Sure.'

Finn had fished a torch from the box. 'Didn't it freak you out, having to light candles here?'

'I didn't have any choice. Candles was all they had in the local store.'

'I'll get the electricity reconnected tomorrow. And we'll take a drive into Galway – stock up on essentials. How do you manage for transport?'

'I had a bicycle, when I was living on the houseboat. But it's handy enough to walk into Lissamore from here.'

71

'Was the bicycle banjaxed in the fire?'

'No. Some gobshite threw it in the canal. Probably the same dickhead who was responsible for burning me out.'

'I guess you can claim everything back on insurance.'

'Nothing belonging to me was insured. The people who owned the houseboat will put in a hefty claim, but I won't get anything. I think they're kind of relieved that the place is gone, if truth were told. Too much responsibility.'

'It wasn't yours?'

'No. I was houseboat-sitting.'

'Of course. I forgot you held Marxist beliefs about property ownership.' Finn aimed the beam of his torch at the kitchen door. 'After you,' he said.

In the sitting room, dustsheets still shrouded most of the furniture, giving the place a funereal appearance. 'What's underneath all that?' Finn asked.

'Furniture. Very Terence Conran. Not my style at all.'

'What is your style?'

'I'm not sure I have one.' Cat bit into her apple. 'I've never cared enough about keeping up appearances to develop a sense of style. My stepmother deplored my lack of interest in fashion.'

'You have a stepmother?'

'Yes. A wicked one. She's tried to poison my father's mind against me.'

'Has she really?'

'Well, it was already pretty poisoned with hooch.'

'You mean he's an alcoholic?'

'Yep. That's why I ran away from home. I could write a misery memoir, except I can't truthfully say I've ever been that miserable.'

'How do you get by?'

'Moneywise?'

72

'Yes.'

'I sell my paintings,' lied Cat. 'Wanna buy one?'

Finn turned his attention to the paintings that Cat had fixed to the wall with masking tape. They looked better by candlelight, Cat decided. You couldn't see the mistakes. The disadvantage of working in acrylic was that it dried faster than oil paint, so mistakes were harder to put right. But because acrylics were so much cheaper than oils, using them made sense to Cat.

'Wow!' said Finn, aiming the beam of his torch at the wall. 'These are great! These are really fine. I mean, I don't know much about art, but I can see that you genuinely have talent. Where did you train?'

'I didn't. My dad wanted me to go to the Slade, in London, but the last thing I wanted was to go back to school.'

'I wouldn't have thought that art college was much like school. I'd have thought art college might be quite a blast.'

Cat shrugged. 'I don't like being taught things. I'd rather learn from my own mistakes. The only good teacher I ever had was my brother.'

'Yeah? What did you learn from him?'

'How to skip stones.'

'Good skill to have.' Finn resumed his scrutiny of Cat's paintings. 'How much do you ask for them?'

'Five hundred euros each.' What!? Where had *that* come from?

'That's a lot. My ma gets about two fifty a pop.'

'Your ma's an artist?'

'An amateur. But she sells quite well during the tourist season. Her stuff's on display in Fleur's boutique in the village.'

'Fleurissima? I wouldn't dare go into that shop! How does she get away with charging those kind of prices?'

He shrugged 'Women are stupid when it comes to clothes. Izzy used to spend a fortune in there.'

Izzy. *Izzy!* Why did Cat hate her so? 'It's the kind of place my stepmother would love, too,' she remarked.

Finn returned his attention to Cat's artwork. 'Five hundred euros a pop? Seriously?'

'Three to you. Special price.'

'Nice try, but no cigar. How much do you charge for your house-painting skills?'

'I told you – will work for food.'

'You mean it?'

Cat nodded. She'd be glad to work in return for a roof over her head. Tomorrow she'd put in a call to her father, and see about getting some money from him. She wondered what she'd need to set up the poste restante thingy Raoul had talked about. She reckoned some form of ID would be required, and she doubted that her fake student card would cut any dice. Shit. Maybe she'd have to go legit and get herself a passport, after all. Oh! Just the thought of filling in the forms made her feel dizzy.

'Tomorrow we'll head in to Galway and pay a visit to B&Q,' said Finn. 'Stock up on DIY stuff. Anywhere else you need to go?'

'Um. I wouldn't mind getting to the art suppliers. I'd love to be able to start painting on canvas again.'

'Is that what you usually paint on?'

'Yes. But if I can't get my hands on canvas, I'll paint on anything. I found a roll of wallpaper in a cupboard here – hope you don't mind. I even took to painting on old shards of slate once, when I ran out of funds. Most of my money goes on art supplies.'

'Most of mine goes on dive gear.' Finn moved toward the window, and turned off the torch. In the plate glass, Cat could see candles reflected and, beyond the glass, the dark hump of Inishclare island. 'There was a dive outfit on that island once,' he remarked. 'That's where I cut my teeth.'

'What age were you when you started?'

'Twelve.'

'So it's your lifelong passion?'

'Yeah.'

'What about your plans to turn this place into a dive outfit?'

His smile was a little rueful. 'Setting up a dive school here would mean infringing on Ma's orchard.'

'The orchard at the bottom of the garden belongs to your ma, does it?'

'Yeah.' He smiled down at her. 'She has no Marxist scruples about owning property. Those two acres are her pride and joy.'

Cat remembered the three women earlier that day who had enjoyed a *fête champêtre* in the orchard, and how carefree they'd seemed. It was an eye-opener for Cat to see women revelling in each other's company: her mother had been the only woman she had ever trusted. And hadn't she every reason to be mistrustful of her own sex? She'd been bullied at boarding school, set upon (on more than one occasion) by gangs of girl thugs (the ones who wore pink were the worst), and cold-shouldered by her stepmother.

Her stepmother. She hoped to God that Ophelia didn't pick up the phone tomorrow when she called the Crooked House to petition her father for cash. Even the sound of Oaf's voice over the telephone line had the power to make Cat want to puke. That sick-making, saccharine, actorish voice that Oaf put on was worse than listening to Burt Bacharach. How had her dad fallen for it? Why had he betrayed the memory of perfect Paloma by marrying that gold-digging has-been?

75

She suddenly felt very tired. But she didn't want to go to bed just yet.

'Let's finish the wine,' she said to Finn, 'and watch the sun come up.'

'Nice idea,' said Finn with a smile. 'I'll get my camera. I've some great shots of the sunrise over Inishclare that I took a couple of years back.'

'I'd love to see them.'

'Coming up.'

Finn disappeared into the kitchen, and Cat settled down on one of the Terence Conran chaise longues and tried to make herself comfortable. Bruce Springsteen was bouncing off the walls, warbling about Candy's room, and Cat wished he wouldn't, because it was such a sexy song. That iPod was a miniature miracle, she thought, especially when compared to her great clumsy brick of a Sony Walkman. It had belonged to her mother, and before the fire Cat had used to plug herself into it every night before she slept, even though it devoured batteries. Cat could ill afford batteries – but, like art materials, they were her essentials, the way make-up or hair straighteners or gossip magazines were for some women.

'More grub.' Finn was back, bearing a tray on which he'd laid out a kind of antipasto. He set it down, and refilled Cat's wineglass. 'Izzy and me used to do this, way back,' he said.

'Do what?'

'Crack open a bottle of wine and watch the sun rise. Here, have a look.' He handed her his camera. 'See? That was taken at around this time of year. With a bit of luck, we might get something similar today – the weather conditions are about the same.'

Cat looked at the picture displayed on the screen of Finn's camera. It showed a breathtaking tangerine sun rising over a roseate sea. Silhouetted against the horizon, a figure was holding a fiendishly difficult yoga pose with seeming effortlessness.

'Who's the yoga master?' she asked, knowing full well what the answer would be.

She wasn't wrong, and there was a smile in his voice when he replied. 'That's Izzy,' said Finn. 'I'll never forget that night. I had exams to take, to do with Nitrox diving. She sat and read and read and re-read the dive manual out loud, so that it would stick in my head. It was the most boring stuff in the world, but she made it sound like poetry. Isn't she gorgeous?'

Chapter Five

Río was looking at pictures of a mobile home on the internet. It was due to be delivered today in two separate sections to Adair's oyster farm, and Río was to be there to meet it.

The 'Bentley' was like no mobile home she had ever seen. Her experience of caravanning had been limited to the Roadmasters of her childhood, when she and Dervla had gone with their parents to spend a fortnight of the summer in a trailer park in Sligo. Those mobile homes had been all Beauty Board and Crimplene curtains and swirly Acrilan carpets, with unreliable water pressure (the shower would peter out just as you were shampooing your hair), and intermittent electricity during storms. She and Dervla had fought over who would get the top bunk in the confined space of the 'spare' bedroom, and entertainment had consisted of 479-piece jigsaws (masquerading as 500-piece jigsaws), back copies of the *Reader's Digest*, and Cluedo with Mrs White and the lead piping missing.

This Bentley yoke was a revelation. Its galley-style kitchen was bigger than the one in Río's apartment, it boasted an en-suite shower room as well as a state-of-the-art tiled bathroom, and a 'bespoke' flame-effect hole-in-the-wall fire. Not only did the Bentley have an integrated washer/drier and a dishwasher, it also featured a Smeg American fridge-freezer, a kitchen island unit complete with built-in wine cooler, and a home cinema and surround-sound system. There was a study kitted out in tan leather office furniture, 'beautiful' bed throws and scatter cushions (Río thought them the most hideous things she'd ever seen), and – ta-ran-ta-ra! to cap it all – there were 'soft-close' toilet seats. Río could not help but notice the plural. The single loo in her bathroom had a seat that slid out of place every time you sat on it, due to the fact that she hadn't got around to replacing a missing bolt.

When he'd asked her to oversee the advent of the Bentley, Adair had made some joke about the fact that he'd gone from being a property baron to being trailer park trash almost overnight. Trailer park trash! This mobile home was fit for a queen: or, at the very least, a princess. And there was, of course, a scratch-resistant quartz vanity unit in the bathroom for HRH Izzy, and a custom-built closet in her boudoir.

Río wondered how much this Bentley yoke had cost Adair. A fraction, she conceded, of what it had cost Shane to buy Coral Mansion; but then, Shane could afford to splash money around now. Back when they'd conceived Finn and lived in a squat, neither of them would ever have dreamed that Shane might one day be in a position to afford as much as a time-share in a crumby bedsit, let alone an apartment in a brownstone overlooking Central Park and a house on Mulholland Drive. She'd had a phone call from Finn first thing that morning to say that, since his flight had landed at one o'clock am (having been held up by mutinous cabin crew on another go-slow), he had decided not to disturb his auld mammy.

'You should know that I can't imagine anything lovelier than being disturbed by you!' she'd told him crossly. 'You're a pig, Finn. I need a hug from you more than I need anything right now.'

'Look on it as delayed gratification, Ma,' he'd told her. And when she'd asked him about the 'surprise' he'd mentioned yesterday, he'd said, 'Hold on tight. You're going to fall off your chair.' He was right. Because she'd been leaning backwards rather precariously when Finn revealed that the Mystery Buyer of Coral Mansion was none other than his dad – Río had done just that.

'Well, I'll be doggone,' she said. 'Shane must be on Monopoly money.'

'I think he got it at a knockdown price.'

'Ha! That's exactly what should be done with that hideous carbuncle. Just knock the joint down and start again.'

'Not a chance, Ma. I'm here to oversee the refurbishment. But you'll be glad to know that the first casualty will be the yoga pavilion. I'm going to demolish it today.'

'That eyesore? Yes!'

'I'll be kipping here, by the way, while I'm working on the joint.'

'That's cool.'

The sleeping arrangements suited Río because, while she adored her drop-dead-gorgeous son, he was six foot two, and her apartment overlooking the harbour was tiny. She'd have him round for dinner tonight: he'd be jetlagged, she guessed, and in need of red meat and red wine after knocking down the pavilion that had been built for Felicity all those years ago, when Adair had been rich, and Shane had been poor. How the tables had turned!

She supposed Shane buying Coral Mansion was a bit like that intrepid mountaineer Mallory trying to conquer Everest 'because it was there', or Richard Burton buying the Krupp Diamond because it was up for grabs, or Imelda Marcos spending a fortune on shoes she'd never wear. She also supposed that he'd finally given in to Finn's badgering about converting the joint into a scuba-dive centre. The badgering had been going on for so long now that it had become a family joke.

Río knew as well that it would give Shane no little pleasure to own the biggest, brashest, most 'fuck-off' residence in Lissamore, particularly since it had once belonged to the man who had been his rival in love. How would poor Adair Bolger, slogging over his oyster beds and slumming it in a mobile home (even one as deluxe as the Bentley), feel when he found out that Shane Byrne was now the owner of the erstwhile Villa Felicity?

Ping! Outlook Express announced the arrival of an email in her inbox. Oh! As if life wasn't complicated enough, the email was from Isabella Bolger, 'Sent from My iPhone', and the subject matter was the Bentley.

Hi, Río, she read, when she clicked on the envelope icon. I understand that Dad has asked you to meet the Bentley people when they deliver to the site. Thank you so much for helping out. Just to let you know that I shall be arriving in Lissamore this evening. I wanted to check out for myself what Dad's accommodation for the foreseeable future is going to be like. I had hoped to be staying in Coolnamara Castle Hotel until the plumbing, etc is taken care of in the Bentley, but I've just found out that they're fully booked due to some fly-fishing event. Would you happen to know if there's anything going in B&Bs in the village?

All best, Izzy

Oh, God. It would be unmannerly of Río to expect Princess Izzy to bed down in a B&B. Should she phone Finn and ask him if he could put her up in Coral Mansion? Um, no. That was so not a good idea. Río didn't pry too much into her son's affairs, but she knew enough about his love life to hazard a guess that he might not welcome Izzy back into her life with open arms. Also, it would be disconcerting – to say the least – for Izzy to find out that Finn was now ensconced in her former home, just down the shore from where the Bentley was to be parked. Life was complicated? Life was *bonkers*!

There was only one thing for it. Hi, Izzy, she typed. How good to hear from you! You're more than welcome to stay with me, if you don't mind sleeping on a sofabed. What time will you be here?

The response was immediate. That's really kind of you. I should be arriving around 7.00. Can I buy you dinner in O'Toole's?

Oh, well. She'd have to delay Finn's roast dinner till another time. Río was just about to type 'Thank you – that would be lovely!' when her phone went. It was Finn, again.

'Hi, Ma,' he said. 'Fancy dinner in O'Toole's tonight?'

'No!' she said. 'I'm cooking for . . . Fleur.'

'Fleur can come, too.'

'No! She's bringing the baby.'

'Oh. Shame. There's someone I'd love you to meet.'

'What? Who?'

'Just a girl.'

'A girl, Finn? What girl?'

'A girl I think you'd like. She's a really talented painter. She's going to help me out with the refurbishment of this gaff.'

'With Coral Mansion?'

'Yeah.'

'She's a house painter?'

'No. She's like an artist painter. But she needs somewhere to stay, so she's giving me a hand here, in return for bed and board.'

'Oh. Is she – um – is she like . . . a *girl*friend, Finn?'

'No.'

'You said that too fast. That means she could *become* a girlfriend.'

Ping!

Or I could cook for you! I've just passed a fish shop and they've fresh langoustines! Shall I stop and get some? Iz. xx

Thank Jesus! **Frsh langustins heaven!** typed Río, and pressed 'Send' without bothering to correct the spelling mistakes.

'Just because she's a girl, Ma, doesn't mean that there has to be a romantic thing going on,' Finn rebuked her.

'Of course not, sweetheart,' said Río abstractedly, wishing that Izzy had chosen another time to descend upon her. She hadn't even been able to give Finn a hug yet! 'I'm glad you've got someone to help you. Now, forgive me. I have to go. I'm running late. Love you!'

'Send my love to Fleur and Marguerite.'

'What?'

'Your dinner guests.'

'Oh, yes. Bye.'

Río put her phone down and picked it up again as her ringtone sounded. It was the Bentley delivery man to say that he was having problems getting the state-of-the-art mobile home down the bumpy boreen that led to Adair's oyster farm, and could she get there ASAP?

83

Life was bonkers? thought Río, as she grabbed her jacket and her car keys. No, no. Life was certifiable!

Some hours later, Río had seen the Bentley safely moored at the rear of Adair's horrible rundown bungalow. (The Bentley had received a bit of a bashing on its way down the boreen: some of the feature Western Red Cedar panelling had come a cropper against a drystone wall leaving it scarred for life, all the knocking about meant that the toilet seats weren't as 'soft-close' as they were supposed to be, and Izzy's custom-built closet had lost some of its bespoke shelving.)

But Río was happy that the thing had arrived reasonably intact. Tomorrow, the two sections would be joined together, and plumbing and electricity would be instated as if by the deft hands of magical elves, and all would be in turn-key condition for Adair. Once he'd wound up his business dealings in Dubai he could come winging his way to the west coast of Ireland, ready to embark upon his ill-advised new career as an oyster farmer.

At seven o'clock precisely, Río's doorbell rang. Buzzing Izzy in, she turned off her phone. She didn't want any calls from Finn interrupting their cosy evening. Well, she *did* want phone calls from Finn – of course she did – but not while Izzy was here.

'Izzy! Hello! Long time!' she said, as she watched the girl climb the stairs that led to her eyrie. 'You look fantastic!'

She could have parroted the words in her sleep, for Izzy always looked fantastic. But this time the words rang hollow as Izzy's cheeks. The girl looked awful – like a ghost of her former self. The minxy, golden babe that lived in Río's memory had turned into a wretchedly thin, pasty-faced spectre.

'Oh, Río! It's so good of you to have me! I can't tell you

how grateful I am. I was dreading coming back to Lissamore – I was – I was dreading everything! And . . . and . . . here are your langoustines.'

Thrusting a carrier bag at Río, Izzy burst into tears.

'Come in, come in at once!' said Río, horrified. To see Isabella Bolger cry – Princess Isabella, who was normally so soignée and so on top of things – was truly disturbing. Bundling her through the door, Río led the girl to the sofa and said 'Sit!' Then she did what most women do when confronted by a weeping compadre: she cast around for the corkscrew.

'Red or white?' she asked.

'White, please.'

Río shoved the bag of langoustines into the fridge and pulled out a bottle of white.

On the sofa, Izzy was rummaging in her bag. 'How stupid! I don't have a tissue . . .'

'Here.' Tearing off a section of kitchen towel, Río handed her a wodge.

'I'm sorry,' sobbed Izzy. 'My car stalled just as I was coming into the village, and a man in a van behind started honking his horn at me.'

What? All those tears because of such a minor upset? Río guessed Izzy must be pre-menstrual.

'And then he started shouting at me. He told me . . . he told me to take driving lessons!'

Río raised her eyes to heaven. *Sweet Jesus! Get over yourself, Isabella!* Sloshing South Africa's finest plonk into a glass, she handed it to Izzy with ill-concealed impatience, resisting the impulse to tell the girl to stop being such a wimp.

'I'm sorry.' Izzy managed a wan smile, then raised the glass to her lips and took a sip. 'I guess I'm just tired after the drive from Dublin. Thanks for the wine.'

'You're welcome.' Río took a seat opposite. 'You're back

85

living in Dublin then?' she asked, glad of a conversational gambit.

'Yes. I've got a position in a marketing company.'

'What made you decide to come back?'

'Not the job satisfaction, that's for sure.' Izzy blew her nose. 'I guess it was . . . well, when Dad told me he was coming back to Ireland, I thought I might as well come home too.'

'What was Dubai like?'

'Bloody horrible. Some good wreck diving, though.'

Río plucked a piece of lint from her sleeve. She didn't want to be diverted on to the topic of diving, because if they went there, Finn's name would be bound to come up. 'When's Adair due back?' she asked, even though she knew perfectly well when he was due.

'Next week. He's just tying up some loose ends.' Izzy took a swig of wine, and then she started crying again. 'Oh, Río!' she wailed. 'Is the cottage really as bad as it looks on the internet? I couldn't believe it when Dad showed me. I couldn't believe that he was serious about buying it.'

'The cottage is pretty bad, all right,' conceded Río. 'But the mobile home is more like a mobile palace!' She invested her voice with gung-ho enthusiasm. 'You needn't have any worries that your dad isn't going to be comfortable, Izzy. It's the Taj Mahal in miniature.'

'Is it? Is it really?'

'Yes. And I'm sure that he can make the cottage into a really lovely home. It'll take a lot of work, of course, but your dad's never been afraid of hard work.' The irony struck her forcibly now, of Adair working like a navvy on a rundown cottage while Río's son and his father swanned around in Coral Mansion.

'How . . . how long do you think it'll take to fix the place up?'

'Six months, or thereabouts, I'd have thought if he hires

86

some help and works flat out.' Río looked at Izzy curiously. Her face had gone an ugly, mottled shade of puce.

'Six months?' she whispered. 'Working flat out?'

Río nodded. 'Are you all right, Izzy? You're looking——'

'My dad can't work flat out for six months on some crappy little house!'

'He's done it before,' Río pointed out. 'Sure, didn't he start his career as a builder?'

Izzy flinched, and tears started to course down her cheeks again.

'I know he's come a long way since then,' said Río. 'But, hey – there are swings and there are roundabouts, Izzy. You win some, you lose some.' God, she was even beginning to talk like Adair! Funny the way clichés came so easily when you were trying to console someone.

'I can't bear to think of him navvying!' whimpered Izzy.

Río got to her feet and moved to the window. She was feeling a tad exasperated with the girl now. Wasn't everybody in Ireland rolling up their sleeves and fielding the flak that life was firing at them? Izzy Bolger's darling daddy wasn't the only ex-property tycoon taking a reality check.

'I think he's kind of looking forward to putting the place to sorts. He was full of beans the last time I talked to him.'

'He's not able for it, Río.'

'*Arra*, he'll be grand.' Río started to busy herself deadheading a geranium. She was beginning to regret her invitation to Izzy to stay the night. Maybe she should have sent her in the direction of Coral Mansion after all, where she could be accommodated in the style to which she was accustomed.

'No. He won't be grand, Río,' said Izzy. 'He's dying.'

'What?' Río turned back to Izzy. The redness had left her face; she was ashen now. 'What . . . did you say? That . . .'

'Daddy's dying.'

The withered geranium blossom dropped to the floor. 'Adair's ill?'

Izzy nodded. 'Cancer.'

'Oh. Oh, God.' Río's hands went to her mouth, and she shut her eyes for a long moment. Then she moved to the sofa and sat down beside Izzy. Putting her arms around her, she gathered the girl against her. 'Oh, God, Izzy. I am so sorry. I am so, so sorry. Words can't—'

'I know. You don't have to say anything.'

No words were adequate. Not even the one-size-fits-all clichés to which Adair was so partial. She remembered the last time she'd seen him, before he left for Dubai. It had been in Dublin: he'd put her up in a splendid room in the Four Seasons, and treated her to the theatre, and bought her dinner in Patrick Guilbaud. Except he hadn't called it dinner. He'd called it a 'slap-up feed', and when his Charolais beef and foie gras had been set in front of him he'd rubbed his hands together with gusto, the way a cartoon character might. That was what was so endearing about Adair: despite his wealth and his very real business acumen and the power he wielded, he was possibly the most down-to-earth, least affected person Río had ever met. And now this larger-than-life, convivial, generous man was dying.

Izzy disengaged herself from Río's embrace and blew her nose again.

'When did you find out?' Río asked.

But Izzy just shook her head, clearly too distressed to answer. Reaching for her bag, she pulled out an envelope and handed it to Río.

'Am I to read this?'

Izzy nodded.

Inside the envelope was a folded sheet of A4 paper.

Dear Dr Rashidya, she read. Thank you very much for being honest with me. I appreciate this, because it gives me a chance to get off my arse and spend the last year of my life doing something I've always wanted to do. It'll amuse you to know that I've bought that oyster farm I was telling you about, so I'm going to realise my dream of living off the fat of the land (OK – the fat of the sea) back in my native country.

It's funny how you get your priorities right when the Big C comes calling. I've realised that living the good life isn't about drinking Cristal champagne or having gold-plated taps in your bathroom. For me, the good life will mean a pint of Guinness in my local pub after an honest day's hard labour, and the sound of the sea on my doorstep. In the best of all possible worlds, the good life might also mean finally marrying the woman I love, if she'll have me. I've always believed that anything is possible, if a man wants it badly enough.

You might write a letter of reference for me to my doctor in Ireland. He can recommend a specialist when the time comes, but until then I just want to truck on as best I can. That medication sure does exactly what it says on the tin, and as long as it keeps kicking in I won't be telling anyone. No point in raining all over someone else's parade – especially not Izzy's. She worries about me enough as it is.

It was nice knowing you, doc. Again, thanks for everything. Next time you have dinner in Burj Al

Arab, order the oysters. They just might have my name on them.

All best,
Adair Bolger

Oh, God. Oh, God! Río couldn't bear it. But if she couldn't bear it, how must Izzy be feeling? With difficulty, she swallowed the sob rising in her throat. Dissolving into tears wasn't going to help: she must be strong for Izzy. *Keep Right on to the End of the Road. Pack Up Your Troubles in Your Old Kit Bag. You'll Never Walk Alone.* Clichés, clichés – keep them coming. There's comfort to be wrung from the commonplace.

'I'm guessing you found this on his computer,' she said.

Izzy nodded. 'Yes. The week before I left Dubai.'

'There couldn't be some mistake, could there?'

'No. I phoned Dr Rashidya. He was as honest with me as he was with Dad. He has pancreatic cancer, Río, probably brought on by stress. As you know, the past couple of years have been tough on him. I suspected something was up, but he's been keeping it well hidden.'

'And he really has just a year?'

'Give or take a couple of months.'

A couple of months! Oh God, how precious a couple of months must now seem to Adair! Ungrateful Río spent half the beautiful winter months in Lissamore wishing them away, waiting for spring to arrive, and with it the all-important tourist trade. How dare she curl her lip at such a priceless commodity as time? How blessed she was to have it on her hands.

'Oh, poor Izzy. Oh, poor Adair! Oh . . . why is life so unfair?'

'I've been saying that to myself every day since I found out. It's like . . . I know Dad had money and was lucky that

90

way, but his quality of life was pretty crap, you know. I mean, he just worked. He just worked really hard. And then the divorce happened and he lost everything – virtually every-thing, Río – that's no word of a lie. But I think losing the Villa Felicity was the biggest blow of all.'

Oh, Jesus! How could Río ever tell Izzy that the Villa Felicity was now in the possession of the Byrne boys? She'd have to keep schtum about that until she dreamed up some way of cladding the iron fist in a velvet glove.

'Does he know that you know? About his . . . about the cancer?'

'No. Like he said in that letter, he doesn't want to rain on my parade. It's been so bloody hard, pretending. I should be up for an Oscar. And then he goes and buys that horrible little house, thinking he's going to be happy living there. How could he ever imagine that he's going to be happy spending the last months of his life working an oyster farm? I remember Finn telling me that he spent a summer working on an oyster farm once, and he said it was backbreaking work. And Finn was – Finn *is* – young, and fit.'

'It's always been your dad's dream.'

Río remembered how Adair had shared with her his dream of maybe one day retiring to Coolnamara and 'living off the fat of the sea', as he had joked in the letter to the Dubai doctor. They'd been sitting on the deck of the Villa Felicity, drinking hot chocolate to warm her up after a swim, and it had been the first time she'd seen a vulnerable side to him. But when he'd told her of his maritime aspirations, Río had laughed and compared him to Marie Antoinette masquerading as a shepherdess. And now Adair really was going to try and live that dream for as long as he had left.

'Where exactly is it? The farm?' asked Izzy, helping herself to more kitchen towel.

'It's about a mile along the beach from Coral— from the Villa Felicity.'

'I'll go there in the morning and check it out. Is it as bad as it looks in the photographs on the internet?'

There was no point in lying: Izzy would see the place for herself tomorrow. 'It's quite possibly worse.'

'Oh, God!'

'But honestly, Izzy – the mobile home is state-of-the-art. I mean, even to call it a mobile home is a misnomer for starters. It doesn't even have wheels.'

Izzy nodded. 'I think they call them leisure lodges now, not mobile homes. I'm glad he'll have some kind of creature comforts.' Swigging back the remains of the wine in her glass, she held it out to Río. 'Could I have some more, please? I did bring some to go with the langoustines – a lovely Loire Valley Chenin Blanc – but it's in the car.'

'I take it your bag's still in the car, too?'

'Yeah. I'll go get it now.'

'You stay there. Give me the keys and I'll bring it up.'

Río didn't want to run the risk of Izzy bumping into Finn on the main street. He'd be likely to be heading into O'Toole's about now, with his new squeeze – if squeeze was what she was. The last thing poor Izzy needed was more emotional aggro. Río topped up their wineglasses, then got to her feet.

'I'll cook this evening,' she said, 'and you take it easy. You're right, that drive from Dublin always knocks the stuffing out of you a bit.'

'Oh, no, please let me cook for you!' said Izzy. She handed Río a key card emblazoned with the Alfa Romeo logo. 'It'll be a distraction – especially if I do a really complicated recipe.'

'Rather you than me, in that case. What had you in mind?'

'Sautéed langoustines with Chardonnay reduction.'

Cripes, thought Río. 'Sounds delicious,' she said. 'I hope I've all the ingredients.'

'I don't imagine you've any truffle oil? Langoustines are divine with a truffle dressing.'

'You imagine right that I've no truffle oil,' smiled Río. 'And I don't fancy you'll get hold of it in Ryan's corner shop, either.'

'I can improvise. I'm quite good at that.'

Río moved to the door, where she'd left her sandals, and slid her feet into them. 'Where did you learn to cook, Izzy?'

'Mummy gave me a course in Ballymaloe for my birthday a couple of years ago.'

Of course she did! Welcome to the rarified world of Isabella Bolger, where you get cookery lessons from a celebrity chef and langoustines come with truffle dressing and wine was a lovely Loire Valley Chenin Blanc, not a cheap and cheerful Obikwa from South Africa. Adair might have lost all his money, Río surmised as she wound leather thongs around her ankles, but his daughter was clearly still high maintenance. She remembered what a beautiful couple Izzy and Finn had made, back in the days when they were full of plans for setting up their dive outfit together. Río had known even then that Izzy was out of Finn's league, just as Izzy had considered her father to be out of Río's league. She remembered the party that Adair had thrown for her in the Villa Felicity, and how Izzy had tried to scupper any notions he might have entertained about a romantic involvement with Río. But then, Isabella was a daddy's girl through and through, and daddy's girls always got what they wanted, didn't they?

What, Río wondered, did Izzy want for her daddy now? That question was easily answered. She wanted him to live out the remainder of his days in peace and contentment, in the best of all possible worlds. And Río could help her. What had Adair said in his letter to Dr Rashidya, when he'd outlined his ideas of what constituted the good life?

The good life will mean a pint of Guinness in my local pub after an honest day's hard labour, and the sound of the sea on my doorstep. In the best of all possible worlds, the good life might also mean finally marrying the woman I love, if she'll have me. I've always believed that anything is possible, if a man wants it badly enough . . .

A year. What was one year? She, Río, was robustly healthy, and had, in all likelihood, loads more years ahead of her. Loads of years and countless months – unless some runaway bus had her number on it. Adair Bolger had been good to her, and she had given him very little in return. It was axiomatic. She had a wealth of time on her hands. She could afford to give him a year of her life.

From the depths of Izzy's capacious handbag came the sound of her phone tone. Río recognised it as 'Poor Little Rich Girl' – Shane had sung it in some revue he'd done years ago, when they'd been penniless students in Galway. It had been one of those jazz baby songs about living life to the max, whooping it up with cocktails and laughter. Adair had had his share of cocktails and laughter, of Cristal champagne and gold-plated taps in his bathroom, of hotel suites and slap-up feeds in the most expensive joints in the world, but they hadn't made him a happy man. Río guessed the least she could do was to allow him to die a happy man. A year. It would only take a year.

Izzy had fished her phone out of her bag, and was examining the display. Turning brimming eyes on Río, she managed a smile. 'It's Daddy,' she said.

Río nodded. Then she finished tying the straps on her sandals, mouthed 'Back soon!' and left Izzy to it.

Chapter Six

Cat was firing water at the peeling aquamarine walls of the swimming pool through a power hose. Yesterday in Galway, she and Finn had bought shedloads of stuff in B&Q. Paint and rollers and overalls and squeegees and tool belts – plus tools to go in them! Lots and lots of tools! Wrenches and pliers and scrapers and Stanley knives and gorilla bars! An angle grinder and an electric sander and a garden blower and a chain saw! Because Cat loved DIY stores the way other women love shopping malls, she'd felt fizzy with excitement as they'd barrelled up and down the aisles, filling their outsize trolleys and sniggering at the couples arguing over carpet samples and tiles. 'Look, Finn! Spray-paint in like – a zillion colours! Oh, wow! A laser saw! Look – an electric shredder! A multi-*multi*-bit screwdriver! A nail gun! *A nail gun!* I used to dream about having one of those when I was small!'

This morning they'd got up early and had a big breakfast – fried bacon and mushrooms and tomatoes courtesy of Finn, French toast courtesy of Cat – done in butter the way her mother had taught her. Now Cat, clad in B&Q heavy-duty overalls (she'd had to roll up the arms and legs by miles because they had only mountainy men sizes in stock), was halfway up a ladder at the deep end of the pool, whistling along to Bruce Springsteen who was crooning through her headphones about dancing in the dark. Finn's beautiful iPod Nano (she'd borrowed it from him earlier to see what all the fuss was about) had proved to be a revelation, and now he couldn't wrest it back from her. He'd promised that he'd download music for her later – all her favourite music in the world! – and she'd promised him that in return she would cook whatever he wanted for supper.

It had been a little rash of him to take her up on the offer, Cat thought, since she wasn't much of a chef, but she guessed that even she could manage steak and oven-ready chips. Yesterday, for lunch, they'd had salad made from lettuce and tomatoes and French beans pilfered from Finn's mother's garden, followed by strawberries. They'd eaten on the terrace, and Cat had felt a blissful sense of liberation sitting there, lunching alfresco in full view of anyone who might pass by on the shore, instead of skulking behind shuttered windows or ducking under the parapet on the roof of the Villa Felicity. She hadn't felt this comfortable or safe since the days when she and her mother had taken refuge in the treehouse in the grounds of the Crooked House, when Paloma had told her tales of how the leopard got his spots and how the camel got his hump. Those were the *Just So Stories*. The other stories, the ones that Cat listened to when she couldn't sleep, had come later.

After lunch Cat and Finn had demolished a rusty old yoga pavilion in the garden, and later in the evening, ravenous after all that hard physical graft, they'd gone to O'Toole's for dinner, and it had been like a date! Cat had never been on a date before! She'd had chowder and Finn had had crab claws and she had to keep reminding herself to stop looking at his mouth as he'd sucked garlic butter from the crab's fleshy pinkies, and to stop looking at his fingers as he'd dipped them in the finger bowl, and to stop glowering at the waitress who had flirted with him.

And now Finn had gone off to Lissamore to buy the ingredients for this evening's meal, and Bruce Springsteen on the iPod was telling Cat that – baby, she was born to run! – and a niggling little voice in her head was nagging at her to do the thing she'd been putting off for days. It was time to phone 'home'.

Unhooking herself from the iPod, Cat climbed to the top of the ladder, swung herself over the edge of the swimming pool, and onto the terrace. Her hateful phone – that link to the so-called 'real' world – was smirking at her from a sun lounger. She gave it a baleful look, picked it up, and dialled.

'Hello,' purred the voice on the other end of the line. 'You are through to the Crooked House. Please leave your message for Hugo or Ophelia Gallagher after—'

'Hello!' Ugh! Oaf's real voice had picked up. 'Hel-lo?' came the voice again. Resisting the impulse to chuck the phone back on the sun lounger, Cat took a deep breath and said 'Hi, Ophelia.'

'Oh. It's you. I was expecting someone else.'

'Yes, well. It's only me. Is Dad there?'

'Why do you want him?'

It's none of your business, thought Cat. 'He's my dad, isn't he?' she said. 'I guess that's reason enough to want to talk to him.'

'Oh. You wish to enquire after his health, is that it?' said Ophelia waspishly. 'Well, I can tell you, Cat, that he's not too good today, so I won't be putting you on to him. I suggest you try calling again some other time.'

'I need to talk to him, Oaf Elia.'

'And I'm telling you that you can't talk to him. Now run along and play, Cat. Goodbye.'

Uh-oh. This phone call was proving more problematic than Cat had anticipated.

'Wait!' said Cat. 'Don't put the phone down. Tell me when would be a good time to get him.'

'Um. How about never?'

Cat was feeling edgy now. She *had* to talk to Hugo. She had to get money. 'Listen, Ophelia. I want to get a poste restante thing set up, so that Dad can send me money. I haven't had any since the houseboat burnt down.'

'Why should he send you money?'

'He's always sent me money. You know that.'

'He sent you money, Cat, when he had some. Unfortunately, he doesn't have any, any more.'

'What do you mean?'

'He's broke. We're broke. You're broke. Conjugate the verb, why don't you, then go out and get yourself a job.'

'But . . . but . . .'

'*But . . . but . . .*' echoed Ophelia in a parody of Cat's voice. '*I don't know* how *to get a job*. Well, let me tell you, Caitlín – don't you think it's about time you did? Who do you think you are – Paris fucking Hilton? Do you think you can spend the rest of your life sponging off your father? You're nineteen fucking years old, and I can tell you that when I was nineteen I'd been gainfully employed for four years. Work it out. Four years is around two thousand days, Cat, and it makes me want to puke every time I hear you whinging on about needing money when you haven't worked a single fucking day in your entire life.'

'Ophelia.' Cat could feel panic mounting. 'Listen to me. You know I've no training, you know I—'

'Your father offered to send you to the Slade, Cat. To the fucking *Slade*. How many wannabe artists would cut their right hand off and learn to paint with their left one if they thought they had a chance of studying there?'

'I couldn't go there. You know I couldn't have hacked it.'

'Why? Because Diddums can't read? I have one word for you, Caitlín. Learn.'

And Ophelia cut her off.

Cat stood looking at the blank screen on her phone. In her mind's eye, she saw spidery text running across it, text that she'd looked at again and again and again on the implacable screen of Raoul's AppleMac, with her brother beside her, making noises of encouragement, his voice infinitely patient as he interpreted the hieroglyphics, trying to help her make sense of the words. She could hear him now, in her head intoning the phrases as they scrolled down . . .

The *Slade* School of *Fine Art* is concerned with con-temp-or-*ary* art and the prac-tice, his-tor-y and the-o-ries that inform it. It approaches the *stu-dy* and *prac-tice* of art in an en-quiring, in-vest-ig-ative, ex-peri-mental and re-search-minded way. Slade fac-il-ities and *infra-struc-ture* for research support the dis-course around painting, sculpture and *fine art* me-di-a . . .

No no no, Raoul! I don't want to go there! I don't want to go there! It's not me! Please don't make me.

It's all right. No one can make you do anything you don't want to do, Cat.

And then there was the look on her father's face when she'd replaced the Picasso reproductions on her wall with posters of Westlife. She'd only done it for a joke, but there had been real fury in Hugo's voice when he had said, very quietly, 'You stupid, stupid girl.'

The sound of footsteps on the shingle below brought Cat

back to the here and now. Could it be Finn, back from Lissamore with the T-bones for tonight's dinner? But why would he come the long way round, by the shore? Tossing her phone back on the sun lounger, Cat padded over to the sea wall and looked down.

Oh! What was America's Next Top Model doing, strutting her stuff along a pebbly beach in Lissamore? The blonde creature below looked as if she had just walked off a photoshoot for Calvin Klein casuals. She was wearing a plain blue shift dress and matching ballet-style pumps. The frames of her sunglasses matched her outfit, and she was texting on a silvery-blue iPhone. She was spray-tanned, manicured and L'Oréal-ed to within an inch of her life. She was *so* worth it!

The silvery-blue iPhone sounded.

'Hi, Río!' The girl's voice came loud and clear to Cat, who was crouching behind a straggly rose bush with her ears on high alert. 'Yes, thank you, I'm feeling much better – I slept really well, and you were sweet to let me lie in . . . Yes, I've had a look . . . It's a dump . . . The Bentley? Oh, the Bentley will be fine, I suppose, once they've licked it into shape . . . No, they're having problems with the plumbing. Something to do with the septic tank. I had promised to pay cash, but I'm withholding payment until I know the job is finished . . . Will you? . . . Thanks so much, I really appreciate it . . . See you later.'

The iPhone was clicked off and dropped into the capacious depths of a blue suede shoulder bag, then the girl moved towards the five-bar gate that led into Finn's mother's orchard and climbed it surprisingly nimbly, given the constraints of her tight-arsed skirt. Cat monitored America's Next Top Model's progress, feeling a tad apprehensive as she glided

100

between the furrows of runner beans, heading straight for the Villa Felicity, as if on castors.

Fight or flight? Or meet and greet? Cat opted for the latter. 'Hi.' Unfurling herself from under the rose bush, she moved towards the overgrown path that ran between garden and orchard. 'Can I help you?'

'Oh!' The girl jumped – literally jumped – back. Wayne Sleep would have been impressed. '*Oh!* Who are you, and what are you doing here?'

'I might ask you the same thing.' Cat folded her arms and gave the intruder an appraising look. 'This is private property, and you're trespassing.' The very useful Marxist principles that Cat had flaunted two days earlier suddenly didn't seem appropriate any more.

'My name is Isabella Bolger,' said the girl, with hauteur. 'And I used to live here. I think I have every right to visit my former family home, don't you?'

Her family home! You'd have thought that the Bolgers had lived in the Villa Felicity since the time of the High Kings, the way she was talking.

'I don't know what rights you have,' said Cat. 'But I'm willing to bet that you could be prosecuted if you take one step further in those pretty blue pumps.'

'Yeah? I'll take them off, so.'

Isabella glared back at Cat, kicked off her shoes, and walked straight onto the terrace of the Villa Felicity in her bare feet.

Touché! Cat felt a grudging admiration for her rival. For rival she was. This was gorgeous Izzy, Izzy of the complicated yoga pose, Izzy who made the Nitrox dive manual sound like poetry, Izzy who had once held Finn's heart in her French-manicured paws.

'Fancy a beer?' said Cat.

'A beer? It's only eleven o'clock in the morning.'

'There's a law against drinking beer at eleven o'clock in the morning?'

Cat strolled round the side of the house and into the kitchen. Taking two cans from the fridge she turned to find Izzy standing in the doorway, gazing round at the room as if she'd never seen it before.

'Do you live here now?' she asked.

'Yes,' said Cat, lobbing a can in Izzy's direction. To her surprise, the girl caught it adroitly. 'I live here with Finn Byrne.'

'Finn Byrne?' said Izzy, her mouth an 'O' of surprise. 'You mean . . . Río and Shane's Finn?'

'Yes. You know him?'

'Yes.' Izzy looked confused. 'I do. But Río didn't mention anything to me about Finn being back! How . . . how long has he been . . . living here?'

'Not long. I've been caretaking the place for him.' Cat pulled the tab on her can. 'We're getting it into shape for his old man.'

'For Shane?'

'Yeah. He's coming over in a couple of weeks, once he's finished with *The Corsican Brothers*.'

'*The Corsican Brothers*?'

'The movie he's working on, with Meryl Streep and Tilda Swinton,' fibbed Cat, just for fun. 'And The Rock,' she added, for extra embellishment. 'They were meant to have finished last month, but poor Meryl broke her toe. Shane's a bit pissed off, actually. He really wanted to get back here ASAP to do some hands-on work on the house.'

Izzy looked around again, and Cat saw her take in the breakfast detritus on the polished granite kitchen island, the half-empty cafetière, the two coffee mugs, the rose petals that had fallen onto the fruit bowl.

'Don't mind the mess,' said Cat. 'I haven't got round to clearing away breakfast yet.'

'That's all right.'

'Come on through to the sitting room.' Cat moved across the kitchen floor, helping herself to an apple on her way past the granite island. Yesterday's shopping list was propped up against the vase of wilting roses, and Cat wished she'd added 'condoms', and maybe 'champagne' – if she'd only known how to spell it.

In the sitting room she was pleased to see that Finn hadn't cleared away the wineglasses from last night. Here, too, rose petals lay scattered where they'd fallen. 'Yikes,' she said cheerfully. 'Those roses really have hit their best-before date. It was awful sweet of Finn to fill the house with flowers for me, but I'm the one who'll end up doing the Hoovering, dontcha know. Housework ain't his strongest suit. Not that I'm complaining.' Cat slanted Izzy a meaningful smile, then plonked herself down on a cushion on the floor. 'So. You lived here once?'

'Yes. This was our holiday home.'

'What brings you back to Lissamore?'

'My dad has bought a house just down the beach.'

'No shit! What made him decide to sell up here and move down the beach?'

'Well, it's a business move, really. He's bought an oyster farm.'

'So he's moving here permanently?'

A sorrowful look clouded Izzy's beautiful blue eyes. 'Yes.'

'But presumably you're not.'

'No. I live in Dublin.'

Cat gave Izzy the benefit of her best smile and waited for her next gambit.

103

'Is . . . is Finn coming to live here full time?' asked Izzy.

Cat shrugged. 'You know Finn. He's a bit of a nomad. What about you? Are you staying here for long?'

'No. I'm driving back tonight. I can't take any more time off work.'

'Shame,' lied Cat. 'What do you do?'

'I work in marketing.'

Cat affected her most fascinated expression.

'And you? What do you work at?' asked Izzy.

'When I'm not cleaning swimming pools?' Cat gave a merry little laugh, and waved a hand airily at her artwork. 'I'm an artist.'

'Are these your paintings?'

'Yes.'

'They're beautiful. They're really beautiful.' Izzy took a step towards the sheets of cut-up wallpaper that Cat had used to paint on when she'd run out of canvas. 'This is really special,' she said, indicating a riotous mass of acrylic paint that Cat had somehow managed to put manners on. It was a depiction of the view beyond the window, of Coolnamara Bay at sundown with Cat's tiny trademark Catgirl sitting on a cloud in the corner.

'Yeah. It's a cutie, all right,' said Cat, carelessly.

'I'd love to buy this for my dad,' said Izzy. 'How much do you charge?'

'Seven hundred and fifty euros.'

'Will you take a cheque?'

Shit. *Shit!* Why hadn't she rounded it up to a grand? 'If you make it out to cash.'

'I have cash, actually, if you'd prefer.'

Had this Isabella Bolger descended from heaven? Cat watched dreamily as Izzy delved into her big blue bag and produced a blue suede wallet.

'But I only have five hundred euro notes.'

Cat pretended to think about it. 'What's a couple of hundred euro between friends? Five hundred is cool,' she said, finally.

Izzy handed over a banknote and Cat stuffed it into the pocket of her heavy-duty overalls, resisting the temptation to inspect it. A Bin Laden, no less! (since everyone knew what it looked like, but no one had ever seen one). Moving to the wall, she peeled away the masking tape and handed the painting to Izzy.

'Thank you.' Izzy held the acrylic at arm's length and gazed at it, and as she did, Cat saw her beautiful eyes start to pool with tears. 'This is the view Dad loves most in the world. But – but he won't be able to see it, because the Bentley is parked behind the cottage. If he wants to see the view, he's going to have to actually go into that horrible place. At least, with this, he can look on his . . . his favourite view any time he likes.'

Cat watched in fascination as the tears started spilling onto Isabella's cheeks. This girl was completely barking! 'I can let you have more views,' she said. 'I got some canvases yesterday. I could do you loads more, no problem.'

'Thank you,' said Izzy, smiling at Cat through her tears.

'I could do a whole series,' said Cat. 'For a special bargain price.'

'That's really kind of you. I'll have a think and get back to you. What's your email? Or can I contact you via your website?'

'The website's under construction. You could just write care of "Coral Mansion".'

'"Coral Mansion"?'

'That's what this house is called now.'

'And your name is . . .? I'm so sorry, I've just realised that we haven't introduced ourselves yet. I'm Isabella Bolger.'

'Cat Gallagher,' said Cat, taking Izzy's proffered hand and shaking it vigorously. She hoped Izzy would go now, before Finn came back. 'And, heavens above and all that jazz! Is that the time? I was meant to phone my agent about my forthcoming exhibition.'

'Oh! Where's it to be? Dublin?'

'No. Barcelona.'

'Oh, how lovely! I adore Barcelona. You might send me an invite? Any excuse, you know, to visit my favourite city.'

'Yes, I will.'

'Let me give you my card.' Izzy produced the blue wallet again, and slid out an embossed business card which was, to Cat's surprise, not blue.

'Thanks.' Without looking at it, Cat stuffed the card in her pocket where it joined the five hundred euro note. How she loved the feeling as her fingers made contact with the cash! 'Well, Isabella. It was nice meeting you.'

'Yes. Say hello to Finn for me.'

'I will. Goodbye. I don't need to show you the way out, I guess, since you used to live here.'

'No. I can let myself out.'

Go, go, *go*!

'But might you have an elastic band or something, so that I can roll the painting up and keep it safe?'

'An elastic band? No. Um, hang on.'

Cat ran into the downstairs loo and unravelled yards of Kitten Soft. Then she returned to the sitting room and handed Izzy the cardboard loo-roll tube. 'Roll it up and put it in that,' she said. 'I hope your dad enjoys it. Now, goodbye.'

'Goodbye,' said Isabella uncertainly. And then she turned and left the Villa Felicity through the back door just as Finn breezed through the front.

'What's all that bog roll doing spilling out of the downstairs loo?' he demanded, poking his head around the sitting room door.

'I was experimenting with an idea for an avant-garde installation,' said Cat. 'Welcome home, Finnster! Did you get the T-bones?'

Chapter Seven

Keeley's lime green Ford Ka bumped along the track that led to the Crooked House, and pulled up outside the front door. Extracting the key card from the ignition, she slid out of the driver's seat and eased herself into a stretch. High on a branch of a silver birch, a blackbird was singing its throaty, liquid song; another took up the refrain from across the lake, and from somewhere to the rear of the house, a cockerel was crowing. Keeley hadn't heard a cock crow since the days when, as a child, she'd holidayed in the cottage on the west coast that now belonged to her, the cottage she was to lay claim to tomorrow. She stood looking around at the bucolic splendour that surrounded the Crooked House – the woods, the hills, the lake – then turned her attention to the residence itself.

It was like an illustration in a children's picture book, all terra-cotta chimney pots and mullioned windows and timber frames. It looked as if it might be full of priest holes and secret chambers and passages. It was the kind of house a child would love to explore, the kind of house in which you might never get found in a game of hide-and-seek, the kind of house in which you wouldn't want to listen to ghost stories too late at night.

When she had done her online research, Keeley had

learned that, before marrying Hugo, Ophelia Gallagher had spent many years living in the vibrant heart of London, in an apartment in Covent Garden. She wondered how a woman who had spent half a lifetime hanging out in a quarter famous for its restaurants, pubs and theatres had adapted to this remote country retreat. It seemed to Keeley that, surrounded as it was by dense forest and ringed by mountains, the Crooked House was as far away from civilisation as any veteran misanthropist could want to get. Even the track that led to it was inhospitable, pitted with potholes and overgrown with weeds.

The cock crowed again and, as Keeley dragged her computer case across from the passenger seat and slammed the car door shut, zapping the lock, a dog began to bark from inside the house.

'Lulu, Lulu – shut up, you silly fusspot!' a woman's voice commanded, and then the front door of the Crooked House opened, and Ophelia Gallagher emerged. The first thing Keeley noticed about the woman was that she was easily as beautiful as the photographs she'd browsed on the net; the second thing she noticed was that she was around six months pregnant.

'Hi! You must be Keeley! I'm Ophelia Gallagher.'

Ophelia descended the steps, and moved towards Keeley, pushing back her hair from her face with one hand and extending the other. She was wearing a floral cotton frock, a cornflower blue apron and polka-dot plimsolls. Her face was bare of make-up and her nails unpainted. Keeley took a measure of her grip (firm, warm), and a measure of her smile (sincere, welcoming), and a measure of her gaze (direct, candid); for Keeley was keenly aware of how very important first impressions could be when conducting interviews. In this instance, however, it was good to keep in mind that the interviewee in question was an actress. Just how competent an actress, Keeley presumed she would find out within the course of the next couple of hours.

'Good to meet you!' fluted Ophelia. 'Come in, come in, you must be tired. Let me help you with that –' she reached for Keeley's computer case – 'and don't mind the dog.' The dog had clearly found a way out through the rear of the house, because an ebulliently barking black Labrador came racing around the corner, and greeted Keeley even more warmly than her mistress had done. 'Lulu – down!' Ophelia scolded.

'Don't worry,' said Keeley, 'I love dogs.' That was a fib. Keeley was actually much more of a cat person, but she knew she wouldn't endear herself to Ophelia Gallagher if she looked askance at the family pet. Conducting an interview was rather easier when the subject under scrutiny warmed to you.

'How was your drive? Did you come all the way from Dublin? Are those hellish roadworks still going on?'

Keeley fielded the routine questions, answering them all politely as Ophelia led her up the steps and through the front door, making mental notes as she stepped into the hallway.

Inside, it took her eyes some moments to adjust to the gloom. She registered a pair of old-fashioned, glass-fronted bookcases flanking a console table upon which more books and periodicals were piled. A marble bust of a woman sporting a straw sunhat stood on a carved Indonesian plinth; an old-fashioned Bakelite telephone nestled in a hatchway in the wall; a staircase carpeted in a worn Turkish runner climbed to the upper storeys. Keeley could hear a clock ticking: looking up, she saw a grandfather clock standing sentinel on the return and a dusty chandelier dripping from the ceiling.

Ophelia opened a door to her right, and stood back to

110

allow Keeley through. 'We won't be disturbed in here, I hope! I'll go organise some tea. Or would you prefer coffee?'

'Tea is perfect, thank you. What a lovely room!'

'Thank you. It's my favourite room in the house, after the kitchen.' Setting down the computer case, Ophelia said, 'I won't be a moment! Make yourself comfortable!' and disappeared, followed by the Labrador. Keeley could hear the clicking of its claws on the flagstoned floor as it trailed Ophelia along the hallway.

Well, she thought, looking around. So far, so predictably bohemian. The room in which she found herself was a sitting room/study. It was much brighter in here than in the hallway – there were windows on two sides, and French doors led to a pretty patch of sunlit garden, where a pair of carved stone discus throwers posed against a background of wisteria-clad wall. There were no paintings on display, Keeley was rather surprised to see: the walls of the room were completely covered with white-painted shelves, crammed floor to ceiling with books. A table in the centre was stacked with volumes bearing the logos of arty imprints: Thames and Hudson, Phaidon, Taschen. On the top of a cabinet to one side of the ornate, smoke-blackened fireplace, was a collection of family photographs. Both books and pictures beckoned Keeley irresistibly.

Her eyes scanned the titles on display. There were biographies of Picasso, Matisse, Mondrian and Miró. There were illustrated alphabets and bestiaries and flora. The *Erotica Universalis,* unsurprisingly. There were dozens of glossy art history books – the kind that even smelled expensive. Keeley spotted a shelf devoted to gardening, and another to photography. Tucked away between the *Complete Works of Shakespeare* and the *Romantic Poets,* she found several volumes of chick-lit. Thanks be to God, she thought – the woman was human!

111

The pictures on the display cabinet told yet another story. They'd all been tastefully mounted in antique frames: many of them were artistic black and white shots. There were several of Ophelia together with the bold-eyed Hugo, and a couple of portraits of the actress on her own that had clearly been taken for publicity purposes. There were photographs of a much younger Hugo – God! he really had been devastatingly good looking! – and some of people Keeley could not identify. Family members, she guessed, many of them dead by now, to judge by the fashions. And there, tucked away in the very back row in a bog-standard clipframe, was a small study in pen and ink of a tousle-haired gypsy of a child with intense dark eyes and angular limbs.

Keeley picked up the drawing. It was the girl she had seen all that time ago – was it ten years? longer, possibly – sitting on the floor of the Demeter Gallery, scribbling with a leaky biro on the back of one of Hugo's price lists. It was Caitlín, daughter of the artist and his second wife, Paloma, who, Keeley had learned during the course of her research, had died of cervical cancer when her daughter was just fourteen years old.

The sound of the dog's clicky nails in the hallway told her that Ophelia and Lulu were on their way back. Keeley set down the drawing and moved to the sofa, where her hostess had left her computer case. Unzipping it, she pulled out the printed list of questions she'd compiled, along with her tiny tape recorder and her trusty stylograph, just as the mistress of the house came into the room, balancing a tray upon which tea-things jostled for space.

'Here we are!' said Ophelia, setting the tray down carefully on a low table. 'I hope you like coffee cake? I couldn't decide whether to do coffee or chocolate.'

Keeley looked at the cake that sat resplendent on a pretty china plate. 'You mean you baked it yourself?' she asked.

'Yes. There are walnuts in it . . . oh, crikey. Maybe you have a nut allergy? I should have thought of that.'

'No,' said Keeley. 'Coffee and walnut is my absolute favourite! You really shouldn't have gone to so much trouble as to bake a cake.'

'Ah. But I knew that you were coming!' quipped Ophelia.

Keeley smiled. 'I'm not surprised that this is your favourite room,' she said, as Ophelia busied herself with cups and saucers. 'It must be lovely to sit curled up here by the fire of an evening, with a book.'

'It is.' Ophelia indicated the piano in the far corner. 'Hugo plays sometimes, too. And sometimes we just sit and listen to Radio 4. It's nice to hear the voices of old friends on the drama slots.'

'Of course,' said Keeley, sitting down on the sofa. 'You must miss all your actor friends from the old days.'

Ophelia shrugged. 'You move on, you know? I'd never have dreamed, in the days when I lived in Covent Garden and spent half my life in rehearsal rooms and theatres, that I'd wind up marrying a reclusive Irish artist and retiring to the back end of beyond!'

'So you really have retired from acting?' Keeley aimed a look at Ophelia's pregnant belly – as subtly meaningful a look as she could manage.

'Yes. I'm going to be a mum, as you can probably see.'

'Congratulations!'

'Thank you.' Ophelia poured tea through a strainer, and offered Keeley milk and sugar, both of which she declined. 'I was beginning to wonder if I hadn't left it too late to have a baby. I was hitting that dodgy age, you know. And then – wow! It just suddenly happened.'

'So, this is your first child?'

Ophelia nodded.

'And Hugo's . . .?'

'It'll be his third. He has a grown-up son – Raoul – and a daughter from his previous marriages.'

'You must be very excited.'

'Yes.' Ophelia prinked. 'I've actually printed out my scan, I'm that excited! I'm having it framed, and it's going to take pride of place in that collection.' Ophelia nodded in the direction of the cabinet, where Gallagher family faces gazed out from their antique frames. Keeley privately thought the notion of including the photograph of a foetus in the collection rather an odd one, but then, she'd heard of women putting pictures of their unborn babies up on Facebook, and tweeting them to their friends and suchlike. Nothing should surprise Keeley, really, in this brave new technophile world.

She watched as Ophelia cut slabs of moist coffee cake and set them on plates, fussing a little over napkins and cutlery. Then, when all was in order, the ex-actress slipped off her plimsolls, and curled her feet underneath her on a chintz-covered armchair.

'Are you ready to get going?' asked Keeley, setting her tape recorder on the table between them.

'Absolutely!' came the warm response.

'OK,' said Keeley, pressing 'Record' and checking to make sure that the green light was on. There was nothing worse, she had learned to her cost, than recording an interview on empty. 'The first question I have for you is this. You're expecting your first child at the age of . . .?'

'Thirty-five,' lied Ophelia. Keeley knew from Wikipedia that Ophelia was actually thirty-nine, but it was common-place for women – especially actresses – to lie about their age.

Keeley sent her subject an encouraging smile. 'So, Ophelia Gallagher, how do you feel about becoming a mother?'

There were only a few crumbs left on Keeley's plate, and the tea remaining in her cup was cold. She'd asked Ophelia all the most innocuous questions on her list – and had got the usual innocuous answers in return.

Ophelia Gallagher, nee Spence, was the youngest of three daughters born to a working-class couple from Brighton. She had started her career as a model before being 'discovered' by a film director, and she had become muse and wife to Hugo Gallagher after they had met at a dinner party (Wikipedia had stipulated a charity event, but Ophelia insisted that it was at Booker prizewinner Colm Tóibín's house). Until she met Hugo, Ophelia had worked her entire adult life, and she was working still, she insisted – the eggs she had used in her coffee cake came from the hens she kept, she grew all her own vegetables and made many of her own clothes, and now she was embarking upon her new career as an author.

But – big yawn – all this stuff (and more) was available to read on the internet. All this stuff would make excruciatingly dull copy. If Keeley was going to get anything substantial enough from Ophelia Gallagher to make an interesting 'Epiphany', she'd have to dig rather deeper.

'Where did the idea for the children's book come from?' she asked. 'Caitlín would have been too old for bedtime stories by the time you became her stepmother. Are there other children in your life who inspired you to write?'

'No,' replied Ophelia. 'I'm estranged from my sisters, so I don't know my nieces and nephews.'

'Oh? How did the estrangement come about?'

'One of my sisters sold dodgy photographs of me to a

redtop,' said Ophelia, with remarkable sang-froid. 'And the other one borrowed a lot of money from Hugo when we were first married, and never paid it back. I haven't spoken to either of them since.'

This was more like it! During the course of her research, Keeley had – unsurprisingly – read about the dodgy photographs on the internet. However, she had been careful not to bring them up at too early a stage in their tête-à-tête today, because she didn't want Ophelia erecting defences and refusing to cooperate.

'The photographs . . .?' she prompted now.

'Were mildly pornographic. The redtops loved the fact that an actress who had appeared in classical productions penned by such literary giants as Chekhov and Ibsen, and who had wound up married to Ireland's answer to Picasso, began her career posing for a lads' magazine.'

'Just how graphic were the pictures?'

'Page three stuff, mostly – tits and ass, you know? The kind of pictures loads of pretty teenage girls get suckered into doing in return for the promise of fame and fortune, and very little hard cash. But my sister made me look ridiculous, and I couldn't forgive her for that.'

'And the other sister?'

'She didn't actually borrow money – she borrowed a painting of Hugo's that she'd admired. I warned her it wasn't hers to sell, but she went ahead and did it anyway. It fetched five hundred thousand at Sotheby's last year.' Ophelia gave a mirthless laugh. 'It would have fetched twice that, before the recession.'

They were playing ball, now. 'Is money important to you, Ophelia?' Keeley asked.

'Yes. Money is important to anyone who didn't have enough of it, growing up. I worked hard for any money I ever made, and it makes me mad to think that people like my sisters profiteer on the back of my success.'

Keeley was seeing a different side now to the woman who romped with her dog and who baked cakes and scattered corn for her hens. She liked it.

'So when you hit upon the idea of writing a children's book, just who were you writing it for? Your unborn baby?'

'No,' said Ophelia. 'I hit on the idea for the book before I even knew I was pregnant. I wrote it . . . I hope you won't think I'm being precious, Keeley, if I tell you that I wrote it for my inner child – for the little girl who wore her sisters' hand-me-downs and who was constantly being told she was a bad girl and who had her hair hacked off when she was five because she had nits. I wrote it for Tracey.'

'Tracey?'

'Tracey was my name before I became an actress. There was already a Tracey Spence in British Actors' Equity, so it seemed an ideal opportunity to change my name to the one belonging to my favourite Shakespeare heroine.' Ophelia smiled, a little sadly. 'I used to read Ophelia's speeches out loud to myself at night, to try and drown out the noise of my parents rowing in the kitchen downstairs.'

Yes! Keeley fucking *loved* it! Already in her mind's eye she saw the strap line for her 'Epiphany' piece: some pertinent quote from *Hamlet,* 'More matter with less art,' or something. Maybe she'd ask the photographer to set up a shot of Ophelia floating on her back in the lake, mirroring the image made famous by Millais, of the drowned tragic heroine. But just as she was about to ask the actress if she'd be up for it, there came the sound of a crash outside in the hallway, and she heard a man's voice boom, 'How many times have I told you not to leave that dog lying there in the hall? It's fucking Stygian without the lights on! Even a blind man could trip over a black Labrador in the dark.'

Keeley and Ophelia exchanged looks.

'My husband,' said Ophelia with remarkable equanimity. 'I have to say, I had hoped he wouldn't be joining us.'

'No worries,' said Keeley. 'This interview is with you, not your husband. I'm turning off my tape recorder now.' And Keeley did just that.

Then the door to the sitting room opened and Hugo Gallagher lunged through. Recovering himself, he placed a hand on the door jamb, and fixed Ophelia with a basilisk look. A lesser woman might have quailed, but Ophelia rose to her feet gracefully, and said, with steel in her voice, 'Hugo, this is Keeley Considine. She's interviewing me for the *Sunday Insignia*.'

Hugo turned the beam of his attention on Keeley. 'The *Insignia*, is it? The *Sunday*-fucking-*Insignia*? Ha! What a load of wankers! What a shower of shits!'

'Nice to meet you, Mr Gallagher,' said Keeley. 'We actually met once before, at an exhibition opening of yours in the Demeter Gallery in Dublin, many years ago.'

'Did I ride you?'

'No. But you rode my colleague, Stephanie.'

Hugo gave Keeley a narrow-eyed look of assessment, and then he smiled the smile that had made hundreds of women go weak at the knees, fall at his feet and beg him to take them to bed – just as Keeley's colleague Stephanie had done. Even in his cups, even at fifty-something, Hugo Gallagher was a fiendishly attractive man.

'Have a drink, Ms . . . *Sunday Insignia* person,' he said, waving his hand towards the laden butler's tray on the other side of the room.

'I've had tea, thank you.'

'Tea? What are you? A journalist or a mouse?'

A journalist. She was a journalist, through and through. No self-respecting hack would turn down an opportunity like this! To be invited to partake of a drink with a major artist – one of Europe's most notorious – was the kind of gig most of her tribe would kill for. Sure, she'd told Ophelia she'd turned off her tape recorder; sure, the interview was now officially over. But the insight she'd get into the way this couple worked would be invaluable if she joined them for a drink. Well – if she joined Hugo for a drink. Ophelia would, presumably, be sticking to tea.

'I'll have a Jameson, thanks,' she said.

'My love?' Hugo smiled at Ophelia. 'Some of your home-made elderflower cordial?'

'Thank you.'

Hugo ambled across the room and proceeded to fix drinks. The bottle of sparkling water to which he helped himself fizzed all over the butler's tray, and as he flailed around, trying to wrench the cap off, his elbow narrowly missed a decanter of amber liquid.

'Oh, let me do it!' said Ophelia, raising her eyes to heaven. 'Sit down, Hugo – and mind that decanter!'

'It's a hideous decanter,' he retorted, gazing at it as if he had never seen it before. 'I've been meaning to put it out of its misery for ages. What is such a hideous object doing in my house, anyway? Who let it in?'

'It was a wedding present.'

'You mean, we're married?'

'Very droll, darling.'

'I have absolutely no recollection of our wedding day,' Hugo told Keeley, unleashing his lethal smile at her before lowering himself on to the piano stool. 'Any requests? Rachmaninov?'

'Something a little less rousing, please,' said Ophelia, testily. 'The baby doesn't like Rachmaninov.'

119

'Oh, yes. The baby. What'll I play? Khachaturian? Caitlín used to love that.'

Caitlín. What had happened to little waiflike Caitlín? Keeley wondered. How did the third Mrs Gallagher feel about little, waiflike Caitlín? It was impossible to tell from her expression, since her back was turned, but Keeley sensed a stiffening at the mention of the name. She guessed that maybe – as often happened when a spouse died and the father remarried – there was little love lost between step-mother and stepdaughter.

'Honestly, Hugo,' scolded Ophelia, rearranging bottles. 'The water's got everywhere. Excuse me, Keeley, while I fetch a cloth.' Giving Hugo a dirty look, Ophelia left the room, Lulu the Labrador padding at her heels.

'Caitlín is your daughter, yes?' Keeley asked, watching Hugo as he riffled through a pile of sheet music.

'As far as I know, Caitlín is my daughter,' he said. 'It's a wise man, as they say, who knows his own father.'

'Where is she now?'

'She should be in London, studying at the Slade. But she's not. She's pissing about on the west coast somewhere.' Hugo raised his eyes from the score he was studying. 'She could have been a contender, my daughter. She had talent. But instead she's wasting her formative years messing about on boats.'

'She sails?'

'Spent every summer of her life at sailing school, far as I know.'

'Do you sail, Hugo?'

'No. Hate the water. Caitlín was a waterbaby, like her mother.'

Keeley remembered the harassed-looking woman who had cast anxious looks at her husband at the Demeter Gallery all those years ago. She was dead now, while her husband – to go by appearances – was intent on drinking himself to death. Half-cut at half-past four in the afternoon! He'd be stotious by dinner time.

What kind of a life did Ophelia Gallagher really lead, marooned in the Crooked House with her chickens and her dog and her soak of a husband? Keeley wondered. What class of a life had Caitlín had, growing up here, beside the lake, beneath the sad cypresses? What class of a life would her baby half-sister or half-brother have, once it was born? She found herself wondering if Hugo might not be a more interesting subject for one of her 'Epiphanies' than his wife, before recollecting that he'd dismissed the staff of the *Sunday Insignia* as a shower of wankers and shits, and would hardly be likely to oblige.

'You don't have a very high opinion of the press, Hugo, do you?'

He laughed. 'The *Insignia* art critic trashed my early work. He called it the "maladroit daubs of a fixated amateur". But that was hardly surprising.'

'How so?'

'He was a fellow Slade graduate, who had had even less success than I did, back in the eighties. He was – is – a mean-minded bollix.'

Keeley knew the critic in question: a man with knock-out halitosis and a bad habit of talking to his female colleagues' tits instead of to their faces.

'He's changed his opinion now, though,' she reminded Hugo. 'He rates your work very highly.'

'Of course he rates it. He'd look like a complete tool if his reviews continued to be out of kilter with everyone else's. It's currently fashionable to rate me.' He leaned forward, and skewered her with a look. 'Tell me this. If my wife were married not to me, but to some two-bit actor or second-rate Sunday painter, do you think she would have got herself a book deal?'

'I can't answer that question, since I haven't read the manuscript.'

'Then let me put it another way. Would you have thought her worthy of one of your in-depth interviews if she was plain Tracey Spence instead of the fragrant Ophelia Gallagher?'

Keeley gave him a level look. 'No,' she said.

'I thought as much. And you wonder why I have such a low opinion of the "ladies" and "gentlemen" of the press?' He leaned back, and rested an arm on the lid of the piano. 'You're a fairly seasoned hack at this stage. How many interviews have you done for the *Insignia*?'

'I've done one a week for the past year.'

'Do you enjoy your work?'

Keeley shrugged. 'I'll 'fess up to feeling tired. Before the *Insignia*, I spent ten years on a paper in New York, and sometimes you learn . . . unsettling . . . stuff about human nature during an interview. It's a little like being a therapist, I guess. People reveal a lot more about themselves than they realise.'

'And do you take advantage? When people spill a few too many beans?'

'I like to think I have integrity.'

'Not a word many people associate with your profession.'

He turned away from her rudely, and resumed his perusal of Khachaturian or Rachmaninov or whatever high-falutin' classical ditties he was into. Keeley felt like telling him to go fuck himself. She was fed up with people curling their lips at her and calling her an unprincipled hack. Not that she'd be a 'hack' for much longer, she thought, ruefully. She had only three interviews left to file before she'd fulfil her contractual obligations on the *Insignia* . . . and then what?

She had, like thousands of other journalists, toyed with the idea of writing a book. Lots of her colleagues talked about the books they were going to write, but none of them had ever managed to get themselves a publishing deal – unlike lucky Ophelia Gallagher, with the high six-figure advance negotiated for her by superagent Tony 'The Tiger' Baines. She wondered if Ophelia was aware of just how hard she would have to work in order to earn out her advance.

Keeley knew the reality that lay behind the glittering masque of book launches and press junkets; the sheer slog involved in hauling yourself onto the bestseller lists. She pictured Ophelia touting her children's book around the London Book Fair; or sitting in a booth at the BBC doing interview after interview after interview until she was sick of the sound of her own name (and that of her book); or languishing behind a table in WH Smiths, hoping that more than one person would ask her to sign the title page – and then she realised that she hadn't asked Ophelia who was going to illustrate the book. Presumably, since it was a children's title, the book would be illustrated – and, given the size of her advance, lavishly illustrated at that? Who, she wondered, did the publishers have in mind? Hardly the saturnine Hugo, who was known for his atmospheric abstracts and esoteric symbolism.

'Who is to illustrate Ophelia's book?' she asked Hugo.

'Who indeed?' he said, opening the lid of the piano and setting a score upon the music rest. 'I know who *should* be fucking illustrating it, that's for sure. But Ophelia won't countenance it.'

'Who?'

'My daughter, Caitlín, that's who.'

'What about Caitlín?'

Ophelia was back, bearing a glass cloth printed with a reproduction of a Rousseau painting and a dish of macadamia nuts.

'I was telling Keeley,' said Hugo, 'that my daughter Caitlín should be illustrating your children's book, not that buffoon your publishers have landed you with.'

'Jasper is not a buffoon. He is a highly respected illustrator.'

'Caitlín could do the job better with her hands tied behind her back.'

'Very funny, Hugo.' Ophelia set about mopping up the spilled water. 'Do you know Jasper Douglas' work, Keeley?'

'I'm familiar with the name, but I can't visualise the style.'

'It's not unlike the quirky style of Jeffrey Fulvimari – you know, the guy who illustrated Madonna's children's books?'

'Oh – how lovely!'

Privately, Keeley thought the pictorial style of Madonna's kids' books saccharine, to say the least. Hugo clearly agreed with her, because he brought his hands down so heavily on the piano keyboard that dust motes rose into the air.

'Hugo! Stop that. Here. Have your whiskey.' Ophelia sloshed a measure into a glass, rather recklessly, Keeley observed. She hoped her hostess wouldn't be quite so liberal when it came to pouring her Jameson, because otherwise she'd be sleeping in her car tonight. 'And you might have had the cop-on to start the dishwasher for me. There'll be nothing to eat our dinner off this evening, at this rate.'

'I didn't start it,' said Hugo, 'because I don't know how to.'

'It's about time you learned. We've had it for four weeks.'

This had the makings of a minor domestic. Maybe it was

124

time to change the subject. 'If your stepdaughter really does have a flair for illustration, Ophelia,' remarked Keeley, 'it could be a very shrewd marketing ploy.'

'Marketing ploy?' sneered Hugo.

'Think of the PR opportunities.'

A closed look came over Ophelia's face. 'I don't think,' she said, 'that Caitlín and I would work well together.'

Another discordant jangle came from the piano.

Uh oh, thought Keeley. Best not to go there. There was clearly some family disharmony going on between Ophelia and Caitlín Gallagher.

Ophelia returned her attention to the butler's tray, then crossed the room and set Keeley's whiskey in front of her, along with the dish of nuts. 'Enjoy,' she said. 'It's Special Reserve. I'm guessing the interview has been well and truly terminated?'

'Yes. If there's anything else I need to know, I can always email you.'

'And you have my phone number, don't you? My mobile number? I rarely pick up the landline.'

'Email sheemail, mobile shmobile,' grumbled Hugo. 'All you communication-obsessive individuals don't know the meaning of a quiet life. "The world is too much with us; late and soon, getting and spending, we lay waste our powers . . ."'

'Please excuse Hugo. He's going to start spouting poetry now. He's a complete technophobe, as you may have gathered from his observation earlier about the dishwasher.'

Keeley smiled. 'Let me just check my contact details.' Retrieving her Nokia from her computer case, she keyed in the PIN code and waited for O2 to welcome her. As the logo shimmered on to the screen, there came a crash from the kitchen.

'Bugger!' said Ophelia. 'Lulu's after the remains of the chicken. Excuse me.'

And she raced through the door just as the phone in the hall began to ring.

Keeley glanced at Hugo, but he was concentrating on some tune he was picking out on the piano, with his foot on the soft pedal. It sounded to Keeley like a lullaby. He'd be playing enough of those, she found herself thinking, when the new baby arrived.

In the hall, the answering machine kicked in and Keeley heard Ophelia's OGM. 'Hello. You are through to the Crooked House. Please leave your message for Hugo or Ophelia Gallagher after the tone.'

The tone sounded and a silence ensued. Then Keeley heard a small voice say: 'Da? Dada? It's Cat.'

Hugo, still absorbed in his lullaby, played on, oblivious.

And then, from the depths of the shadowy hallway, came a soft click as the phone line went dead.

Chapter Eight

Río was waiting in the Bentley for Adair to arrive. The mobile home was shipshape now, all hooked up to water, electricity and the internet. Río had set a jug of weigela blossom on the dining table, and put a lasagne in the oven and a bottle of champagne in the fridge. Under her jeans and T-shirt she was sporting the fabulous underwear that Adair had bought her half a lifetime ago, and she'd made an effort with her make-up and spritzed herself with Jo Malone grapefruit.

Earlier in the day she'd signed on Adair's behalf for delivery of the spanking new tractor that he'd bought from the Massey Ferguson High Horsepower range. It boasted a six-cylinder AGCO SISU power engine and Dyna-VT transmission – whatever they were – and it came with a matching fire-engine-red trailer. Río was dying to have a go on it. She'd cut some extra weigela blossoms and fashioned them into a wreath with which she'd festooned the steering wheel.

There was, unfortunately, not a lot she could do with the dismal cottage (apart from demolish it and start again) but she had asked Finn to come by at some future stage to help Adair clear the surrounding detritus. She wondered if he would bring his new girlfriend. She wasn't sure what exactly his relationship was with the girl he called Cat, but she could tell that Izzy had been badly fazed by a run-in with her rival. Poor Iz – as if she didn't have enough on her plate without getting grief from her ex's new squeeze. She'd returned to Dublin with the promise that she'd be back in Lissamore at the weekend to lavish TLC on her dad.

In the meantime, she'd left something for him in the Bentley. A rolled-up sheet of what looked like wallpaper stuffed into a loo-roll tube, upon which she'd written the words: 'A House-Warming Present for the Best Daddy in the World, with All Love from His Darling Izzy-Biz XXX'. Río had resisted the temptation to sneak a look at what was contained therein; she also thought the girl might have gone to a bit more trouble with the giftwrap. And then she gave herself a mental slap on the wrist and reminded herself that she shouldn't be thinking such uncharitable, sarky thoughts.

The sound of an approaching car engine sent Río in the direction of the mirror on Izzy's polished quartz vanity unit. She looked tired, despite the care she'd taken with her make-up. She'd had her fair share of sleepless nights recently. When she'd told Dervla about her decision to marry Adair, her sister had been aghast.

'But you don't love him, Río!' she'd said.

'I care for him.'

'That's hardly a reason to marry the man. I mean, I don't want to sound heartless, given that he's dying, but you could simply draw the line at sleeping with him.'

'That doesn't show the same level of commitment, Dervla. While I'm married to him, he'll know that I belong to him, and him alone, for the rest of his life. That'll afford him real comfort.'

She had debated whether or not it was kosher to share with Dervla the news that Adair was dying. In the end, she'd decided that the strain of keeping the knowledge to herself would be too great: she would need someone close to confide in and seek advice from over the course of the next twelve months, and who closer than her sister? She'd toyed with the idea of letting Fleur in on the secret, too, but then reconsidered. As a single working mother of a small baby, Fleur had worries enough of her own to contend with, and as a consummate romantic, she would find the notion of marrying a man whom one didn't love profoundly shocking. No. Fleur did not need to know.

Even as she had picked up the phone to call Dervla, Río had had second thoughts about betraying Izzy's confidence. Izzy had sworn her to secrecy, after all. But she knew that she would go to pieces without someone to talk to, and she needed to be strong for both Adair and his daughter. *Keep Right on to the End of the Road. Pack Up Your Troubles in Your Old Kit Bag. You'll Never Walk Alone . . .* This was the music to which Río must march now.

But she hadn't banked on Dervla's reaction. The horror she heard in her sister's voice over the phone line had been palpable.

'Just think what it's going to do to Shane!' Dervla had said, sounding like some doomy soothsayer.

'What's Shane got to do with anything?'

'It'll break his heart.'

'Nonsense,' returned Río briskly.

'Jesus! You just don't get it, Río, do you? It's been staring you in the face your entire life.'

'What has?'

'The fact that you and Shane were meant for each other.'

'Ach, that's crap, Dervla. You know I'd never marry Shane. I've told you a zillion times before that I could never go and live in LA.'

'Doh. Why do you think he's bought the most palatial house in Lissamore?'

129

'It's not for him. It's for Finn to turn into a dive centre. Now shut up, Dervla – you're doing my head in. My mind's made up, and there's nothing you can say or do to change that. *Capisce?*'

And Río had put the phone down on her sister, feeling rattled.

Outside the Bentley, the car engine shut off. Río took a last look in the mirror in the state-of-the-art bathroom, fixed a radiant smile on her face, and walked out on to the deck.

'Hello, Adair,' she said, as he shut the driver's door of his Mercedes. 'Welcome home!'

He looked up, and Río kept the radiant smile glued to her face with an effort. Adair looked ten years older than when last she'd seen him. The most jovial man she knew was now gaunt and grey, with a haunted expression about the eyes. But those eyes became luminous with love when they lit on Río.

'Río! Río – is it really you? My dream girl's come to greet me! Come here to me, darlin', and let me give you a hug!'

And Río danced down the red cedar steps of the Bentley and into the outstretched arms of her future husband, laughing and crying both at the same time.

Later, after they'd cracked open the champagne, and eaten their fill of lasagne ('Lovely grub!' Adair had said, rubbing his hands together with glee), and made very relaxed love in the very comfortable bed in the Bentley's master bedroom, Adair turned to Río and asked the question she'd been waiting for.

'Río?' he said. 'I know I'm not a rich man any more, but I know . . . well, I know too that you are not the kind of woman who cares much about material stuff, so this makes me, you know, dare to hope. This is presumptuous of me – Jesus! it's presumptuous in the extreme – but nothing ventured, nothing gained, as they say, and if you find what I'm about to propose unacceptable, well . . . we'll forget I even asked, OK?'

She nodded. 'Shoot.'

He looked at her levelly. 'Río, would you do me the honour of marrying me?'

'Yes,' said Río, unhesitatingly.

'What?'

'You heard me,' said Río.

'Are you serious?' said Adair.

'Yes.'

'But . . . but what . . . I mean . . . I . . . Dear God, I never really dared to dream that you'd say yes! I mean . . . why? Why would a beautiful woman like you want to marry an auld eejit like me?'

'Because I love you.'

'You do?' Adair looked even more astonished. 'What's there to love? Like I said, I'm not even rich any more.'

Río smiled straight into his eyes. 'I love that you make me laugh. I love that you love me. I love that you are one of the most decent, honourable men it has ever been my privilege to know, Adair Bolger.'

'And you are an angel from heaven, and I am blessed, blessed!' Scooping up her hand, he pressed his lips against the palm and held them there for many moments; and then his demeanour changed abruptly. He laid Río's hand very gently on the counterpane and said, as he traced a finger along her life line, 'Río, *acushla*. There is something I have to tell you.'

'I don't want to know,' said Río. 'I don't want to know any of your secrets. If I am going to marry you, Adair, I am

131

marrying you for better or for worse, for richer or poorer, in sickness and in health, till death us do part. That's what marriage means. And if you don't agree, then the deal's off.'

He gave her a searching look. 'You really mean that? What if you live to regret it?'

Río closed her fingers over his hand. 'Allow me to tell you a story. I had a conversation with Izzy once, when she told me that she did not know a single couple of our age who were not already on their second or third marriage. I found it shocking, and not a little sad. I know your marriage to Felicity wasn't a happy one, Adair, but if you're going to commit a second time round, you are going to have to commit to a woman who will stick by you. For Izzy's sake.'

'When did Izzy tell you this?'

'She told me the morning after you threw that birthday party for me at the Villa Felicity. Remember?'

He nodded. 'How could I forget that party? I was going to ask you to marry me that night.'

'I thought as much. But then Izzy threw that wobbly and you changed your mind. And you were right. Things would have been complicated if we'd got married then. It wouldn't have been . . . appropriate while Izzy and Finn were an item. But things have changed, and the time *is* right now. And I think Izzy would approve.'

'I'd like to think she would.'

Río smiled. 'I've never forgotten the heart-to-heart we had that morning. It was early, before anyone else had got up, and we were swimming in the bay. And two swans passed overhead, and Izzy asked if it was true that swans mated for life.'

'Is it true?'

'Yes. They are aggressively loyal. So if we're going to do this thing, Adair Bolger, we're going to follow the example set by the pair of mute swans that flew above the bay the morning I swam with your daughter.'

Río could tell by the expression on his face that she'd nailed it. She released his hand and watched as he traced her life line again, and her head line and her heart line, and then he took her face between his hands, and kissed her.

'I love you, Río Kinsella,' he said. 'I love you so very, very much. Thank you. Thank you for making me the happiest of men.'

After they had finished making love for the second time in as many hours (Río was *impressed*!), Adair – back in ebullient form – said, 'Well, isn't this cause for a celebration! Where did we put that bottle?'

'We actually finished it.'

He winked. '*Arra*, but amn't I the cute hoor? There's a bottle of Veuve Clicquot in the car. I bought it in the unlikely event that you'd say yes, *acushla*, never dreaming that I'd actually be cracking it open.' Throwing off the duvet, Adair reached for a towel and wrapped it around his waist. Then he stopped in his tracks and gave her a doubtful look. 'Just a thought. I'm guessing you won't want to be called Río Bolger?'

She considered, then shook her head. 'You're right. Río Bolger is a stupid name. It sounds like a mountain range in Mexico. I'll stick with Kinsella.'

He laughed, and bounded off. She heard the boot of the Merc open and close, and within minutes came the pop of another champagne cork from the kitchen of the Bentley.

Río turned over onto her tummy and laid her cheek on her forearms. It was true, in its own way, that she loved Adair. She didn't love him with mad white-hot passion, the way she had once loved Shane; she loved him in a more measured, mature way, with her head as well as her heart.

Did she love him with her whole heart? No. Much of the love contained within the harbour of Río's heart was, and always would be, reserved for Shane, who had fathered the other great love of her life.

She thought again about what Dervla had said, about how she and Shane were meant for each other. Well, yes . . . maybe once upon a time they had been. Back in the days when they'd been young and carefree and irresponsible, before Shane had carved a career for himself as a shit-hot actor in LA, before Río had realised that her son was more important to her than any lover. But she and Shane were worlds apart now. And yet, and yet . . . any time he came to drop in on Finn in Coral Mansion – Adair's erstwhile pride and joy – Shane would be just a stone's throw down the shore. How weird!

She'd hardly seen Finn since he'd arrived back in Lissamore, she realised now: they'd had a quick pint in O'Toole's on Sunday, he had dived into her flat to mend the bolt on the loo seat yesterday, and they'd run into each other on the main street this morning, purely by accident. It was almost as if he was avoiding her. Why? Was it because, if the scuba-dive dream was at last to become a reality, her adjacent orchard would perforce become part of the equation? She remembered the plans he and Izzy had come up with once, the plans he had outlined to her so enthusiastically, about felling some of the fruit trees to make way for a kit room and an air room, and she remembered the relief she had felt when those plans had come to naught, because to have relinquished her orchard would have devastated Río. Was Shane planning to make her an offer for the orchard, in order to make way for *An Ghorm Mhór* – The Big Blue?

Too much speculation! Too many hypotheses! Chief among her concerns now should be Adair, their forthcoming wedding and the state of his health. Shaking the thoughts of Finn and Shane and her orchard and *An Ghorm Mhór* from her head, Río slid out of bed and into the panties and T-shirt that had been unceremoniously discarded earlier.

In the kitchen, Adair had poured champagne into flutes and inserted the bottle in the nifty wine cooler integrated into the kitchen island. He was standing with the scroll of wallpaper in his hand, reading the legend Izzy had inscribed on the loo-roll tube.

'Listen to this, Río. "A House-warming Present for the Best Daddy in the World with All Love from His Darling Izzy-Biz." Isn't she a sweetheart?'

Privately, Río thought she would withhold judgement until she saw what the loo-roll tube contained. She watched as Adair slid the wallpaper out of its casing and unfurled it.

'What is it?' she asked.

'It's a painting. It looks like the sea view from the Villa Felicity.'

Río joined him, and looked over his shoulder at the brush strokes jostling for space on the improvised canvas. Her eyes went to the bottom right-hand corner where she saw, as she fully expected to, the tiny signature: 'C A T'.

'You're right,' she said. 'It's the southerly aspect. And it's by the same person who left a painting behind in your cottage. Remember? I sent you a photograph when I recced the joint.'

'I wonder who the artist is?'

Río took the painting from Adair and looked at it appraisingly. It was easily as good as the one she'd found in the ramshackle house down the lane. 'I think I know who the artist is. I think it's a girl Finn has hooked up with.'

She remembered Finn's phone call of three days ago.

There's someone I'd love you to meet . . . A girl I think you'd like . . . She's a really talented painter . . .

'Finn? You mean, Finn is back in Ireland?' asked Adair.

'Yes. He's . . . Oh, shit . . . There's no easy way of telling you this, Adair, and you're going to find out sooner or later. Finn is refurbishing the Villa Felicity.'

'*Finn* is?'

'Yes. Shane has bought it.'

'Shane. Shane Byrne? Your ex – the Hollywood film star – has bought my old house?'

Río nodded. Adair looked puzzled for a moment, as if trying to do some complicated calculation, and then a smile spread across his face. 'Well, whaddayaknow?' he said, with a robust laugh. 'Good luck to him, the bollix!' Reaching for the champagne flutes, he handed one to Río and chinked his glass against hers.

'You're not upset?'

'Why should I be upset? Sure, doesn't it mean I'll get an invitation to the housewarming party?'

'Except . . . I don't think there'll be a housewarming party.'

'What makes you think that?'

'It's not Shane's intention to live there. Finn's converting the place into a scuba-dive centre.'

'The way Izzy and Finn planned to do, once upon a time?'

'Yes.'

Adair looked thoughtful; then he shrugged. 'I wish them well. Sure, it was always far too grandiose and rambling a joint to be a home. I'm glad to see some enterprising spirit is prepared to take a chance on the place. I'm just sorry I was never able to do it for Izzy.' Raising his glass to his lips, he took a sip; and for the first time since she'd broken the news, Río saw hurt in his eyes. 'My girl deserves better than to be working for some narky git in marketing.'

'She seems to be doing well for herself.' Río remembered the nifty Alfa Romeo and the designer handbag.

'She's doing all right. But money isn't everything. I know that, Río, to my cost. I wasted years of my life making it, only to lose it all.'

'Are you really poor now, Adair?' asked Río, curiously. 'Things can't be that bad if you can afford a state-of-the-art Massey Ferguson.'

'Things are complicated. I've had to sell a lot of assets in order to get my life back on track. But you needn't worry that I can't keep you in the style to which you have become accustomed, Ms Kinsella.'

'That wouldn't be hard,' smiled Río. 'I'm very low maintenance.'

He pulled her into him. 'And once the oyster farm is up and running at full throttle again, won't we be laughing? The added plus is that we can dine on Pacific gigas every night.'

'Hm,' purred Río, raising an eyebrow. 'You know what they say about their aphrodisiac qualities?'

'I don't need no aphrodisiac when it comes to you, sweet thing. You're the sexiest woman I've ever met. Just looking at you turns me on.' He took her hand, and held it against his crotch. 'Let's go back to bed.'

'*Again?* No, Adair. I've things to be doing.'

'Such as?'

'Such as organising a wedding.'

'When'll we do it?'

'ASAP. We could have a Celtic ceremony, somewhere lovely. How about barefoot, on Coolnamara Strand?'

'Sounds good. Means I won't have to bother with a tux.'

'I'll have to get myself a pedicure,' said Río, contemplating her unpainted toenails. 'But aside from that, let's not go to

137

a huge amount of trouble. We can put "Shabby Chic" on the invites.'

'We're inviting people?' said Adair.

'But of course,' Río told him with a smile. 'Everybody's coming. It's going to be the best damn party Lissamore has ever seen.'

Chapter Nine

Cat was on the roof, helping herself to some rays. Finn was below on the terrace, mending a gate. She could hear him banging away and whistling lustily, if tunelessly. The Villa Felicity was getting there. Between the two of them, they were putting manners on the place, and Finn was sending his father progress reports on a regular basis.

Cat was completely fascinated by Skype. To watch Finn and Shane talking together on the screen of Finn's MacBook Pro was like nothing she'd ever seen. In the Crooked House – before the advent of Oaf – there had been no broadband, no satellite television, no wi-fi. There'd not even been a phone, effectively, since the ancient Bakelite yoke in the hall was not conducive to having laidback chats like the ones Finn conducted with his father.

These chats were a revelation to Cat. She found it astonishing that a person could talk so openly to a parent. Any 'chats' Cat had ever had with her own father were comprised of either maudlin ramblings on his part, or lectures, or rants, and Cat's input had been negligible. She'd just glowered, taciturn and contemptuous, waiting for Hugo to run out of steam.

She remembered one of the last conversations (actually, it had been a flaming row) that she'd had with him shortly before she'd left the Crooked House to go and live on the houseboat, during the course of which he'd told her that she was a bird-brain and a good-for-nothing and a bitter disappointment to him, and how dared she squander the talent that had been his bequest to her. He'd used words like 'prodigal' and 'profligate' and 'ingrate'; and then – when she'd finally told him to fuck off to hell and back in a handcart, and stormed up to her bedroom and locked herself in – he'd languished on the landing for an hour with a bottle of Jameson, begging her to come out and sobbing about how much he loved his baby girl. And indeed, Cat had come out, finally, and put a blanket over him and snuggled down on the floor beside him, and told him the stories she knew off by heart – the ones that her mother had told her. And he'd smiled and stroked her hair and said that sometimes he felt as if he were the baby and she was the parent. And the next day he had, of course, forgotten all about it.

How other-end-of-the-spectrum was Finn's relationship with Shane! Finn called his father 'punk', his father called him 'dude'. Finn didn't bat an eyelid when Shane lit up a joint, and Shane didn't bat an eyelid when Finn told him that the girl he'd found squatting in Coral Mansion was living there still. He'd just said, 'Introduce me, why don't you?' and when Finn turned the webcam on Cat, his father had flirted shamelessly with her. Cat had flirted back, thrilled to be shooting the breeze with a Hollywood star (even one as ancient as Shane) and hoping to piss off Finn, but Finn was as laidback as ever when they finally cut the Skype connection and went back to work.

Finn was highly amused by the fact that Cat was such a Luddite. He'd laughed at her phone when he'd first seen it, and told her it was like looking at some antiquity from the Iron Age. Cat couldn't take or send photographs on her phone, she couldn't access the web, she couldn't even play any games. Whereas Finn seemed to spend half his life when he wasn't working doing esoteric phone-centric stuff, or lounging in front of the screen of his MacBook Pro, living a vicarious virtual life out there on the worldwide web.

'Let me teach you the basics,' he'd suggested to Cat. 'It'll change your life once you get internet savvy.'

But Cat had demurred, and continued to shy away from all things technical, with the exception of Finn's iPod, which she adored. 'You do know,' she had told him, 'that every time you log on to the internet or hook up with someone on your phone, Big Brother is monitoring your every move?'

'So?'

'So they get loads of information about you that way. Like, what kind of subversive literature you're into, or the deviant porn you're accessing.'

But Finn just smiled at her – that lovely, lazy smile he'd inherited from his father. 'I don't do deviant porn,' he said. 'I just do the bog-standard stuff.'

'And they know where you're going and where you've come from. They're like Santa Claus. They know when you are sleeping. They know when you're awake. They know when you've been bad or good . . .'

Finn finished the lyric for her. 'My ma used to sing that song to me every Christmas. It really pissed me off. I was always convinced I'd get no presents.'

'And now you should be well pissed-off that Big Brother's going to be on to you every time you commit a misdemeanour.'

'Big Brother holds no fear for me,' said Finn, with equanimity. 'I'm a law-abiding citizen. Unlike you, Cat burglar, going around breaking into houses all over the place.'

'I'm not a burglar. I never steal stuff.'

'Liar. You stole my iPod.'

'I'll buy you a new one,' she said airily, 'when I sell another of my paintings.'

'And like, when is that going to happen? Have you booked yourself a slot in the Museum of Modern Art or something?'

'The Museum of Modern Art doesn't sell paintings,' she told him. 'It buys them.'

'Maybe you should stick a couple of your wallpaper doodles in the post to them then, and ask them to make you an offer.'

'Ha ha.'

'Although . . .' He gave her a thoughtful look. 'That's not as outrageous an idea as you might think. You might think about circulating JPEGs—'

'What are you on about?'

'You could send JPEGs—'

'What's a J-peg?'

'Oh, Jesus.' Finn had put his head in his hands. 'I won't even begin to try to explain.'

'Do. Please. I like the sound of a J-peg. Like J-Lo, only Irish. J-Peig.'

'Honestly, Cat, you're hopeless. It's like talking Klingon sometimes, talking to you.'

'Go on, Finnster,' cajoled Cat. 'Tell me what a J-peg is.'

'Well, when you send an email, you can attach an image to it.'

'Like, a photographic image?'

'Yeah. And the person at the other end opens the JPEG—'

'Kind of like opening an envelope?'

'I guess so, yeah – a virtual envelope – and then they get to see the image you've sent. I could take a picture of this view, for instance,' he said, waving a hand at the picture window, 'and send it to Da in LA. Or I could take a picture of your painting of this view, and send it.'

'So you could send images of my paintings through the internet, to galleries and places?'

Finn had nodded. 'Except I was thinking more along the lines of sending them to Da.'

Cat gave him an interested look. 'Why him?'

'He has loads of contacts in LA. Rich ones. One of them might take a fancy to your paintings and offer to buy one. Artists are selling stuff through the internet all the time, now.'

Cat threw him a sceptical look.

'It's true. Take a look at this.' Finn typed something on the keypad of his laptop, and then – lo and behold – the screen became a display case for a series of rather lovely linear images – most of them female nudes. 'It's the website of the mother of a friend of mine, who does etchings.'

'Hm. Show me more.'

Finn clicked again, and some words came up on the screen. 'I don't want the words,' said Cat, leaning closer to the screen. 'I just want to look at the pictures.'

'They're good, aren't they?'

'They're grand,' said Cat, noncommittally. She was more interested in the prices than the paintings. 'How much do they fetch?'

'The price list is on another page.' Finn clicked again. 'Two, three hundred euros. Cheaper than yours. But I suspect you'll have to bring your prices down, to stay competitive. There are an awful lot of other people out there with their wares on display.'

Cat gave him a look of hauteur. 'Someone was prepared to pay seven hundred and fifty euros for one of my paintings the other day.'

'What do you mean, the other day? You haven't been anywhere you could flog your paintings.'

143

'It was a stranger passing on the beach. She came in when you were off getting the T-bones.'

'You let a stranger into the house? Are you out of your mind, Cat? She could have been a psychopath!'

'Oh, she was fine. She was just a little old lady from a neighbouring island. A bit like Peig Sayers. Tell me more about these J-peg thingies. Do you really think it could work?'

Finn shrugged. 'It's worth a try, ain't it?'

'Cool! Why don't you do it, then? Take some pics and send them to your dad.'

Finn yawned. 'OK. I'll do it in the morning.'

'Can't we do it now?'

Cat was impatient, thrilled by the notion of so-called JPEGs of her paintings flying through the ether across the ocean to Los Angeles and all Shane Byrne's film star friends. They liked Irish artists in LA. She'd heard that Sylvester Stallone and Robert de Niro owned a fair few of Graham Knuttel's paintings, and Tom Cruise and Colin Farrell had bought stuff from Rasher. OK, so Graham Knuttel had earned a diploma from the art school in Dun Laoghaire, but Rasher was a self-taught maverick, like her.

'I'm not doing it tonight,' Finn had told her, categorically. 'I'm knackered. And if I leave off until the morning I can take them in natural light.'

'I can't wait!' said Cat, hugging herself.

And the next morning she had set up her paintings to their best advantage in the light-filled sitting room, and watched excitedly as Finn took the pictures with his iPhone.

'But shouldn't you be doing it with a proper camera?' she asked. 'Wouldn't you get better quality images?'

'Nah. These'll work perfectly.' Finn had connected his phone to his computer and droned on about how it was connecting via Bluetooth to Windows Live Mail and blah

blah blah, and Cat pretended to listen until she was finally satisfied that, by some arcane and mystical process, her paintings were now safely ensconced on Shane Byrne's hard drive in the Hollywood Hills.

'How long before we know for sure?' she asked.

'We'll Skype him tonight,' said Finn.

And then he had lectured Cat some more about how she ought to get internet savvy, and droned on about packets and bandwidth – whatever they were – and now Cat was taking her ease in the sun listening to Finn banging and whistling below, indulging in a fantasy of getting a phone call from Johnny Depp (who, Finn had told her, was a friend of Shane's) or Keira Knightley or Helen Mirren, or even Oprah Winfrey, to say that they wanted to buy all her paintings. She'd have to put her prices up. She pictured herself on *Oprah*, and was glad that Oaf had insisted on having a Sky Box installed in the Crooked House, because it meant that Hugo could watch her on the show.

'So, Cat,' Oprah would say, 'how does it feel to have Hollywood at your feet? I'm told you can hardly keep up with the demand from the stars who are clamouring to own one of your paintings. Your father Hugo must be very proud of you. I hear your work is selling for twice as much as his and—'

'Finn!'

It was a woman's voice, calling from the beach. Uh-oh, thought Cat. Could that Izzy girl be back in Lissamore so soon? Buggeration. She'd get into trouble now for not telling Finn she'd called in to the house the other day, especially since she had lied and said that Izzy was like Peig Sayers, the original cranky auld wan. Crawling to the parapet, Cat looked over.

It wasn't Izzy on the beach. It was one of the women Cat

145

had seen having the *fête champêtre* in the allotment, the one who'd gone in swimming.

'Hey, Ma!' said Finn. 'What brings you here? Are you on your way to the Bentley?'

Aha! thought Cat. This must be the famous Río that Finn had told her about.

'No,' said Río, moving from the beach to the orchard gate and pushing it open. 'I've just come from the Bentley.'

The Bentley! That was the posh mobile home that Finn had told her about, the one that had recently been delivered to the junk yard a mile or so down the beach. Cat wished it had been there ten days ago. She'd much sooner have stayed overnight in a state-of-the-art mobile home than in that poxy cottage she'd broken into. She'd never jemmied the lock on a mobile home before; she reckoned it would be a piece of piss.

Making herself comfortable on the hammock that Finn had strung up on the roof, Cat closed her eyes against the sun and lay back. She was glad when she heard hammer blows ringing out again. There was nothing nicer than listening to someone else grafting when you were taking your ease.

Río moved across the shingle to the embankment and pushed open the gate to her orchard as Finn resumed work, raining down hammer blows on something tinny. She wished he'd come racing down to wrap his arms around her as he'd done earlier that day when they'd bumped into each other in the middle of the main street, but she could hardly expect a touchy-feely demonstration of affection from her son every time they met. He'd done a good job of demolishing the pavilion, she noticed: there was nothing left of it, apart from the concrete base. Maybe that could serve as the foundation for his air room? That would mean fewer trees would need to be cut down to make way for new buildings. Río knew she was clutching at straws, but the less Finn's project encroached on her land, the better as far as she was concerned. Leave her with at least one of her two precious acres!

She saw that there was a widening gap in the fence by the gate where a new rabbit trail had been established – she'd have to get that mended soon, otherwise stray sheep would find their way through, and her vegetables would end up as organic fodder for her neighbouring farmer's ewes. But she'd hardly find time between now and the wedding.

The wedding! She and Adair had done a bit of online research and made a few phone calls, and they'd found a lovely Celtic priest who had a window for a wedding next Monday. If they were going to hold out for a civil ceremony, they'd be waiting months before they could make it legal. A Celtic wedding on a beach would be more romantic anyway, Río decided, and Adair could do with a little romance in his life.

What would she wear? she wondered now, as she passed along the rows of runner beans she'd planted last March, pulling away dead pods here and there. There was no time to get a wedding dress, and anyway, she hated all that palaver so. She could ask Fleur to step up to the mark and organise a suitable frock, but really, Río would rather get married in scarlet. White was *so* wrong a colour for her! Why not just wear the red dress she'd bought in Fleurissima for the birthday party Adair had thrown for her, all those years ago? It might just about fit, still. She'd try it on when she got home this evening. Stooping, she retrieved a tomato from where it had fallen at the root of a vine, and inspected it for signs of alien invasion. There were none. That organic pesticide was clearly doing the trick.

Finn had stopped his hammering, and was squinting down at her, shielding his eyes from the sun with a tanned hand. 'How's Adair settling in?' he asked, as she stepped onto the terrace.

'Very well,' she replied, biting into her tomato. 'I think he likes living in a mobile home much better than living in a real home. I have to say, I could get used to it, too. It's a bit like playing house. How are you getting on?'

'We're getting there. But there's no rush.'

Río looked around at the tool-strewn terrace, at the power-hose snaking over the cracked Indian sandstone slabs, the peeling paintwork on the walls of the pool, the ivy that was running riot all over the rusty railings, and she thought that really, Finn ought to have more cop-on than to think he could do this job on his own, even with the help of his Cat-friend. 'When are you getting the pros in?' she asked.

'The pros?'

'Well, you're hardly going to be able to do all the work yourself. Presumably there's a lot of specialist stuff involved?'

Finn shrugged. 'Not really. It's all pretty straightforward painting and decorating. A bit of plastering, maybe. The pool's the only area where we'll need professional help.'

'Oh?' Río moved towards the big picture window and peered through. 'I'd have thought you might have enlisted a team of interior designers.'

'Nah. You know Da. He's pretty laidback about that kind of stuff. He's happy enough with the place the way it is, with Adair's old furniture. It's still in real good nick. I gave him a tour on webcam so he could check it out.'

Río gave him an 'as if' look. 'It's hardly in good enough nick for paying guests,' she said. 'Presumably you're after people with a few bob to throw around if you want to turn a profit.'

'What do you mean, paying guests?'

'You know – the ones who'll be coming on scuba safari.'

'Scuba safari?' Finn looked baffled. 'What makes you think there'll be people coming here to dive?'

'But that's the reason Shane bought the place, isn't it? To set up a scuba-dive outfit, like the one you and Izzy planned, when it belonged to Adair.'

Finn shook his head. 'No, Ma. He didn't buy it for a scuba-dive outfit.'

Río took off her sunglasses, and narrowed her eyes at Finn. 'Why did he buy it, then?'

'I guess – I guess he just wants to be able to spend more time in Lissamore.'

'But he lives on the other side of the world!'

'Even Lissamore's accessible from the other side of the world, Ma. Especially when you can afford to fly first class, like he can.'

'So . . . you're not doing up the joint for yourself, Finn? You're not going to be the one living here?'

'No. Da is.'

'But . . . but that's ridiculous!'

'Why?'

'Because it . . . because it just *is* ridiculous! Shane can't come back to Ireland and live! He can't!'

'I think you'll find that Da can live anywhere he damn well pleases, Ma. It's not as if the tax on second homes is going to bankrupt him.'

Río's sunglasses hit the deck suddenly, and her hands went to her mouth. 'Oh! *Oh!* The stupid, stupid man! Why didn't he *tell* me! Why didn't he tell me before I . . . Oh, God.'

'*I* told you,' said Finn equably. 'Practically the first thing I told you when I got back was "Surprise! Dad's bought Coral Mansion", and you did get a surprise. Remember? You told me you got such a surprise you fell off your chair.'

'But you said he'd bought it – I'm *sure* you said he'd bought it for you to do up.'

'And I am doing it up. Look.' Finn held up the hammer. 'I'm doing it up to the best of my abilities. But hey, Da's not fussy. If the work ain't done to professional standards, he's not gonna fire me. He'd rather I trousered the dosh than some rip-off merchant from Galway.'

'I just assumed that you were going to convert it,' Río said, sitting down very suddenly on the sun lounger. 'I never dreamed that Shane would ever come back to Lissamore . . . Oh. Oh! What have I done? I've done the wrong thing, when I so thought I was doing the right thing.'

'You've made a mistake, that's all,' said Finn. 'I suppose it was an easy enough conclusion to jump to. The scuba-dive outfit seemed like a good idea once upon a time. But then, you know, Ma, when Iz and me split up, and when I thought about it, I realised it would actually make a lot more sense – if you *were* going to set a scuba joint up in Lissamore – to refurbish the old one on Inishclare. The diving there would be way better for novices because of the – Ma? Are you all right?'

When Iz and I split up . . .

At the mention of Izzy's name, curiosity finally got the better of Cat. She swung herself out of the hammock, shimmied over to the parapet, and peered over.

Finn's ma was sitting on the sun lounger, looking a bit green around the gills, the way a girl in her boarding school had done once, just before she'd projectile-vomited all over the classroom. Cat wondered if Río was going to be sick, and hoped she wouldn't do it into the swimming pool that she'd spent an entire day power-hosing. Finn was hunkered next to her, holding her hand.

'What's up, Ma?' he asked.

150

Cat had to strain to hear the response. In a voice trembling with emotion, sounding a bit like the way Peig Sayers might talk, she heard Río say, 'I'm getting married.'

'What?' said Finn. '*What* did you say?'

'I'm getting married next week.'

Cat laughed. What fine larks were to be had in Lissamore!

Finn looked utterly baffled. 'But . . . who are you getting married to, Ma? I didn't even know you had a boyfriend!'

'I'm getting married,' said Río, 'to Adair Bolger.'

Later that evening, when Finn had come back from seeing his mother home, Cat asked him if they could Skype Shane, and see if the JPEGs had arrived. Finn was sitting at the kitchen table, trying to cheer himself up on YouTube, with Cat perched cross-legged next to his laptop. Cat didn't blame him for feeling a bit glum. If his da had bought this stonking great mansion in order to be reunited with his family, it *was* a bit of a bummer that his ma was getting married to somebody else. But, hey – Cat knew what it was like to be dealt a crap hand when playing Happy Families. Finn would get over it, the way she had.

'I can't Skype him,' Finn said. 'I wouldn't know what to tell him about Ma.'

'But isn't she going to tell him herself?'

'Not yet. She says she wants it to be a *fait accompli.*'

'What's a *fait accompli*?'

'You know – already done, so that she can't back out of it.'

'Why would she want to back out of it? Doesn't she love this Adair bloke?'

Finn looked uncertain. 'I . . . well, I guess she must. It's not as if she's marrying him for his money, now that he doesn't have any. I mean, you'd *have* to love someone, wouldn't you, if you were going to go and live in a mobile home with them?'

'I'd like to live in a mobile home,' said Cat. 'I'd like to live

151

in one of those real luxury motor homes that you see German tourists zooming around Coolnamara in. You have every-thing in those motor homes – telly, fridge, power showers, everything. Imagine, Finn! You could drive off to anywhere you liked any time you felt like it. Not even the television licence inspector would be able to get you.'

'If you could afford one of those motor homes, I don't think you'd have any problems paying your television licence fee. I suppose I'm going to have to get one for this joint. I wonder how much they cost.'

'A television licence? Chill, Finn. You haven't even got a telly yet.'

'I'll have to organise one. Da's going to need one for all the DVDs he gets given.'

'He gets free DVDs?'

'Millions of them. It's one of the perks of his job.'

Cat uncrossed her legs and hugged them to her chest. 'Imagine having a job as a film star! Is that what he puts on forms? You know, like "Job Description: Film Star"?'

'I don't know what he puts. What do you put? Artist? Or painter? Or vagabond?'

'None of the above. I put "Visionary",' lied Cat, who had never filled out a form in her life. 'My dad puts "Academician".'

'"Academician"?'

'He's a member of the Royal Hibernian Academy of Artists. He only puts it to piss people off. It's his favourite hobby.'

'Pissing people off?'

'Yeah. Me included.' Cat slid down from her perch on the table. 'Can we Skype now? Come on, Finn. Have a beer, and we'll put in a call to your dad.'

'But I don't know what to say to him, Cat, about Ma.'

'Don't say anything. It's not your problem.'

Why should he want to waste time and energy getting

involved? How stupid boys were, sometimes! They had all the cop-on of an elephant seal. Moving to the fridge, Cat took out a couple of cans of beer, and set them on the table. On YouTube, Kingsford the cutest piglet on the planet was going swimming.

'It's kinda weird to think that Ma getting married means Izzy'll be my stepsister,' said Finn contemplatively, gazing at his computer screen as if it was a crystal ball showing him a cloudy future, instead of Kingsford swimming.

Cat didn't want to talk about Izzy. She snapped the tab on Finn's beer and handed it to him. 'When is the wedding going to happen?'

'Next Monday, on Coolnamara Strand. She's getting a Celtic priest or monk or something to do it.'

'A Celtic priest?'

'Yeah. She's asked me to give her away.'

'Jiminy. That's a bit weird, isn't it? Giving away your own mum.' Perching herself up on the table again, Cat took a swig from her can. 'Is there going to be a party?'

'Yes. In O'Toole's.'

'Can I come?'

'Sure.'

'The only wedding party I was ever at was my dad's. It was horrendous. He got smashed and tried to drag Oaf's maid of honour off to bed.'

'Who's Oaf?'

'My stepmother. It's short for Ophelia, but her real name's Tracey. I don't know whether it's more embarrassing to have an Oaf for a stepmother, or a Tracey.'

'Parents really can be embarrassing, can't they?'

'Your dad's pretty cool.'

'Yeah. I actually thought my ma was pretty cool, too.'

'Was?'

153

'Well, it just seems so out of character, this whole wedding thing. I mean, she didn't even marry my dad – and back in the days when I was a kid it was kind of frowned upon to have a child out of wedlock.'

'Wedlock!' Cat shuddered. 'What a horrible word. Imagine promising to lock yourself to another person till death do you part. It must feel like locking yourself in a dungeon.'

'That's just what I don't understand. Ma was always such a free spirit. She never belonged to anybody. I mean, that Duran Duran song kind of sums her up.'

Cat didn't know what Duran Duran was and she didn't care. It was getting late, and she was determined to get Finn to Skype his dad before bedtime, because if he left it till the morning it would be the middle of the night in LA, and she wouldn't be able to find out what Shane thought of her paintings, and whether he'd be able to find buyers for them. She'd been thinking all day about Finn's idea of sending her stuff out on the internet, and the more she thought about it, the more excited she became. What a fantastic feeling it would be, to have her own income . . . to never have to pick up the phone to her father again and ask for money! To never again have to grovel to Oaf to be put through!

But just as she was wondering how best to persuade Finn to talk to his dad, funny music started coming from his computer.

'What's that?' asked Cat.

'An incoming call. Shit. It's Da.'

'Pick up! Pick up!' urged Cat.

'Oh, God.' Finn took a deep breath. Then he clicked on a little symbol of a green telephone receiver, and said, as Shane's face materialised on the screen, 'Hi, Da.'

'Hey, Finn!' In LA, Shane was Skype-ing alfresco. His eyes

154

were concealed behind aviator shades, and Cat fancied he was poolside because there was a marine-blue shimmer going on in the background. 'I've someone here who wants to say hello.'

'Who is it?'

'It's . . . ta-ran-ta-ra!' The webcam wobbled slightly as Shane adjusted it, and then another face appeared alongside Shane's.

'Hello, Finn!' A velvet voice oozed through the speaker.

'Elena!' said Finn. 'Hey! How's it going, beautiful?'

Cat recognised the face smiling at them, magically beamed into a kitchen in the west of Ireland courtesy of the world-wide web. It was Elena Sweetman, glamorous star of *Silver Vixens*, one of Oaf's favourite television series.

'Well, holy shomoly!' gasped Cat. 'Oaf, eat your heart out!'

'Hi, Catkin,' said Shane, sending her his great smile. 'You're looking very fetching today. Meet Elena.'

'Hello, Elena.'

Cat actually felt shy, greeting Elena, which was not an emotion she was familiar with. She hadn't felt shy when she'd met Finn's dad over the internet because he was only Finn's dad, even if he was a shit-hot Hollywood star. But meeting Elena Sweetman was a bit like meeting the Queen of Sheba, or Catwoman. Elena had been a legend forever: Cat even remembered going to see her films with her mother.

'Hi, Cat.' Elena leaned a little closer, and looked straight into Cat's eyes. 'Nice to meet you! You're the artist, right?'

The artist! Because Cat had never been called an artist before in her life, she wasn't sure whether to answer yes or no. But as she dithered, Finn answered for her. 'Yes,' he said. 'You got the JPEGs, Da?'

'I did. Nice work, Cat,' said Shane. 'Elena's a big fan.'

'You mean, you like them?' Cat demanded.

'I love them,' said Elena. 'They brought me right back to that corner of Ireland. I made a film there once, near Lissamore.'

'*The O'Hara Affair*?'

'That's right.'

Ha! *The O'Hara Affair* just happened to be Oaf's favourite film, too! How Cat would love Oaf to see her now, talking on Skype to Hollywood royalty. A future scenario flashed across her mind's eye, of Cat sitting with Hugo and Oaf, and casually dropping Elena Sweetman's name into the conversation. *Elena's loving my new work! Elena and me . . . Elena says . . . My new best friend, Elena Sweetman . . .*

'I'd like to buy one of your paintings, Cat, if I may?' said Elena.

'What?' answered Cat, rudely.

'I'm sorry? I'm assuming they're for sale?'

'Oh! Sure!' No shit! This was getting better and better! 'Which one would you like?'

'The one with the dolphins? Is that available?'

'Yes.'

'How much?'

'A thousand.'

Beside her, Finn stifled a guffaw.

But Elena didn't bat one of her beautifully painted eyelids. 'A thousand seems very reasonable. Consider it a done deal.'

'Um . . . How will I get it to you?' asked Cat, thinking fast. She could hardly stick it in a loo-roll tube, the way she had with the painting she'd sold Izzy.

'That won't be a problem,' said Elena. 'Shane can pick it up for me when he's in Lissamore next.'

Dammit. That might not be for ages, thought Cat. And she could hardly ask Elena Sweetman to send her a cheque until after she'd received delivery of the goods. A cheque.

She supposed that was how people paid for pricey stuff. Could she cash a cheque in the pub? That's what her father had always used to do before he got famous. Or would she have to open a bank account? No! Maybe she could ask Elena to give Shane cash to bring over with him? But that didn't look very professional, and Elena clearly thought she was dealing with a professional artist . . .

Hm. This was getting complicated, and Cat liked to keep things simple. She was on the verge of asking how long it would take for Meryl Streep's toe to get better when she remembered that all that stuff about Shane and Tilda Swinton and Meryl Streep making a film together called *The Corsican Brothers* had been made up to confound Izzy, and that Shane was actually 'resting' between films right now. Maybe she could persuade him that a holiday in lovely Lissamore would be just the ticket?

'Lissamore's looking lovely at the moment,' she began. 'The . . . er, sun is shining and the sea is . . . um, blue and . . .'

But further cajolement was unnecessary because: 'I'm glad to hear it,' said Shane. 'I'll be over there next week.'

Beside her, Cat felt Finn stiffen. 'You what?' he said.

'I'm coming over to inspect my new property in person,' said Shane. 'I'll pick up Elena's painting from Cat then.'

'Cool. How . . . um, how long are you staying, Da?'

'That depends,' replied Shane, 'on how energetic I'm feeling. I might like to do some hands-on work myself on the joint. Or I might just like to take things easy for a while.'

'Oh, fuck. What day are you arriving?' asked Finn.

'Name a day,' said Shane.

'Monday?' suggested Cat.

'Monday it is.'

Cat couldn't help it. She started to laugh.

157

Instantly, Finn clicked on the picture of the little red telephone receiver, and that funny noise came through the speakers – that sound between a plop and a whoosh that told Cat the call had been terminated.

'Why did you do that?' she scolded, turning to Finn.

'Why do you think?' he said. 'Why do you fucking *think*? The shit's just hit the fan.'

'Yes! That's exactly what it sounds like!' said Cat, with a delighted smile.

'What? What are you on about now?'

'That noise the computer makes when you end a call. It's like shit hitting a fan.'

Hopping down from the table, she skipped over to the fridge. 'Fancy another beer, Finnster? I'm having one, to celebrate. And no worries – I'll treat you to the next crate when we go to the supermarket to stock up. I'm a rich girl. A thousand! A *thousand*! I wonder, did she mean dollars or euros? Which is worth more, Finn? Finn?'

But Finn wasn't listening. When she set the can on the table he had that stupid staring-into-a-crystal-ball face on again. Except this time his expression was darker.

Pah! He was clearly going to be no fun for the rest of the evening. Plugging herself into his iPod and grabbing her beer, Cat shimmied up on to the roof to do some stargazing.

Chapter Ten

'Look at this one! "The Lady Galadriel". You could get married as an elf, Río!'

'Or Queen Guinevere. It says you will be sure to feel like a graceful nymph as you walk and dance in this lovely design.'

'Or Snow White. Get a load of that *gúna*!'

'I told you gals – I'm getting married in my red dress.'

Dervla, Fleur and Río were sharing a bottle or three of wine (while the eminently portable Marguerite slept soundly in her Silver Cross Pop Vogue), browsing internet sites to do with Celtic weddings. Fleur had hit upon one specialising in outlandish fairytale wedding dresses that had her in fits of giggles. Río had come to realise that getting married barefoot on a beach wasn't going to be quite as straightforward or simple as she'd expected, and now Fleur and Dervla kept coming up with stuff to complicate matters even further.

'What about music?' said Fleur.

'Um. I guess I could ask Padraig Whelan to play his fiddle. 'She Moves through the Fair', or somesuch,' Río said, off the top of her head. She hadn't given a single thought to what music should be played. 'That song's all about a wedding, ain't it?'

'It says here that you can do a dance after you make your vows, as a couple,' observed Dervla.

159

'I'm not dancing with everyone looking on! I'd feel like a complete eejit.'

'You could have Padraig play that Duran Duran song,' suggested Fleur. 'That would be really appropriate, since you're getting married on a beach.'

Río shook her head. 'I'm sick to death of that song.'

'Have you booked O'Toole's yet?'

'Yes.'

'Ordered champagne?'

'Yes.'

'OK. So what else needs to be done?' said Dervla.

'Um. The rings.'

'Get them in that silversmith's in Galway. He does lovely Claddagh rings.'

'You think I should go for a Claddagh?'

'For sure. It's a Celtic ceremony.'

'What's the symbolism behind a Claddagh ring?' asked Fleur.

'Well, the heart is a symbol of love, of course,' explained Dervla, reaching for the wine bottle. 'The hands on either side are for friendship, and the crown means loyalty and fidelity. And you have to wear it with the heart turned inward, because that means you've committed your lives to each other forever. It's more of a statement than your common or garden engagement or wedding ring, isn't it, Rí?'

There was something very significant about the way Dervla was looking at Río, and Río knew that she was making an oblique reference to the engagement ring that Shane had given her once, a solitaire diamond she'd never got round to returning. Río tried to ignore her sister, and returned her attention to the screen, where a woman was pictured modelling a hideous confection of nylon lace.

'More romantic, too, to have a Claddagh ring!' said Fleur.

'Remember, you'll have to get a cake, Río. They can be really expensive – someone I know paid five hundred euro for her wedding cake.'

'What? Was it coated in gold leaf, or something? I'll bake my own cake.'

'Will you have time? You'll want to get your hair done, and your nails – and a facial, of course. Oh, listen to this: "If the bride's mother-in-law breaks a piece of cake on the bride's head as she enters the house after the ceremony, they will be friends for life."'

'If anyone broke a piece of cake on my head after I'd forked out a fortune on my hair, I'd hit them a dig,' said Río. 'Anyway, I'm not going to be entering a house. I'm going to be entering a mobile home. Or a leisure lodge. Or whatever it calls itself.'

'Will Adair carry you over the threshold?' asked Dervla.

Río gave her an 'as if' look. 'He'd need to embark on a serious weight-training programme if he was going to do that.'

'D'you remember our childhood dreams, Río?' said Dervla. 'About the kind of houses we were going to live in?'

'Tell me,' said Fleur, refilling their glasses.

'Well, I was going to live in a Great House, and Río was going to live in a cottage by the sea. Coral Cottage was her dream house, before the Bolgers knocked it down and turned it into Coral Mansion.'

'It was the prettiest place then, Fleur,' said Río. 'You wouldn't have known it, the way it was when we were kids. Mama used to take us to visit the old woman who lived there, to buy free-range eggs. And Dervla and I used to have picnics in the orchard – squashed tomato sandwiches and MiWadi, Dervla, do you remember? And we used to do balancing tricks on the sea wall, and pretend we were circus acrobats, and lie under the trees and dream about the men

161

we were going to marry, and the babies we were going to have. You married your dream man, Dervla.'

'Yeah. But you got the baby.'

Río smiled. 'It's funny to think that Finn was ever a baby.'

'Wasn't he conceived in that orchard?' asked Fleur.

'Yes. In the garden of my erstwhile dream cottage.'

Oh! To have a little house! The lines of the Padraic Colum poem that she'd learned at school came back to Río:

> *Oh! To have a little house!*
> *To own the hearth and stool and all!*
> *The heaped up sods upon the fire,*
> *The pile of turf against the wall!*

It had been her favourite poem, so simple, and yet so full of yearning. And it was true that that was all Río had ever wanted from life. A little house of her own, and a plot of land to tend as a garden.

There was a silence, as they all reflected on their past, and then Dervla hauled them back to the present.

'What are you going to do about this place?' she asked Río. 'Let it?'

'This place?' Río looked around at her apartment, her lovely little eyrie above the harbour that had been gifted to her by her sister after their father had died, having left Dervla the bulk of his estate. 'No. I'm going to need it as a bolthole. I'll want somewhere to escape to from time to time as long as we're living in the Bentley. I won't be able to paint there.'

'What about when you do up the cottage?'

'There's an outhouse I could convert into a studio. But it would break my heart to leave here.'

Río's eyes went to the embroidered sampler that Dervla

had given her when she'd first moved in, the one worked in French knots and featherstitch and herringbone that bore the motto 'Home is where the Heart is'. Something told her that she wouldn't be bringing it with her when she moved into the Bentley.

Since she'd agreed to marry Adair, and since she'd found out that Shane was coming back to live in Lissamore, Río had felt as if she were going through an out-of-body experience. She'd spent an hour after Finn had left her last night sitting in front of an enormous glass of wine, staring at the palms of her hands. Her life line, her heart line, her head line . . . Had she allowed her heart to rule her head, or vice versa? She hadn't a clue. Nothing made sense any more. And then she'd retrieved the diamond ring that Shane had given her when he'd asked her to marry him once upon a time, and slid it on to her finger. It was worth a lot of money. Río had had a notion, once, that she might sell it to help set Finn up in business; but then plans had changed, as they had a habit of doing, and she hadn't had to sell it after all. She'd have to give it back to Shane ASAP. She couldn't keep his ring, now that she'd promised to marry Adair.

Shane coming back was a disaster of the highest order. Dervla had been right when she'd said that Río and Shane were made for each other. She'd also been right when she'd said that Río had never faced up to it. Right until now, she hadn't. While Shane was on the other side of the Atlantic, any kind of rekindling of their relationship had been out of the question. Out of sight, out of mind had been the principle that informed their *modus vivendi*. And now he'd be within a stone's throw of where she was to live with her new husband.

How she'd love to throw, hurl, pelt and sling stones at Shane – thousands of them. How she'd love to send all the pebbles on the beach raining down upon the one-time love of her life. Why – *why* – hadn't he told her himself that he'd bought Coral Mansion? If she had been in possession of this knowledge a week ago, would she now be contemplating marriage to Adair Bolger? Oh, God . . . it was a head wreck of a situation, a cat's cradle of a conundrum, a complete fucking *bitch* – and she could confide in no one. Not even Dervla was in a position to advise her now.

What would she say, anyway, if she were to seek advice? I'm marrying a man I cannot claim to love with my entire heart and soul, and the reason I'm marrying him is because he's dying. And now the man I do love with my entire heart and soul, the man whom I have always loved, and who is the father of my child, is coming back to Ireland, and what can I tell him? Should I come clean and reveal to him that the real reason I'm getting married to someone else is because my husband-to-be has terminal cancer, and – hey – if we can just hang on for a year, he'll more than likely be dead and I'll be a free woman again? Chill, Shane – it's just a year! Oh, it was unthinkable. *Unthinkable!*

And now Fleur was saying something about buying ribbons for the handfasting, whatever that was, and Dervla was looking on her phone for the number of a florist in Galway, and Río just felt like running away and diving into the sea and swimming off to an island where she could live on her own for the rest of her life like W.B. Yeats on his Lake Isle of Innisfree.

Her despondency must have registered on her face, because, 'Have some more wine,' said Dervla, giving her a sympathetic look. 'And tell us, where is Adair taking you on your honeymoon? Somewhere *uber*-luxurious? Or is it a surprise?'

Río shrugged. 'It's a surprise. And I doubt he can afford anywhere *uber*-luxurious now.'

'Are you sure about wearing that red dress, Río?' said Fleur, typing 'wedding cake recipes' into the search engine bar. 'I have the loveliest little eau-de-nil number in stock.'

Río shook her head. 'No. It's unlucky for a bride to wear green.'

'What'll you do about the old, new, borrowed, blue thing?'

'Well, my red dress is old. Maybe I'll get myself some new blue underwear. And you might lend me one of your pashminas, Fleur? I know you've got about a zillion of them.'

'My pleasure!' Fleur raised her wineglass at Río. 'A wedding! What fun! I haven't been to a wedding in ages. It's a pity Marguerite isn't old enough to be a flower girl. Can Dervla and me be official matrons of honour?'

'Sure. What do matrons of honour do, exactly?'

'Get drunk and flirt with the best man. Who's going to be Adair's best man?'

'I don't think he has one.'

'Thanks be to Jaysus,' said Dervla. 'No boring best man speeches.'

'But Finn is giving you away,' Fleur pointed out. 'So he'll presumably make a speech.'

'I guess so. Poor Finn. He hates public speaking. He didn't inherit the show-off gene from his dad.'

At the mention of the words 'his dad', a silence fell. Shane was suddenly the elephant in the room.

'Is . . . um . . . is Shane coming?' said Fleur, finally.

'No. I haven't told him.'

'You haven't told him you're getting married, Río?' Fleur looked aghast. 'Why not?'

'It's none of his business.'

'But . . . don't you think he has a right to know?'

'No,' said Río categorically. 'He forfeited any rights to be involved in the complexities of my life when he fucked off to LA and left me holding the baby.'

'But that was more than two decades ago, Río!' Fleur looked bewildered, now. 'You're not still angry with him over that – didn't the pair of you get over all that shite yonks ago? You're best friends, still. And look at the fantastic son you reared. Shane's been a brilliant father, even if he was an absentee one. He's entitled, surely, to be involved in—'

'Oh, look!' said Dervla, deftly changing the subject. 'It says here that in the olden days, couples ate salt and oatmeal at the beginning of their wedding party as a protection against the power of the evil eye.'

Río sent her sister a grateful look for her intervention. She really, really didn't want to talk about Shane any more. She didn't even want to think about him until after Tuesday, when she would be bound irrevocably in matrimony to Adair Bolger.

She remembered the way Dervla had looked at her when she'd told Fleur about the symbolism surrounding the Claddagh ring. *You have to wear it with the heart turned inward, because that means you've committed your lives to each other forever . . .*

But Adair didn't have forever. He only had a year. Just under a week ago, Río had thought a year such a small sacrifice to make for the sake of his happiness. Now the lyrics of that lovely ballad that had won the Eurovision way back kept coming into her head . . . *What's another year, for someone who's lost everything that he owns?* For Adair, who had lost everything, another year *was* everything now. Another year would not just be a gift, it would be the most significant twelve months of his life, twelve months to be crammed brimful with living, twelve months in which he deserved to be made truly happy. That knowledge was what she had to stay focused on.

'Salt and oatmeal?' she managed brightly. 'I wonder might O'Toole's rustle up some salt and oatmeal *amuse-bouches*. Which reminds me – I'd better get back on to them. They need to know how many guests we're having.'

'How many are coming?'

'As many as they can fit. We've decided to take the entire restaurant. The whole village is invited.'

'Good for you!' said Fleur. 'Way to go, Río!'

'Yeah,' said Río. 'We just reckoned – well, you know – the more the merrier.'

The More the Merrier. Keep Right on to the End of the Road. Pack Up Your Troubles in Your Old Kit Bag. You'll Never Walk Alone . . . There surely was comfort to be had in squeezing the life out of those old clichés.

Some time later, Marguerite having awoken and become fractious, Fleur decided it was time to take her home.

'Bed and bath time for you, *bébé*,' she said, draining her wineglass and swinging her daughter onto her hip. 'Home again, home again, jiggedy jig.'

'Oh! Can I do it?' asked Dervla.

'Put Marguerite to bed? *And* give her a bath?'

'Yes. You stay here and have another glass of wine, and I'll do the needful. I'd love to!'

Fleur looked uncertain. 'Are you sure?'

'Sure I'm sure. It gives me enormous pleasure watching your baby splashing around and playing with her rubber duckies. Beats watching my old dears being given a blanket bath any day.'

'That's damn decent of you, Dervla. I must say I'd love another glass of wine. Let's see . . . You know where everything is? All her changing stuff is in the bag –' Fleur indicated the changing bag on the floor bursting with baby paraphernalia

'– and you'll find a clean Babygro in the chest of drawers. *Kiki à la Mer* is her current favourite bedtime story, but have a root around in her toybox for something in English.'

'*Ulysses*?'

'We've done that already.'

'It'll have to be *Finnegan's Wake*, so.'

'That should have the desired soporific effect. *À la Recherche du Temps Perdu* worked wonders.'

Fleur busied herself with the bundle that was Marguerite, manoeuvring her flailing arms into a pompommed matinée jacket (courtesy of Osh Kosh) before tucking her under a harlequin-patterned quilt (Babylicious), and fitting on Calvin Klein bootees. Then she did a checklist of the contents of the Baby Vuitton changing bag – 'Wipes, Sudocrem, mug, rusks, nappies . . . Oh! Where's her soother?!' – until Dervla grabbed the bag and said, 'Relax, Fleur! Trust me: I'll manage.'

'All right. Any problems, just phone. And I know that blanket she sleeps with is minging, Dervla, but unfortunately she's got to have it. Any time I wash it she throws a tantrum – like she's a master parfumier and I've contaminated her signature scent. You know where the steriliser is, don't you? There are spare soothers in there – and remember to wash your hands before you fish one out. And dry them on kitchen paper. What else? Her favourite lullaby CD is in the player, and . . .'

Río stopped listening as Fleur followed Dervla through the door of the flat and hung over the banister, issuing further orders as Dervla descended the stairs with Marguerite and all her designer baby accoutrements. What a fusspot she was! It made Río smile when she remembered how different things had been for her when Finn had been a baby and they'd lived in that squat in Galway. She'd never had to bother with sterilisers because she'd breastfed Finn for the first year of

168

his life. His clothes had been cast-offs donated by other mothers, or charity shop purchases, or quirky little garments knitted and crocheted by friends. He'd never had a soother, and his bedtime stories had been improvised by Shane or whichever of their actor or musician friends happened to be around at bedtime. More often than not, Finn had fallen asleep in a fuggy pub, passed from one pair of arms to the next, lulled to sleep by traditional Irish music and the raucous voice of the barman crying, 'Time, gentlemen, *plis*! Have yis no homes to go to?'

A wave of nostalgia washed over her. Moving to her bureau, Río pulled open the drawer where she kept her memorabilia, and took out a bulging manila envelope. Then she went back to the couch and curled her feet up beneath her before upending the contents of the envelope on to the coffee table. Photographs spilled everywhere.

The more dog-eared were of Dervla and Río as children, and as teenagers. To look at them, you wouldn't think they were sisters. Río was all freckles and red-gold hair, Dervla was sallow and dark, with Giaconda eyes. Some of the photographs featured their parents – holidays in Kerry and Sligo, a trip to the zoo in Dublin, the St Patrick's Day parade in Galway – but most of the photographs were of the sisters together, presenting a united front against the world, arms linked and fingers entwined.

There were, unsurprisingly, very few of them together as adults, since Dervla and Río had been estranged for most of their adult life. The most recent one – cut from a local newspaper – showed them at the opening of Dervla's upmarket retirement home. And there was a picture of Shane – the devil who had been responsible for their estrangement. No wonder both girls had fallen for him! Río had forgotten what killer looks he'd had back then when, with breathtaking insouciance, he'd broken the heart of one sister and made a baby with the other. Finn was the image of him: father and son had the same wicked green eyes, the same unkempt dark hair, the same sculpted bone structure, the same Michelangelo mouth. They shared identical laughs, an identical rangy, loose-limbed demeanour and the same dangerous devil-may-care attitude – like modern-day gun-slingers, Río thought.

'Is that Shane?' said Fleur, dropping back on to the couch beside her. 'Or Finn?'

'It's hard to tell, isn't it?' said Río with a smile, sliding another photograph in Fleur's direction. 'That's actually Shane – taken around the same age Finn is now. And look – here's you.'

'Oh, my God!' exclaimed Fleur, affecting a nauseous expression. 'What was I *wearing*?'

'Vintage Balenciaga, probably.'

'No,' said Fleur, tossing the photograph aside. 'It's Dior. I found it in that stuff we got at the house auction, d'you remember? Lord somebody-or-other was getting rid of his ex-wife's wardrobe, and we were in like Flint when we heard.'

'I remember. That was the first time we turned a profit.' They'd opened a bottle of Asti Spumante to celebrate, Río remembered, sitting on the floor of the old grocer's shop they'd converted into a vintage clothing store. Río had painted trompe l'oeil French café scenes on the walls, and Fleur had improvised changing cubicles from cuts of timber retrieved from a skip, draped with yards and yards of World War II parachute silk.

'And look!' said Fleur. 'Here I am in one of Philip's very first hats. How amazing to think he's designing for royalty now.'

'And how amazing to think that you are now the owner of one of the chicest boutiques in Coolnamara,' said Río.

'The *only* boutique in Coolnamara,' Fleur corrected her. 'Anais had to shut her place last week. That's three retailers gone in the last nine months. Nobody can afford to stay afloat.'

'What about you?' asked Río. 'How are you coping?'

'I'm lucky,' said Fleur. 'I have a little private income from my investments – *merci, merci sacrés Maman et Papa, pour la bénédiction!* But if it hadn't been for my inheritance I'd be in trouble. Right now, it's costing me to keep the shop up and running.'

'Is it worth it?'

'Oh, yes! It would break my heart to close up. Apart from Marguerite, that shop is my *raison d'être*. More wine, please, Río.' Fleur held out her glass. 'Thank you. How lovely for a gal to be able to indulge when a pal like Dervla volunteers to oversee baby beddy-byes. How's her business doing, by the way? I meant to ask earlier, but all those horrific wedding sites distracted me.'

'She's doing all right. Retirement homes must be cleaning up, now that we're all living longer. And she's cornered the grey vote, of course. I'm guessing she'll be running for Taoiseach next.'

'I'd love to be like Dervla when I grow up.'

'I don't know about that. She's so run off her feet we rarely get time to talk these days. I'm glad I have you to advise me on . . . stuff.'

Río remembered that she didn't want Fleur's advice on her forthcoming marriage, that she'd suspected it might make for uncomfortable listening. No. There must be no reminders of *temps perdu*, no recriminations and no room for regret. Río had made her proverbial bed, and she was going to make damn sure that – for as long as she had to lie in it – it would be as comfortable as possible. Anyway, what woman wouldn't envy her? Her husband-to-be was a gift – good looking, generous and dead set on making her happy.

'I'm not so sure that a woman who has embarked upon motherhood without even an absentee father for support is grown-up enough to offer advice to anyone,' said Fleur, looking thoughtful. 'That divine zipless fuck was probably the most irresponsible thing I've ever done.'

'I managed.'

'Ah, but you had Shane. He might have been absentee, but he was always there for you. Every woman should have a Shane in their lives.' Río felt her heart do a tumble-turn. Her eyes skimmed away from Fleur's, and then both women looked abruptly back down at the photographs. 'Or an Adair!' added Fleur, brightly.

Río stapled on a smile, and changed the subject. 'Look at you! You're like Dorian Gray, Fleur – forever young. You've hardly changed since that photograph was taken.'

Fleur wrinkled her nose. 'I guess I've my mother to thank for those genes. Her and Eve Lom.'

'Who's Eve Lom?'

'A doyenne of skincare.'

'Expensive?'

'Yes.'

'I'll stick to Simple, so. But French women do say that an occasional glass of wine is as good as a spa treatment.'

'I'll drink to that,' said Fleur, raising her glass.

Río refilled her own glass, then continued rummaging through the photographs. It was funny, she thought, that there were so many of Shane, and so few of Adair. In fact, she realised that the only photographs she had of Adair were on the hard drive of her computer. The one that she especially loved had been taken at the party he had thrown for her in Coral Mansion some years earlier, when they'd embarked upon their short-lived affair. Adair had been laughing to camera, his arm slung around her. He had then been at the height of his career, having just wrapped up some property deal in London's Knightsbridge – an audacious pincer movement that had had his name trumpeted by Forbes. Río remembered that in those days he had exuded almost palpable wealth and power. She knew that most women found that irresistible in a man, but dirty sexy money had never done it for Río. If it had, she would have married Shane yonks ago and moved to LA.

Oh, stop it, stupid girl! Stop thinking about Shane! To distract herself, she grabbed another photograph from the pile – one of Finn this time.

'Ooh!' said Fleur. 'Look at your gorgeous boy! I saw him in Ryan's last week, with a stunning dark girl.'

'That must have been Cat. I haven't met her yet. What does she look like?'

'*Jolie-laide*, I guess, would be the way to describe her.'

'*Jolie* what?'

'It's a French term – it means pretty, in an unusual way. She has Armada eyes.'

'Armada eyes? Like a pirate?'

'Yes. You Irish would call them "bold" eyes. Are she and Finn an item?'

'I don't know. Twenty-something boys don't tend to talk to their mothers about their love lives.'

'But he and Izzy are history now, are they?'

'Yeah.'

Fleur set her glass down. 'Río? Do you mind if I ask you something . . . personal?'

'Shoot.'

'Do you love Adair? I mean, do you love him the way you loved Shane?'

Río didn't need to think about it. 'No,' she said. 'Of course I don't. Shane was white heat. Adair and I are more . . . I dunno. Glowing embers, I guess. It's a cosy thing, like wearing comfortable shoes. The kind of love you'd never read about in a romance novel, but that you appreciate when you stop believing in the Mills & Boon myth.'

'When you grow up, you mean? Like Dervla?'

'I guess.'

Fleur looked down at Río's bare feet, and then at her own Blahnik-shod ones. 'Comfortable shoes?' she mused. 'Seems like a contradiction in terms, somehow.'

Chapter Eleven

Cat was enjoying a Guinness in O'Toole's when she saw Río Kinsella walk past the window. For a bride to be, she looked pretty grim. Cat couldn't understand why Río was marrying this bankrupt Bolger geezer when she could have married a Hollywood hotshot who was mad about her. Shane had proposed loads of times, according to Finn. Maybe Río felt sorry for Adair, and was marrying him out of pity? Somebody in the pub earlier had been talking to the barman about an article in today's *Sunday Insignia* about how loads of the top bankers and developers who had once been Celtic Tigers couldn't even find anyone to play golf with any more because they'd been abandoned by all their former friends and nobody wanted to know them, let alone be seen playing golf with them. And the barman had said that it was a bit rough on Adair because he was a decent skin at heart, and wasn't it grand that he had decided to stay on in Coolnamara and was even marrying a local girl – not like some of those shysters who had all sold up their country cottages and buggered off to Spain instead of weathering the storm and contributing to the ailing economy.

And the geezer at the bar had said, 'Bad cess to the lot of them! And isn't it the fault of that shower of shites up in Daíl Éireann? This government has . . .'

And then Cat had zoned out for a bit because talk about the economy and the government bored her senseless, and she fixed her attention instead on the stuffed fish in the glass cases that were displayed on the walls of the pub, wondering who had ever thought it a good idea to stuff a fish in the first place instead of eating it. The next thing she knew, Río and that French woman who ran the posh boutique had come into the pub and made themselves comfortable in the corner. Now might be a good time to introduce herself to Río, Cat thought, especially since she was going to her wedding tomorrow – but then she heard Río say, 'How did Elena find out?' and her ears pricked up.

'Twitter.'

'Twitter! So Shane knows now.'

'Yes. Once something's tweeted, everybody in the world knows your business.'

Río gave a heavy sigh. 'I should have known I couldn't keep it quiet for long. When's he due?'

'She didn't say.'

'Did you actually talk to her?'

'No. We had a confab on Facebook.'

'Oh? How long have you and Elena been Facebook friends?'

'Since *The O'Hara Affair* wrapped. Don't you keep in touch with her?'

'I don't do Facebook much.'

Facebook! Cat narrowed her eyes speculatively. Now there was a thought! Maybe Finn could do a Facebook page for her artwork. Hm. She'd have to find out more about Twitter, too. She'd ask him this evening all about social networking – and she could tell him then too that he wouldn't have to bite the bullet and Skype his dad about Río's wedding, since Shane already knew. Cat was just about to get up and go

176

over to Río to say hello when she heard the French woman say 'That journalist is in town. You know, the one who does the interviews in the *Insignia*? She did a piece on that actress in today's edition – Ophelia Gallagher.'

'The one who's married to the painter?'

'Yes. Apparently she's signed a book deal.'

'The journalist has?'

'No. Ophelia Gallagher. She's . . .'

Cat didn't want to hear about Oaf. She drained her Guinness and left the pub, noticing as she crossed the road to the sea wall that there was a lovely display of hydrangeas growing on the little triangle of grass that locals liked to call the village green. Cat had been wondering what she could get Río as a wedding present. Mauve and white hydrangeas would be perfect, she thought, perching herself on the sea wall where she could check out the boats bobbing about in the harbour.

There was one she hadn't noticed before. Moored next to an ostentatious motor launch, looking as though it were cocking a snook, was a pretty little yacht. And cock a snook it should. To sail a boat like that would be much more fun than ploughing through the sea propelled by horsepower on a so-called pleasure craft, Cat thought, craning forward to see if she could make out the names painted on the hulls. She couldn't discern the name of the yacht, but the pleasure boat was called the *Sting Ray*.

A bloke on board was posing for her delectation in cargo pants and sunglasses and nothing else. He was well fit, but Cat didn't like that bronzed, gym-toned look; it spoke of trying too hard. She liked the way Finn looked – muscular without the body-sculpture thing going on, and tanned by exposure to sun and sea rather than a sun booth or chemicals. She knew he'd seen her looking the other day when he'd stripped off his T-shirt; but then, she'd seen him looking that same afternoon when she'd undone her overalls and tied the arms around her waist in an attempt to cool off. The T-shirt she had been wearing underneath was one that she'd stolen from Oaf, and was two sizes too small. Since then, they'd both stayed covered up, and last night when Finn had accidentally made contact with her hand on reaching for the corkscrew, he'd reacted as if he'd been burnt, and said, 'Oh – sorry, Cat.'

She knew what that meant. They both did.

Cat smiled, and swung her legs off the wall. Maybe it was time to treat herself to something new to wear for Finn's ma's forthcoming wedding.

After a weekend spent writing up her next 'Epiphany', Keeley was out power-walking through the dunes by Coolnamara Strand. She'd got into an exercise routine since settling in Lissamore: sometimes the bog road beckoned, sometimes the beach. The Coolnamara air was so heady that it put a spring in her step, and while the fine weather lasted she was determined to make the most of it, working off calories that in Dublin would be burned on her cross-trainer in front of Sky News. Today she'd spent the morning spring-cleaning her cottage and now she needed to blow away the cobwebs in her head.

She'd delivered her piece on Ophelia Gallagher (it had appeared in yesterday's *Insignia*), and conducted an interview with an ageing rock god via an intermittent Skype connection, and now she was casting around for another subject. There were lots of potential candidates living in the Lissamore region: artists and writers and musicians tended to gravitate towards Coolnamara, presumably for the inspiration it afforded them.

The village itself was full of intriguing individuals. There was Fleur, the French woman who owned the gorgeous boutique on the main street, and who was the mother of a small baby – rather surprisingly, given her fairly advanced age. There was Dervla Vaughan, who was running as an independent in the forthcoming elections, and who was garnering support from older voters on account of her proactive stance on the ageing demographic. There was Dervla's sister Río, whose son was the love child of the actor Shane Byrne, now a major player in Hollywood. A rumour was circulating that he had bought a house in the area, and Keeley was keeping her fingers crossed that he might move in soon. Shane Byrne would make a great interview: if she could persuade him to talk to her, her swan song for the *Insignia* would be unforgettable.

Just one more 'Epiphany' to nail, and then Keeley would join the ranks of the unemployed. She wondered now if she hadn't been a bit hasty in her decision to quit the paper and go freelance. She'd spoken to a journalist friend on the phone last night, and he'd told her that his commissions were way down on last year. But Keeley had hated the duplicity going on in her life: she knew that word of her affair had leaked out, and she hated the idea that her peers might assume that the only reason she had won her prestigious weekly slot on the *Insignia* was because she was fucking the editor.

The notion of writing a book was – as always – an appealing one, but practically everyone she knew was writing a book. Everyone was aiming to be the next Maeve Binchy or Dan Brown or J.K. Rowling, and Keeley knew very well that unless you had a Unique Selling Point, the chances of your book being published were as slender as cheese wire. She also knew that six-figure advances, such as the one extended to Ophelia Gallagher, were now the stuff of legend. One writer of her acquaintance was taking in ironing to supplement the meagre income generated from her royalty payments; another worked evenings on a sex chatline.

No, there was no money to be made in writing . . . and on reflection, she didn't think she could hack the solitary nature of life as a dedicated writer, stuck inside her own head all day. But there might be money to be made somewhere along the line in the publishing world. Tony 'The Tiger' Baines was said to have bought himself a nice little pad on the French Riviera on the strength of the deal he'd brokered for his newest client, a stunning twenty-something who was writing a trilogy aimed at young teens. Her USP (aside from her fortuitous good looks) had been that she came from a famous musical family – both her parents were platinum-selling recording artists – and it hadn't been hard to get a bidding war going. But the most important factor, according to Mr Baines, was that the book had merit. A USP could only get you so far up the ladder that led to publishing success: you needed genuine talent if you wanted to climb right to the top.

Did Keeley have the nous to become an agent? She had contacts in publishing, and she was passionate about books – had been since she'd turned the first thick cardboard pages of the Mr Men series with impatient baby fingers. Had been since, as a student, she'd got a summer job packing books in a big literary agent's in London. Each package of books constituted the dozen free copies to which authors were entitled under the terms of their contracts, and if Keeley had enjoyed the book, she always inserted a little note between the pages saying as much, and signing it 'From the Book Packer'. On her last day at the agency, she had written a note to a celebrity author that had read 'Don't give up the day job.'

Keeley also had an instinct for what would sell, having spent hours going through the slush pile of manuscripts that reared higher than the Manhattan skyline, recommending and discarding. She'd read an interview recently with a top agent who spoke of her career as a 'vocation', and of the strong relationships she'd forged with both clients and publishers. Keeley was good with people – her 'Epiphanies' were proof of that. She loved the wining and dining aspect of her job – what was not to love? – and there'd be plenty of wining and dining involved in being a literary agent. Maybe she'd put in a call to Tony's people and see if she might take him to lunch, pick his brains?

But in the meantime, there was the question of her remaining 'Epiphany', and who might be the subject of her final grilling.

The strains of a violin made Keeley stop in her tracks. Who was playing a violin alfresco? It sounded like a lament, and then Keeley recognised the melody. It was 'She Moves Through the Fair'. Climbing to the top of the dunes, she looked seaward. There, on the beach below, a party had congregated. It appeared some festive event was underway: a wedding, perhaps? A man wearing a snowy white surplice was standing in the centre of a circle of people, who were all gazing in the direction of a couple moving towards them along the sand. The woman was barefoot, clad in a dress of fluid red silk; the man accompanying her looked like a younger version of the film star Shane Byrne. It was Río Kinsella, Keeley saw as she drew nearer, with her son, Finn.

The journalist in Keeley was curious. Making her way down the dunes, she ambled towards the party until she was within eavesdropping distance. She hoped she didn't look like a crasher, but something told her it was OK to be a bystander in such a public place. Anyway, there was a kind of 'more the merrier' vibe going on: a look around told her that most of the village had gathered here on the beach. She recognised several of them: Mrs Ryan from the corner shop was looking colourful in a fuchsia pink dress and matching hat with silk flowers, the barman from O'Toole's was wearing a pinstriped suit that looked as if it might have been trendy in the eighties, and the postmistress was looking extremely put out by the fact that she was being obliged to wield a pooper-scooper at such a solemn event, because her Airedale had just crapped in the sand.

Río and Finn were now encompassed in the circle of onlookers, and the fiddle player had come to the end of his solo. A light wind had got up: the priest's surplice was fluttering like the pinions of a seabird, and above them clouds were racing across the sky, casting shadows on the beach. Keeley watched as Río moved alongside a man whom she took to be the groom. He was clad in loose linen trousers with a matching Jodhpuri jacket, the kind of smart-casual look favoured by boho-inclined bridegrooms. Keeley had read about weddings like this, and had often thought that if she were ever to get hitched, alternative would be the way to go. A curlew called, low and fluting as it skimmed over the scalloped shallows, and then she heard Finn clear his throat nervously as he began to address the assembled company.

'Um. Welcome to you all,' he said. 'I'm not much of an orator, but Ma asked me if I'd say a few words, and I came up with this. As many of you may remember, my grandfather was a great man for reciting W.B. Yeats. This poem was a big favourite of his.

> When you are old and grey and full of sleep,
> And nodding by the fire, take down this book,
> And slowly read, and dream of the soft look
> Your eyes had once, and of their shadows deep;

How many loved your moments of glad grace,
And loved your beauty with love false or true,
But one man loved the pilgrim soul in you,
And loved the sorrows of your changing face;

And bending down beside the glowing bars,
Murmur, a little sadly, how Love fled
And paced upon the mountains overhead
And hid his face amid a crowd of stars.

'It's a sad poem, but a happy one at the same time,' Finn told his listeners. 'And I think that's fitting, because while weddings are occasions of great joy, tears are often shed. Tears of happiness, it has to be said. I know I'll probably end up crying into my pint later, and I can see that Ma has already started.'

There was some laughter at this, and Keeley could see that it was indeed true – Fleur had had to pass Río a handkerchief to mop up the tears that were streaming silently down her face.

'I never dreamed that I would end up giving my mother away to another man,' continued Finn. 'She's been mine, and mine alone since I was born. So, Adair, this has been a tough ask. All I need say now is that you had better take good care of her, or I will hunt you down and kick your ass. Joking aside, I know that you have admired Ma for many years, and I have to thank you for making an honest woman of her at last. I hope you will both be very, very happy together. Um . . . that's basically it.'

Finn stepped back, and Keeley watched as Río made an effort to recover herself. Her face was pale, apart from two hectic patches of red on her cheeks. Taking a couple of deep breaths, she reached for the groom's hand, then said, in a faltering voice, 'You cannot possess me, Adair, for I belong to myself. But while we both wish it, I give you that which is mine to give. You cannot command me, for I am a free person, but I shall serve you in those ways you require and the honeycomb will taste sweeter coming from my hand.'

Admirable sentiments, thought Keeley. And barefoot on a beach certainly beat the mobile meringue thing. The last wedding she'd been at, she'd come across the bride in tears in the loo because her corset was so tight and her feet were hurting so badly that she hadn't been able to enjoy a single moment of her own wedding.

It was the groom's turn, now. In a voice that was as robust as Río's was weak, he said, smiling down at her, 'I pledge to you, Río, that yours will be the name I cry aloud in the night and the eyes into which I smile in the morning. I pledge to you the first bite of my meat and the first drink from my cup. I pledge to you my living and my dying, each equally in your care. I shall be a shield for your back and you for mine, and I shall honour you above all others. This is my wedding vow to you. This is the marriage of equals.'

A marriage of equals! Keeley liked it. She watched as the priest took up his cue. Stepping forward, he reached for the couple's hands.

'May the light of friendship guide your paths together, as one, in caring for the other above all else on your life's journey,' he intoned, winding a silk ribbon around their conjoined hands. 'And when eternity beckons, at the end of a life heaped high with love, may the good Lord embrace you with the arms that have nurtured you the whole length of your joy-filled days together. And, today, may the Spirit of Love find a dwelling place in your hearts. Amen. Adair, you may kiss the bride.'

Very gently, the groom caressed Río's cheek with a finger.

Then he tilted her chin, and lowered his mouth to hers, and as he did so, applause rang out, and cheers and whistles, and a man beat out a drumroll on a *bodhrán*, and children popped party favours and blew vuvuzelas, and firecrackers went off.

And when the newlyweds broke the kiss, the groom – Adair? was that his name? – smiled broadly at the assembled wedding guests and said, 'The Milky Bars are on me! And the Guinness and the Veuve Clicquot. I hope I'll see each and every one of you in O'Toole's within the hour. Let's get the party started!'

There were a couple more whoops, and then the fiddle player launched into a lively rendition of 'The Arrival of the Queen of Sheba in Galway', and rice was thrown as Río was claimed by her friends.

Adair. Adair . . . Why did the groom seem so familiar? And then Keeley remembered where she'd seen him before. It had been at a fundraising event in New York, in the days when the Celtic Tiger was running rampant, and when pressing the flesh was mandatory as deals were brokered on both sides of the Atlantic. Adair Bolger. Of course! He'd been one of the biggest, brashest wheeler-dealers of them all; and one of the ones who had crash-landed hardest, in spectacular fashion. How different he looked now, here on a beach in Coolnamara, linen-clad and stripped of the power suit that had been his armour for so long! He seemed shrunken, half the man he'd used to be. So that was what happened when you plunged, like Icarus, earthward. And, Keeley thought as she watched the guests disperse, he'd make a perfect subject for her final 'Epiphany' . . .

Instantly, she made a beeline for him, across the sand. 'Adair!' she said, extending a hand. 'Keeley Considine. You may remember that we met at a fundraiser in New York, about five years ago?'

Adair had clearly lost none of his people-skills. 'Keeley!' he said, shaking her hand warmly and segueing directly into full-on charm mode. 'Of course I remember. That was a great night. And I've been following your career closely ever since. Your "Epiphany" piece is the first thing I turn to in the *Insignia* every Sunday. What brings you here to Coolnamara?'

'I've inherited a very modest little cottage. This is actually my first time back in Lissamore since I was a child.'

'Well, you're very welcome,' Adair told her, with manifest sincerity. 'You'll join us, I hope, in O'Toole's? You may have realised that there's a celebration going on. I'm after marrying the woman of my dreams!'

'Congratulations! And thanks for the invite. I'd love to join you. I don't know many people in the village yet, and it'd be a great way of getting to meet the locals.'

'Well, boogie on down with us. Do you need a lift?'

'No, thanks. I'll nip home first, and grab a shower – I've been spring-cleaning, which explains the state of me.' Keeley indicated her dirty jeans and elderly T-shirt.

'You're welcome to join us at any time of the evening. We'll be there till all hours. I intend to throw a party that'll go down in Lissamore folklore!'

'And I'm thrilled to be here for it. It's very kind of you to include me. I'll catch you later!'

Adair raised a hand to salute her, then dropped it suddenly, and sucked in his breath.

'Are you all right, Adair?' asked Keeley.

'I'm fine. Touch of heartburn is all.' He took a pill box from his pocket. 'These mojos should do the trick.'

'My granny used to swear by cider vinegar.' And Keeley flashed him her best smile and backed away down the beach, heading for home, humming the tune of 'She Moved Through the Fair', knowing that it would be stuck in her

186

head for the rest of the day, with that lyric on a loop: *The people were saying, no two e'er were wed, but one had a sorrow that never was said . . .*

Later, when she had showered and changed into something a little smarter, she took extra care when applying her make-up. It would work to her advantage to make a good impression at her first social event in the village, and the wild-haired guy who had played the fiddle had actually been rather tasty. Spritzing herself with a little scent and tucking a wild rose behind her ear, Keeley locked her front door behind her before heading in the direction of Lissamore village and the wedding party.

Chapter Twelve

Cat had been extravagant. In Fleur's shop yesterday she had helped herself to a new dress. She'd spent thirty minutes moseying around Fleurissima, inspecting – as well as the clothes – the paintings displayed on the walls that Finn had told her were the work of his mother. They weren't anywhere near as good as hers, Cat had decided. They were too . . . whimsical. Río's wishy-washy watercolours had none of the panache of Cat's acrylics, none of the vigour. But Cat could see why tourists would like them, as holiday souvenirs.

Now, *there* was a market worth tapping into! All those Yanks and Germans who spent a fortune hanging out in Coolnamara Castle Hotel. Maybe she could get Finn to send some JPEGs to the hotel manager? He'd had the cheek the other night to say that he should be charging agent's commission on any paintings she sold. After her slogging her ass off, sugar-soaping walls in preparation for the arrival of his dad!

She wondered if she could interest the French woman who owned the boutique in some of her work. They could put a sign saying 'As Bought by Elena Sweetman'. Maybe Cat could get some business cards done up, with 'Painter to the Stars' on. But the French woman had been kept busy by her customers, and Cat had resolved to approach her another time when the shop was less crowded.

In the end she'd hit on a dress that was reduced to half-price because it had some buttons missing. Cat didn't care about the buttons – she'd have left most of them undone anyway. It was a kick-ass little frock in black crepe de Chine that put her in mind of a Gothic Lolita. It wasn't dead kosher to wear black to a wedding, she supposed, but then Finn had told her that his mum was getting married in red, and how kosher was that? She supposed they'd play that cheesy Chris de Burgh song endlessly at the party.

Although, to be fair, it hadn't come on yet. In O'Toole's, Cat was tapping her feet in time to the rhythm of the fiddle player's upbeat version of 'My Lagan Love', loving the feel of the silk against her skin for, beneath her frock, she was stark naked apart from her stay-ups. The fiddler had been joined by a *bodhrán* player, and Finn had said more musicians were arriving later. He was cute, the fiddle player – though not as cute as Finn.

She hadn't seen much of Finnster today, sadly: he'd been distracted – up to ninety with nerves about his speech. That poem he'd read had been a bit of a weird one to read at a wedding, Cat thought. All that stuff about getting old and grey. She was sure that Río didn't want to be reminded on her wedding day that she was well past it. No wonder she'd started crying. Still, if it had been her dad's favourite poem, maybe it was hers, too.

She wondered if maybe Finn's grandpa and Hugo were similar types: Hugo often droned out W.B. Yeats and Seamus Heaney poems when he was drunk. Cat had actually met Seamus Heaney at one of her dad's exhibition openings once. He was a gent, with the twinkliest eyes Cat had ever seen. Kind eyes. And he was rich, Seamus Heaney. Maybe he'd be kind enough to buy one of her paintings? Maybe she could get his email address from the Demeter Gallery woman and ask Finn to fire off a JPEG.

Izzy had wanted to read something at the ceremony too, Finn had told her, but she'd been held up by the roadworks that were a permanent feature on the N6 between Dublin and Galway. How did Izzy feel about her dad getting married again? Cat wondered. At least it was unlikely that she'd be landed with a baby half-brother or sister, the way Cat would be soon, since Río was a lot older than Oaf. Cat wondered if there'd be much bonking going on in the Bentley. The bride and groom were currently still stuck on Coolnamara Strand, having their picture taken. Cat hoped that someone had advised Río to repair her make-up.

'Is this seat taken?'

Cat glanced up to see a woman looking down at her. She had an interesting face, and a friendly smile, so Cat said that no, the seat wasn't taken, even though she knew the old woman who'd been sitting there a moment before had only gone to the loo.

'What lovely hydrangeas.' The woman indicated the massive bunch of mauve and white blooms on the banquette beside Cat.

'They're a present for Río.'

'Are they from your garden?'

'No. I bought them in a flower shop in Galway.'

'It's unusual to see hydrangeas in flower shops,' said the woman, sitting down beside Cat. 'They must have cost a fortune. I'm Keeley Considine.'

'Keeley Considine!' said Cat. 'That's a great name. Isn't there a page three girl called Keeley?'

'Yes. Keeley Hazell. She was voted one of *FHM* magazine's hundred sexiest women in the world, three years in a row.'

'Where did she come?'

'Second, third and fifth.'

'Who came first?'

'It was Cheryl Cole last year. And this year, too, I think.'

'Cheryl Cole.' Cat considered. 'Yeah. I suppose she is quite sexy. I must ask Finn.'

'Finn? You're a friend of Finn Byrne's?'

'Yes. I live with him.'

Cat saw a gleam of interest ignite in Keeley's eyes, and she took a guess as to what the next question would be. She guessed right.

'So in that case you must know Finn's father, Shane?'

'Yeah. Shane and me are good mates.'

'Really?' The gleam intensified. 'I was hoping to maybe set up an interview with Mr Byrne.' Keeley rummaged in her bag, and produced a business card, which she handed to Cat. 'I'm a journalist – I work for the *Sunday Insignia*.'

The *Sunday Insignia*! That was the paper that Hugo said he'd rather use than Kitten Soft.

'So, you could use an introduction?' said Cat, pocketing the card without looking at it.

'That'd be great.'

Cat was wondering just how desperate this woman was, and how much an introduction might be worth to her, when she saw Izzy walk into the pub. She was decked out ladylike in a cream jersey dress, cream platform sandals and a double string of pearls, and she had a cream cashmere cardigan draped around her shoulders. She cast around, clearly at a loss, until she saw Cat.

'Hello,' she said, making her way towards her. 'I nearly didn't recognise you there.'

Cat guessed she scrubbed up well in black bombazine. The last time Izzy had seen her, she'd been wearing outsize overalls from B&Q.

191

'Mind if I park myself?' said Izzy, perching on the arm of Cat's chair. 'I don't seem to know anyone else here. Where's my dad, do you know?'

'He and Río aren't here yet. They're having their picture taken on the beach by a bloke who thinks he's Mario Testino.'

'And where's Finn?'

'Upstairs, organising the seating for the meal.'

'The *placement*?' said Izzy in a French accent.

'No. The seating for the meal,' said Cat. Cat had already decided that she was going to shuffle around some of the name cards on the tables. She wanted to make sure that she'd be sitting next to Finn.

'There's *placement*?' remarked the woman called Keeley. 'I hope I won't be *de trop*.' What was this? A Francophiles' convention? 'Adair invited me on the spur of the moment,' Keeley added. 'I've just moved into the village, and he's the only person I know here.'

'Oh – so you're a friend of Daddy's?' said Izzy, leaning across Cat and extending a hand to Keeley. 'I'm pleased to meet you. I'm his daughter, Isabella.'

'Keeley Considine. Pleased to meet you, likewise, Isabella.'

Cat noticed that the rose stuck behind Keeley's ear had some greenfly on it. She watched, fascinated, as one of the insects ambled into Keeley's lovely blonde hair.

'How do you know Daddy?' asked Izzy.

'We met in New York, at a fundraising dinner, a few years ago.'

'Oh – was that the one at the Guggenheim, with the fashion show afterwards?'

'Yes.'

'I was there, too! That was a fabulous evening wasn't it? The Stella McCartney stuff in particular was blah blah blah . . .'

Cat zoned out, and instead looked around with interest at the people thronging into the pub. There was Mrs Ryan who owned the corner shop, and who was always nosing about asking questions any time Cat went in. She was even more curious now that Cat was buying for two people instead of just one, and her curiosity would go into overdrive, Cat suspected, when Shane arrived and Cat started shopping for three. Maybe she should start flinging intriguing items like pregnancy tests and Nuts magazine and Rizla roll-up papers into her wire basket next time she went in.

There was that woman who owned the boutique, Fleurissima, looking pretty snazzy in her party gear, passing around her baby to be admired. It was funny the way people went all googly-eyed over babies, and came out with coochie coochie crap. Cat had babysat once for a cousin, and had run out of the joint at the end of the evening feeling like the figure in the Munch painting. The baby had been monstrous – flailing its arms around and hollering like a mini version of that actor in *King Lear* that she'd gone to with her school once.

There was – hm. Interesting! – a guy she'd been on a sailing course with once, in Galway. They'd got on well – he owned a nifty Kawasaki, and riding pillion had been fun . . . But they hadn't got on well enough, Cat decided, to make her renounce Finn, who she had determined she was going to have to seduce some time soon. And it would have to be very soon, otherwise pretty cream and pinky clawed Izzy might wise up to what she was missing, and stick those manicured talons into her Finnster.

Across the crowded bar, the sailing course guy made eye contact, but clearly didn't make the connection between the girl sitting perched on the banquette in her kick-ass party gear and the hoyden who'd ridden bareheaded and barefoot on the back of his motorbike. That Galway sailing course had been one of a series she'd embarked upon every year since she was seven years old, when she had announced it was her intention of crewing her own ocean-going yacht some day. If she sold loads more paintings, maybe she could buy herself a neat little sloop-rigged sailboat. She hadn't been sailing since the last summer she'd lived in the Crooked House, when she'd spent virtually all day every day on the lake, in her dinghy.

And there was Finn now, coming in through the door of the pub. Funny. She'd thought he was upstairs helping to organise the seating arrangements. But then Cat looked again, and realised that it wasn't Finn standing on the threshold looking around with a thunderous expression. It was Finn's dad, Shane.

She smiled, and gave him a merry wave. Well, good show and good luck, chaps! Chocks away, and break a leg and all that! Cat almost wished she had a camera phone, because it looked like the shenanigans were about to begin, big time.

Keeley stiffened, and her small talk about Stella McCartney petered out. Shane Byrne had just walked into the pub. All around her, camera phones were going off like small-arms fire, and girls were nudging each other in the ribs and giggling. As Shane stood in the doorway, looking grim-faced, the bridal car bedecked with ribbons pulled up directly outside the pub window and Río Kinsella stepped out, followed by her new husband.

Keeley's journalistic antenna stood to attention. Murmuring excuses to Cat and Izzy, she rose from her seat and made her way through the crowd towards the entrance, where she would have a grandstand view of the scene outside. Río had clearly had her make-up retouched before her photoshoot, because she was looking less haggard than she had at the ceremony. Whatever brand of eyedrops she used had done exactly what it said on the tin, her foundation was dewy, and her hair was as swishy as a shampoo commercial. Her freshly lipsticked mouth was smiling (Clinique's Red Drama, Keeley thought abstractedly) and she was now sporting fabulous scarlet heels to match her bridal gown. She was laughing at something Adair was saying, and as she moved towards the door, Keeley heard the fiddle player launch predictably into 'The Lady in Red'.

Keeley resisted the prurient impulse to take her phone from her bag, but she was the only one who did. Even as the events that followed unfolded, YouTube was waiting, open-armed, for camera phone footage to be uploaded.

And this is what Keeley heard and saw when she sat down in front of her iPad later that evening, courtesy of someone called 'Lizzie Moore'. Simon Beaufoy couldn't have scripted it better.

EXT. O'TOOLE'S BAR, LISSAMORE.

DAY.

FADE IN.

We are CLOSE on RÍO's face. She is laughing, enjoying her day.

As the CAMERA pulls back, we find SHANE lounging in the doorway. There is a definite sense of danger.

Through the window, we see that O'Toole's is heaving with PARTY-GOERS and WELL-WISHERS. Pints are being pulled non-stop behind the bar, and there is a palpable feeling of celebration. Outside on the village street, the sun is shining and seabirds are wheeling joyfully in the cerulean blue sky. A FIDDLER is playing a reel, the rhythm picked out by a *BODHRÁN* PLAYER. As RÍO moves along the pavement, the FIDDLER changes his tune to 'The Lady in Red'. RÍO starts to sing along, then freezes. Her expression changes.

RÍO
Shane! How . . . how nice to see you!

SHANE
(*saturnine*)
Congratulations, Río.

ADAIR
(*jocular*)
Howrya, Shane! Glad you could make it, mate!

ADAIR's smile falters as SHANE declines to take his extended hand.

SHANE
Why didn't you invite me to the party, Río?

RÍO doesn't answer. A passing PARTY-GOER showers her with confetti.

PARTY-GOER
Yay!

SHANE
(*with menace*)
You might have paid me the courtesy of telling me you were getting married.

ADAIR
(*genially*)

Didn't think you'd be able to make it, mate. What with the short notice and your busy schedule hobnobbing with the stars. But you're very welcome.

SHANE
(*to RÍO*)
I wouldn't miss your wedding for anything, Río. I asked you often enough if you wanted one.

ADAIR
Hey! I think that's a little out of order, pal.

SHANE
(*to ADAIR*)
Don't call me pal. I am not your pal.

RÍO
(*distraught*)
Shane, I wasn't expecting you. If I'd known that you were coming—

SHANE
You what? You'd have baked a cake? But sure isn't there a grand one waiting to be served? A grand big wedding cake.

A beat, as SHANE shakes his head in sorrow and disbelief. RÍO doesn't answer.

SHANE
You stupid, stupid woman. What have you done?

ADAIR
(*indignant*)
Don't you talk to my wife like that! Who do you think you are?

SHANE
(*snarling*)

I'm only the father of her son. Which is more than
you'll ever be.

RÍO

Stop it, Shane!

SHANE turns, stares haggardly at RÍO.

SHANE

Well, ain't it the truth? I gave you Finn – the love of
your life. I gave you everything you ever wanted, Río
Kinsella. I gave you good times! I gave you a diamond
as big as the Ritz. I bought that fucking mansion for
you.

RÍO

What?

SHANE

That fucking mansion on the beach. I bought it for
you, Río, because it was your cherished childhood
dream to live there. Remember?

RÍO

You thick eejit! I never wanted to live in a mansion. It
was my dream to live in a *cottage* by the beach. It was
Coral *Cottage* I wanted.

RÍO begins to cry.

RÍO

It was only ever the cottage I dreamed of, and the
orchard.

SHANE

The orchard! I remember the orchard. Remember that night, Río? The night that Finn was conceived?

ADAIR

(*warningly*)

Too much information, buddy. You're well out of line.

SHANE grabs ADAIR by the lapel.

SHANE

Don't call me buddy, you – you bulldozer!

ADAIR

Don't call me bulldozer!

ADAIR smashes his fist into SHANE's face. SHANE staggers back, then recovers his equilibrium. He rubs his jaw ruefully, then narrows his eyes at ADAIR.

SHANE

That's rather untidy conduct, my friend.

SHANE aims a punch at ADAIR, who ducks nimbly out of the way.

ADAIR

Ha! You're not in one of your B-movies now, pal!

RÍO

Stop it! Stop it, the pair of you!

RÍO is joined by a troubled FINN, who clearly does not know which side to take. He insinuates his way between the two men and receives an accidental blow to the side of his face from SHANE.

FINN

Da! For fuck's sake.

FINN's friend DECLAN grabs ADAIR by the collar, and forces him across the road. They are followed by SHANE, whom FINN is trying unsuccessfully to restrain. The postmistress' Airedale DOG, intent on joining in the fun, bounds – barking – towards them, and starts trying to hump SHANE's leg. SHANE shakes the DOG off, and lunges again for ADAIR, backing him against the sea wall.

ADAIR

Ow! Get off my foot, you – you luvvie prat!

The WEDDING GUESTS have left the pub *en masse*, and are standing on the pavement, clutching their pints. The FIDDLER has launched into 'Toss the Feathers', the *BODHRÁN* PLAYER is battering away at his drum.

RÍO

Someone call the Guards!

SHANE grapples ADAIR into a chokehold, and ADAIR, red-faced, is doubled over the sea wall. But the DOG is dogged, and has again wrapped his forelegs around SHANE's shin. SHANE loses his balance and flails wildly as he stumbles against the wall. It just takes one shove from ADAIR. There is an almighty splash as SHANE hits the water, and then we hear the sound of an approaching siren.

RÍO

Shane!

ANOTHER ANGLE showing the consternation of the crowd across the road. A GIRL in a bandana and a black dress is clearly enjoying the spectacle, dancing from foot to foot, and laughing out loud. IZZY runs across to the sea wall and flings her arms around ADAIR.

> IZZY
> (*frantic*)
> Daddy! Daddy – are you all right?

The BYSTANDERS surge towards the sea wall. From their POV, we see SHANE floundering in the sea.

> FINN
> (*urgent*)
> Throw him a life buoy, someone! Hang on, Da! Here it comes!

The buoy lands next to Shane. He clutches it, and grim-faced and muttering imprecations, sets out on the long, ignominious doggy paddle that will take him to the pier.

> DISSOLVE TO BLACK.

Chapter Thirteen

It had been even better than Cat expected. Shane had ended up in the drink, and Adair had had to be carted off to A&E with a suspected broken toe. She watched the clip over and over again on YouTube, pausing at the bit that showed her gleeful tapdance on the footpath outside O'Toole's.

'I wonder who "Lizzie Moore" is, who posted this?' she mused out loud.

'You're perverse, you know that?' Finn told her, setting a bowl of pasta in front of her. 'My da could have ended up seriously hurt.'

'But isn't he grand? Sure, no one got hurt really, apart from you.'

Finn was nursing a mother of a black eye from the accidental dig his da had given him. They were back in Coral Mansion, in their wedding finery still, sitting at the kitchen table. Finn had made spaghetti bolognese for all three of them, but Shane wasn't hungry. After he'd showered and changed, he'd disappeared off up to one of the palatial bedrooms with a bottle of Jameson. Cat was disappointed, because she'd wanted to talk to him about selling more paintings to his wealthy pals.

'Adair got hurt,' Finn pointed out, helping himself to

Parmesan cheese. 'If he really has a broken toe, he won't be going anywhere fast. They'll have to cancel the honeymoon.'

'Yeah, well, he kind of deserves it, for stealing your ma from your da. Pass the Parmesan, please, Finnster. Did Shane really buy this house for Río?'

'Yes. I think he thought it was the ultimate romantic gesture – the one that would finally send her hurtling into his arms.'

'What'll he do now?'

'I haven't a clue. It's unlikely he'll get a buyer for it.'

'So in the meantime, we can stay on here, and just carry on doing it up?' Cat finished piling on the Parmesan, and gave him a winsome smile.

Finn shrugged. 'I guess. As long as he keeps paying me. I've no other work lined up.'

'You could try getting a scuba-diving gig somewhere.'

Finn shook his head. 'I don't want to move too far away from Lissamore right now. I've got a feeling that something's up with Ma.'

'Like what?'

'I dunno. She just seems in really weird form. Didn't you notice that she was in bits during the wedding ceremony?'

'Well, that poem you read probably didn't help. Reminding her about growing old and grey, and all that jazz. Maybe she's going through the menopause. They say women can get awful depressed when that happens. Maybe she needs HRT or Prozac, or something.'

Finn looked gloomily into his bowl, and swizzled spaghetti around his fork. 'I'd say Da could do with Prozac after today.'

'Yeah,' agreed Cat. 'He must feel like a complete, com*plete* tool. And he'll feel like even more of a plonker when he finds out he's all over YouTube.'

'Oh, fuck. And the press'll be after him like a herd of hyenas.'

'A *pack* of hyenas, Finn, I think you'll find they're called.' Cat remembered the woman she'd met earlier in the day in O'Toole's, before the fisticuffs on the street had scuppered the wedding party. 'You might be interested to know that I met a member of the press today. She was called Keeley: she's a friend of Izzy's dad. She gave me a card. She's just moved into the village.'

'Oh, shite. It will not be music to Da's ears, to hear that a journo witnessed today's goings-on. What paper does she work for?'

'The *Sunday Insignia*.'

'Show me her card.'

Cat produced it, and handed it over.

'"Keeley Considine",' read Finn. 'I know that name. She does in-depth interviews every week.'

'Yay! She can interview me when I'm famous, so.' Cat helped herself to more Parmesan.

'What do you mean, when you're famous?'

'Like when I've sold loads more of my paintings.'

'I admire your self-belief.'

'No one else ever believed in me. I might as well do it myself.' Cat smiled sweetly at Finn. 'Can we have some champagne? It seems a shame to waste it.'

After Río had had to drive Adair to A&E, Finn had taken it upon himself to salvage several cases of champagne intended for the wedding celebrations, since it looked like half of them would never be opened. He had dumped them by the fridge in Coral Mansion, and they had a forlorn look about them. Cat thought that it was kind of unfair on the champagne: it deserved to be drunk, since it had, after all, been bought for a special occasion. She wondered how those freeloaders who had opted to stay on in O'Toole's were getting on with the masses of food that had been ordered. It would be a bit weird to dig in to a wedding banquet and toast the happy couple when the bride and groom weren't even there to cut the cake.

'Sure,' said Finn, in lacklustre tones. 'Let's crack a bottle.'

'Yay! I'll do it!' Cat danced across the room and extracted one from a crate. 'I'm a dab hand at opening champagne. My dad taught me when I was ten.' Deftly, she stripped away the foil from the neck of the bottle. 'Get the glasses, Finn.'

'What was your dad celebrating?'

'An exhibition opening.'

'He's an artist, too?'

'Yeah.' Unwilling to volunteer further info, Cat deftly changed the subject by saying, 'Did you know that those old-fashioned champagne glasses – the saucer-shaped ones – were inspired by Marie Antoinette's breasts? That's useful trivia for a pub quiz. Do they ever do pub quizzes in O'Toole's, Finn?'

'Yeah. Izzy and I went to one once. She was brilliant – she knows everything.'

Cat didn't want to hear about Izzy's brilliance, so she changed the subject again. 'You know, when you open a bottle of champagne, you're meant to twist the bottle, not the cork,' she said, doing just that. 'Most people do it the other way round, which means it happens too fast, and loads gets wasted.' The cork came away with a sigh and the gentlest of pops, and Cat proceeded to pour fizz into flutes. 'Cheers,' she said, when she'd topped up the glasses to her satisfaction. 'Pity it ain't chilled. Maybe we should put a couple away in the fridge.'

'Cheers, Catkin.'

205

Finn touched his glass to hers, and Cat sat back down at the table, and took up her fork.

'This is excellent grub, Finn. You're not a bad cook, you know.'

'Ma taught me.' He drooped a bit. 'Poor Ma.'

'And your poor pa,' she reminded him.

'Hopefully he's comatose now. I'd say he took a couple of sleeping pills. I saw a packet of Ambien in the bathroom.'

'He'll have a stonking hangover tomorrow. I could make him Buck's Fizz, as a cure. Or a Black Velvet.'

'I'm sure he'd appreciate that.'

They carried on eating in silence for a while, and then Cat's ears pricked up. 'What's that noise?'

'It sounds like the doorbell.'

'How weird! I've never heard the doorbell go in this house before.'

Finn set down his glass and rose tiredly from the table. Cat sprinkled more Parmesan onto her pasta as she listened to the sound of his footsteps crossing the cavernous hall, and the front door being unlocked.

'Hi, Ma,' she heard him say. 'Come in.'

'No. I won't come in. I just came to find out how you are.' It was Río's voice. 'After . . . you know. Oh God, Finn! That's some shiner.'

'I know. It looks worse than it is. It hardly hurts at all. Are you sure you won't come in for a drink? Da's upstairs, asleep. It's just me and Cat.'

Cat prinked a little. She liked the sound of that! *It's just me and Cat . . .*

'No. Honestly, I'll have to get back to Adair.'

'How's his toe?'

'It's not broken after all, just badly bruised.'

206

'So he'll be able for the honeymoon?'

'He will. How . . . how's your da?'

'Like I said, he's sleeping – courtesy of jetlag and several very large Jamesons.'

There was a long pause, and then Río said something in a mangled voice that sounded like, 'Will you give him this from me?'

'Sure. What is it?'

'It's the ring he gave me once.'

'Oh, fuck, Ma!' Finn sounded upset. 'Don't you think you should give it to him yourself?'

'No, Finn. I can't – I just can't. Please do it for me. I'm so sorry to ask, but I really don't want to see Shane again.' Her voice had gone even sobbier. 'I mean . . . I do, but I can't.'

There was a silence, and then Cat heard Finn sigh and say, 'OK. I'll do it.'

Oh, poor Finn! First he had to give his mum away against his better judgement, and now he was going to have to give his pa back the ring he'd bought her. What a prize cow that Río was, going around messing up people's lives all over the place! Finn deserved cheering up. He deserved a treat. Rising from the table, Cat took a good swig of champagne, then started to undo those buttons on her dress that were not already undone.

'Thanks,' said Río. 'Thank you so much, Finn. I know it's a tough ask.'

'No worries. Are you heading off to Coolnamara Castle tonight?'

'No. We're booked in for tomorrow. We're staying in the Bentley tonight.'

'Well, have a good time when you get there.'

'Yeah.'

'Is there . . . is there any message you want me to give to Da?'

'No, Finn. Thank you – you're a star. But there's nothing I can say to him.'

'OK.'

'I'll be off, so.'

'Good night, Ma.'

'Good night, darlin'. I love you very much.'

'Love you too, Ma.'

There was another silence, and then came the sound of the front door closing.

Cat undid the last button, slid her arms out of the sleeves of her frock, and allowed the silk to shimmer to her feet just as Finn came back into the kitchen.

He stood speechless in the doorway, and then Cat stepped out of the pool of black silk and moved towards him. Standing on tiptoe, she closed her eyes, and presented her mouth for a kiss. After what seemed like an eternity, Finn obliged. Many long moments later, he still had not uttered a word.

'What's up, Finnster?' asked Cat, slanting him a smile. 'You seem lost for words. That's unusual for you. Cat got your tongue?'

Still Finn said nothing. He simply returned the smile, raised an eyebrow, then lowered his mouth to hers once again, and licked her lips.

Much later, Cat was sitting up in Finn's bed, drinking champagne.

'This is the life!' she said. 'I could easily get used to a champagne life style. And we've masses to keep us going, Finn. We could fill a bath with the stuff, like Johnny Depp and Kate Moss did once.'

'They did?' Finn was lolling back against the pillows, watching Cat with amused eyes.

'Yeah. Apparently they filled the bath in their hotel with, like, a grand's worth of Mumm, and the chambermaid pulled the plug when she came in to turn down the bed. Imagine! A thousand quid down the plughole!' She drained her glass, then set it on the bedside table. 'Your dad's mates with Johnny Depp, ain't he?'

'Yeah. And you're not to start giving him grief again about showing all his mates your paintings. You're going to have to cut him some slack, Cat. Allow him to chill for a couple of days.'

'Sure, I can do that. We could pamper him. I'll be his maid, and bring him breakfast in bed in the morning. And maybe pour him a champagne bath. Except it would be no fun having a champagne bath all by yourself.'

'I liked that idea you had about Buck's Fizz. Why not bring him a glass on his breakfast tray? He's going to need a hit of alcohol before I do the dirty deed. So am I, come to think of it.'

'What dirty deed?'

'The reason Ma called round earlier was to give me this.' Finn reached into the pocket of his jeans which lay discarded by the bed, produced a ring box, and handed it to Cat.

She opened it, and went, 'Wow!'

Nestling against a white satin cushion was a solitaire diamond, set in gleaming platinum.

'Da gave it to Ma a few years ago, in one of his attempts at persuading her to marry him. She's never worn it.'

'Why not?'

'Too scared she might lose it.'

'How much is it worth?'

'I dunno. All I know is that Ma can't even afford the cost of insuring it.'

'Then it must be worth a *lot* of money. Mind if I try it on?'

'Go ahead.'

Cat slid the diamond on to her finger, and held out her hand, the better to admire it. As she angled her hand to and fro, the stone flashed pale fire. 'It's real pretty,' she said. 'But I think I'd rather have the cash. D'you mind if I ask you something, Finn?'

'Shoot.'

'Your mum has your dad on her case, right? And your dad is pretty damn hot for an elderly geezer, plus he's famous and loaded. And he's, like, showering her with diamonds and a mansion and all. And yet your mum goes and marries a man who is follically challenged in the hair department and who ain't that hot, and who's lost loads of money and lives in a mobile home. I mean, what's all that about?'

'I guess my ma's like most women,' said Finn.

'And what are most women like?'

'They're riddles wrapped up in mystery inside an enigma.'

'Wow! Profound! Did you make that up?'

'No, Winston Churchill did. Except he probably wasn't talking about women.'

'Who's Winston Churchill?'

'You mean you don't know? What kind of an education had you, Cat Gallagher?'

'A crap one.' Unlike brilliant Izzy, thought Cat darkly, who excelled at pub quizzes and had probably been educated at the Sorbonne or somesuch.

'Where did you go to school?' asked Finn.

'Kylemore Abbey, in the arse-end of nowhere. But then the so-called authorities said I had to be home-schooled because I kept running away.'

'You were home-schooled? By your mother?'

'No, Finnster. My mother died when I was fourteen.'

'Oh. I'm sorry, Cat.'

'So was I.'

'So you never got a chance to be teacher's pet. Poor Pusscat. You can be my pet, instead.'

'I'd like to be your pet! I love being petted by you. What'll my pet name be?'

'Pusscat, of course,' he said, tucking a strand of hair behind her ear and kissing the tip of her nose. 'So what was it your father home-schooled you in?'

'In – among other subjects – the arcane art of opening bottles of champagne. Which is why I'd be rubbish at pub quizzes.'

'I dunno. I think you're a pretty smart chick.' He smiled, and pulled her back against the pillows. 'That was a pretty smart thing you did earlier, after all.'

'What smart thing did I do?'

'You seduced me, minx. Let's do it again. God! Look at you! I just *love* your naked loveliness!'

'But I'm not naked,' Cat told him, twinkling her ring finger. 'I'm wearing a small fortune's worth of jewellery.'

'Take it off, Pusscat,' Finn told her. 'I want you stripped bare. I've never had a woman before who was naked as the day she was born.'

'What do you mean? You've never seen a woman naked? Don't make me laugh.'

'Any woman I've ever had has had piercings somewhere on her body. Or tattoos. How come you have no piercings at all – not even for earrings?'

Cat wasn't about to tell him that she had a pathological fear of needles. So she said, 'I think piercings are dead common.'

'Posh totty! How I love classy girls,' said Finn, dropping kisses on her ears.

Hm. That was too true, if Izzy was anything to go by. Cat remembered the cream ensemble and the double string of pearls Izzy had been sporting this evening. Cream looked expensive because it was expensive to keep clean. Izzy's dad might be broke, but his daughter evidently had money of her own. Pah! If Cat ever had money, the last thing she'd be tempted to spend it on was designer clothes or jewellery. The diamond glittering on her finger caught her eye. How much, exactly, might it be worth, she speculated, as she slid it off her finger and set it carefully on the bedside table. Six figures? Seven? That anyone in their right mind would spend that kind of money on a ring for any woman struck Cat as being absurd. Shane Byrne must be totally cracked over that Río Kinsella.

But then she was distracted by Finn doing something so very delicious to her with his fingers that all thoughts of money went out of her pretty head. Which was no mean achievement, she conceded with a blissed-out smile, stretching luxuriously to allow him access all areas. Oh! *Oh!* Clever Finn! He seemed to instinctively know exactly what she wanted, and how, and when, and where . . . and Cat simply *adored* getting the cream. Double cream. Whipped. With a cherry on top.

Chapter Fourteen

In the Bentley, Río and Adair were watching *EastEnders* on Sky Plus. Río had made tea and was sipping it without tasting it, wishing it was laced with alcohol. She thought of all that surplus champagne, languishing in Coral Mansion. All those revellers in O'Toole's, toasting an absent bride and groom with forced cheer. The cake she had cobbled together from Mr Kipling Battenbergs waiting to make its entrance, the giftwrapped presents waiting to be opened, the bridal posy jettisoned on the village main street . . . She hoped that somebody had rescued it, and that it was now gracing some local mantelpiece, not lying trampled ignominiously underfoot by cavorting wedding guests.

Stupid Shane! What had he been playing at, ruining her wedding day? The eejit! The stupid, stupid eejit. On *EastEnders*, Phil and Shirley were screaming at each other. They did a lot of screaming in *EastEnders*. Was that a reflection of how the scriptwriters perceived marriage in real life? Trouble and strife and endless screaming matches? Did nobody in soap opera live happily ever after? Were there no Richard and Judys, no Barack and Michelles, no Darby and Joans to act as role models for disaffected viewers? When writers scripted weddings, had they nothing but disaster planned for the participants?

And then she remembered that her own wedding day had effectively been ruined, not today, but a week ago, when Finn had told her that Shane was coming back to Lissamore, to live. She should have been on high alert when she'd heard that; she should have expected Shane to swagger into her life again, in his usual inconsiderate fashion, without thinking of the consequences. In her mind's eye, she saw the haggard expression on her ex's face when he'd looked at her today, heard his voice say, *You stupid, stupid woman. What have you done?*

He was right. She, Río, was the eejit, not Shane. She had plunged headlong into this marriage with Adair, propelled by some ill-considered altruistic impulse, with no regard for her own happiness and scant regard for the happiness of the other two men in her life – her son and his father. Why hadn't she listened to Dervla, who knew her better than she knew herself? If she had paid her sister some heed, she might not be sitting here now, watching *EastEnders* and drinking tea with a man she barely knew. She might be cosied up in her own nest, watering her roof garden or priming a canvas. She might be in her orchard, sweeping up in her little greenhouse or swinging in her hammock. She might be in Coral Mansion, laughing with Finn and his father . . .

To be fair to Adair, he had tried to keep her spirits up. He had joked about not being able to carry her over the threshold, and he had apologised profusely about the spat with Shane. He had made an effort to make love to her earlier, but his toe was giving him such grief that he had kept whimpering in pain, and they'd aborted the act.

She thought of Shane lying comatose in Coral Mansion, all on his own in the master bedroom that he had hoped to share with her. *I gave you everything you ever wanted, Río. I bought that fucking mansion for you . . .* How typically

214

quixotic of him, to buy Río a dream home as a surprise present! But Coral Mansion had never been Río's dream home, any more than an ostentatious LA lifestyle had been her idea of the good life. Her dream home had been the modest cottage Coral Mansion had supplanted, and a simple life had always been her ideal. Goats and chickens and beehives and fruit trees and bean rows constituted Río's idea of a girl's best friend. Not diamonds.

On *EastEnders*, Shirley was in full-on rant mode. *Get a grip, Phil, who d'ya fink you're fooling, why d'ya fink your kids all ran a mile from ya . . .*

She and Adair were luckier than Shirley and Phil, that was for sure. Despite the catastrophic wedding, despite the banjaxed toe, despite the shit stirred up by Río's jealous ex, she and Adair had the love and respect of their kids still, and their regard for each other. And then Río remembered that there was a bottle of wine in the boot of her car, and that there were tapas in the fridge, and that *Mamma Mia!* was about to start on another channel, and hey – maybe they could salvage their wedding night and have a little fun after all, even though there was no champagne or cake or sex to be had. And just as she was about to suggest to Adair that they rustle up a little supper and switch channels and open a bottle of wine, a knock came at the door.

'Our first visitor!' said Adair, struggling to his feet.

'I'll go,' said Río. 'The doctor said you were to rest your foot.'

She set down her mug (it had a silhouette of Sheikh Zayed on it – Adair's gift from Dubai), then found herself stalling a little before she opened the door, bracing herself in case it might be Shane on the other side. But it wasn't Shane. It was John-Jo Maloney, a local farmer.

'Good evening, John-Jo,' she said.

'A good evening, is it? It's well for some, so. There's nothing very good about this evening as far as I'm concerned, Río Kinsella.'

'Oh? What's the problem, John-Jo?'

'I'll tell you what the problem is, if you'll be so kind as to accompany me up the boreen.'

'Sure,' said Río. 'Just let me put on some shoes.'

'What's up?' asked Adair, when she returned to the sitting room.

'I don't know. It's our neighbour, John-Jo Maloney. You haven't met him yet, I don't think?'

'No. I called in when I saw the damage that had been done to his gate, to offer to reimburse him, but there was no one in.'

'What damage?' Río stooped to tie the thongs on her sandals.

'The lads who delivered the Bentley accidentally knocked into one of Mr Maloney's gateposts on the way down the lane.' Adair aimed the remote at the television, to mute it. 'Ask him in, and we'll have a chat.'

A chat? Something told Río that it was more than a chat that John-Jo was after. She wished the delivery men had seen fit to tell her about the accident, instead of Adair. Being familiar with locals taking territorial umbrage, she would have known better how to handle the situation. 'I'll just nip up with him now to have a look. Maybe he can join us afterwards for a neighbourly cuppa.'

Oh, God, thought Río as she finished strapping her sandals. She fervently hoped that she'd be able to persuade John-Jo to join them for a cuppa. He was a notoriously belligerent man, who relished nothing better than stirring the shit. And Río really, really didn't want any more shit to hit the fan today. Adair had had more than his fair share of knocks; he needed some breathing space. She couldn't wait until they were in the car tomorrow, on their way to Coolnamara Castle and some badly needed R&R.

When she went back out on to the deck, it was to see that John-Jo was already trudging up the boreen that led to the main road. Río ran to catch up, plastering a pleasant smile onto her face as she drew level with him.

'Were you away, John-Jo? I noticed your car was gone over the past couple of weeks.'

'Yes. I was away. And you want to see what I came back to.'

'Oops. Adair told me that there'd been a bit of damage done to your gate, is that right? He called in to have a word, but of course, you haven't been around.'

'A bit of damage, is it? Divil a *bit* of damage.' John-Jo trudged manfully on. 'My gateposts are destroyed.'

'Oh . . . I'm sorry to hear that. I know they had some trouble getting the mobile home down the lane. But don't worry – Adair will be glad to cover the cost of repairing them.'

'It's not repairing they need. It's rebuilding. And it's a brand new gate I'll be after.'

'I'm sure Adair—'

'Adair. Adair! The Bolger boy, with his grand notions and his big feckin' mansion! I remember well the days when I used to cut his grass for him, and feck manure over his flower beds. *Arra* – how the mighty have fallen, eh?' John-Jo gave an unpleasant laugh.

'Well . . . you're neighbours, now!' she said, brightly. '*We're* neighbours, now, come to think of it!'

The smile he gave her was twisted. 'I heard you got married. What got into you, Río Kinsella, marrying a blow-in like him? Were none of the local *gossoons* good enough for you?'

Río didn't like the turn this conversation was taking. On another occasion she'd have told John-Jo to mind his own bloody business, but something told her to tread carefully here.

'Oh, you know, John-Jo, I just felt a change was as good as a rest,' she said, evasively. What the fuck did *that* mean? She could see that she was going to have to call upon her cache of useful clichés to help her through this contretemps.

'A change is it?' said John-Jo, mirthlessly. 'And a big change it will be, I'd say. From hobnobbing with the likes of film stars to slumming it in a mobile home. Pah! That gobshite! What made him think he had the right to haul that great monstrosity across my land? If I'd been here, I'd never have allowed it.'

'Your land?'

'That's right,' said John-Jo. 'My land. This boreen belongs to me.'

'But there's a right of way, surely?'

'There's a right of way – within reason. No person has the right to go lumbering up and down over my land in trucks and trailers and what have you.'

'But Madser Mulligan used to be up and down every day on his tractor, to get to his shed beyond!'

'Ah, now, Río. Don't be calling poor Patrick names. Patrick Mulligan was a dacent schtick, and one of our own. That's why he had special dispensation to use the thoroughfare.'

'Special dispensation?'

'From me. I gave him permission to use it.'

'So . . . Adair will need your permission, John-Jo, to use the boreen to access the main road?' Río was feeling panicky now. The shed where the oysters were packed was on the other side of the main Lissamore road, and the only way to get at it was via the boreen.

'He will. And I can tell you now that there'll be no trac-tors or trailers allowed.'

'But—'

'No tractors or trailers or heavy plant will be allowed on my land, after the damage that's after being done to my gate.'

'But, John-Jo! How will Adair get his oysters up from the farm?'

'Arra, Río, isn't that a problem for Mr Bolger himself to be solving?'

'You mean . . . you won't grant him access?'

He fixed her with a gimlet look. 'I'm not an unreasonable man, Río. Yiz can travel up and down in your fancy cars as much as ye like. But cars is where I'm drawing the line. No plant. That's final.'

'Oh, for God's sake, John-Jo! Have a heart! Adair's invested a lot of money in the farm, and in his equipment! He's bought a brand new Massey Ferguson—'

'Didn't I see it? The big shiny yoke parked down by the shore? And isn't your husband the fortunate man to be able to afford a grand tractor like that, and a trailer to go with it?'

Oh, Jesus!

'I'm not prepared to run the risk of another accident happening, Río Kinsella,' John-Jo resumed. 'The next time, it might be more than a gate that gets in the way. There could be health and safety issues involved. And we don't want the authorities getting involved, do we now? Because if the authorities get involved, they might rescind planning permission for that oyster farm. It's in a designated area of outstanding natural beauty, so they say, and it's an unsightly blot on the landscape. It's a cumberground, so it is. There could be complaints. And then where would yiz be?'

'But, John-Jo, don't you see that if Adair has no access to the road, he won't be able to work the farm?'

'Ah, now, Río, don't be telling me that he has no access to the road. Isn't there a right of way not a mile along the beach?'

'There is? Where?'

'Down by Coral Mansion, Río, to be sure. Through the land there that's belonging to you.'

'You mean through . . . through my orchard?'

'That's the very spot that springs to mind. You'd just need to fell a few trees, and lay down some hardcore and ye'll be sorted. Now, take a look at that.'

John-Jo stopped, and pointed towards the gate that opened on to his farmyard. There was damage, yes, but nothing that couldn't be put right in a day. Río looked at her neighbour. There was a smirk on his face that the Mona Lisa might have envied. The bastard! The fucking malicious, bastarding bastard! Río knew now that he was privately delighted by the damage done to his gate, because it gave him a wholly plausible excuse to block Adair's access to the road.

She gazed numbly at the gate, and then she turned back to John-Jo. He was looking down at her with that malicious little smile on his lips, still. 'You, John-Jo Maloney, are a nasty, vicious prick,' she said. And then she turned on her heel and stumbled back the way she'd come.

She didn't go directly back to the Bentley. Instead, she let took herself down onto the shore, where the sun had dipped below the horizon, rimming the ocean with crimson. Venus, the evening star, had already climbed high above Inishclare island, and the clouds that were making their way westward were big, puffy ones – the kind of clouds a child might draw – tinged with pink. Red sky at night, thought Río. *Red Sky at Night over Lissamore* was the title of one of her paintings. And she thought again of the canvases in her apartment that were waiting to be primed, and how, if recent events had not happened, she could be there now, taking a shepherd's pie from the oven and setting the table for herself and Finn, and then maybe Skypeing his father in LA, as they often did at this hour of the evening.

To the west, only the islands and the earth's natural curvature interrupted the view to America; to the east, Río's orchard glimmered, golden. Her orchard! Her most precious possession, her pride and joy, the solitary jewel in Río's nondescript crown! Her retreat, her sanctuary, her panacea for all ills: her very own private Eden, where peace came dropping slow between the beanstalks and the beehives.

She watched as, high above the orchard, a light came on in Coral Mansion, and she thought of Finn and Shane rattling around in that preposterous palace, drowning their sorrows. What wouldn't she give to be able to run there now, and join them! What wouldn't she give to sit down with her son and his father – the two people in the world she loved the most – and unburden her weary soul? What wouldn't she give to be able to crawl into bed beside Shane and sleep easy, instead of lying prone beside Adair, staring hot-eyed into the darkness, as she knew she would tonight, wracked with worries.

Another light came on, and she saw two figures stroll hand in hand on to the terrace. Finn, and his Catgirl? She hoped so. She hoped that whatever they had going between them was good, and that they were happy. Somebody in the cast of characters that made up this bizarre scenario deserved to be happy! She remembered the anxious look in Finn's eyes earlier, when he had invited her in for a drink, and knew how concerned he must be, for both her and for Shane. And she thought of Shane, clutching a bottle of Jameson and drinking himself into oblivion in his great big fuck-off mansion. And she thought of Izzy, holed up on her own in some hotel bedroom before facing the gruelling drive back to Dublin tomorrow, her head crammed with sorrowful thoughts of her father. What would become of Izzy when her darling daddy died? Río knew that the girl despised her mother, and that she had no siblings. Izzy would be as lonely as Río when Adair died. Lonelier; at least Río had Finn.

And Río had wine, she reminded herself, and with a glass or two she could try and drown a few sorrows of her own. Turning back towards the Bentley, she retrieved the bottle from the boot of her car, and climbed the steps to the deck. Inside, the television was still on mute, and Adair was asleep. Beside him lay a copy of *Irish Tractor & Machinery* magazine.

Fetching two glasses from the cupboard, she uncorked the wine, then sat down beside her new husband, and kissed his cheek.

'What?' he said, struggling back to consciousness. 'Whoa. That was some dream.'

'What were you dreaming about?' asked Río.

'I was dreaming that I was at an all-Ireland in Croke Park, taking a free kick.'

'What a lovely dream! I'm sorry I woke you.'

'No worries,' he told her with a smile. 'The reality is much better. I woke up to find you.'

'What a charmer you are! Look,' she said, nodding at the bottle she'd set on the table, 'I remembered that there was wine in the car. We can toast our wedding at last.'

'Aren't you the grand girl! And did Mister Maloney not care to join us?'

Río shook her head. 'I decided not to ask him. I'd rather spend our first evening here just the two of us together.'

'What's the story about the gate?'

222

'I told him that we'd foot the bill, of course, and that I'd get Finn round to mend it for him.'

'So it's all sorted?'

'It's all sorted. There is one problem, though.'

'What's that?'

'He can't allow you to use your tractor on the right of way.'

'What right of way?'

'The boreen belongs to him, and there's some problem with insurance.'

'Shit!'

'It's OK, Adair – he doesn't mind us bringing the cars in and out, but commercial vehicles and plant won't have insurance cover.'

'*Shit!*' Adair struck his forehead with the heel of his hand. 'Why didn't that gobshite who sold me the joint tell me?'

'You didn't know about the right of way?'

'No. The *sleveen*, the rogue – bad cess to him!' Then Adair slumped. '*Arra* . . . there's no use blaming him. I was in too much of a hurry to buy the place – it's something I should have checked out for myself. I'm sick with myself, now, Río. Pure sick!'

'Don't worry – there's an obvious solution. It'll involve a bit of a detour, but only a minor one. There's a right-of-way up to the road further along the beach.'

Adair looked at her miserably. 'But sure, I'll have the same problems with insurance wherever I go, won't I? I'm banjaxed, whichever way you look at it.'

'No. The land in question belongs to me. I'm not going to sue you if anything happens on my land, Adair.'

'You're not talking about your orchard?'

Río nodded.

'But, darlin', that's your pet project! I can't be barging through your precious allotment in a tractor!'

'Of course you can,' she told him, crisply. 'It'll simply mean cutting down one or two trees and broadening the existing thoroughfare. I'll take you down there tomorrow before we go to Coolnamara Castle and show you. It's the obvious solution to your problem.'

Río avoided pointing out that it was the *only* solution to his problem, and that if Adair didn't grab it with both hands, his dreams of working his oyster farm would be about as realistic as his dream of taking a free kick at Croke Park.

'And you would seriously do this for me?'

'But of course. Didn't I tell you earlier today that – while we both wish it – I will give you that which is mine to give. Those were my very words.'

'And didn't I tell you,' said Adair, taking her hands, 'that I shall be a shield for your back, and honour you above all others? It's not much, in the light of what you have given me. Ach – this is never a marriage of equals, *acushla*. I have married way above my station. I am not worthy of you, Río Kinsella.'

'Will you go away out of that!' said Río. She gave him a minxy look. 'You might remember that you also pledged to me the first drink from your cup. Would you ever get your finger out, Adair Bolger, and pour us some of that wine?'

And later that night, after they'd finished the bottle and decided to call it a day, Río lay prone beside a fitfully sleeping Adair, gazing into the darkness as she'd predicted she would, hot-eyed and wracked with worries.

Chapter Fifteen

Keeley was taking her morning power-walk along the beach beneath the battlements of Coral Mansion, wondering how she might gain access. She wished she'd had a chance to get hold of the phone number of that girl she'd met in O'Toole's yesterday, the girl in the Harajuku get-up who was living with Shane Byrne's son, Finn. Of course, she could always put in a call to Shane's people and try and set things up the regular way, but something told her that a less formal approach was what was required here.

Keeley was now dead set upon getting this interview. The YouTube video of Shane's spat with Adair had received countless hits since it had been uploaded only hours earlier, and to be granted an audience with the man himself would afford her serious kudos. She reckoned that she was possibly the only journalist in the world right now who knew where Shane Byrne was holed up.

A voice from further along the beach made her stop in her tracks. There, standing next to a five-bar gate that opened on to some kind of allotment, was Adair Bolger with his new bride.

'It's dead straightforward, Adair,' Río was saying. 'We get a bulldozer in and clear a track between here and the access point up the hill. All we need is a few tons of hardcore, and some galvanised steel gates. The gates should have been replaced yonks ago, anyway.'

'Are you sure about this, Río?'

'I've told you twenty times and more, that I'm sure. I'll put in a call to Pat Brennan.'

'Who's he?'

'He's a local builder. He has a dozer and all the gear, and he'll have the job done for us in no time. It'll be finished before we get back next week.'

'You're a star,' Adair told her. 'And you deserve a lovely lunch and afternoon tea with scones and jam and cream and a long soak in a bath and a glass of Coolnamara Castle's finest champagne before we go downstairs to a slap-up dinner.'

'Are you mad, Adair! If I'm going to eat like that on our honeymoon you'll rue the day you ever married me by the time it's over! I'll be the size of a house.'

'Our wedding day is practically the only day of my life I'll never rue,' said Adair, as they turned and made their way back across the sand. 'What about some pampering, too? There's a spa, where you can get massages and manicures and facials and stuff.'

'I've never had a manicure or a facial,' Río told him. 'I don't see the point of paying someone to do something you can do perfectly well yourself. But I have to say, I'd love a massage. Fleur says they do great hot-stone treatments and . . .'

And Río's voice trailed away as the couple meandered around a bend in the bay.

'Hello!'

A voice from above made Keeley look up. There, sitting on the parapet of the roof of Coral Mansion with her feet dangling over the edge, was Finn Byrne's girlfriend.

'Hi, there,' said Keeley, shading her eyes against the sun. 'Fancy a drink?'

'Sorry?'

'I said, d'you fancy a drink?'

'Do you mean later? In O'Toole's?'

'No. I mean here. Now.'

The girl rose to her feet as casually as she might have done had she been on terra firma, not perched on a parapet thirty feet up.

'I'd love one, thanks!' replied Keeley.

She wasn't about to protest that it was not yet midday, and that the sun was far from being over the yardarm. If gaining access to Shane Byrne meant swigging back alcohol at an inappropriate hour, then so be it.

'Come on up, then.' Taking a nonchalant step backwards, the girl disappeared from view.

Keeley looked around, unsure as to how to find her way up to the villa. The most obvious route appeared to be through the allotment, which clearly belonged to Río Kinsella. Moving to the gate and pushing it open, she stepped through. She was reasonably confident that the natives were friendly and that she wouldn't get done for trespassing if she took a short cut.

Wow! Luxuriant was the word that came to mind, as she made in the direction of Shane Byrne's villa. Keeley didn't know much about market gardening, but she could see that this place had been treated to a lot of TLC. There were rows of courgettes and leeks and onions and cabbages. There were potato drills. There was a polytunnel and flower garden, where roses and gladioli and frilly petunias grew. There were apple and pear trees, and Keeley could tell by the burgeoning fruit that there'd be a bumper crop later in the year. It made her wonder if she shouldn't think

227

about getting her own hands dirty and start scraping out a vegetable patch in the corner of the garden that had been sadly neglected since her grandmother died, and the cottage had been taken off the Coolnamara Hideaways rental books. She wondered why Río had been talking about commandeering a bulldozer, and laying hardcore here. A hardcore track going through this lovely place struck her as akin to a switchblade slash across the face of a beautiful woman.

There seemed to be no real boundary where Río's allotment ended and the grounds of Shane Byrne's villa began, except for a haphazard line of raspberry canes. The grass here was nearly waist-high, and the steps that led up to the massive deck that fronted the villa were overgrown with moss. On the deck itself, a variety of tools lay around. Restoration work was evidently underway.

Finn's girlfriend was standing at the far end of the deck next to a table upon which two glasses were set. She was dressed today not in quirky high fashion as she had been yesterday, but in oversized work overalls. Her feet were bare, and her black hair was piled loosely on the top of her head. In her hands she was holding a bottle of champagne.

'Champagne!' said Keeley. 'Marvellous.'

'Here's some champagne trivia for you,' said the girl. 'Did you know that the pressure inside one of these bottles is the same as the pressure of a tyre on a double-decker bus?' With a deft twist, the cork came away from the bottle, and the girl began to pour.

'My mother always said that, while drinking alcohol before six o'clock in the evening was reprehensible, it's perfectly acceptable to enjoy a glass of champagne at any time of the day,' said Keeley with one of her most winsome smiles.

'Try telling that to my father.'

'Oh . . . He's teetotal, is he?'

The girl laughed. 'He thinks it's perfectly acceptable to enjoy a bottle of whiskey at any time of the day. Mind you, so does Shane, by the cut of him.'

Aha! This was the cue Keeley was waiting for. 'Shane Byrne?'

'Yeah. He's dug into the Jameson already, hoping a hair of the dog might do the trick.'

Keeley cheered inwardly. This girl was going to be indiscreet! A bonus!

'I'm sorry,' she said. 'I didn't catch your name yesterday when I introduced myself.'

'That's because I didn't tell you it.' Smiling, the girl handed Keeley a glass.

'Well . . . If we're going to share a glass of champagne, I'd rather like to know.'

The girl considered. 'I guess that's fair enough. I suppose you need to be able to quote your sources. You could call me "a friend of Shane's", or "an insider", or "a source close to the troubled actor", but I guess they're all too much of a mouthful. People call me all kinds of things. You can call me Cat. *Sláinte.*'

'*Sláinte*,' echoed Keeley, taking a sip from her glass.

'Sit down,' said Cat. 'Make yourself at home.'

'"Make yourself at home"! I haven't heard anyone say that for yonks! It was a favourite saying of my grandmother.'

'It's kinda my motto.'

Cat sat down and swung her feet up onto the table, and Keeley sat rather more decorously on the chair opposite.

'What a fabulous view!' she said.

'Yeah. I've been painting it.'

'You're an artist?'

229

'Yeah. Wanna see some of my stuff?'

'I'd love to.'

'Finish your champagne first, and then I'll give you a sneak preview.'

'A sneak preview – you mean, prior to your *vernissage*?'

Cat laughed.

'What's so funny?'

'That pompy word – *vernissage*.'

'It means "exhibition opening", doesn't it?'

'It does. But not many people know that, apart from artists.'

'Funnily enough,' said Keeley conversationally, 'I interviewed the wife of an artist, just last week.'

'Oh? What's her name, and why did you interview her?'

'I interviewed her because she's going to be bringing out a book soon. Her name's Ophelia Gallagher.'

'Oaf!' Cat spluttered into her champagne.

'Are you all right?'

'Yes. It's just . . . I've heard of her. She's married to Hugo Gallagher, ain't she?'

'Yes.'

Cat narrowed her eyes, which had the effect of making her look a little like her namesake. 'So, tell me. How is good old Hugo these days?'

'You know him?'

'Everybody in the art world knows Hugo Gallagher.'

'Well, I found him very charming,' said Keeley, diplomatically. 'I spent a very pleasant couple of hours in their home.'

'In the famous Crooked House?'

'Yes. It's quaint. Not the kind of place I can imagine a child being brought up, though. It's rather isolated. Ophelia's expecting, you see,' she added, for Cat's benefit.

'I'd heard. So. You were interviewing her about her so-called book? What's it about?'

'I haven't read it yet – there are no advance copies available. I was really just talking to her about her past life, and the fact that she's embarking on a brand new career.'

'She could probably do with the money.'

'I'm sorry?'

'I said she could probably do with the money. Rumour has it that Hugo's blocked and they're skint. I heard that he can't even support his own daughter.'

'But Caitlín's nineteen!' protested Keeley. 'No self-respecting nineteen-year-old expects to be supported by their parents.'

'Maybe. But Caitlín hasn't any qualifications for anything. She's really dense. I heard from someone that she's been begging on the streets of Galway.'

'Oh, God!' Keeley recalled the drawing of the waiflike child that she'd seen in the sitting room in the Crooked House, and felt a tug of pure pity. 'That . . . that's dreadful!'

'Yes, it is. It's really, *really* dreadful. You might mention it to Hugo next time you're talking to him, and tell him to do something about it.'

'It's unlikely that I'll be talking to him any time soon,' said Keeley. She gave Cat a concerned look. 'Do you know Caitlín well? Is there any way you can help her?'

'No. Now, hurry up and finish your champagne, and come and see my pictures.'

Cat drained her glass and jumped up from the table, and Keeley felt obliged to follow suit. Following the girl across the deck, she entered the villa through a pair of massive, sliding glass doors. On the walls of what Keeley took to be the sitting room, rows of vibrant acrylics were taped.

'Well, I have to say your paintings are a revelation!' said Keeley, with a smile. 'Where did you train?'

'I didn't train. My father taught me.'

'He was an artist?'

Cat shrugged. 'An amateur.'

'And tell me,' said Keeley, examining one of the land-scapes more closely, 'why have you used the back of wallpaper as your canvas of choice? Is it some kind of artistic statement?'

'Yes. It's a statement about the rip-off prices charged by art suppliers. It's a statement that says: you don't need to fork out a fucking fortune in order to find a way to express yourself artistically. All kinds of creative alternatives are available to those who are gifted with imagination, like I am. I could paint on a binbag.'

'I'm impressed. Do you mind me asking how much you charge?'

'One thousand five hundred. Twelve hundred to you.'

A laugh came from the doorway. Lounging against the jamb was a man Keeley recognised as Finn Byrne.

'Shut up, Finn!' said Cat. 'There is a serious chat about art going on here, and since you know bugger all about it you're not welcome to join in.' Cat turned back to Keeley. 'It may interest you to know that Elena Sweetman is one of my patrons.'

'Elena Sweetman? The film actress?'

'Yeah. She adores my work. She's one of my biggest fans. Well, Keeley? Can I interest you in one of my paintings? How about this one? Elena Sweetman's dead keen to buy it, but if you like it, I'll let you have it COD.'

'Keeley?' Finn gave her a look of scrutiny. 'Are you Keeley Considine?'

'Yes.' Keeley extended her hand. 'And you are . . .?' she said, doing that vague tailing-off thing as an invitation to him to introduce himself.

'He's Finn,' said Cat. 'He's Shane Byrne's son – Shane who you want to interview.'

'I . . . I never said that I wanted to interview Shane Byrne!' said Keeley, colouring.

'Yes, you did. You said it yesterday in the pub. I thought that's what you were here for when I saw you on the beach earlier, snooping around. I thought you were probably trying to find a way in. That's why I invited you up.'

'You invited a journalist into the house, Pusscat?' said Finn. 'Jesus Christ! It's one thing to invite an old woman from the islands—'

'What old woman from the islands?'

'The one you invited in last week, who you sold a painting to, that you said was like Peig Sayers.'

'Oh, yeah,' said Cat dismissively. 'Her. Anyhoo, I just thought it was probably safer to invite Keeley in, in case Shane discovered her trespassing in the grounds and shot her.'

'What? Dad doesn't have a gun!'

'Yes, he does. He showed it to me last night. And can you imagine if he did shoot her? It would go straight to the top of YouTube.'

'Well, not courtesy of you. You wouldn't even know how to upload the video.'

'You could do it, easy peasy.'

'Yeah, and you really think I'm going to stand around making a video of my da shooting an intruder? Anyway, knowing him, the gun is just a replica. Just how many YouTube hits would that get? My da waving a replica gun at some random hack?'

'Still. There'd be a fair few bob involved, wouldn't there? How much do you get if you get to the top of the YouTube charts?'

'Nothing,' said Finn.

'Nothing?' Cat looked gobsmacked. 'Are you serious? Then why do people *bother*?'

'They do it for fun.'

'Fun? Well, blow me if that's a person's idea of fun. That sucks. I'm getting the champagne.' And Cat stomped off.

Keeley could not believe that she was standing here listening to this couple bickering about which of them was going to upload footage of her murder at the hands of a drunken film star on to YouTube. She thought it was possibly the most surreal moment of her life. But then things got even more surreal, because there came a crash from the hallway beyond the sitting room door, and a man's voice yelled, '*Noooooooooooooooooo!*'

'What's up, Da?' said Shane, looking over his shoulder.

'That was my last fucking bottle of Jameson,' came the mournful reply.

And then Shane Byrne, star of *The Faraway* and *The O'Hara Affair*, and sundry other Hollywood epics, shambled into the room.

'It's OK, Shane,' said Cat, coming back in with the bottle of champagne. 'There's loads of Veuve Clicquot. And there's brandy somewhere, Finn, ain't there? I mix a mean champagne cocktail. All we need are sugar cubes.'

'I suppose you learned how to do that when you were ten too,' said Finn. 'And may I remind you that that fizz isn't ours, Pusscat. Adair bought it for the . . . um . . . the festivities.'

Shane gave Finn a saturnine look. 'All the more reason to drink it, then,' he said.

Finn shrugged. 'I suppose we could always pay Adair back.'

Shane curled his lip. 'Pay him back? Bollocks to that for a game of soldiers. We'll drink the entire case.'

'Yay! I'll get more glasses!' And Cat danced out of the room, singing 'Hey diddle diddle, the cat and the fiddle,' just as someone's phone tone jangled. It was the theme tune to *The O'Hara Affair*.

'Your phone, Da,' said Finn.

Sliding it from his pocket, Shane squinted at the display, then slung the phone onto a calfskin Buddha bag. 'Fuck off, my friend,' he said. '"No comment" is the catchphrase du jour.'

'I'd turn it off, if I were you.'

'I can't. I'm expecting a call.'

Shane stretched and yawned and said 'Ow', then realised belatedly that there was someone else in the room. 'Who's this?' he asked, peering at Keeley through bloodshot eyes.

'The name's Keeley Considine,' said Keeley, presenting a hand with her best smile.

'Nice to meet you.'

'She's a journalist, Da,' Finn warned.

Shane withdrew his hand as though he'd touched a hot iron. 'A journo? What's a fucking journo doing in my house?'

'I invited her,' said Cat, returning with champagne flutes and another bottle.

'You've really embraced that *mi casa es su casa* ethic, Catkin, haven't you?' said Shane. 'Next thing you know, you'll be inviting *all* your friends to stay.'

'That won't be a problem,' said Cat, giving him a look of hauteur, 'since I don't have any friends. "The little dog laughed to see such fun, and the dish ran away with the spoon, la la."'

'So,' said Shane, skewering Keeley with a look. 'What *are* you doing in my house?'

'She wants an interview,' said Cat, helpfully. 'She does in-depth stuff for the *Sunday Insignia*. She did Ophelia Gallagher last time.'

'Who's Ophelia Gallagher?' asked Shane.

'Good question,' said Cat. 'I wonder what the dish *saw* in the spoon?' she mused, as she set about filling glasses and

235

handing them around. 'She must have been on drugs. It was probably a cocaine spoon.'

Tch! Keeley was beginning to regret that she'd ever met this girl. It might have proved less torturous to go through the usual channels. And then she remembered what Shane had said, about 'No comment' being the catchphrase of the day, and she guessed that actually, she was pretty damn privileged to be here.

'An "in-depth" interview, eh?' Shane stroked his jaw. Even unshaven, hungover and dishevelled, Shane Byrne was a damn sexy man. 'What's it worth to you?'

'Well, that's axiomatic,' she said with a laugh. 'It's how I earn my living.'

'I'm not a very "deep" individual.'

'In the course of my work, I've found out that everyone has hidden depths.'

'That's a pretty facile answer, if you don't mind my saying so.'

'Touché.'

'I suppose they were all on drugs. The cat and the fiddle and the little dog. I mean, how else would you explain the cow jumping over the moon?'

The O'Hara Affair ringtone sounded again. 'I'm fucking beleaguered!' moaned Shane. 'Why can't they all bog off and leave me alone?'

'Who is it this time?' asked Finn.

'It's my press agent. Again. He's phoned about fifty times this morning.'

'Da?' said Finn, very gently. 'Allow me to make a suggestion. Talk to him. Tell him you've offered the *Insignia* a world exclusive and then he can send all the others packing. One answer fits all, if you get my drift. You know it makes sense.'

'You think?' said Shane.

'It makes very good sense to me,' said Keeley.

'Well, of course it would make sense to *you*!' returned Shane.

'If you don't speak out, you won't be left alone, Mr Byrne,' Keeley continued, unruffled. 'And you'll be subject to the most prurient kind of media speculation. As will Ms Kinsella.' *Gotcha!* It was clear to Keeley from Shane's expression that she'd played her trump card. 'You can trust me to set the record straight any way you want. And I'll allow you to approve the copy before I file it.'

'Can I have that on record?'

'Sure.' Her editor wouldn't like it, but then, since she'd handed in her notice, Keeley didn't much care what Leo thought.

'Old King Cole was probably spaced out on drugs, too. He called for his pipe in the middle of the night, didn't he? It could have been an opium pipe.'

Shane looked into his glass, then downed the contents in one and handed it to Cat. 'Slosh some more fizz in there like a good Kitty Cat,' he said. 'And then I'll go and make some phone calls.'

'Number one being your press agent?' asked Keeley, daring to hope.

'No. He's number two.'

'Who's number one?' asked Cat.

'You know what curiosity did to the cat,' Shane told her.

'Doesn't worry me,' said Cat. 'I'll still have eight left.'

'Will you sit in on the interview with me, Finn? You can be Patroclus to my Achilles.'

'Sure.'

'And you can keep Ms Considine entertained while I talk trans-Atlantic, Catkin.'

'But she might want to find out stuff about you!' protested Cat.

'In that case, you have my permission to tell the sweetest lies. Come with me, Finn. I could do with your strategic advice.'

237

'Honestly!' protested Keeley. 'I'm not some kind of many-headed Hydra, out to get you!'

'I have a deep-rooted mistrust of the press,' Shane told her. 'Have done since the *National Enquirer* set a rumour in train that I was a drunk.'

Cat laughed. 'A rumour! That's a good one.'

'You, Catkin, are the cheekiest madam it's ever been my misfortune to encounter. You're bloody lucky that I haven't thrown you out of my house yet.'

'You can't throw a cat out of a house if she doesn't want to leave,' Cat told him. 'She just finds her way back in. And it doesn't suit me to leave just yet.'

'You'll go with my boot in your hole if you don't mind your manners.'

'Did you hear that, Keeley? You can put in your interview that Shane Byrne threatens vulnerable females.'

'Vulnerable! Ha!' And Shane strolled from the room armed with his phone and his wineglass, followed by Finn.

God, Keeley thought wearily, as she took a swig of champagne, she'd be bloody glad to finally doff the 'hack' label once and for all! She was fed up of people treating her as if she were some kind of virulent succubus.

'What's it feel like to have people so suspicious of you?' Cat asked her.

'Bloody awful, if truth were told. I can't wait to get started on my new life. Can I have some more of that?' she added, indicating the champagne bottle. If everybody else in this house was going to get roaring drunk, she might as well join them, even though it was highly unprofessional conduct. But, hell – who cared? It would appear that the rule book had already gone through the window today.

'Here we go,' said Cat, pouring with a practised hand. 'What's your new life going to be?'

'I'm thinking about becoming an agent.'

'An agent?' Cat turned interested eyes on her. 'Like, an artists' agent?'

'No. A literary one.'

'Because if you were thinking about becoming an artists' agent, I might consider taking you on.'

'Thank you. That's quite a compliment. But I don't know enough about art.'

'Unlike Shane Byrne. He *loves* art. That's why he has my paintings all over his house. He even has one in his en-suite bathroom, so he can look at it while he's taking a dump. He's what they call an aficionado.'

Keeley decided that it was time to start doing a little preliminary digging. 'You seem to know Finn and Shane very well, Cat. How did you meet them?'

'We go way back. We met when I worked as a scenic artist on a film called *The O'Hara Affair*.'

'Oh, yes. That was made near here, wasn't it?'

'Yeah.'

'Elena Sweetman was in that too, wasn't she?'

'Yes, she was. Poor Elena.'

'Why so?'

'I don't know how I'm going to break the news to her that I've sold one of her favourite paintings.'

'Who did you sell it to?'

Cat looked put out. 'I sold it to you. Didn't I?'

'Oh. I . . . I'm not sure I can afford it, Cat.'

'I think you'll find you can,' said Cat with a sweet smile. 'After all the trouble I went to, to set up this world exclusive interview for you. And you know, it would take just one word from me in Finn's shell-like to scupper the whole caboodle. Caboodle – that's a word, isn't it?'

Keeley nodded. Honestly, the girl was shameless! But she

had to admit a grudging admiration for her. She studied Cat over the rim of her glass as she held the bottle up to the light to gauge the level of the contents. There was something vaguely familiar about her, but she couldn't place her. It would come to Keeley, sooner or later. It was there, lurking somewhere in the box-file of her journalist's mind.

'Here – have some more,' said Cat cheerily, even though Keeley's glass was still half-full. 'We may as well finish the bottle, and there's loads more where that came from. In the meantime, while Shane and Finn are planning their strategy, is there anything else you'd like to know about life here in idyllic Coral Mansion?'

'Yes, indeed,' said Keeley. 'I'd love to ask you a few questions. Just let me find my notepad and pen . . .'

Much later the following evening, dazed, confused, and monumentally hungover, Keeley typed in the final sentence of her first draft, attached it to an email, and sent it winging its way through the ether to the other side of the bay, where, from the dormer window of her cottage, she could just see the lights of Coral Mansion glimmering through the branches of the fruit trees in Río Kinsella's orchard.

She wondered what antics might be going on there now in that extraordinary villa, and whether champagne was still being randomly popped. She'd lost count of how many bottles had been popped there yesterday. Popped . . . it was a funny word, when you thought about it. Pop . . . pop . . . pop! goes the weasel. Why did the weasel go pop? wondered Keeley. Could he have been on drugs, too? Could the half pound of tuppenny rice have been a euphemism for hash? Could the treacle have been best Lebanese Black? Was there a clue in the words 'That's the way the money goes . . .? Pop! goes the weasel . . .' It was a puzzle.

And then Keeley caught herself on and dragged herself to bed.

Chapter Sixteen

'Listen to this! "They may have called him 'Slow' Byrne at school, but Shane Byrne is actually one of the most nimble-witted actors it has ever been my pleasure to interview. He is laidback with it, and utterly devoid of ego – and, yes, he is easily as sexy in the flesh as he is on celluloid." Sheesh! How much did you pay Keeley to write this, Da? It's practically a hagiography.'

'What's a hagiography?' asked Cat.

'A kind of lick-arse "too good to be true" type of piece, like you'd find in *Hello!* magazine.'

Shane, Cat and Finn were lounging on the deck of Coral Mansion. Shane was nursing a Bloody Mary; Cat and Finn had opted for pink grapefruit juice. Keeley's email had arrived some time in the middle of the night, and Finn had printed it out and was reading it aloud to his father.

'Did they really call you "Slow" Byrne at school?' asked Cat.

'Yep.'

'I was called Puddy,' said Cat.

'Because you were fat?' asked Finn.

'No!' Cat gave him a disdainful look. 'Because of Puddy Tat – you know, of Sylvester and Tweety fame. Go on reading about Shane.'

'I couldn't be arsed. It's the usual crap. Read it yourself if you're so interested.'

'No,' said Cat.

'Oh, look! There's something here about you.'

'What?'

Finn handed her the printout. 'Here you go. It's halfway down.'

Cat shook her head.

'What? Don't you want to know the lovely things Keeley has said about Shane Byrne's taste in artwork?'

'I can't.'

'What do you mean?'

'I mean just that, OK? I can't read.' Cat threw the pages back at him, then turned over on the sun lounger, and lay on her tummy.

'Oh,' said Finn. 'Oh, God, I'm sorry, Cat. I didn't realise . . . you're dyslexic?'

'I told you. I can't read. I'm like, "Special Needs".'

There was a hiatus, then: 'There's no shame in being dyslexic,' remarked Shane. 'Loads of actors are dyslexic. Tom Cruise and Orlando Bloom are dyslexic. And so is Keira Knightley.'

'And . . . um . . . Winston Churchill was dyslexic,' said Finn helpfully.

'I knew about Keira Knightley and Orlando Bloom,' said Cat. 'But I didn't know about Tom Cruise.'

'He blames it on his father,' Shane told her. 'His pa used to come down hard on him for the slightest thing – that's why he disowned him, when he was twelve.'

Cat gave him an interested look. 'Tom Cruise disowned his father?'

'Yep.'

'How do you know that?'

'He told me himself.'

'Picasso was dyslexic,' said Cat. 'And even Leonardo da Vinci might have been, too.'

'See?' said Shane. 'You're in illustrious company. Loads of really artistic people are dyslexic. Elena is.'

'Elena Sweetman?'

'Yep.'

'Cool!'

'Duncan Goodhew!' said Finn. 'There's another famous dyslexic person!'

'Who's Duncan Goodhew?'

'He's an Olympic swimmer. They called him Duncan the Dunce at school.'

'See?' said Cat, crossly. 'Everyone thinks dyslexics are dense. I used to get that all the time. The teachers kept telling my parents that I was lazy, and that I should try harder. Nobody understood.'

'Not even your dad? When he was home-schooling you?'

'Especially not my dad! He thought I was as thick as two planks plus one. Raoul was the only one who had a clue. He rocked.'

'Who's Raoul?'

'My half-brother. He taught me everything I know.'

'Including breaking and entering?' asked Finn.

'Yes, actually.'

'I'd like to learn how to do that. Will you teach me, Pusscat?'

'She will not teach you how to break and enter!' said Shane. 'The tabloids would have a field day if they got hold of that.'

'Breaking and entering's been way more useful to me than anything my dad taught me,' said Cat. 'He used to read me poetry until it felt like it had bunged up my brain and was coming out of my ears. I could recite practically the entire works of Shakespeare.'

'You're right. Breaking and entering's way more useful

than poetry,' conceded Shane. 'And I'm speaking as a professional actor.'

'You could get a job as a locksmith,' suggested Finn.

'Talking of locks,' said Shane, 'what does Goldilocks have to say about the famous YouTube fiasco, Finn?'

'Goldilocks?'

'Keeley Considine. Our roving reporter.'

'No, no – first tell me what she says about me!' pleaded Cat, sitting up straight and hugging her knees. 'Please, Finn! I'm dying to know.'

'OK.' Finn reached for the discarded printout. 'She says that . . . um . . . Oh, yeah. Here we are. "Shane also has a discerning eye when it comes to art. Hanging in his new home are numerous works by a young artist who goes by the name of 'Cat', whose work invites comparison with the naïve French painter, Henri Rousseau."'

'Rousseau!' breathed Cat, feeling starry-eyed and all aglow. 'My hero!'

'"Among Cat's notable patrons,"' continued Finn, '"are the actress Elena Sweetman, and Shane's great pal, Johnny Depp."' Finn gave her a stern look over the top of the A4 pages. 'Bad Cat! Telling lies to the press.'

Shane laughed. 'I'll buy one of your paintings and give it to Johnny as a birthday present. That'll take the harm out of the lie.'

'Oh – would you, Shane? Ta muchly!' Cat, feeling greatly cheered now, slid off her sun lounger and plonked a kiss on Shane's cheek. 'I'll even give you a discount if you buy two.'

'How much are they?'

'Two thousand each. I'll give you two for three grand.'

'Jesus, Cat! You are incorrigible,' said Finn.

'You still haven't told me what she says about the YouTube lark,' said Shane.

'Oh, yes! Go on,' said Cat, jumping up onto the sea wall and promenading along it. 'Let's hear how she gets Shane out of that one.'

'Um . . . she says the "fracas" was down to some misunderstanding to do with the title deeds of the Villa Felicity.'

'Good,' said Shane. 'There's absolutely nothing there about your ma? I specifically asked her to keep Río out of it.'

'No. Ma isn't mentioned.'

'Well, good on Goldilocks, to stay true to her word.'

Cat had come to the end of her catwalk. 'And here she comes now,' she said, looking up the garden towards where the old yoga pavilion used to be. An elegant woman was gliding down the path towards them. 'Oh, no – it ain't Keeley, actually. This one's goldy locks are even goldier.'

'Then it'll be Elena,' said Shane, getting to his feet.

'Elena Sweetman?'

'Yeah. She phoned yesterday to tell me she was coming.'

'Fucking ace!' Cat jumped down from the wall and scooted towards the house.

'Where are you off to, Pusscat?' asked Finn.

'To get champagne, of course,' said Cat, 'to celebrate the arrival of my new best friend! Will you take a picture of us together, Finn, and put it up on the internet? Then I can text Oaf with the link.'

And Cat scampered off, humming the theme song to *The O'Hara Affair*.

Cat was in love. Elena Sweetman was the most beautiful person she had ever met. She had the face of a Botticelli angel, she was svelte as a leopardess, she smelled like a flower shop, and her smile was a benison: like her namesake, Helen of Troy, men would die for her, thought Cat. Never before in her life had Cat wanted to please another person, just to

246

see them smile. Elena was rangy, she was radiant, she was game for anything. She threw together a lunch made from store cupboard staples, she helped Cat sand down a window frame, she played a mean game of rounders, she made Shane laugh. And, after dinner and a swim in the sea, she beat them all at poker.

'Why did you never get married, Elena?' Cat asked her. They were sitting together on the sea wall, listening to the sound of the waves whispering on the shingle below. Cat had lit candles liberally all over the deck, which had the effect of enhancing Elena's golden beauty; Cat felt as though she was worshipping at the shrine of a goddess. 'Are you gay?'

Elena laughed her wonderful, throaty laugh. 'No, I'm not gay. I've just never met a man I wanted to spend the rest of my life with. And I'm the kind of old-fashioned gal who believes that marriage is for life.'

'Wasn't there even one man you'd have considered?'

'Yes. There was one. But he wasn't available.'

'What about George Clooney?'

That laugh again. 'He asked me, but I had to say no. I couldn't trust George not to stray.'

'You turned down George Clooney? But every woman in the world wants to marry him! I mean, even I think he's quite tasty, and he's old enough to be my dad.'

'I don't mind not being married. I'm rather set in my ways, like an old spinster with her cats.'

'How many cats do you have?'

'Three beautiful blue Burmese. I love them like they were my own children.'

'And do you mind not having children?'

Elena shrugged. 'It would have been nice. I like to think I'd have made quite a good mother.'

247

'You'd have made a brilliant mother! Why don't you think about adopting, like Angelina Jolie?'

'I'm not keen on the idea of single parenthood. I think a child needs a father figure. Like I said, I'm an old-fashioned gal.'

Shame, Cat thought. She'd have loved to have been adopted by Elena Sweetman.

'Now,' said Elena, 'let's talk about something a lot more important.'

'What?'

'You. More specifically, your artwork. We've got to get you launched, Cat. Why don't you think about coming out to LA?'

Cat shook her head. 'I . . . I can't, Elena.'

'Whyever not?'

'I couldn't fly.'

'Have you a fear of flying?'

'Yes. There are really only two things in life that scare me rigid. Needles and aeroplanes.' And fire, Cat might have added, since the incident on the houseboat.

'Did you have a bad flying experience once?'

'No. I've never flown in my life.'

'You might find you enjoy it, you know. I love it. I would have applied for a pilot's licence if I weren't dyslexic.'

'Tom Cruise is dyslexic, but he flies a plane, doesn't he?'

'Ah – but Tom claims that Scientology cured his dyslexia. I'm not so desperate to be cured that I'd turn to that kind of claptrap. Anyway, we're veering away from the subject. You're adamant that you won't come to LA?'

Cat nodded. 'I'm sorry.'

'No worries. There a solution to every problem if you look hard enough. What if I take your paintings with me when I go back, and hold a private view in my house?'

'You'd do that?'

'Of course. Any excuse for a party.'

'And do you think you'd get buyers?'

'For sure. The LA film community loves anything artistic to do with Ireland. That's why Irish actors do so well there. I could invite the usual suspects – Neeson, Farrell, Gleeson – and ask for their support. If you volunteered to donate a portion of the price of each painting sold to a charity, you'd be guaranteed sales. People like to think they're contributing to a good cause.'

Privately, Cat thought her own fight for financial survival was a good enough cause, but she could hardly say so to a woman she'd compared to a Botticelli angel.

'Um. I suppose I could donate something to the Dyslexia Association,' she said, trying to inject a little enthusiasm into her tone. She'd have to put up her prices again.

'Perfect!'

'I don't like to sound mercenary, Elena, but how will I get the money?'

'I'll lodge it in your bank account.'

'I don't have one. I have a fear of filling out forms.'

The list was getting longer. Maybe Hugo Gallagher's fearless daughter – the kick-ass loner who walked by herself – was actually a scaredy-cat at heart?

'Hm. We'll have to find a way around that. I'll drive you into town tomorrow, and we'll see about setting one up for you.'

'But you need ID for that, and I don't have any, apart from a fake student one.'

'You've no ID at all? Not even a passport?'

'No. I've never needed one.'

Elena gave a delighted laugh. 'So you're a complete floater! The ultimate vagabond! There's something wonderfully romantic about that.'

It suddenly didn't feel very romantic to Cat, especially if it was going to get in the way of her making some money.

'In the days when my dad supported me,' she told Elena, 'he used to send me cash in a card – you know, like a greeting card. Maybe you could just send me dollars that way?'

'It's unorthodox,' said Elena, thoughtfully, 'but I guess it could be done. What about tax, though?'

'Tax, Shmax. You know that artists in Ireland didn't have to pay tax once upon a time?'

'I'd forgotten what a civilised country Ireland is. Maybe I should think about coming here to live.'

'Would you really like to live here?' Cat gave her a sceptical look. 'There's loads of disadvantages.'

'Tell me about them.'

'Well, we're governed by a shower of shites—'

'A shower of shites! I love it!'

'And the weather's mostly crap – apart from this summer. We've been lucky this year.'

'It's beautiful. So balmy.'

'And we're broke on account of all the corrupt bankers.'

'Sadly, there's corruption everywhere in the world. Where would you most like to live, Cat, if you could live anywhere you chose to?'

'I'd like to live on a Greek island,' said Cat without hesitation. 'In a white house by the sea – one of those houses that has Aegean-blue painted doors and window frames – with a beautiful dark-skinned boy. That's what I'd like from life.'

'And I wish I could be your fairy godmother, darling,' said Elena, 'and make it happen for you. Ping!' She tweaked an imaginary wand, then gave Cat a curious look. 'But how will you get to Greece if you can't fly? Overland?'

250

'I would sail. I could get myself a little blue water cruiser and navigate my way there.'

'How are your map-reading skills?'

'I know how to navigate by the stars. My brother taught me. And you can get something called GPS that practically takes you straight to wherever you want to go.'

'GPS? What's that?'

'Um . . .' Thankfully the arrival of Finn meant that she was let off the hook.

'GPS,' he said, 'stands for Global Positioning System. Without GPS there'd be no such thing as satnav and . . .'

Cat zoned out.

'How do you learn your lines, Elena, for your films?' she asked, when Finn had done boring them both to death with stuff about GPS.

'It's not as difficult as you might think. Once I've mastered reading them, I record them and play them back over and over and over. I get there in the end.'

'Ill met by moonlight, proud Titania!' he said in an acto-rish voice as he joined them by the wall.

'What! Jealous Oberon,' responded Elena. 'Fairies, skip hence: I have forsworn his bed and company.'

'Tarry, rash wanton! Am not I thy lord?'

What the fuck were they on about? thought Cat.

'Then I must be thy lady.' Elena rose and, sweeping into a graceful curtsy, looked up at Shane and laughed. 'Remember the night you dried stone dead, and I had to improvise iambic pentameter?'

'What's iambic pentameter?' asked Cat, and then wished she hadn't because it reminded her of being schooled by her dad. Shane started droning on about Shakespeare and some-thing called accentual syllabic verse, and saying more stuff in that funny voice: 'Yet mark'd I where the bolt of Cupid

251

fell: it fell upon a little western flower, before milk-white, now purple with love's wound, and maidens call it Love-in-idleness.'

'We were cast together in *A Midsummer Night's Dream*,' Elena told Cat, 'as Oberon and Titania in a production on Broadway.'

'Who's Oberon and Titania?'

'I thought you knew Shakespeare backwards?' said Shane.

'Only the tragedies.'

'Oberon and Titania are king and queen of the fairies,' Elena told her. 'I got to wear some fabulous gowns.'

What a weird job for grown men and women, thought Cat, poncing around all dressed up in fancy garb, spouting crap about Cupid and flowers and maidens!

'But you also got to wear no clothes at all,' Shane reminded her.

'You did a nude scene?' asked Cat.

'I did, believe it or not. I was in better shape back then.'

'I think you're in fantastic shape now,' said Cat, loyally.

'Thank you, darling! Aren't you kind!'

'I'm not saying it to be kind. It's true. Look at her! Look at her, Finn and Shane!'

Shane smiled as he allowed his eyes to roam over Elena's body. 'She's right, Ms Sweetman. You are still in fantastic shape.'

And then it struck Cat that – now that Shane was no longer betrothèd (as Shakespeare would have put it) to Río – wouldn't it be great if Elena and Shane got it together? They'd be a perfect couple, like a storybook prince and princess, or the ones you see on the covers of Mills & Boon books.

But Cat wasn't sure that anybody really did live happily ever after, the way they did in the stories her mother had used to read her. And that didn't really surprise her because, apart from Paloma, all women were monsters and harpies

252

in Cat's experience. Her schoolmistresses had mocked her, her fellow boarders had bullied her, the local girls had beaten her up. Since her mother had died, Elena Sweetman was the first woman Cat had met who actually deserved to live happily ever after. Hm. She wondered if there was some way of arranging a love match between Shane and Elena. She vaguely remembered a production of *A Midsummer Night's Dream* that the sixth formers in school had done, and how one of the characters squeezed some magic juice from a flower into the eyes of one of the fairies so that the fairy in question ended up falling in love with the first person she saw, who just happened to be a bloke with a donkey's head on him. Some of that juice would be handy enough now, to squeeze into Elena's eyes and make her fall in love with Shane.

'Let's have more champagne!' said Cat, jumping to her feet.

'It's two thirty in the morning, Cat,' said Finn.

'My mother always said that, while drinking alcohol before six o'clock in the evening was reprehensible, it's perfectly acceptable to enjoy a glass of champagne at any time of the day,' said Cat, quoting what Keeley had said to her just the other day.

'And my body clock doesn't have a clue what time it is,' said Elena, 'since I'm on a different longitude.'

'And I seem to be on another planet,' remarked Shane.

'That's because you've been drinking too much, bad boy,' Elena reproved. 'You're going on the wagon tomorrow.'

'Am I?'

'Yes. That's one of the reasons I flew over – to set you back on the straight and narrow.'

'Straight and narrow's no fun.'

'And neither's drinking yourself to death. I'll allow you a couple more glasses of champagne, and then you're detoxing. Now. How about another game of poker?'

And Elena sashayed back into the house. The way she moved made Cat wonder how any man could resist her, and indeed, she saw that Shane was checking out her rear view with interest. Hm. Maybe they could make it a game of strip poker, thought Cat. Maybe if Shane saw Elena in the nude again, his desire would be inflamed, and they'd end up in bed together. It would be a very acceptable set-up, Cat decided, Shane and Elena and her and Finn together under the same roof. Like playing Happy Families. Happy Families! Now there was a card game she had never mastered. Maybe it was about time she did.

Chapter Seventeen

'How much do you actually know about oyster farming?'
Río asked Adair.

The pair were strolling through the grounds of Coolnamara
Castle, being bombarded by birdsong. They were having to
take things at a fairly leisurely pace, since Adair's toe was
still giving him grief. Río had managed to get a run in earlier,
while her new husband was still asleep: she'd pelted at full
tilt around the lake, running as though her life depended
upon it. She would have loved a swim, too, but swimming
in the lake was frowned upon. The last time she'd done it,
some years ago, it had been after midnight, naked, with
Shane. That had been the night he'd given her the ring . . .

She wondered what Shane was up to now. Was he still in
Lissamore, or had he gone back to LA? She'd heard nothing
from Finn, and had decided against phoning him for news,
because as long as she and Adair were holed up in Coolnamara
Castle, she wanted no real-life complications to spoil their
time here. This honeymoon period would be beset by no
worries, no stress and no regrets. It was a week for relaxing
and eating and getting pampered and making love. It was a
week for her to get to know her new man better.

And what a new man he was! Adair was courteous and
kind and respectful. He had a sense of humour, a lust for

255

life and a genuine curiosity about people – and he worshipped her. He was attentive to Río's every whim, but he also sensed when she needed space to herself. He was altogether an ideal husband, but for one thing. He wasn't Shane . . .

No! Río mustn't allow herself to go there. Ever. No regrets. *No regrets!*

'How much do I know about oyster farming?' mused Adair. 'Not a huge amount, it has to be said. But I'll have the two lads helping me out. And it's not rocket science.'

The 'two lads' were part-timers who had worked for Madser in the past. Río knew them both. They were village boys, unafraid of hard work, reliable, glad to be in employment, and they'd been keeping the farm operational since Adair had bought it.

'It's hard work,' Río pointed out. 'Turning and shacking those oyster bags is backbreaking.'

'It is,' he conceded. 'But the lads'll be doing most of the hard graft. I'll man the shed and take charge of the tractor.'

'Crushed oyster shells are a great slug repellent,' Río told him. 'I'll take all your cast-offs for my orchard.'

'And if you find any pearls while you're at it, you might make yourself a fine necklace.'

Río remembered the double string of pearls belonging to Izzy. No seed or cultured pearls for Isabella, she conjectured, only the real thing would do for Adair's princess, bought as they had been in the days when Adair had had money. She knew well that there'd be no money to be got from his oyster business. She'd heard that Madser turned over somewhere in the region of twenty thousand a year, even though his oysters had routinely won awards in Ireland's Oyster Oscars. But of course, for Adair it wasn't about money. He was doing this for love; he was doing it so that he could die a happy man.

And, sneaking a sideways glance at him now, it was happy he looked.

'What are you thinking about?' she asked.

'I'm thinking about you, and that lovely dress you had on last night. And I'm thinking about you, and that lovely dress I took off you last night, after dinner. And I'm thinking about what we might have for dinner tonight.'

'Dinner, Adair? What are you like? We've only just had breakfast!'

'And some breakfast that was! That black pudding has got to be the best I've ever tasted . . .'

And as Adair waxed lyrical about the black pudding and the potato cakes and the rashers he'd demolished that morning, Río couldn't stop thinking about the proverbial condemned man, and the hearty breakfast he'd consumed.

Some days later, the honeymoon period was over, and the newlyweds were back in the Bentley. It was Adair's first day in his new job as oyster farmer. Río watched as he donned his waterproof bib and brace trousers, his heavy-duty wellington boots and his baseball cap, and then she kissed him goodbye and watched him clamber happily aboard his shiny new tractor and trundle off down to the shore.

What to do now? What to do, now that she was a married woman, after seeing her husband off to work? She supposed that she ought to think about what to cook for his dinner. He'd be hungry after a day spent outdoors: there was nothing like Lissamore sea air to give a man an appetite. So, what to cook? Something substantial, something special. All her cookery books were in her apartment; she'd have to go online.

Outlook Express beckoned: not having bothered to check her email while she was on honeymoon, Río had a rake of new messages waiting for her. The usual spam suspects, something from Dervla, a circular from Fleur (Fleur was a complete sucker for them!), a message from Shane.

Subject: WTF??? she read.

Well, she knew what WTF stood for: What the Fuck. So what the fuck did Shane want to know the fuck about? What the fuck was she doing, getting married to Adair Bolger, that's what the fuck he wanted to know. She didn't want to respond to his email, she didn't even want to open it. Instead, she typed 'Hearty Meals' into her Google search bar and hit 'enter'.

Brisket with Stone-Ground Mustard Sauce; All-American Beef Stew; Bacon and Tomato Mac 'n Cheese; Barbecue Beef with Cornbread Topping . . . Oh, God. There was something so dispiriting about this. She pictured women in kitchens all over the world click-click-clicking on recipes, and then posting reviews such as the following: 'Yum yum yummy!!! I had already marinated pork medallions cut from a whole pork tenderloin in a marinade I found on the bottle of Montreal Steak Seasoning, decided I wanted a sauce & went searching. I cooked them quickly to med-rare & made the sauce in a flash in the pan drippings. Thx for sharing this keeper recipe w/us ☺'

Or this one: 'Very tasty and easily made. I was a little confused over the inclusion of dinner rolls AND pie crust until I figured out that you only need one or the other. Didn't have cream of celery so subbed cream of mushroom and added a little Velveeta to augment the cheddar.'

Or this: 'I added a dollop of ketchup in with the cheeses, I had also debated sweet chilli sauce, which I think would be quite yummy too! I ALSO debated (such a lot of debating!) slicing a tomato in there, but didn't, perhaps another time. Or fried onions . . . yum, the possibilities are endless, lol!!'

Maybe Río should write something along the lines of: 'I

debated adding a pinch – or maybe two! – of salt. Hubby who is dying of cancer asked for second helpings, so it must be good!! Thx for sharing! LOL!!! ☺'

In the end she decided to opt for Italian Chicken Pie because she was assured that even 'picky eaters will go back for seconds', and wrote a shopping list to take into the village later. But what to do now? Housework? The Bentley was spick-and-span. Ironing? She rarely ironed any of her own clothes, and now that Adair wasn't going to be attending board meetings and think tanks and such, there wouldn't be any Thomas Pink or Russell and Hodge bespoke shirts to press. She could go home to her apartment and get some painting done, but if she were to abandon the Bentley on her first day of proper married life, Adair might misconstrue it as a kind of betrayal or belittling of her new home. She'd go for a swim, that's what she'd do.

Unfortunately, her favourite place to swim was in the bay, directly under Coral Mansion. What if Shane was there, still? Well, bollocks to him! She couldn't allow him to stymie her life style. If her ex was going to carry on residing in Lissamore, he'd just have to get used to the fact that she lived there too. Río helped herself to a towel, and then remembered that – now that Coral Mansion was occupied – there could be no skinny-dipping in the environs: with a vexed 'Tch!' she grabbed the swimsuit she'd bought in Coolnamara Castle to wear in the hot tub there, then hit the beach.

The 'lads' were at work on the oyster beds, shifting bags of shellfish before the tide turned.

'Where's Adair?' she called to them.

'Up beyond in the shed,' came the response.

'Save me any pearls you find, will you?' Sending them a smile, she continued along the beach, thinking back to the first time she'd ever laid eyes on Adair. It had been here on this very stretch of shingle, and she marvelled now at the extraordinary train of events that had led her to marry a man, who – back in that faraway time – she had completely taken agin. She remembered how she'd thought him arrogant and bumptious, a real *Fianna Fáil*-er, a Galway tent merchant, a bit of a *sleveen*. Maybe back then he had been all those things: it had taken Río many years to overcome her antipathy for him. But the man she knew now was so very, very different. She guessed that that's what happens when you find yourself coming face to face with your own mortality – he'd said it himself, in his letter to the Saudi doctor: *It's funny how you get your priorities right when the Big C comes calling . . .*

Arriving at the slipway she used to dive from, Río looked across at where the new galvanised steel gate was lying open, like an invitation to stray sheep to come and help themselves to what her husband would call a 'slap-up feed'. She supposed she couldn't expect Adair to be perpetually getting up and down from his tractor in order to shut gates behind him, but still . . .

The hardcore track leading to the main road was, as she'd known it would be, an eyesore. Four of her apple trees had been cut down to make way for it: she'd have to hire someone with a chainsaw to come and saw them into logs. And two of the trees had been damaged, she saw now, their branches dangling limply, like broken arms. With a sigh, Río set her beach bag down on the slipway, and took off her sunglasses; as she did, she heard a voice from above shout, 'What the *fuck* is going on?'

Squinting against the sunlight, she shaded her eyes with a hand to see Shane standing on the sea wall of Coral Mansion, looking down at her.

'I'm going for a swim, that's what,' she told him.

'I don't mean that. I mean, who authorised some prick in a dozer to come and lay a hardcore track at the bottom of my garden?'

'Don't shout at me, Shane. Come down here if you want to talk.'

She watched as Shane leapt from the wall and started to stride down the orchard towards her, dust rising from the hardcore with each step he took.

'So? What's the story, Río?' he said, as he drew abreast with her. 'I came back from lunch the other day to find an access road running through my garden.'

'If you take a look at the title deeds, I think you'll find that that tranche of land belongs to me,' Río told him, coldly. 'It was necessary to lay a track through it to facilitate my husband's business.'

'His business?'

'His oyster-packing shed is up on the main road.'

'So how many times a day is your *husband* likely to be chugging along my boundary belching fumes from his tractor?'

'You'd need to ask him that.'

'There are laws about this kind of thing,' Shane told her. 'It's an infringement of my privacy, for starters—'

Río dismissed him with a baroque gesture of her hand. 'Build a wall. Grow a hedge. Erect a fence.'

'And then there's the pollution aspect.'

'Pollution?'

'The engine noise. The petrol fumes.'

'You're living in the country now, Shane. I think you'll find that the tractor is a fairly commonplace mode of transport here.'

'So I'm expected to relax on my deck with that buffoon perpetually trundling through my view, am I?'

261

'How dare you call Adair a buffoon! How *dare* you, Shane Byrne! He's ten times the man you are!' Río raised her hand to smack him, but Shane grabbed hold of her wrist.

'What happened, Río?' he hissed. 'Why did you do it? Why did you marry him?'

'I love him.'

Shane shook his head. 'I don't buy that. I don't buy that at all.'

'Let go of me,' said Río. 'You're hurting me, Shane.'

'Not as badly as you hurt me. Broken hearts don't mend easily. But then you don't know that, do you? Because you've never had one.' He glared into her eyes for a long moment, and then he released her wrist, turned, and strode back the way he'd come, leaving Río standing on the slipway with tears streaming down her face.

Oh! *Oh!* She knew too well the pain of a broken heart, for behind the cage of her ribs her heart felt as though it had been squeezed by a fist in a chainmail glove. Maybe . . . maybe she should confide in Shane, explain the reason behind her hasty decision to marry Adair? She owed him an apology, at the very least. She owed him *some* kind of explanation.

'Shane!' she called. But her voice was drowned out by the sound of an approaching engine. Looking up at the hardcore track, she saw Adair bouncing along it in his tractor, grinning broadly. Quickly, Río wiped the tears from her face with her towel.

'Off for a swim, my little mermaid?' Adair said, jocularly, as he drew near.

'No. The water's too cold,' she lied. 'Let me climb up beside you and you can give me a ride home.'

'Home again, home again, jiggedy jig!' quipped Adair. 'Better fasten your seat belt, Río! We're in for a bumpy ride!'

262

And as Río climbed aboard, she took one last look back up at Coral Mansion. Shane was nowhere to be seen. But there on the wall was a girl dressed in oversized workmen's overalls. Cat. Finn's friend, workmate, helpmeet . . . bedfellow? She, Río, had been all those things to Shane once. Now, she was just a housewife. Worse than that, she was a leisure lodge wife.

'"The little cat laughed to see such fun",' sang Cat on the wall. '"And the dish ran away with the tool".'

'Get back to work,' said Finn crossly, flicking a fragment of wooden dowling at her. 'And stop spying on people.'

'I'm not spying,' Cat told him. 'If I were crouched down behind the wall, peeping over, I'd be spying. I'm just standing here enjoying the view. Oh, look, there's our roving reporter, roving along the shore.' She pointed to where Keeley was strolling along the shoreline, talking on her phone. 'Roving. Roving! It's a daft word, ain't it? I mean, when would you ever use it, except for "roving reporter". You'd never say "I roved down the street", would you? And now there's Shane hoving into view. Hiya, Shane!'

But Shane just threw her a black look as he passed through into the house.

'He's in a bad mood,' observed Cat.

'Why?' asked Finn. 'Did you do something to annoy him?'

'Me? Never! I'm little Miss Sunshine. Hey, Keeley! Enjoying your rove?'

Below on the shore, Keeley paused in her roving and looked up. 'Hello there, Cat. How are you?'

'Wait there! I'm coming down.'

Cat slid off the wall and scampered down to join Keeley on the beach.

'Thanks for saying nice things about my paintings,' she said, admiring her reflection in Keeley's mirrored sunglasses.

'You're welcome. Is Shane happy with the piece?'

'Yeah. He's over the moon. Like the cow. And so will you be when I tell you who's arrived in Coral Mansion. It looks like you might have another worldwide exclusive on your hands.'

'Oh? Who?' asked Keeley.

'Elena Sweetman,' said Cat.

'No shit!'

'Yes shit.' Why did people wear mirrored sunglasses? wondered Cat. They were dead distracting, and she really wanted to concentrate on her spiel. 'Um. Sweetiepie's notoriously reclusive, as you probably know. But I think I might just be able to persuade her to talk to you.'

'Could you, Cat? That would be fantastic!'

'Text me your phone number. I'll have a word with her and get back to you. And I won't charge you an introduction fee if you give my paintings another big plug.'

'An introduction fee?'

'Yeah. A publicist would charge a fee for this kind of thing. Max Clifford didn't get rich by being selfless, did he? So, promise me that you'll rave on about my paintings, and I promise you an interview with Sweetie.'

Keeley looked uncertain. 'I . . . I don't really see how I could find a way of promoting your paintings in an interview with Elena Sweetman,' she said.

'Oh, you most definitely will be able to,' Cat told her, 'because she's going to be holding a big exhibition of my work when she goes back to LA, and inviting all the stars.'

'Is she really?'

'Yes. And all the proceeds are going to charity.'

'My word! That's remarkably altruistic of you, Cat.'

'I know. I'm a big-hearted gal. And like I say, I won't even charge you an introduction fee. Now, take down my number. It's 086 . . .'

When Cat had finished dictating her phone number to Keeley, she gave her a cheery salute, and danced back up to Coral Mansion, where Finn was leaning on a spade, waiting for her. 'Get back to work shovelling, Pusscat,' he said. 'You've done enough skiving for one day.'

Cat gave him an indignant look. 'All I did was have a bit of a rove,' she said. 'I wonder why so many dogs are called Rover? I mean, dogs don't really rove at all, do they? They stay at home mostly, or go for walks on leads, and that could hardly be described as proper roving. Cats are much more roving types than dogs. Aha! There you go! There's your new pet name for me, Finnster! I'm getting bored with Pusscat.'

'Sorry? What's your new pet name?'

Cat stood on tiptoe and gave him a kiss on the cheek. 'Rover, of course,' she said. And then she took the spade from Finn, and set to work. 'Did you give that ring to Shane, by the way? The one with the diamond?'

'Yes,' said Finn, gloomily.

'How did he take it?'

'With very bad grace.'

'So he didn't really want it back?'

Finn shrugged. 'I guess he doesn't know what to do with it.'

'If he really truly doesn't want it back, I know what he can do with it.'

'What?'

Cat sent Finn a dazzling smile over the spade handle. 'He can give it to me of course,' she said.

Chapter Eighteen

Keeley was in Ryan's corner shop, buying more cleaning products. Now that she had delivered her last 'Epiphany' and was a free agent (the interview with Shane had been very well received, Leo had told her, and sales figures for the *Insignia* had shot up that particular Sunday), she had the luxury of time on her hands. She had scrubbed her little cottage until it was cleaner than the house in the Mr Muscle ad, and she'd hung new curtains and bought new bed linen and lots of cushions and scented candles and pretty little jugs that she'd taken to filling with wild flowers. The place felt like home now, and after nearly a month in Lissamore Keeley was feeling less than enthusiastic about going back to her flat in Dublin, with its view of an identical apartment across the way, furnished – just as hers was – by Ikea, where the flowers came courtesy not of Mother Nature, but from M&S, and where there was no open fire in which to burn driftwood.

But beckon Dublin did. Keeley needed to forge some kind of financial future for herself, and the notion of becoming a literary agent was becoming more and more attractive. Most of the agents she knew seemed to spend most of their time in their French *gîtes* or their Tuscan villas, and if Keeley could set herself up with the help of Tony 'The Tiger' Baines, she liked to think that she could spend most of *her* time in her Coolnamara cottage.

In Lissamore, Keeley had settled into a brand new life. The cosmopolitan girl who had once partied and dined and experimented with sex toys with her very sophisticated, very married lover, had morphed into a singleton who was actually quite happy to be single. Her usual routine of book launches, exhibition openings and theatrical first nights had been supplanted by evenings spent in front of the fire with a book or a radio programme after a power-walk along a beach. Except her power-walks had become more like strolls, during which she listened to birdsong rather than news on her iPod, and took time out to peer into hedges and study cloud formations and breathe in the ozone. She was dressing differently, too. Instead of the smart-casual look she favoured in the city, she'd adopted a more feminine boho look – not dissimilar, she supposed, to the look espoused by Río Kinsella. She'd bought herself a pair of espadrilles and a pair of flowery-patterned wellingtons and a pair of walking boots and a pair of gaiters for hill-walking. She was even thinking of getting a dog, so that she'd have to go walking in all weathers. A dog would be company, too, for the long winter evenings. Or would it be cosier to curl up on her couch with a cat?

Speaking of which, she hadn't heard from that girl, Cat. She'd texted her her phone number, but had had no response, and on the couple of occasions that Keeley had tried contacting her, the phone just rang on and on, without even allowing her the option of leaving a voicemail. Oh well, Keeley had thought with a mental shrug, you win some, you lose some. Maybe the 'notoriously reclusive' Elena Sweetman had been immune to Cat's powers of persuasion, after all. And anyway, her final 'Epiphany' was done and dusted so there was no call for her to go trekking after celebrities any more. For which relief, much thanks . . .

'Grand day, thank God,' Mrs Ryan said, as Padraig Whelan, the tasty wild-haired fiddle player, came into the shop.

''Tis.'

Padraig joined Keeley in the cleaning products aisle, where he tossed a bottle of Ecover into his wire basket. On the shop radio, a female voiceover was waxing orgasmic over the cleaning prowess of Cif. Hm. Cif would do the job, but maybe Keeley should be going for the more ecologically friendly option, like Padraig? She had just helped herself to a bottle of natural wood floor soap and was perusing the label, trying not to be distracted by Padraig who had moved on to scented drawer liners (Gay! He was gay! Just her luck), when she saw on the other side of the aisle that Río Kinsella was doing her shopping too. Her new husband was going to be well fed, observed Keeley. Río's basket was piled with provender, including sausages and rashers and eggs and black pudding: Adair was clearly the kind of man who liked to start his day with a cooked breakfast. There was a tub of cream there, too, for his Crunchy Nut Cornflakes. Not great for the cholesterol, though.

Keeley wondered if it was maybe about time she had people round for supper. Maybe she should introduce herself to Río, and ask if she and Adair would like to come round some evening? It would be good to get to know Río. Keeley still didn't have any friends in the village, and she liked the look of Ms Kinsella and her gal pals.

She was just about to cross aisles and say hello, when the woman rhapsodising about Cif shut up, and a chirpy voice on the radio said: 'News hot in from Hollywood! Irish actor Shane Byrne and *Silver Vixens* star Elena Sweetman were married yesterday in the Little Wedding Chapel of the

268

Flowers in Las Vegas. Heartthrob Shane said in a press release—'

But Keeley wasn't to hear what heartthrob Shane said in his press release, because there came an enormous crash as Río Kinsella's wire basket fell to the floor.

'Río!' said Mrs Ryan, scurrying out from behind the till. 'Are you all right?'

'Río!' said Padraig, dropping his purse. 'What's the matter, love?'

Río looked like death, white-lipped and wretched. 'I'm fine,' she managed. 'I'm sorry about the mess. I'll pay for everything next time I'm in.' And then she fled the shop, leaving Mrs Ryan gazing after her, shaking her head in concern as cream and eggs spread in a thick puddle on the floor.

'Don't worry,' said Keeley, rounding the aisle and stooping to pick up the cartons. 'I'll help you clean it up.'

'It's not the spillage I'm worried about,' said Mrs Ryan. 'It's Río.' She and Padraig exchanged meaningful looks.

'I knew it would all end in tears,' said Padraig, shaking his head mournfully. 'That Shane!'

Cat was watching a re-run of *Silver Vixens* on Sky Plus. Finn had had the biggest plasma screen in the world installed in the entertainment suite of Coral Mansion, and in the evenings after work the pair of them would curl up on the leather upholstered sofa and surf channels looking for programmes about DIY disasters, which always cracked them up. Occasionally they'd come across old films featuring Shane before he'd got famous, which cracked them up even more, or Elena in her starlet phase looking so breathtakingly beautiful that Cat would press the pause button just so she could gaze at her idol. They'd seen footage of Shane and

269

Elena too, on the Smile channel, walking hand in hand at some red-carpet event, telling the world how happy they were, and smile, smile, smiling for the cameras.

So, sly boots Elena had been in love with Shane all along! Cat liked to think that maybe she had been instrumental in getting them together. While the pair had been staying in Coral Mansion, Cat had engineered it so that they were left to their own devices as often as possible. She had sent them off in a row boat to a neighbouring island to pick mushrooms, she had packed them off with a picnic to Coolnamara Strand, she had even played soppy love songs over the sound system when they were relaxing on the deck of an evening. And then, very early one morning, she had come across them on the beach, Shane with his head on Elena's lap while the actress stroked his hair and murmured words of wisdom in his ear: well, Cat couldn't actually hear the words, but she just knew that any words murmured by Elena would be wise.

And lo and behold! the very next day they had announced to Cat and Finn that they were going back to the States, and just a few days after that they had announced to the media that they'd been married in a place called the Little Chapel of the Flowers in Las Vegas.

The episode of *Silver Vixens* Cat was watching was called 'Love on the Rebound'. In it, Elena was getting married to someone who had been jilted, and really, wasn't life aping art, as they so often said? In real life Shane had crashed and burned and then bounced into Elena's arms like an India-rubber ball, the way Hugo had bounced into Oaf's arms after Paloma had left him – although of course, Elena was much more deserving of love than Oaf. Why did men do that rebound thing? Was it any port in a storm? Her father certainly needed looking after, and Cat thought rather begrudgingly that at least Oaf cooked and looked after the

270

house and stuff, even though it was perfectly obvious that she had only married Hugo for his money. It served her right that he was broke again. Why couldn't Hugo have married someone who was as good and true and beautiful as Paloma had been, someone more like Elena?

Elena had looked lovely on Smile TV, radiant in a silvery, shimmery gown, like a real star that had dropped down from heaven. And Shane had talked about how Elena had made an honest man of him at last (why did people who got married always say that? Cat had wondered), and had even managed to get in a plug for his next film.

And now Cat was hoping to hear from her new best friend about the exhibition of her paintings that she'd promised to organise in LA. She had taken the precaution of buying some sturdy cardboard tubes for her artwork in an art suppliers in Galway, and had carefully rolled up each painting and labelled each tube with her signature C A T, and packed them into the boot of Shane's hire car before the star-crossed lovers had taken off back to the States.

Cat had started painting again on her days off. She'd used some of the money that Elena had given her to pay for new art materials, and she was working a blinder. She routinely headed down to the beach to paint her landscapes, always including in them a tiny self-portrait – a little catgirl perched on a gate or on the branch of a tree or the roof of a cottage. Her days off were more frequent now that there was less pressure on Finn to get the house finished. They worked rather desultorily now, and Cat secretly wondered if there was really any point in refurbishing the great white elephant that was Coral Mansion. Was Shane ever going to come back here to live with his beautiful bride? And if so, how would Río countenance it? She'd seen Río crying on the beach the day she'd had the run-in with Shane about the access road through the orchard, and she suspected that there was unfinished business between Finn's parents. But she didn't think too hard about it. It made her much happier to think about Shane and Elena and the stellar Hollywood connections that were being lined up for her on the other side of the ocean.

Beside her, Finn's phone went. Cat glanced downward to see 'Izzy' on the display. She picked up the phone, pressed the green button, and said, 'Finn Byrne's phone. How may I help you?'

'Oh,' said Izzy. 'Is Finn there?'

'He's in the bath,' said Cat. 'Hold on. I'll take you to him.'

'Oh, no – please don't disturb him. I'll call back another time.'

'I'll take a message, if you like.'

'Um. No . . . it's nothing. Nothing important. Goodbye.'

'Goodbye.'

Hm. What did that Izzy want with her Finn, and should Cat tell him that she'd called? She didn't think she'd bother. After all, Izzy had said it wasn't important, and Finn was busy playing some game on his laptop. So Cat pressed 'play' on the remote control, and resumed watching *Silver Vixens* instead.

In the Bentley, Río and Adair were watching *Who Wants to be a Millionaire?*

'I think I might have a bash at going on this show,' said Adair. 'I've got all the questions right so far without having to lose a single lifeline.'

'But you *were* a millionaire once,' Río pointed out. 'And you didn't like it.'

'That's true. Maybe I should apply to go on *Mastermind* instead.'

'With your specialist subject being . . .?'

'My wife.'

Río smiled back at him. 'You're so sweet, Adair Bolger! OK, let's give it a bash. What's Río Kinsella's favourite colour?'

'Purple,' said Adair.

'You're right!' said Río, whose favourite colour was green. 'What's her favourite item of clothing?'

'Shoes!'

'Right again,' said Río, who seldom wore shoes except when she had to. 'What's her favourite food?'

'Oysters!'

'Clever clogs!' Río only ate oysters to please Adair. Shane would have known that her favourite food was fish and chips from McDonagh's in Galway. 'We should go on *Mr and Mrs*,' she said, linking her husband's arm.

Adair winced.

'I'm only joking! Adair? Adair, are you OK?' Río sat bolt upright, looking at him in concern. Adair's face had gone a strange shade of mottled grey and pink.

'Yes,' he said. 'I'm fine. Just a touch of – of heartburn or something.'

Río jumped to her feet. 'What can I get you? There's nothing in the house. Dammit – I should have got some antacid when I was in Ryan's the other day . . . I know! Celery. I used to chew on a celery stick when I was pregnant with Finn. I know it helped Fleur, too, when she was pregnant. And I mean, I know you're not pregnant, Adair, ha ha ha, but heartburn tends to affect pregnant women and someone told me that . . .'

And Río gabbled on and on as she took a head of celery from the fridge, cutting a stick from it and scrubbing it under the tap, because talking and keeping busy meant that she was buying time for Adair to manage the pain he was in. For Río knew that the pain he was suffering was not

273

heartburn. And she knew that while her back was turned, Adair would be helping himself to one of the pills that had been prescribed for him by the doctor he was seeing in Galway, the doctor he had visited today. He'd made some excuse about checking out the oyster scene in nearby Clarenbridge, but when Río had hit the redial button on the landline to talk to Dervla, it had been picked up not by her sister, but by a doctor's receptionist.

Some minutes later she was back sitting next to her husband on the sofa, and he was chewing obediently on his celery stick. His face was back to its normal colour, and the *Who Wants to be a Millionaire?* theme music was coming to an end; and then the ads came on, followed by a trailer for a forthcoming special on quickie weddings. Río found herself gabbling again as the voiceover said something about the most recent example being Shane Byrne and Elena Sweetman, trying to pretend she wasn't seeing a picture of her ex and his bride flashing up on the screen in front of her, gabbling, gabbling on about how Dervla had got married in the Little White Wedding chapel in Las Vegas and had gone on honeymoon to some place in Mexico, gabbling on and on and *on* about anything other than what was staring them both in the face.

There was no cure for heartburn in the Bentley. There was no cure for heartache, either. And there was certainly no cure for terminal cancer.

Later that evening, when Río couldn't sleep, the notion of lying beside her dying husband staring into the darkness for yet another night filled her with horror. Instead, she slid out of bed, and made her way down the shore to the slipway. There she stripped off and lowered herself into the frigid, wine-dark sea.

Swimming always did it for Río. She could swim off fear

274

and worry and stress and anger. The rhythmic strokes of her limbs as they levered her through the water, the regular in – two, three, four; out – two, three, four of her breath calmed her. It was as though her body was an engine working on autopilot, leaving her mind free to go problem-solving. But this time swimming didn't work. When she emerged from the sea, her mind was in turmoil still, and she could hear her father's voice reciting that line of Yeats over and over, the line from the poem called 'The Song of Wandering Aengus': *I went out to a hazel wood because a fire was in my head . . . because a fire was in my head . . . because a fire was in my head . . .*

And then, as she was standing naked on the beach, towelling herself dry, Río heard another voice – a high light voice, like that of a child, singing in the darkness over by Coral Mansion, singing what might be a nursery rhyme: and no amount of vigorous rubbing with a towel could take the chill from Río's bones, or assuage the ache in her heart, or put out the fire that was in her head.

Chapter Nineteen

Cat was painting. She'd decided today that she liked the way the shiny new fire-engine red tractor belonging to Adair Bolger kind of blinged against the rust-coloured bladderwrack exposed at low tide. At this distance, Adair's Massey Ferguson looked like a toy tractor, the kind that ought to be driven by someone in *Postman Pat*. She'd decided to call her painting 'Catgirl, Tractor and Bladderwrack'. She'd asked Finn to look up bladderwrack on the internet, and had so loved the other names it went by that she'd taken to chanting them like a mantra or a nursery rhyme: bladderwrack, black tang, rock rack, bladder fucus, dyers fucus, red fucus.

She was chanting this tongue twister now, as roving reporter Keeley Considine hove into view. Keeley was sporting flowery wellies today and a flowery pink frock: she looked like something off the cover of a glossy country lifestyle mag that Cat had seen in Eason's in Galway last week.

In Eason's, Cat had kept herself amused by looking at the covers of all the bestsellers on the bookshelves while Finn searched for the latest Super Mario game. She didn't think much of the jacket designs – why did so many women's books have cartoony type 'cute' crap going on? Cat remembered how Oaf had once remarked upon the genius of Jeffrey Fulvimari – who had designed Madonna's book jackets – and how she and her father had looked at each other and then looked back at Oaf with stark incomprehension.

The bestseller chart had made Cat wonder when Oaf's book was going to be out, and what it might be about. She remembered what Raoul had said, about not needing imagination to write a book any more, just needing to be a celebrity instead, and she thought how awful it must be to be challenged in the imagination department! Not to be able to escape to jungles or deserts or coral reefs or the Planet Zog or the Greek islands, or put yourself in a lighthouse or a circus ring or travelling on a jaunty red tractor, the way Cat was travelling now, in her painting. She added the last stroke of Anthracite Black to her Catgirl's pointy ears and set down her paintbrush just as Keeley Considine drew abreast with her.

'Hello, Cat,' said Keeley. 'You never returned my calls.'

'Well, there wasn't much point, was there? Elena disappeared before I could put the proposal to her. Fecking Shane jumped the gun by getting there first.'

Keeley looked bewildered for a moment, then laughed. 'Oh! I see what you mean. You mean he got in with his proposal first!'

'He sure did.'

Cat stepped back from her painting to give it a critical onceover. Hm. There was something missing, some imbalance there. A gull, perhaps, in the top left-hand corner? Or a cloud? A gull. Cat started rooting in her paintbox for a tube of Titanium White.

'That's a beauty.'

Keeley was looking at the painting over Cat's shoulder. Cat

wouldn't bother trying to sell it to her. She'd get more money if she pimped it via Elena to Johnny Depp or suchlike.

'I love the juxtaposition of the starkly modern gas-guzzling behemoth against the eternal vista of sky, sea and islands. You could call it "Time and Tide".'

Not just 'Catgirl, Tractor and Bladderwrack'?

'There's something so ephemeral, isn't there, about . . .' droned Keeley.

Cat zoned out. Keeley was going to start spouting artspeak, the most boring language on the face of the planet. Cat had sat at numerous dinner tables where some gobshite had bored the assembled company to death by analysing her father's paintings and showing off how many big words he knew. She had coped with it by falling asleep like the dormouse in *Alice in Wonderland*, her father had coped with it by getting blind drunk, and her mother hadn't coped at all. She'd just ended up having to put both of them to bed and do the washing up by herself.

'There was a wonderful exhibition at IMMA once – you may have seen it – in which half a dozen conceptual artists . . .'

Noooooooooooo! Cat would have to shut Keeley up, other-wise she'd be in danger of having Titanium White or Anthracite Black accidentally squeezed all over her lovely flowery frock.

'You know Oaf?' she said, interrupting Keeley's drone. 'Ophelia Gallagher? When's her book out?'

'Um, I think it's due out next month,' said Keeley. 'There's a sneak preview in this month's *RSVP* magazine.'

'There is? I must get Finn to buy a copy when he's next in town, so we can have a good laugh.'

Keeley looked puzzled. 'Why would you want to have a laugh at Ophelia Gallagher's book?'

'Oh, look! There's Finn over there!'

278

'What? Where?'

'Just getting on to that island, see, in the distance.' Cat pointed at a random drumlin. 'He's gone off fishing. We'll be having lemon sea trout with capers tonight courtesy of Marco Pierre White. Why do they say "cut capers" when they mean dancing? You're a writer; you should know.'

'Um. I think it comes from the Latin for "goat". Goats tend to leap about a lot.'

'I'm a Capricorn,' said Cat. 'What are you?'

'Virgo.'

Cat laughed.

The sound of the tractor starting up further down the beach made them turn. Adair waved at them from the driver's seat, the picture of the jolly farmer in his canary-yellow oilskin bib and braces.

'Oh! Hello, Adair!' called Keeley, waving back. 'I must go and have a word with him.'

'Río had several words with him earlier,' said Cat, who had overheard the pair rowing that morning. 'She was giving out about the fact that he was lugging sacks of oysters around by himself.'

'I thought he had employed someone to help him?'

'The lads have taken the day off. There's a big funeral in the village today. Río was on her way to it.'

After her spat with Adair earlier, Río had passed Cat by on her way along the beach. She had not done that rude thing of peering over Cat's shoulder at her easel, as Keeley had just done. Instead, she had smiled and said: 'You're working, so I won't interrupt. But maybe you'd call round and have a glass of wine with me some time? Finn will tell you where to find me.'

And Cat had said: 'I'd like that,' and watched as Río had kicked off her funeral footwear and continued on her way along the beach barefoot, pausing occasionally to pick up a shell or a pebble or some pretty scrap of flotsam.

'I saw the cortege earlier,' said Keeley. 'Looks like the whole village is on its way to that funeral. I wonder who died.'

'Dick Head.'

'I beg your pardon?'

'Richard Head. He was a local county councillor.'

It was true. For once, Cat wasn't winding Keeley up. Dick Head really was the name of the retired politico. A screech from above reminded her of her seagull. Squeezing a dollop of Titanium White on to her palette, she thought about adding a touch of Indian Yellow for the sunlight that was bouncing off its wings.

'I'd better leave you to it,' said Keeley. 'Enjoy your trout.'

'What?'

'The trout you're having for supper tonight.'

'Oh yeah.'

Cat picked up her paintbrush, squinted at the canvas, and then all she felt was comforting oblivion as she lost herself in her landscape.

'Help! Help, Cat – help! Over here!'

What? Who was over where, and who needed help? Cat came to, emerging from her painterly trance back into real life. Keeley was standing over by Adair's tractor, and Adair appeared to be asleep on a bed of seaweed. Setting down her paintbrush, Cat shielded her eyes with her hand.

'Do you have a phone?' Keeley was yelling.

Cat had no phone on her, and no idea where it was since she'd last spoken to Raoul about a week ago.

'Can you phone for an ambulance, Cat?' shouted Keeley. 'Quick!'

An ambulance! Something was wrong. Cat sprinted down

the beach, to where a distressed Keeley was crouching by Adair, checking to see if he was breathing.

'Is he dead?' asked Cat.

'No. I think he's had a stroke. We have to get him to hospital right now. Have you a phone?'

'No.'

'Fuck,' said Keeley. 'Neither have I. How stupid of me to leave it behind. Is there a landline at Coral Mansion?'

'No. There's broadband. Could we Skype?'

Keeley shook her head. 'No. That's no use, no use – too slow – the broadband connection's crap here. We'll have to try and do it ourselves.'

'Get him to hospital?'

'Yes.'

'How?'

'Have you a car?'

'No. Yes. Well, it's Finn's. I can't drive.'

'I can. Let's go.'

'How will we get him to the house?'

'We'll have to carry him somehow.'

'No way! He's too heavy. Let's put him in that wheelbarrow.'

'We can't do that!' protested Keeley. 'It's . . . it's undignified!'

'There's nothing dignified about dying on a beach. You take his feet. Come *on*!' commanded Cat.

Together they hoisted Adair up and into the wheelbarrow. He was surprisingly light for a big man, but it still took Keeley and Cat many long minutes to get him as far as the porte-cochere of the house where Finn's Renault was parked, and into the back seat. Cat ran into the kitchen, praying that the car keys would be where Finn usually left them, in the fruit bowl. They were.

'You stay with him in the back seat,' said Keeley, when Cat emerged from the house.

'What'll I do?' asked Cat, crawling in beside Adair while Keeley strapped herself into the driver's seat.

'Just hold his hand, and talk to him.'

So Cat did. She talked to Adair about Kylemore Abbey, the boarding school she'd been to, and the wild mountain goat that had followed the girls home one day, and slept on the backdoor mat for the best part of a week before a ranger from Coolnamara National Park had come to reclaim it. She talked about how she'd used to go climbing the mountains that were part of the school's grounds, and swimming in the lake there. And she talked too of the lake by the Crooked House, and how she'd swum there as a child, and sailed her little boat called *The Catkin* that she had painted pea-green like the one in 'The Owl and the Pussycat'. And she talked about the treehouse called the Heron's Nest that her mother had built for her, and how she and her mother had used to lie there at night, and how her mother would tell her stories.

'Would you like to hear one?' she asked Adair. 'I remember them all.'

And when she thought she saw Adair manage a nod and a kind of weird lopsided smile, Cat launched into one of the stories with which her mother had regaled her as a child, not just at bedtime or in the treehouse, but also during the time when Cat had had to spend many, many nights on and off for a year in a hospital bed with bandaged eyes after an accident with nitric acid. Her mother had often slept beside her, on a low camp bed, and Cat would lie with her hand dangling limply over the side of the mattress so that her mother could hold it while she told her the tale of the little Catgirl who lived in a fabulous palace called Sans Souci which was built by the King of Prussia to be his pleasure dome.

In Sans Souci – which was French, her mother had told her, for 'no worries' – Catgirl roamed from chamber to fabulous chamber through colonnaded galleries, accompanied by naughty cherubs who had flown down from the dome of the palace to befriend her. Outside, she explored the parklands: the richly decorated gazebos and temples and pavilions, the labyrinthine mazes, the greenhouses in which exotic fruits grew. Catgirl ate her fill of melons and peaches and figs and bananas, she kicked up sprays of water with the cupids in the fountains, and she swooped low over the terraced gardens with brightly coloured parrots and macaws, spitting cherry stones down on the heads of the courtiers as they ponced around below, paying obsequies to the king.

Her mother had painted such a vivid word picture of the palace that Cat felt as if she was actually living there, not lying blind and bandaged in a hospital called Sans Souci that smelt of disinfectant and boiled cabbage. It was the stories that had got her through that dark, dark time; the stories that she listened to still on the ancient Sony Walkman her mother had given her, stories she knew by heart.

She was in the middle of the story of Catgirl and the Monkey when Keeley pulled up at the main entrance to Galway University Hospital.

'I'll go get help,' Keely said. 'You stay here.'

Cat nodded, watching as Keeley sprinted into the foyer.

'Of course, Adair,' she resumed, 'Catgirl was very angry with the ape who had stolen her bananas. And she swore she'd get her revenge. And that night she waited until the king and his courtiers had gone to bed, and then she crept into the secret, cedar-lined library, and took a big, leather-bound book of magic from one of its cedar shelves, and leafed through it until she found the very spell she was looking for, the How to Be Revenged on Monkeys spell . . .'

And Cat carried on telling her story as she waited for the paramedics to come and take Adair away to perform CPR, and she knew even as they took him from the car and laid him on the gurney that there was no point in performing CPR, because just as she had been about to embark upon the spell that told you How to Be Revenged on Monkeys, Adair Bolger had laid his head on Cat's shoulder and died.

The place where they went to wait for news of Adair was horrible. The walls were snot-green, the plastic chairs grubby. The hospital smells made Cat feel sick, and brought back painful memories of bandages and needles and inedible food. She tried zoning out, but there was so much going on around them that escaping to a jungle or a lighthouse or a Greek island was out of the question. Keeley got coffee from a vending machine that was so disgusting it made Cat feel even sicker.

She hadn't told Keeley that she knew Adair was already dead. She felt that that was the kind of news that should be delivered by a healthcare professional. When did people stop calling hospital workers doctors and nurses and start calling them healthcare professionals instead, she wondered? And when did nurses stop wearing neat uniforms and start dressing in drab overalls? Some of the nurses were obese, she noticed. In fact, lots of the people sitting around the waiting area were obese. One child who was stuffing his face with Coke and crisps was clearly suffering from ADHD. He was lying on his back on the floor kicking his legs and embarrassing his mother. He was probably Special Needs, like her. Except Cat had never made a show of her mother when she'd been in hospital.

'So, you're Caitlín? Hugo Gallagher's daughter?' said Keeley, taking a sip of coffee and making a face when she got a load of how vile it was. 'I put two and two together when I heard you talking to Adair in the car.'

'Yes.'

'Why didn't you tell me, Cat? What made you keep it to yourself?'

'We're kind of estranged since he married Oaf. And if I'm going to make it as an artist I want it to be because of what I do in my own right, not because I'm somebody's daughter.'

'Well, you're doing that, all right. You've had amazing success. It looks like you can charge whatever you like for your paintings.'

'Yeah. I don't know where to draw the line, though. Excuse the pun. I mean, sooner or later I'm going to want to exhibit here in Ireland, and Irish buyers aren't going to have the same spending clout as Elena's pals. I'll have to decide on a ballpark figure.'

'That's when you're going to need an agent.'

'But they take like fifty per cent commission! My father hates his agent, but he can't do without him now. He's painting again, by the way.'

'Hugo is?'

'Yeah. My brother Raoul told me.' Raoul had told her last week that during a visit to the Crooked House, Hugo had been ensconced in his studio painting up a storm – much to Ophelia's relief.

'Does he often suffer from creative block?'

'The odd time. "Odd" being the operative word.'

'How does he get the flow going again?'

'Creative Ex-Lax. Why are you asking me?'

'Your father's very proud of you, you know,' remarked Keeley.

'He is?' Cat gave her a sceptical look.

'Yes. He told me he would have loved for you to illustrate Ophelia's book.'

'Ha! She wouldn't have asked me in a million years to illustrate her fucking book. She hates me. She's the genuine article.'

'What do you mean?'

'She's the original wicked stepmother. I bet she was all sweetness and light when you interviewed her though. She ain't a half bad actress. She certainly performed well enough to fool my dad. Oh – look! There she is, on the cover of *RSVP* magazine. That must be the one that has the preview of her book in.'

On the other side of the room, the mother of the ADHD boy was trying to calm him by reading to him. Was it Oaf's story, Cat wondered? She strained to listen, and then she heard the following words: '"The macaw kept up a running commentary as she flew with Pussy Willow over the pleasure garden. 'See, over there – that's where the king sits and plays Canasta. He cheats, you know . . .'"

Oh! *Oh!* '". . . but everybody pretends not to notice. The only person who stands up to him is the learned philosopher, Voltaire.'"Cat found herself automatically mouthing the words of the story that she knew by heart, the story her mother had told her all those years ago, the one that she told her still on those nights when Cat could not sleep and the yearning for her mother became so intense that she had to plug herself into the ancient Walkman on which Paloma had recorded the Sans Souci stories for her daughter. '"You'll get a load of the king playing his flute tonight in the music room. He plays really badly, but the lick-arse courtiers always ooh and ah. The monkey does a great impersonation of him . . .'"

'Sorry?' said Keeley. 'Are you talking to me, Cat?'

Cat didn't answer. She rose to her feet and crossed the room. 'Excuse me,' she said, taking the magazine from the startled woman, 'this is my story. It's mine.'

Keeley watched in astonishment as Cat rose to her feet and crossed the waiting room. 'Excuse me,' she said, taking the magazine from the startled woman, 'this is my story. It's mine.'

The woman clearly thought that Cat was mentally deranged, because – although her mouth went into an 'O' of surprise – she declined to protest. Cat returned to her seat, and sat with her eyes closed, holding the magazine against her chest.

'What's up, Cat?' asked Keeley gently.

'This isn't Oaf's story. It's mine. My mother made it for me when I was a little girl.'

Keeley felt the excited stirring she always got when scenting a scoop. 'Hang on. Are you telling me Ophelia has plagiarised it?'

'What's plagiarised mean?'

'Stolen.'

'Yes,' said Cat. 'She's stolen my story. I told you she was a wicked stepmother.'

'But what made her think she could get away with it?'

'Nobody else knows about it. Except me. Mama wrote the stories down in exercise books for me and me alone, but when it was obvious I was never going to be able to read them, she recorded them onto a Sony Walkman. I know them off by heart.'

'You're dyslexic, Cat?'

'I never learned to read properly.'

'So Ophelia presumed you'd never be able to read her stories—'

'They're not her stories!' hissed Cat. 'How many times do I have to say it? They're my stories!'

Cat laid the magazine on her lap, and Keeley looked at the cover, at the image of Ophelia smirking up at her. What a duplicitous bitch! What a cunning cow! She remembered the spiel Ophelia had spun her, about writing the book for her inner child, and felt a surge of indignation. She, Keeley, who prided herself on her insightful journalism, had been taken for a ride by an ex-bit-part actress and topless model whose real name was Tracey Spence. She had been duped and made a fool of. How dared she think she could get away with it! Keeley Considine was *nobody's* fool, and Tracey Spence, Ophelia Gallagher – Oaf! – would rue the day she'd concocted her lie-fest!

Turning to Cat, Keeley said: 'Doesn't your father know about the stories?'

'Him? No no no! I told you. Mama made them for me and me alone. They were our secret stories, to get us through the time in Sans Souci.'

'Sans Souci . . . you mean, the hospital?'

'Yes.'

Something about Cat's tone warned Keeley not to probe further.

'Ophelia's not going to get away with this, Cat,' she said, with assurance. 'Mark my words. Plagiarism is a serious crime. Her publishers are going to be very, very angry with her.'

'But how do we prove that she didn't write it?'

'I have an idea. Listen . . .'

Keeley took the magazine from Cat, finding the extract easily. Spread across five pages, were big colour pictures of Ophelia taken in various poses in the Crooked House: Ophelia at the piano, Ophelia with cupcakes in her kitchen,

Ophelia walking her Labrador . . . There was a cutesy illustration from the book, too, of Pussy Willow and the macaw.

'Pah!' said Cat, curling her lip at it. 'What a piece of crap. Catgirl doesn't look remotely like that.'

'Catgirl?'

'Catgirl is the star of the stories. Not Pussy Willow. Excuse me while I barf.'

'Listen,' said Keeley again, choosing a random paragraph. '"Pussy Willow – I mean, Catgirl – was standing on the roof of the palace . . ." Can you finish the sentence, Cat?'

'Of course I can,' said Cat, giving Keeley a disdainful look. '"Catgirl was standing on the roof of the palace, watching the monkey, who was today dressed in a little red suit and a fez." A fez is a hat with a tassel, like they wear in Egypt.'

'So, you really do know this book off by heart?'

'Yes.'

'Then we rest our case. Have you a lawyer, Cat?'

'No.'

'I do. We're going to take Ophelia Gallagher to the cleaners.'

'I don't want her money,' said Cat. 'I just want my story back.'

And I want to wipe that smirk off her face, thought Keeley, looking down at the magazine, and have one last *coup de théâtre* before I wave goodbye to the world of journalism and go looking for my first literary client. She smiled. She didn't have to look very hard. Her first client was sitting right here beside her. She was about to turn to Cat and ask if she had any qualms about exposing her father's wife as a con merchant, when a discreet cough made her look up.

'I have bad news, I'm afraid,' said the young intern. 'Your friend Adair Bolger didn't make it.'

And all thoughts of Ophelia Gallagher and revenge and money evaporated, as Keeley listened to the grave words that followed, and realised that she had just stared death in the face.

Chapter Twenty

I went out to the hazel wood,
Because a fire was in my head,
And cut and peeled a hazel wand,
And hooked a berry to a thread,
And when white moths were on the wing,
And moth-like stars were flickering out,
I dropped the berry in a stream
And caught a little silver trout.

When I had laid it on the floor
I went to blow the fire a-flame,
But something rustled on the floor,
And some one called me by my name:
It had become a glimmering girl
With apple blossoms in her hair
Who called me by my name and ran
And faded through the brightening air.

Though I am old with wandering
Through hollow lands and hilly lands,
I will find out where she has gone,
And kiss her lips and take her hands;
And walk among long dappled grass,

And pluck till time and times are done,
The silver apples of the moon,
The golden apples of the sun.

Río didn't know why she had chosen 'The Song of Wandering
Aengus' to read at Adair's funeral, until Fleur explained her
own subconscious to her.

'The fire in Adair's head was the stress he had been under,
when he went bust. He goes fishing – that's him buying his
oyster farm – and the fish he catches becomes a glimmering
girl. The glimmering girl is you, Río – his prize, with blossoms in your hair from your apple trees. You were his unat-
tainable ideal, he never dreamed that you would marry him.
And now he'll worship you until the end of eternity, and
walk with you through your beautiful orchard. You did a
wonderful thing, by marrying Adair Bolger, you know,
darling. You should be very proud of yourself.'

'I'm not proud of myself at all,' an anguished Río told
her. 'I should never have allowed him to lug those great heavy
bags around without help. I should have stayed with him
that day. I am wracked with guilt, Fleur. Wracked.'

'But think, Río! If he was already terminally ill, wasn't it
better that he went as he did, on a beach in glorious sunshine,
doing the job he'd always dreamed of doing? You once told
me that his real vocation in life was to be a fisherman. You
wanted him to die a happy man, and that's exactly what
happened. He'd achieved his ultimate dream of marrying
you!'

Río and Fleur were in Río's apartment, waiting for Dervla
to arrive. Río couldn't go back to the Bentley; she'd asked
Dervla to pick up her things and bring them back here,
where she belonged. The funeral was to take place tomorrow,
in the graveyard where Río and Dervla had buried their

parents. Río had liaised with Izzy on this, and Izzy had agreed that that was the final resting place her daddy would have chosen.

Río had invited Izzy to join them here for dinner tonight; Fleur had made cassoulet, and it was slow-cooking in the oven. Finn was due, too, and Río had asked him if he wanted to bring his new friend Cat, who had played such a blinder, helping Keeley get Adair to the hospital. But Cat had declined, and Río was glad about this because she didn't want to run the risk of Izzy being upset.

Poor Izzy! Her own mother wasn't going to be attending the funeral: her divorce from Adair had been acrimonious, and they hadn't spoken in years. Few of his old business associates would be attending either, according to Izzy. It looked like none of those threadbare, toothless Celtic Tigers could be arsed making the journey to the west coast to say goodbye to their erstwhile golf buddy. They were all soaking up the sun on some Costa somewhere.

Had Adair died happy? Río hoped so. She had found herself wondering, in the short time they'd lived in the Bentley, just how much longer he would have been able to continue masquerading as a well man. She'd noticed on occasion the expression on his face when he thought she wasn't looking – the expression that told her he was in considerable pain. And sometimes he had let a groan escape him, which he'd constantly claimed was merely down to heartburn. Pain made people tetchy, Río knew that from her own experience: in the months before her mother had died, she had become uncharacteristically irritable. Perhaps she and Adair might have started to bicker; perhaps his glass-half-full view of the world might have become skewed; perhaps the marriage would have gone pear-shaped, living as they were in such close proximity. You needed space, for a relationship to flourish. Maybe Fleur was right, and it was good that Adair had had a sudden, unexpected death.

Since their marriage had not been registered, he had left her nothing in his will. Not that Río cared. Everything had gone to Izzy – who had very decently volunteered to cover the cost of the funeral. Funerals were expensive and Izzy wanted the best for her daddy, who was now lying in a silk-lined Italian ash coffin in a funeral parlour in Galway, waiting to be transported to Lissamore in the morning. Río had arranged to travel into the city with Izzy: neither woman wanted Adair to embark upon his final journey alone.

The fire in Río's head had burnt out. Ashes were all that remained, and the embers of love.

As she reached for the wine bottle, the doorbell went. It would be Dervla, come to bring Río her belongings from the Bentley. Releasing the lock on the front door, Río went to the top of the stairs to welcome her sister. But when she looked down at the landing below it wasn't Dervla she saw climbing the stairs to her apartment. It was Shane.

'*Acushla*,' he said, when he joined her at the top of the staircase. 'I am so sorry for your trouble.'

And Shane enfolded her in his arms and allowed Río to cry like a little girl. It was the first time she had cried since her wedding day.

Cat didn't accompany Finn to the funeral. She had other things on her mind, and plans to hatch with Keeley. But first she wanted to check out a dreamboat.

She'd first seen her on the eve of Río's wedding, and had fantasised about her ever since. She was called *The Minx* and she was a classic twenty-nine-foot yacht. She'd been built in 1970, the present owner told her, and she had journeyed down from Stockholm seven years ago, and sailed on Coolnamara Bay every summer since.

'Construction?' asked Cat.

'Mahogany on oak ribs. Teak deck.'

'Weight?'

'Three and a half ton.'

'Mind if I take a look around?'

'Be my guest.'

Cat explored the little boat with mounting excitement, ticking things off on a mental checklist as she went. Autopilot? Check. Solar battery charger? Check. Navigation lights? Check. Sail furling system? Check. Satnav? Check.

Below, in the compact fore cabin, were two berths, and two more in the saloon, which also housed a galley with sink. *The Minx* was well fitted out with shelves, a folding chart table, and a chain locker. Her upholstery was pristine, she had been scrubbed to within an inch of her life: she was in shipshape nick.

Cat climbed back on deck with a fluttery heart, trying not to look too lovestruck.

'How much?' she asked.

'Twelve grand.'

'The mast needs repairing above the spreaders.'

'Consider it done.'

'The price is still too high.'

'I'm in no hurry to sell.'

Cat shrugged, and climbed back onto the quayside, expecting – as she sauntered off in the direction of the corner shop – to hear the man call after her, expecting him to drop his price. But the call didn't come.

On the noticeboard in Ryan's, more boats were on offer. *The Merlin* could be had for nine thousand, *Rum Runner* for nine and a half. But neither *The Merlin* nor *Rum*

Runner did anything for Cat. She wanted *The Minx* so badly it hurt.

She was painstakingly deciphering the details of *The Gina* – 2 bat-ter-ies, amp-meter, sep-tic tank and toi-let, depth sound-er, v-d-o log-ic log, 2 an-chors, chain and warp – when Keeley came into the shop.

'How was the funeral?' Cat asked.

'Bloody awful,' said Keeley in an undertone, so that Mrs Ryan couldn't hear. 'Loads of Río's friends came, but hardly any of Adair's. A journalist mate of mine wrote an article recently about ex-Celtic Tiger CEOs becoming social outcasts, and it looks like he was right.'

'Oh! Poor Adair!' lamented Cat. Although she hadn't attended the funeral – Cat just didn't *do* funerals – she had dressed in black today, to honour the memory of the man who had died in her arms. It was the little black party frock she had bought to wear for Adair and Río's wedding, just last month. How ironic that she should be wearing it again so soon, on such a very different occasion.

'Río tried to read a Yeats poem, but she couldn't manage it, and Shane had to take over,' Keeley told her.

'Shane? Why Shane?'

'Well, he is a professional actor. And you could tell that he couldn't bear to see Río in such a state: he just *had* to help her. He read the poem beautifully, I have to say. Are you thinking of buying something?' Keeley nodded at the noticeboard.

'No. I'm thinking of putting up a notice myself, for a web designer. I'd like to be able to showcase my paintings.'

'That's a bloody good idea, Cat. I can help with the wording, if you like. I'll write a lovely eulogy for you.'

Cat remembered the eulogy that Keeley had come droning out with the other day on the beach – all that crap about time and tide and behemoths (whatever they were), and said, 'No, thanks.' And then, when Keeley looked put out, Cat felt a bit sorry for her, and added by way of improvisation, 'I like to think the paintings tell their own story. Didn't someone say something once about a picture being worth a thousand words?'

'Napoleon said it. *Un bon croquis vaut mieux qu'un long discours*. Talking of stories, I had a word with my solicitor. He says you're going to have to act fast, to get an embargo put on Ophelia's book.' Cat gave her a look. '*Your* book,' Keeley amended.

'OK,' said Cat. 'Let's go there now.'

'Go where?'

'To the Crooked House, to confront Oaf. You'll take me, won't you? It would mean another scoop for your paper. I'm responsible for giving you a lot of them, aren't I?'

'Don't you . . . well, don't you think we should have a solicitor with us?' suggested Keeley.

'What do we need a solicitor for? It's what they call an open and shut case, ain't it? Oaf doesn't have a leg to stand on. Solicitors cost money, and I'm not about to spend a load of my hard-earned dosh on one.'

'But when you go to court—'

'Court? Who said anything about going to court? I'm not going to a court of law. That would be a complete bore and a waste of time and money. I told you before, I just want my stories back. I don't want Oaf to have them.'

'But you could sue Ophelia for megabucks, Cat!'

'She doesn't have megabucks. Presumably she's gonna have to pay back her advance to her publishers when the shit hits the fan. And then she'll be poor again, and Hugo'll have to sell a load of his new paintings to pay for the court case, and that doesn't make sense. I don't need my dad's money any more. I can make my own way in the world. Plus they've got a new baby coming, and babies are expensive.'

'That's very generous-spirited of you, Cat.'

Cat laughed. 'I don't know about that. I'm just not prepared to stoop to Oaf's level, you know? Let's go.'

'Where?'

'To the Crooked House, of course. Fancy an ice?' Cat marched up to the counter, where Mrs Ryan was shaking her head lugubriously.

'Dreadful business about Adair Bolger, wasn't it? I understand you took him to the hospital.'

'Yeah, I did. Two 99s, please, Mrs Ryan. And a pack of Pleasuremax Durex.'

Cat asked Keeley to go via Coral Mansion. She wanted to pick up her Walkman and the cassette recordings of her mother's story, as evidence of Oaf's plagiarism. There was no one around: Shane and Finn were at the post-funeral party that Río was throwing in O'Toole's. Before leaving the house through the kitchen, Cat wrote a note for Finn, which she propped against the fruit bowl. 'GON ON A JONT' it read. She didn't care to elaborate about her jaunt. It was nobody's business bar hers. And Keeley's, she supposed. It was good of Keeley to offer to help, but she reckoned the journo wasn't doing it out of the goodness of her heart. She was just after another world exclusive story.

The drive to the Crooked House took more than an hour, during which time Keeley listened to political pundits droning on the radio, and Cat visited her favourite places in her head. The Planet Zog, the coral reef, that Greek island . . . As they approached the house, Cat saw to her surprise that there were cars parked all along the driveway. Posh cars, mostly.

'Seems there's a party in progress,' remarked Keeley. 'Wow.

298

There's some dignitary in attendance, by the look of things. That's got to be a government Merc. It's unlikely we'll get a parking space anywhere.'

Cat looked in the direction indicated by Keeley. A sleek black Mercedes was pulled up outside the entrance, a chauffeur in the driver's seat.

'I know where you can park,' said Cat. 'Go on round to the back of the house.'

As Keeley manoeuvred her Ka past the Merc, a goon with a security badge stepped forward. 'I'm sorry, Miss,' he said, when Keeley pulled down the window. 'You can't go that way.'

'Why not?' asked Cat, leaning over from the passenger seat.

'Parking's restricted to the main driveway. And may I ask if you have an official invitation?'

'I don't need an invitation to anything in this house,' Cat told him. 'My dad lives here.'

'You're the daughter of the house?'

'No. I'm the daughter of my dad. Let us through, mook.'

'I'm not sure I like your attitude, Miss. May I ask you for your ID?'

'Don't be ridiculous,' said Cat, who had just caught sight of her father through the open front door of the house. 'I don't need ID to get into my family home.' She opened the door and made for the front steps. 'Hey – Hugo!' she yelled. 'Call off your guard dog and let me in.'

'Miss . . . Miss!' shouted the mook.

'It's cool.' Hugo emerged from the house and addressed the security man. 'This is my girl. How are you, Catkin?' He put an arm around her shoulders, and Cat saw that there was paint on his hands. She breathed in the familiar scent of Windsor & Newton as he stooped to kiss her, and knew

299

all was well in Hugo's world now that he was painting again. 'Don't tell me Ophelia relented and invited you to her birthday party after all?' he asked.

'It's Oaf's birthday? Well, knock me sideways with a shuttlecock. I'd never have guessed she had so many friends.'

'Try and be mindful of your manners, Caitlín. What brings you home, then, if you haven't come to help us celebrate?'

'I'm here to cause trouble.'

Hugo smiled down at her approvingly. 'Of course you are. How did you get here?'

'Keeley Considine drove me.'

'Keeley Considine? Why does that name sound familiar?'

'You met her when she came to interview Oaf for the *Sunday Insignia*. There she is, in that green car. Can you help her find a parking space? I told her to go on round to the stable block, but that ape won't let her pass.'

Hugo glanced down at Keeley, whose progress was still being blocked by security. 'It'd be easier if she backed down the drive. The stable block's been converted into party central. I'll take care of her.'

Cat watched as Hugo descended the steps, then slipped into the house and went straight up the two bockety staircases that led to Hugo's studio.

The moment the door closed behind her, she was a child again, assailed by the scents and the sounds and the colours that meant her father was at work and at peace. Linseed oil and French cigarette smoke. Stan Getz on the sound system. The colours he'd taught her, that she could chant off by heart like a mantra. Monestial Blue, Yellow Ochre, Raw Sienna. Chinese White, Burnt Umber, Rose Madder. Crimson Lake, Red Vermilion, Permanent Magenta. Hugo's paintings were stacked around the room, glowing with all those shades, and myriad more.

Walking the length of the room, Cat felt as though she were moving through a wash of colour, and memories came back in a rush. Her father, cigarette between his lips, hog-hair brush between his fingers, squinting at a canvas. Her mother, wineglass in hand, laughing with her head thrown back. Both of them, wrapped in each other's arms, slow-dancing to Ella Fitzgerald, moonlight streaming in through the studio skylight above.

Those were the happy days, the state-of-grace days, the halcyon days before alcohol had claimed her father and disillusion, her mother. Those were the days when to live in the Crooked House had been a wondrous thing, when her father had helped her paint pictures and her mother had told her endless stories, and both of them had delighted in their only daughter, who was the most beautiful, talented, intelligent, imaginative, intrepid girl on the face of the planet. And then, of course, shortly after Hugo had made his first major sale, the accident had happened that had put Cat in hospital, and everything had changed.

Hugo had blamed himself, but it hadn't really been his fault. It had been Cat's curiosity on a day when, bored by grown-up conversation over endless bottles of wine at a lunch party given by an artist friend of her parents, she had gone to explore the studio at the bottom of the garden. The artist was experimenting with etching, a discipline unknown to Cat, who thought all art was processed through the medium of paint. She wasn't to know that etching was a rather more complicated business involving nitric acid. Her screams had brought Hugo and Paloma running, and after that she remembered very little – just the pain and the sensation of being scooped up and hearing voices shouting and sirens wailing and then the hospital smells and the pain and the needles and the darkness and the pain that lasted

301

on and off for a year until new corneas were grafted over the scar tissue. And the stories, of course. She remembered the stories very well.

On the far wall of the studio, a familiar portrait hung. It showed Cat and her father and mother and half-brother together, regarding the viewer dispassionately. Paloma was wearing a yellow dress that Cat remembered so well she could almost smell the perfume that clung to it, the chypre and jasmine and oakmoss that compounded Mitsouko. Raoul wore a T-shirt with 'Fuck Art – Let's Dance!' emblazoned on it, Hugo a faded indigo blue French workman's shirt, and Cat duckling-patterned dungarees and a cardigan her grandmother had knitted for her from leaf-green cotton bouclé. Hugo had nicknamed the painting 'The Smugs', because they were, after all, the happiest family that ever were. Happy Families. She remembered a rhyme Raoul had made up one Christmas, to make her laugh: *Mr Chip the Carpenter, Mr Pipe the Plumber; happy families do not last, life really is a bummer.*

Cat wondered if her new sibling would be a boy or a girl. Would Ophelia produce another half-brother for Cat, or a new half-sister – another Gallagher girl? Whichever, she wished the infant well. She had no axe to grind with Ophelia's sprog. In her present serene mood, she even bore Oaf herself no ill will. But – and now Cat screwed her resolution to the sticking place – *her stepmother would not steal her stories*, and it was time to tell her so.

Taking one last look at the portrait, Cat turned on the heel of her black Doc Marten boot, and set off to find the party.

Chapter Twenty-One

'Keeley! So glad you could make it! I wasn't sure whether or not you were still contactable at your *Insignia* email address.'

Keeley had to presume that she'd been sent an invitation to Ophelia's party: she hadn't been able to access her email lately on account of her dodgy broadband connection; she was also fearful of finding mail there from Leo scheduling a pay rise for her if she stayed on with the *Insignia*. She'd had a couple of phone calls from him, hinting that a pay hike could be in the offing (this when virtually everyone else she knew was taking pay cuts!) and during which he'd tried to initiate phone sex. He had been hard to resist. Leo was *very* good at phone sex.

'Thanks, Ophelia,' she told her hostess. 'You're looking great.'

It was true. Ophelia had about her that bloom that so many attribute to pregnant women, and which so few pregnant women are actually ever blessed with, since most are perpetually knackered.

'Your *Insignia* piece was lovely. Thank you,' said Ophelia.

'You're welcome.' Keeley privately thought that the piece was a rather anodyne puff, and not her best effort. In retrospect, she wished she'd come down harder on her interviewee.

'It's just a shame they ran with it so early. The book won't hit the shelves until next month. Would you care for an advance copy?'

'I'd love one,' said Keeley, feeling a twinge of *Schadenfreude*. She knew damn well that the book wouldn't be hitting the shelves next month, but she wasn't about to let Ophelia know that her career as a children's author was about to crash and burn before it had even been launched. She wondered where Cat the avenging angel had got to. Keeley hadn't seen her since she had joined the party half an hour ago. Nor was there any sign of Hugo.

A marquee had been set up to house Ophelia's birthday celebrations in the stableyard to the rear of the Crooked House. It was heaving with the kind of names seen in the more upmarket periodicals: movers and shakers from the legal world, a couple of well-known actors, a boy band member, a television presenter, a government minister (who really shouldn't be using a state car to attend a private function, Keeley observed) and a fashion designer. Keeley had interviewed several of those present for her 'Epiphany' column, and those she hadn't were trying to catch her eye, clearly intent on fishing for an 'Epiphany' of their own. Over by the drinks table, a famous artist was deep in discussion with an even more famous poet; over by the canapés, a celebrity chef was deep in discussion with a renowned restaurateur; and over by the stage a journalist colleague of Keeley's was observing the goings-on with a view to a kill.

'Allow me to introduce you to my editor,' said Ophelia, steering Keeley in the direction of a formidable-looking woman who reminded Keeley of Meryl Streep in *The Devil Wears Prada*. She looked as if she should be editing Salman Rushdie as opposed to an ex-actress purveyor of children's fiction. But if Keeley had learned anything in her career, it was never to judge a book by its cover. Speaking of which, Keeley had spotted an actress famous for her audio book recordings some minutes earlier, perusing a copy of Ophelia's book with its cutesy cover image of Pussy Willow, and Cat's voice had come back to her, dripping with disgust as it had the other day in the A&E department of Galway University Hospital: *Catgirl doesn't look remotely like that* . . . The book's jacket also had the title emblazoned upon it in a bubblegum-pink font: 'Pussy Willow and the Pleasure Palace of Peachy Stuff'. It was a pretty execrable title, thought Keeley. Kind of Harry Potter meets Barbie.

As she exchanged small talk with Ophelia's editor, Keeley felt the stirrings of excitement in the pit of her belly; she badly wanted to make a pre-emptive strike. Instead of 'How was your journey over from London?' she wanted to be able to say: 'I've got a potential publishing coup for you!' Instead of 'The Dordogne? How lovely!' she wanted to be able to say: 'I've got a marketing sensation on my hands!' Instead of 'The Frankfurt Book Fair?', she wanted to be able to say: 'We're going to head for the top of the bestseller list faster than you can say Exocet missile!'

But her cue to initiate dialogue had not yet come. She could look forward to having that particular conversation on a more appropriate occasion. In the meantime, it was Cat Gallagher's prerogative to shout 'Action!', and call some shots.

She made her entrance in unobtrusive fashion. Well, as unobtrusive as a stunning girl dressed in a Harajuku frock, black bandana and Doc Martens can get. The boy band member performed a classic double take, as did the famous artist, and the fashion designer looked as if she wanted to start stealing some style. But Ophelia didn't notice Cat. She was on her way up to the stage where the band had launched into 'Happy Birthday to You', graciously accepting compliments and bestowing smiles as she went.

'Hello, everyone, and welcome to my birthday party,' she said, when the band finally finished telling her what a jolly good fellow she was. 'I won't make a long speech because I have no talent as a speech maker. I'm glad to say though, that I've discovered I do have talent as a storyteller. And today I got the best birthday present imaginable – advance copies of my first book. Look! Isn't it pretty!' Ophelia raised aloft the copy she was holding, so that her audience could admire it. And admire it they did. There were cheers and wolf whistles, and another round of 'For She's a Jolly Good Fellow', and then someone called out: 'Treat us to an extract!' and someone else said 'Yes! Do! Tell us a story!' and suddenly the entire company was exhorting Ophelia to read to them from her book.

Ophelia demurred beautifully, lowering her eyes and blushing becomingly before acceding to the demands of her public, and as she began, Keeley knew with the certainty of a soothsayer what was coming next.

'Once upon a time . . .' said Ophelia, 'in a faraway place and a faraway era—'

'There was a girl who was more of a cat than a child.' By the entrance to the marquee, Cat took up the story in a high, clear voice. 'She didn't have a name because she had no parents to give her one. No parents that she knew of, at any rate. So everyone just called her Catgirl.'

The crowd parted as Cat peeled herself away from the doorway and proceeded to saunter towards her stepmother on the stage. Keeley found herself smiling at the expressions on the faces of the assembled party guests, who clearly assumed that this was some kind of charming familial double act.

306

'Catgirl was clever,' continued Cat. 'She was so clever that the learned philosopher Voltaire used to ask her for advice. And that was how she ended up living in the fabulous palace that belonged to a great king, the palace called Sans Souci, where painted cherubs came to life and parrots strutted their stuff among the cherry trees.'

On the stage, Ophelia stiffened. Keeley could tell from the look in her eyes that she knew she'd been hoist on her own petard. But Ophelia was nothing if not resilient. She stapled a smile onto her face and said, 'My stepdaughter just loves to make mischief! Don't you, Caitlín?'

'Shakespeare calls it "michin malecho".'

'You're an authority on Shakespeare, are you?' asked Ophelia, sweetly.

'I'm not an authority on anything. As you know, I can't even read. But I have a facility for learning by rote, the old-fashioned way. My dad used to read me Shakespeare. And Yeats. And Heaney. All the greats. And my mama used to read me stories that she made up herself. They were beautiful stories. But you know that, don't you?'

'I haven't a clue what you're talking about.'

'I'm talking about my legacy. You have no right to do what you're doing.'

'What am I doing? Having a little fun is all, spreading a little happiness. That's what Pussy Willow's all about.'

'Pussy Willow doesn't exist.'

'Oh, lighten up why don't you, sweetie?'

'You know what I mean, Oaf.'

Ophelia suddenly broke out of character. 'Don't call me that!' she snapped, as Cat stepped on to the stage. 'Anyway, what do you think *you're* doing? Come to scrounge off your daddy again? You're not welcome here.'

'I bet I'm not.'

307

'I think you should make yourself scarce, Caitlín.'

'I bet you do,' said Cat, advancing on her stepmother.

'So, get your ass out of my party.'

'Not before I claim what's rightfully mine,' returned Cat.

'What are you on about?'

'I'm here to reclaim Catgirl,' said Cat, taking the book from Ophelia.

'What on earth makes you think—'

'This is my story. It's mine.'

'You're talking crap.'

'You may be fluent,' said Cat, calmly, 'but crap ain't a lingo I'm familiar with.'

'Give that back!' Ophelia lunged for the book, but Cat took evasive action. 'What the fuck do you think you're doing, Caitlín? You're mad. You're stark, staring mad!'

'Yes,' agreed Cat. 'I am mad. I am mad as hell.'

And then she descended from the stage, and left the marquee.

As she wove her way through the crowd, Ophelia's editor said 'Excuse me! Is this some kind of prank?' and one of the actors said 'Hey! It's an installation, man!' and the other actor said 'Right!', starting to applaud, and people began taking photographs, while the journalist took a notepad from her handbag and began scribbling.

'Too late,' Keeley told her colleague with a smile. 'I've got the insider gen.'

'No shit! Share!'

'Not a chance,' said Keeley. 'It's gonna be one hell of a scoop. You could call it a *coup de grâce*.'

She watched as Cat crossed the stable yard to the back door of the Crooked House and went inside. In the marquee the furore began to subside, but before it died down completely, something even more theatrical happened. On the stage, Ophelia clutched her belly, doubled over, and gave an anguished cry.

Alarmed, the band leader rushed forward. 'Is there a doctor in the house?' he shouted.

'Yes, I'm a doctor! What is it?' A party guest, a distinguished surgeon who had clearly been waiting all his life to be asked that particular question, leapt onto the stage.

'The baby!' whimpered a white-faced Ophelia. 'The baby's coming! Call an ambulance! Get me out of here now!'

Keeley sensed that Cat would want to be left alone for a while. So before she set out to find her, she took the opportunity to approach the Prada-clad she-devil, who was looking uncharacteristically unnerved.

'As Ophelia's editor, I think you ought to know what's going on,' said Keeley, segueing into confidante mode.

'That would be a help. Can you enlighten me?'

'Yes. But now is not the time. Do you have a card?'

A classy, gold embossed card was produced from a Birkin bag, which also contained, Keeley deduced from a glimpse of lurid pink, a copy of *Pussy Willow and the Pleasure Palace of Peachy Stuff*. The legend read: 'Camilla Featherstonehaugh. Commissioning Editor, Pandora Publications.'

Featherstonehaugh! Keeley was glad that she knew that the surname was pronounced 'Fanshaw' by posh people, just as Cholmondely was pronounced 'Chumly'. 'When will you be back in London, Camilla?' she asked.

'I'm flying back tomorrow. But I shan't be in the office for quite some time. We're off to the Dordogne . . .'

Keeley didn't think so!

'. . . but if you can throw some light on all this, I'd certainly appreciate it. Perhaps you could contact me on my BlackBerry?'

'I'll do that,' said Keeley. 'I'll call you tomorrow.'

'And you are . . .?'

'Keeley Considine.'

The woman's rather arrogant demeanour changed abruptly. 'Oh! Keeley Considine! I'm very pleased to meet you. You wrote that marvellous piece on Ophelia, didn't you?'

'Yes. That's actually one of the last pieces I'll be writing. I'm changing career.'

'Oh? Into what area are you thinking of moving?'

'I've been doing some homework on becoming a literary agent.'

'Really? Well, if I can be of any help I'd be delighted.' Camilla didn't look delighted. She was probably sick to death of literary agents pimping their clients to her.

'Thank you.'

'Do you know who that girl was?' asked Camilla, clearly anxious to return to the subject with which she was currently principally concerned. 'That extraordinary-looking girl who caused all the fracas?'

'Yes. I do.'

'What's her name?'

'Her name,' said Keeley, 'is Cat Gallagher.' And it's one you won't be likely to forget, she wanted to add, but didn't.

'Cat Gallagher. Is she anything to Hugo?'

Keeley hesitated. She remembered what Cat had said to her in A&E that time, about how she'd kept her identity to herself because she wanted to be successful in her own right, not on account of who her father was. And then she realised that there was no point in keeping it a secret any longer, because the events that had unfurled here today at Ophelia's birthday party would soon be making headlines all over the world, thanks to Twitter.

'Yes. She's Hugo's daughter.'

'Oh. Her mother died, didn't she?'

'Yes. When Cat was just fourteen.'

'Tragic.'

'Yes. It was tragic.'

And Keeley wondered just how gutted Camilla would feel when she learned that the bubblegum-pink book cocooned in her Birkin bag had not, in fact, been penned by the fragrant Ophelia Gallagher, but by a woman who had been dead for over five years.

Later that evening, Keeley poured herself a glass of wine, and went into the garden to replay the events of the day, fast-forwarding the boring bits (although now she thought about it, there hadn't been any boring bits), and pressing 'pause' on any she wanted to dwell on.

She had found Cat sitting in the kitchen of the Crooked House, drinking lemonade and talking to the catering staff. She didn't appear at all fazed by the showdown in the marquee, and had been amenable to Keeley's suggestion that maybe it was time to hit the road. But when they were halfway down the drive, Cat had suddenly said: 'Stop.'

'What's up?' Keeley asked.

'You go on. I'm going to stay here.'

'You're going back to the house?'

'No. I'm staying here.' And Cat had pointed at a tree.

'I'm not sure I understand . . .'

'It's my old treehouse. I'm going to spend the night in it.'

'Oh. OK. You're sure?'

'Yes.'

'How will you get yourself back to Lissamore?'

'I'll hitch.'

Keeley had been about to say, 'You'll do no such thing!' but had stopped herself just in time. She wasn't Cat's mother, and she wasn't Cat's keeper. Instead she said, 'Give me a call any time if you want me to come and pick you up.'

'No. I won't do that,' replied Cat. 'Goodbye. Thanks for the lift.'

'You're welcome.'

And Keeley had watched as Cat slid out of the passenger seat and put her foot on the first rung of the rope ladder that would take her high into the branches of an ancient cypress.

'Wait!' Keeley called, reaching for the copy of *Pussy Willow and the Pleasure Palace of Peachy Stuff* that she'd left lying on the passenger seat. 'Your book!'

'I don't want it,' said Cat. 'I've got the real thing.' And she held up a brick-like Walkman and gave Keeley a hawk-like look from those astonishing Armada eyes before disappearing into her treehouse.

What an extraordinary girl Cat was, Keeley thought now, as she sipped her wine in the gloaming, listening to a bee doing overtime in the lavender. And how very, very marketable. She had read random pages of *Catgirl*, and knew that it passed more than muster. That, and the fact that the story behind the story was so compelling, meant that it was destined for bestsellerdom. She would set her alarm for early the next morning and speed-read the book from cover to cover before phoning Camilla Featherstonehaugh. She would have read *Pussy Wil – Catgirl* tonight, if she hadn't been so wired to the moon by today's events. Right now, she just needed to regroup.

Cat, of course, would illustrate the book herself. That was axiomatic. She wouldn't need an image overhaul because her look was so fresh and funky. She clearly had no problems with public speaking or she couldn't have done what she had done today in front of an audience of such

312

scarily illustrious individuals. She was talented, articulate and beautiful in a *jolie-laide* way. She was a PR's dream, she was her own USP, and Keeley was very, very lucky to have found her.

And as for the wicked stepmother? Keeley had phoned the Crooked House an hour earlier and spoken to one of the catering staff, who had told her that Mrs Gallagher was well, thank God, and that the premature arrival of her baby had been a false alarm. Why am I not surprised? Keeley had thought. Going into premature labour had been a convenient way for Ophelia to sidestep the fan when the shit hit it. But tomorrow she was going to have to face up to the inconvenient truth about the authorship of her book. Keeley almost felt sorry for her.

Beside her, her phone sounded. 'Leo' lit up in the display. Keeley relented, and answered.

'You've been stonewalling me,' he said.

'I've been busy.'

'Let me guess. You've bought chickens and you're growing your own veg.'

'I haven't become completely countrified, Leo. There's still a lot of city girl in me. And I'll be back in the big smoke next week.'

'I'm glad to hear it. What's bringing you back?'

'I'm setting up a business.'

'What class of a business?'

'I'm sold on the idea of setting up a literary agency. What do you think?'

There was a pause while Leo considered. 'I think it's a great idea,' he said. 'I think you'd make a very good agent. Aside from the fact that you're an omnivorous reader, you have contacts in the publishing world – that's invaluable – and you're smart, you're ambitious, and you drive a hard bargain. I suppose you haven't reconsidered my last offer?'

'Sorry, Leo. I need a change. And working with you is *so* not a good idea.'

'You know I'd leave Rachel tomorrow if it weren't for the kids, Keeley.'

'I know you would.'

Actually, Keeley wasn't at all sure about that. It was the perennial excuse trotted out by married men: it had been the excuse that her editor in New York had come up with too. She wondered how many times women all over the world had heard it. Now that she thought about it, it would make a good title for a novel. *If It Weren't for the Kids . . .*

'Can I see you when you're in town?' Leo asked.

Oh, God. This was going to be tough. 'No.'

'Not even for old times' sake?'

'That's facile, Leo.'

'Yeah. I guess it is.' He sounded uncharacteristically down-beat. 'But you'll stay in touch?'

'Of course. I need brains to pick, and yours are the best brains I know.'

It was true. Leo had the brains of a *Mastermind* champion and the nous of Simon Cowell. He'd been right when he'd said that connections were invaluable: Keeley was excep-tionally lucky that Leo was so extremely well-connected.

'I'll help you in any way I can. Have you spoken to Tony Baines?'

'Yes. He's been very helpful. He compares the slush pile to panning for gold. It can be tedious and frustrating and time-consuming, but when you come across a new talent it's like hitting pay dirt.'

'I'll let you have my novel when it's finished.'

Keeley smiled. Leo had been writing a novel for the past five years. 'Thanks. I won't hold my breath.'

'Are you going to actively seek clients, Keeley, or do you want to discourage no-hopers?'

'I'll encourage submissions to begin with. Once I'm established I can afford to be pickier. I've actually already got my first client.'

'Who's the lucky man or woman?'

'It's a girl.'

'Good looking?'

'Very.'

'That's one of the first questions publishers ask agents now, did you know that? Marketability is almost more important than talent.'

Keeley felt ineffably smug. 'This girl has both, in spades,' she told him.

'Who is she?'

'I'm not saying anything just yet. I don't want to hex myself – she may decide to go with someone more established. But we've a good rapport, so, fingers crossed.'

'Who are you approaching first?'

'Camilla Featherstonehaugh.'

'Wow! I am impressed, Ms Considine. You're taking aim at the big guns.'

'I might as well start at the top.'

'What about practical considerations? You're going to need premises.'

'I know. I'm being very brave and going for an upmarket address.'

'City Centre?'

'Yes. Dame Street. I'm recceing an office on Monday.'

'Expensive.'

'I want to keep up appearances. This is going to be a classy set-up.'

'Maybe you should put an ad in one of the trade papers to trumpet your arrival.'

'Good idea.' Keeley checked out the level of her wineglass. She'd have one more before bed, she decided.

'Are you going to hire a PA?' Leo asked.

'I thought about poaching Donna.'

'Hands off my Donna, Keeley! She's the best PA in the business.'

'Relax. I only said it to annoy. I'm interviewing some people next week.'

'We could do lunch next week. There's no harm in that.'

'Leo! Stop it.'

'Keeley. Lovely Keeley.' The timbre of Leo's voice had changed: it became lower, darker, more dangerously charged, and Keeley knew what was coming next.

'What are you wearing this evening, darling? That under-wear I bought you for your birthday? That bra with the rose buds? Those knickers with the ribbons?'

'Leo. No dice.'

He laughed – a laugh that Keeley found way too seductive – and then resumed his siren song. 'Lace-topped hold-ups? And what about those love eggs I gave you, hm? I bet your pelvic floor muscles are in pretty good shape now, baby. Don't you just love it when—'

Keeley pressed 'End Call' with a firm thumb. She couldn't allow Leo to insinuate himself back into her life. She needed to make a fresh start.

Turning off her phone, she got to her feet and went back into the cottage to replenish her wineglass. She was hugely excited now about her brand new career. She'd taken a virtual tour of the office space in Dame Street, and it certainly looked the business. It was in a restored period building, fully modernised with CCTV camera coverage, an air-conditioned meeting room and state-of-the-art IT systems. It was carpeted in cream, with cream suede sofas, and floor-to-ceiling display units in pale sycamore and glass. Keeley imagined the books of all the authors she was going to represent lining the shelves, covers facing out to show them to their best advantage.

She wondered what Cat would come up with as the cover look for *Pussy Willow and the Pleasure Palace of Peachy Stuff.* (Oh! That title *had* to go!) Something as vibrant and eye-catching, she hoped, as the painting she was looking at now, the one Cat had finally agreed to sell her for six hundred euros. Keeley had made a bloody good investment, she realised. In the not-too-distant future, this painting would be worth substantially more. Like her father, Cat would be able to name her price.

Wandering back out into the garden, she activated her iPad, and Googled 'literary agents' for the second time that evening. She routinely checked out other agents' sites now, and had found that a lot of them seemed rather dull: old-fashioned and lacking in imagination. She'd have to get a cracking web designer on board. Keeley knew she wanted something different, something that said, 'Choose Me!' She'd also have to get some really classy business cards designed, something along the lines of Camilla Featherstonehaugh's.

Picking up a pen and a notepad, she began to word her ad using an established agent's blurb as a template. 'Keeley Considine, literary agent. I can help you devise a strategy at every stage of the writing process, from conception, to editorial, to publication. I am seeking long-term relationships with writers and illustrators whose career paths I can forge and whose talent I can nurture.'

Nah. Ditch that. Scribbling it out, she substituted: 'Keeley Considine, authors' agent. I kick ass, and I take no prisoners.'

Then she leaned back in her chair, reached for her wineglass and smiled into the gloaming.

In the gloaming, Cat was lying on the floor of her treehouse, listening to her mother's voice. Paloma had included lullabies on the tape, and snatches of songs and nursery rhymes. 'Hey diddle diddle'. 'Old King Cole'. 'Star light, star bright'. All the classics. But the one that was playing in Cat's head now was 'Rockabye Baby'.

Chapter Twenty-Two

Cast a cold eye on life, on death. Horseman, pass by.

Those were the words that were carved on Yeats' tombstone. Her father had used to utter those eleven words lugubriously when he was in his cups: unsurprisingly, therefore, they were words that Río had heard frequently while she was growing up.

The words that were to be carved on Adair's tombstone had not yet been finalised, but Río would allow Izzy to make the ultimate decision. She felt she had no claim on either Adair's life or his death: she felt she had barely known him. She felt like a faux wife, an impostor, a selkie. Oh, God! That was what Adair had called her once, years before, when they had first embarked upon their on/off courtship. *You're beautiful, Río. A goddess. A selkie . . .*

The selkie shed her seal skin in order to seduce men. Legend had it that if a man could steal a selkie's pelt, he could prevent her from ever returning to the sea. Without her pelt, trapped on land, the selkie swims forever in the shallows, yearning to return to her ocean home. That, now, was how Río felt. She had a yearning for home, but the hellish thing was that she didn't know where home was. It certainly wasn't the Bentley, and while she loved her little eyrie on the main street of the village, it bore no relation to

319

the home she had dreamed of living in as a child, the little house with a ticking clock and speckled china on the dresser and a fire burning in the hearth and a pile of turf against the gable wall.

Right now Río was in the home that had been bought for her by Shane, the home that would never be hers. It had gone through so many incarnations. Coral Cottage. The Villa Felicity. Coral Mansion. A motley crew had taken possession of the house this evening: Río, Finn, Shane and Izzy. Wanting to keep herself occupied, Izzy had cooked up a storm in the state-of-the-art kitchen earlier – roast chicken with new potatoes and summer herb dressing courtesy of Rachel Allen – and now the four of them were sitting on the deck, nursing wineglasses.

Shane had been a rock. After Adair's sendoff in O'Toole's yesterday, he had gone to Río's apartment and packed a bag for her, and then he'd driven her in his hire car to Coral Mansion. He'd allowed Río to cry herself ugly, he'd given her a foot massage, he'd made her cheese on toast, and he'd tucked her up in bed. 'You'd make somebody a great husband,' she told him as he'd kissed her on the forehead, and they'd both laughed until the tears came. Shane had slept beside her in the bed, but there had been no question of amorous activity. It was purely so that Río did not have to lie there alone.

She'd hoped he would come. And in a way, she hadn't been surprised when she'd opened the door to her apartment and found him there on the stairs, because Shane had always been there for her when she'd needed him. And when she'd asked about Elena, and how his new wife felt about him jetting off halfway round the world on a mercy mission to an old flame he had said, 'Elena told me she'd respect me more if I came than if I stayed away. She knew what a lonely time you were in for, and that you needed more men in your life right now than just the one.' And when Río had looked puzzled, Shane had reminded her that Finn was a man now, not a little boy.

And now Río was lying alone with her thoughts on the recliner at the far end of the deck, listening to Shane and Finn and Izzy hatching plans for the future. She knew that Izzy was the type to just get on with things: that was why she'd insisted on cooking for them all earlier. Izzy had been solely responsible for organising the funeral, and the aftermath in O'Toole's, and she'd already talked to an auctioneer about the viability of selling the oyster farm as a going concern. She'd done her homework – Adair's business had been doing better than expected. He'd been selling oysters not only locally to eateries like O'Toole's and Coolnamara Castle, but had been exporting them too, to the UK and France, and Izzy had announced with pride that her daddy had been hoping to take part in the famous oyster festival in Clarenbridge later that year. Busy Izzy was all go. It was her way of coping with grief.

Río, on the other hand, just wanted to die.

'This place would never have been viable as a scuba-dive venture, Iz,' Finn was telling Izzy on the other end of the deck. 'It would make more sense to refurbish the old place on Inishclare. The visibility's much better there – you sometimes get a red tide on this side of the bay, and there's too much weed.'

'But there's a pool here for confined water training,' Izzy pointed out.

'C'mon, Iz! Let's face it – how many people are going to come to the west of Ireland to learn to dive? The kind of diver we're after is the seasoned one, who can handle dry suits, and who's into wrecks and deep dives. Kids nowadays go to warmer climates to train. We'd never have attracted amateurs. What do you call them? Debutantes?'

'Dilettantes.'

'And if you were going to turn this joint into a dedicated dive resort you'd have to hire staff. Gardeners, chefs, cleaners,' observed Shane. 'Chambermaids in frilly frocks with petticoats.'

'Yeah,' concurred Finn. 'Can you imagine the cost involved? It just wouldn't make financial sense, Iz. And we'd have had to buy Ma's orchard—'

'Nobody's buying my orchard,' Río told them.

'I know, Ma. And I wouldn't dream of asking you to sell, now your market garden's established.'

There was a pause, and then Izzy said, 'I could do the food, if we set up a scuba centre. I have my cert from Ballymaloe. That could be a real selling point, Finn. Divers are always starving after a day spent blowing bubbles.'

Río heard Finn laugh. 'You're talking about it as though we were really going to do it,' he said.

'Well, why not?'

'Hello? You have a job in Dublin. And Dad's promised to line up more stunt work for me in LA.'

'Lucky you, to have a challenging job.' Izzy sounded glum.

'Don't you enjoy what you do, Izzy?' asked Shane.

'No. I'm good at it, but I hate my job. I just *hate* it. And I saw what doing a job that you hate did to Daddy. It killed him. And I have no intention of dying without having a little fun in my life. It could be fun, Finn, couldn't it?'

'Could we afford it?' Finn's voice was dubious. 'I have no money.'

'I have,' said Shane. 'I'm fucking loaded. I'll buy shares in your dive outfit.'

'Would you, Shane?' said Izzy. 'Maybe you could go

guarantor, or something? We won't be entirely without capital. I'll have money from the sale of the oyster farm—'

'*If* you can sell it,' said Finn.

'Oh, don't be so negative!' Izzy told him. 'And I have a trust fund that Daddy set up for me, that kicks in on his . . . on his death.'

It was brave of Izzy to use the 'D' word, Río thought. Most people who had spoken to her yesterday at Adair's funeral had used euphemisms like 'passing' or 'at rest', or that one that she especially hated – 'gone to a better place'. But then, Izzy *was* brave. She and Río had had their run-ins in the past, but beneath the spoilt princess façade, Izzy reminded Río of a little bantam cock, feisty and full of fighting spirit. She and Finn had been good together. Maybe they *should* have a stab at setting up a business. A business here, in Lissamore, meant that Río would have her son near her indefinitely. And Finn was the only man in Río's life, now and forever. Had been since he was born, and would be until the day she died.

She wondered what had happened to his current girl-friend: Finn had said something about Cat going off on a jaunt, and that he didn't know when she'd be back. Río wondered how the girl would feel if she came back to find Isabella ensconced in the house. Finn had invited Izzy to stay when he'd learned that she was holed up in a local B&B, not in Coolnamara Castle, as he'd assumed. A B&B was no place for a girl who'd just lost her daddy.

'A trust fund? I thought your dad was broke,' said Finn, cautiously.

'You know Daddy. He had ways and means.'

Izzy said it with great pride. Ways and means, thought Río, like the ways and means of numerous other developers who'd prospered during the years of the Celtic Tiger and who were now residing in their villas in Spain and Portugal, thanks to NAMA and the put-upon Irish taxpayers who had had to bail out the big boys, the bankers and the builders. Just how legit had Adair's business dealings been? Río realised now that she really, really hadn't had a clue about the man she had married. Had there been shady stuff – offshore accounts and tax breaks and all the kinds of nefarious goings-on that Joe Citizen wouldn't have a clue about, but which were standard behaviour for the kind of movers and shakers that Adair had fraternised with? And then Río remembered that none of those movers and shakers had bothered to attend their buddy's funeral yesterday. Izzy was right. *Gather ye rosebuds while ye may.*

'We could go over tomorrow,' Izzy said.

'Go over where?' asked Finn.

'To Inishclare, and check out the old dive centre. I wonder why nobody snapped it up before now?'

'Because nobody's mad enough to plough money into the leisure industry in the current economic climate,' said Shane.

'You are,' Izzy pointed out.

'That's true. But then, I have money to burn.'

'There's a pun there somewhere, Shane Byrne,' said Izzy, 'but I'm too knackered to go looking for it.'

'I'm knackered too,' said Finn. 'Maybe we should call it a day. Beddy-byes! Come on, you. You deserve some sweet dreams.' And Finn held out a hand to Izzy, and hauled her to her feet.

'There's a pun there somewhere, Shane Byrne, but I'm too knackered to go looking for it.'

'I'm knackered too. Maybe we should call it a day. Beddy-byes! Come on, you. You deserve some sweet dreams.'

Then there was silence, apart from the hush-hush lullaby wash of the waves on the shore.

324

Below the sea wall, Cat was sitting motionless, legs hugged against her chest, chin on her knees. She'd been there for some time, listening to the plans being hatched above, about reinstating the old scuba-dive joint on Inishclare island.

So. Izzy and Finn were going into business together – and by the sound of it, they were going beddy-byes together as well. Oh, well. All good things come to an end, and she'd known that Finn wasn't forever: Finn was just for fun. And it had been fun, while it lasted.

Cat had walked the last mile of the journey back to Coral Mansion along the shore, having said farewell to her lift in the village. A dude had picked her up, and made it clear that he was interested. She'd allowed him to key her phone number into his Nokia, making sure that she substituted a '6' for '9'. Nobody had Cat's number, except Raoul. And – now that she thought of it – Keeley Considine had it, too. But that was no bad thing. Keeley might be useful at some time in the future, if Cat wanted publicity to sell more paintings.

Cat was hungry, not having eaten since the breakfast she had taken with her father in the Crooked House. She'd moseyed up there from her treehouse at around eight o'clock that morning and, having ascertained that Ophelia was tucked up in bed after her baby scare, had accepted Hugo's invitation to join him in what he'd called his 'repast'.

Her father had done the thing he was so good at – scrambled eggs with cheese and bacon on toast: the breakfast he'd used to cook for her as a child. And they'd had a grand chat. They'd talked about their mutual loathing for conceptual art, and they'd talked about Raoul, and they'd talked about Paloma. And Hugo understood – of course he did – why Cat had had to do the thing she'd done yesterday.

'It was your story, baby, and no one else's. It was really

stupid of Ophelia to think that she could get away with it. She underestimated you – and nobody should underestimate my Catgirl.'

'That's not what you thought once upon a time,' Cat had told him. 'You didn't have a very high opinion of my intellect when you were home-schooling me.'

'Oh, Catkin! That's because I'm not a teacher. I don't have the patience for it. I should never have taken on the responsibility of educating you, but somebody had to do it. And I was scared – so scared that if you went to a state school you'd have ended up on drugs – a corner girl, lost, a loner. That would have been textbook, given your circumstances, given all the shit you'd gone through. And given the fact that your father's a substance abuser. Jesus Christ!' Hugo had slumped so much his face had almost hit his scrambled eggs. 'I've been a crap father.'

'Yeah, you were pretty crap all right,' said Cat. 'But you were good about sending me money, when you had it. Thanks for that.'

'I'm painting again. I'll have a show soon – I'll send you a bonanza.'

'Nah. Don't worry about me, Hugo. I'm managing. I've sold a few paintings myself.'

'That's my girl!' Hugo rose to his feet and fetched a tea caddy from a cupboard. He opened it and took out a wad of cash. 'How much do you charge?'

'Three grand per canvas.'

'I'll commission two,' said Hugo, peeling off banknotes.

Cat accepted them, then handed some back. 'Special price. Family discount. I'll get them to you as soon as they're finished.'

'Done deal.'

And Cat had said: 'One day, maybe we'll show together.'

And Hugo had said: 'Let's shake on it. Here's to our first group exhibit.'

And now Cat was sitting on the beach, hatching plans of her own that would rival those of Izzy and Finn. Rising to her feet, she made for the gate that led into Río's orchard, vaulted it, and set off up the slope towards Coral Mansion. On the deck, Río was lying fast asleep on a recliner. Shane was sitting at the table, wineglass and bottle in front of him, smoking a joint.

'Shit!' he said, when Cat sat down opposite him. 'You gave me a fright. Where the fuck did you come from?'

'I'm like the Cheshire Cat in *Alice in Wonderland*,' Cat told him. 'I tend to materialise from nowhere.'

'I like your dress.'

'Thanks.'

'Fancy a toke?'

'No, thanks. But I'd like some wine.'

'Stay where you are. I'll get you a glass.'

Shane disappeared into the house, and Cat sat back in her chair, regarding the sky over the bay. It was a clear night, and all the constellations were out. The Plough. Canis Major, Canis Minor, Cassiopeia. Cat could navigate her way to her Greek island by that stellar map in the sky. She could set sail to Byzantium, if she liked, as Yeats had claimed to do in one of the poems her father had used to read her.

It had been good to talk to Hugo today. It had been good to be able to tell him that he didn't have to look out for her any more, now that she was earning her own crust. It had been good to see the look of pride in his eyes. But then, she knew that her father had always been proud of her. He just hadn't been very good at talking about his feelings, like most men. Cat guessed that that was a trait she'd inherited from him. She had never been touchy-feely, like the girls at her boarding school, who had talked endlessly about the pyjama parties they held during holidays when they'd watch rom coms and gorge on cupcakes and paint each other's nails and giggle over the text messages they'd send to boys. Cat had longed for a mate with whom she could compare the cut of a spinnaker, the shape of a keel. Someone who didn't mind getting their hands dirty. Someone like Finn. Finn would have become a great mate, had they more time to get to know each other. But Cat knew that, while the sex had been very, very good, she wasn't right for Finn in a romantic sense. She had known from the first time she'd heard him talk about Izzy that whatever he had had going on with her was as good as it could ever get for him. And wasn't it right that, with one of the main men gone from her life, Izzy should look for her own port in a storm? Finn could be that for her. Maybe Cat could send them a painting as a wedding present.

Shane was back with the wineglass. He poured, then passed an envelope across the table to her.

'What's that?' asked Cat.

'It's the proceeds from the sale of your paintings,' said Shane. 'Elena knew you'd prefer payment in cash.'

'Wow.' Cat hefted the envelope in her hand. 'I must have sold a fair few. Feels good.'

'Time to get cracking on some more,' Shane said, with a yawn. 'What'll I do about Sleeping Beauty over there? Should I wake her?' He indicated Río with a nod of his head.

'No. Cover her with a pashmina or something. There's nothing worse than being woken up when you're dog-tired, and told to lay your head somewhere else.'

'You sound like you're talking from experience.'

'I am. I've done my fair share of sleeping rough.'

'You can afford hotel rooms from now on, Catkin. Or a

deposit on a little flat somewhere. There are a lot of dollars in that envelope.'

Cat laughed. 'I've better things to spend my money on than hotel rooms and mortgages,' she said, draining her wine and rising to her feet. 'Good night, Shane. It was nice knowing you.'

And Cat scooped up the envelope on the table, and took herself off into Coral Mansion, detouring via the kitchen to pen some notes on a Post-It pad before helping herself to a chicken leg and an apple.

Upstairs, in the bedroom she'd earmarked as hers – the one she didn't share with Finn – she packed her backpack methodically, rolling items of clothing into bundles so compact they could have been balled socks. Cat was a seasoned packer: she knew better than most how to travel light. Double checking that she hadn't forgotten anything in drawers, cupboards, under the bed – her compass, her Nalgene, her Swiss Army knife – she made for the balcony and the steps that would take her down to the garden. And then she halted, and struck a mental fist to her forehead. She had forgotten one of the most important tools of all. Setting her backpack down on the bottom step, she slinked back to the bedroom. On the window ledge, where she had carelessly left it after some work done several days ago, was her right-angled screwdriver.

Cat would need somewhere to sleep tonight.

Chapter Twenty-Three

Río woke to find that someone had laid her pashmina over her. There was no one else around: her menfolk must have retired. She slid off the recliner and eased herself into a stretch. Her body felt as though it didn't belong to her: she had an overwhelming longing to reclaim it. Unzipping her dress, she let it fall to the deck, and stepped out of it. Bra next, then knickers. The night air on her skin felt like a caress, the grass – when she stepped barefoot on to the floor of her orchard – like a merino carpet.

Beyond the orchard gate the susurration of the waves called to her. The water, as she waded in to waist level, was like cold silk. Plunging, Río swam several strokes underwater before surfacing to gulp lungfuls of salt air. Then she turned over on to her back and floated, gazing up at the star-spangled sky. The Plough. Canis Major, Canis Minor, Cassiopeia.

What was written in the stars for her? What did her destiny hold? Río wasn't superstitious, but right now destiny for her was a throw of the dice. Her life was a tabula rasa – a bit like those magic slates she'd played with as a child, the ones you drew upon and then wiped clean, so that you had a blank sheet upon which to draw something else. She thought of her sister, Dervla, who seemed to have everything mapped out. There was nothing haphazard in Dervla's universe. She had taken knocks in her time, sure, but Dervla was resilient, Dervla bounced back. She was busy, she was motivated. Fleur? Fleur had her shop to keep her occupied, but more importantly, Fleur had her baby, the dotiest of dotes to care for. As for Shane – he had his career, not to mention his beautiful new wife.

Shane had said something over supper earlier about finding Finn more stunt work in LA. If he did, that would mean that Río would be on her own again. She remembered when Finn had first left her, to go travelling, and the awful, awful aching emptiness that had claimed her then. Those days of being unable to get out of bed, to wash, to eat. The days when dying seemed a better option than living, the days of the Black Dog. And Río was full of fear suddenly, that the Black Dog might return and seek her out. The Black Dog liked company. She could see it now, hiding under Canis Major, winking at her.

How could she keep it at bay? Her orchard. Her painting. She'd have to work hard at nurturing her smallholding, and work hard at being creative. The Black Dog hated creativity. And because the Dog had a keen nose for physical frailty and would use it to his advantage, she would have to maintain the machine that was her body. Río would have to swim every day, come rain, come shine.

Right now, the flexing of her biceps, the tensing of her pectorals, the strain on her calf muscles as she turned and furrowed through the water felt good. She wanted to feel all her muscles tauten, all her sinews stretch, she wanted to feel the entire tissue of her body contract and expand as she tested it. She wanted to be comfortable in her own skin, she wanted to make her senses sing. She wanted to make love. *She wanted to make love . . .*

Río wanted Shane. She wanted him one last time.

He was waiting for her, on the shore, with her pashmina, and a towel.

Wordlessly, she took his hand as she emerged from the water, and together they walked into the orchard and found the tree under which Finn had been conceived. Río was trembling with cold, and with desire. Neither of them spoke as Shane spread the pashmina on the grass, and settled Río upon it, arranging her limbs just so. Her left leg crooked a little, her right arm outstretched, her left hand over her mons veneris. He stood over her for a long moment, looking down at her, taking her all in, and then he lowered himself to his knees and began to kiss her as he towelled her dry. He kissed her forehead first, and then he kissed her eyelids and her cheekbones and the tip of her nose and her chin. He kissed the hollow made by her collarbone, and then he kissed her nipples and her navel before removing her hand and kissing her sex. He angled her leg a little more so that he could kiss the soft place behind her knee, and then he kissed the dip below her ankle, and the arch of her foot and all ten of her toes. And by the time he'd finished kissing her all over, and she was wet only where she wanted to be, and her goosebumps were all gone, Río felt as though she had dissolved in water.

'You taste of salt,' he told her, as he entered her. 'You taste of the sea.'

But the salt that Shane tasted on his tongue when he trailed it along Río's cheekbone and traced the contour of her ear was not sea salt. It was the salt of her tears.

And later, when the glimmer of Canis Major, Canis Minor and Cassiopeia had evanesced in a sky the shade of faded denim, in a place somewhere between living and dying, Río told Shane how much she loved him, how she had always loved him, and how she always would.

*   *   *

Propped next to the fruit bowl in the kitchen of Coral Mansion was a note from Finn saying 'Iz & me gone to check out dive outfit on Inishclare. Iz says she'll bring back crab claws for lunch. Love you, Ma. Hi-five, Pa.'

'I'll do pancakes for breakfast,' said Shane, setting a cafetière on the table.

Río smiled up at him. 'With lemon and sugar?' she asked.

'Of course. And with honey from your beehives. If that ain't too OTT?'

'Not OTT at all. I'll need a big sugar rush to get me through the next few days. And lots of caffeine. Thank you. Thank you for everything, Shane.'

'Everything? What have I done?'

'You've looked after me. You've been there when I needed you.'

'Sure, I've always done that.'

'I know. Fleur said as much, just recently. She said that every woman should have a Shane in their lives.'

Shane looked horrified. 'Fleur? You've been talking girly stuff about me to your mates?'

Río laughed. 'Girly stuff! Don't imagine for a minute that we sit around over cupcakes and pink fizz and giggle and share sex tips.'

'Sex tips? Jesus – don't scare me, Río. What did you say to Fleur?'

'I said nothing. She just knew.'

'Knew what?'

'That I was still in love with you.'

'You are?'

Río threw him a look. 'I told you so, didn't I? Just as the sun was coming up this morning.'

'Yeah.' Shane looked uncomfortable. 'I kinda feel the same way, Río. I mean – I never stopped loving you.'

333

'I guess it's a bit like that Alanis Morissette song, isn't it?'

'What? Now you *are* going all girly on me.'

'"Isn't It Ironic?"'

'Isn't what ironic?'

'Oh, you're useless, Shane. You'd make a crap girl.'

'I'm glad to hear it.'

'And I was about to start a meaningful talk with you.'

'I don't do meaningful.'

'I know. I've just remembered. But we have to.'

'Have a meaningful talk?'

'Yes.'

'Oh, crap. You go first.'

Río plunged the cafetière, and poured them both very strong mugs of coffee. 'We shouldn't have done that.'

'Done what?'

'What we did earlier this morning.'

'Why not?'

'Because you are now a married man.'

'But I only married Elena on the rebound.'

Río covered her ears with her hands. 'Don't say that! That's a shocking thing to say.'

'It's true.'

'It doesn't matter. I don't want to hear it.'

'So just because you don't want to hear it means I can't say it?'

'Yes! I've gone through a really hard time recently.'

'And I haven't?'

Río stood up abruptly. 'OK. That is now officially the end of our meaningful conversation.'

'Just because you say so?'

'What? You want more?'

He skewered her with a look. 'Yes. I want to know why you married Adair.'

334

'I loved him.'

'You're a really rubbish liar, Río. You married him because you felt sorry for him, didn't you? Izzy told Finn that Adair would have been dead within the year – that he had pancreatic cancer. You knew that, didn't you?'

Río sat down again. 'Yes. I did know that.'

'You didn't love him.'

She shook her head. 'I . . . I guess I didn't love him, really. Not in the way I love you.'

'In other words, it was an act of charity.'

'No, no! Don't say that,' wailed Río. 'It diminishes him, and he was such a lovely man.'

'It was an act of charity, Río,' said Shane categorically. 'It was an incredibly altruistic thing to do, and very big of you. But you really didn't think it through, did you?'

'Think it through! There wasn't anything to think about. It was . . .' she made a helpless gesture with her hands '. . . impulsive of me, maybe.'

'And ruinous consequences are generally the result of impulsive gestures.'

'Oh, come on! What about you? I didn't know you were going to go and get married, you too! Why didn't you warn me?'

'And what would you have done? Would you have said "Oh, no, hang about, Shane. Just wait until I'm available when my hubby dies in a year's time."?'

Río wanted to slap him, but instead, she slumped. 'You're right. I'm sorry. I don't know what I would have done.'

Shane took a swig of coffee and set the mug down on the table with a thud. 'Fuck. It's like something out of a Greek tragedy, minus the ornate dialogue.' There was a long, loaded moment of silence before Shane said, rather sheepishly: 'I suppose we could just carry on the way we always have. As fuck buddies?'

335

Río threw him a look. 'Well, you sure are right about the dialogue, pal. Fuck buddies! That is *hideous*. That is *undignified*.'

'Sorry. You're right. And I couldn't do that to Ellie. If I'd married some plastic bimbo on the rebound, things would be simple. I mean, if I'd married someone like . . . um, Jordan, who'd love the publicity of a quickie divorce—'

Río couldn't help it. She started to laugh.

'What's so funny?' asked Shane.

'The idea of you marrying Jordan. Sorry for laughing, but there's not much else to laugh about right now.'

'No, there ain't.' He gave a humourless smile. 'Cat once suggested that we call this house "The Smugs", after some painting her dad did. We could call it "The Glums", now.'

'You've nothing to be glum about, really, Shane. Elena's a wonderful woman.'

'Yeah,' said Shane, glumly.

Río looked at him over the rim of her mug, assessing. Then: 'She really loves you, doesn't she?' she asked.

'Yeah. She told me she's been in love with me since we first met. But she always knew that you were The One. It wasn't until you married Adair that I became fair game.'

'She seduced you?'

'No. She . . . consoled me. She was a real port in a storm during those hellish few days after your wedding. And I found myself thinking about how pointless life is without a soul mate and a partner to share it with, and when I knew I couldn't have you, it just felt right to be with Elena. I seduced her.'

That wouldn't have been difficult, thought Río. Poor woman, loving Shane from a distance for all those years. Lucky woman, to have landed him at last! She remembered the picture she'd seen in *Hello!* magazine, of a stunning Elena with Shane at some red carpet event in LA. The smile

336

on her face had said it all: it was the blissed-out smile of a woman in love, a woman who'd bagged her main man.

Whereas love had only ever brought Río grief and heartache and tears. To express it in words less than ornate: love sucked.

'Did your assistant organise a flight for you?' she asked Shane.

'Yes.'

'When are you going back?'

'This afternoon.'

Río started to cry. 'Oh, no! How can I live without you in my life, you stupid person?'

'We've done it before, *acushla*.'

'It won't be the same. It just won't. Oh, God!' She dashed tears away with the back of her hand. 'What a stupid mewling crybaby I've turned into. I was feeling earlier that I was dissolved in water, and I am. I'm made of tears, like the man in that poem by Brendan Kennelly, the man made of rain.'

It was true. She remembered how the first verse of the poem went, and it seemed to her to express so precisely her feelings, that long poem written 'between living and dying', after open heart surgery. Because that was how Río felt now: she felt as though she were undergoing open heart surgery without an anaesthetic.

> 'What is my body?' I asked the man made of rain.
> 'A temple,' he said, 'and the shadow thrown
> by the temple, dreamfield, painbag, lovescene,
> hatestage . . .

Hatestage. That was the stage that Río was at now. She loved Shane so much she hated him. She hated him for loving her and leaving her and loving her still, and for leaving her again, and taking her heart with him. Her heart! Her heart was here. *Her heart was here.* Of the two men remaining in her life, it was Finn she loved the most; Finn was the one without whom she could not live. She was a lucky woman. She had a man in her life still.

'Don't take Finn with you to LA, Shane,' she said abruptly.

'What do you mean?'

'You said something last night about getting him more stunt work over there. I don't think I could bear it if he went away again. I don't think my heart can take any more cuts to it.'

Shane reached for her hand. 'Listen, to me, Rí,' he said. 'It's my turn to get meaningful, and for me "meaningful" means putting my money where my mouth is. If Finn and Izzy are serious about setting up this dive joint, I'll invest. That Izzy's real savvy. You know she has a degree in business studies? If they want a backer, I'm their man.'

Río clutched Shane's hand, then covered it with kisses. 'I love you. I *love* you!'

'There is a fly in the ointment, though,' he told her when she stopped kissing him. 'What about Finn's girlfriend?'

'You mean Izzy?' said Río, confused.

'No. I mean Cat. She came back last night, after you fell asleep on the terrace. If I were in her Doc Martens I wouldn't much like the idea of my boyfriend setting up a business with his ex.'

'I don't know Cat,' she said.

'You've never met her?'

'We said hello once. But she was painting, and I didn't want to disturb her.'

'She's a talented painter.'

'Yes. She is.'

And Río thought back to the cottage where she had first seen one of Cat's paintings – the one of the curious Catgirl

338

peering into a rock pool – and she remembered the vibrant acrylic that Izzy had bought for her father, so that he could have a beautiful view before his eyes even though The Bentley was parked in a junkyard, and she remembered how she, Río, had come across Adair once, sitting on an upturned crate in the derelict cottage, gazing at his view with his hands on his lap and a smile on his face, and how she had backed out of the cottage on soundless feet, and left him to his thoughts. And she knew now that she had been right to have married him.

Her phone started flashing at her.

'Go and introduce yourself,' suggested Shane, as she reached for it.

'Sorry?'

'Go and introduce yourself to Cat.'

'Where is she?'

'Upstairs, I guess.'

'I wouldn't want to disturb her,' said Río, checking out the display on her phone. Finn's name was illuminated; she picked up at once. 'Hey, darlin'. How's my main man?'

'It's looking good, Ma. If Da is serious about investing in the joint—'

'He is!'

'Then we could be in business by the New Year.'

'We?'

'Me and Iz.'

'Um. What about Cat?'

'Cat's gone.'

'Cat's gone? What do you mean?'

'All her stuff's gone. I went into her room this morning and there was nothing left.'

'How weird. Was . . . d'you think her nose was put out of joint?'

'What do you mean?'

'By Izzy.'

'By Izzy? Oh. I never thought of that. You mean, she might have thought that Izzy and me were – you know . . .'

'Yes, Finn.'

Why were men so *thick*? She glanced across the table at Shane, who had taken up a pen and was defacing a photograph of George Clooney on last week's *Sunday Insignia*.

'Anyway, the only thing she left was a painting for Elena,' said Finn. 'And an envelope of cash for me.'

'Why did she leave you money?'

'To pay for the iPod she nicked from me.'

'And what makes you think the painting's for Elena?'

'Because it's a portrait of her. Cat did it when she was staying here. I saw it on the table in the hall when we left this morning. Where were you, by the way?'

'Oh . . .' Río got up from the table. 'Your dad and I . . . went for a walk.'

She looked at Shane, but he was engrossed in scribbling snot on George Clooney's upper lip.

'Fantastic dawn, wasn't it?' said Finn. 'Izzy came in and dragged me out of bed to take photographs. I'd forgotten what an early bird she was.'

Thank God, thought Río, that Izzy's early bird photoshoot hadn't taken her in the direction of the orchard. Curious about Cat's painting, she wandered across the kitchen and out into what Felicity – the woman for whom this house had been built – had called the 'Atrium'. There, on the console table was a portrait of a woman who could only be Elena, dressed in a gown embroidered with stars. Río picked it up. In the bottom right hand corner were the carefully worked letters 'C A T'.

'There's no message?'

'What?'

'From Cat.'

'No. She's the kind of gal who comes and goes as she pleases.' There was the sound of a voice calling in the background – Izzy's voice – then: 'Gotta go, Ma,' said Finn. 'See you lunchtime. Crab claws, remember? Your gaff?'

Río considered. Shane would be on his way to the airport: she didn't want to stay on in Coral Mansion by herself.

'Yes. My gaff. Bye, love.'

Río picked up the painting of Elena and studied it more closely. Cat had got the blissed-out, loved-up smile just right. But Finn had been wrong about the message: there was one, on the back of the canvas, painstakingly printed in Anthracite Black capital letters. 'I HOP U GET THE BABY U WANT'.

Elena wanted a baby! She wanted Shane's baby . . . But of course she did.

Life went on.

'Serendipity,' said Río, out loud.

'What's that?' Shane's voice came from the kitchen.

'It's when good things start to happen,' said Río, setting the painting back down on the table for Shane to find. 'It looks like Izzy and Finn might be onto something.'

'Serendipity, eh? Bring it on,' said Shane.

And as Río walked back into the kitchen, to where the one-time love of her life was adding nerdy glasses on to George Clooney, she knew that the white heat had consumed itself, and the fire in her head had finally gone out. She found herself hoping that Elena got the baby she wanted, too.

Chapter Twenty-Four

It was ten twenty-five in the morning. Having set her alarm for six o'clock, Keeley had finished reading the book she had taken the liberty of provisionally renaming *Catgirl and the Pleasure Palace of Adventure*, and was hugely excited. Paloma Gallagher had written a classic children's page-turner: all the right ingredients were there: cliffhanging chapter endings, an engaging heroine and subsidiary characters, and a pacy narrative. It was cinematic, too. Keeley was looking forward to negotiating the film rights. Film rights, television rights, audio book rights, large print rights, book club rights, translation rights, anthology and quotation rights, serial rights, electronic rights – the list was endless. Cat Gallagher was going to become a very rich young woman. And Keeley would be entitled to fifteen per cent of those riches. Not including the percentage of the advance and royalties she would negotiate for Cat's illustrations. And the percentage of the advance and royalties generated by the next author she signed, and the next, and the next. And sign she would, until her wrist hurt. Once news hit the trade publications that Keeley Considine was representing Cat Gallagher, bright new star in the biblio firmament, talent would come tearing at her from all directions, knocking other agents aside like nine-pins in a rush to seek her out.

Picking up the phone, she punched in Cat's number. There

was no reply. Bummer. But Keeley was certain that Cat would have no objection to her, Keeley, putting the record straight on Cat's behalf regarding the authorship of *Catgirl*. If she didn't do it, it would give rise to prurient speculation in the media, and Keeley was sure that that would be the last thing Cat would want. Or Hugo. Or poor, stupid, mortified Ophelia, who was going to have a lot of crow to chew on for the foreseeable. It was just as well she'd have a baby soon, to take her mind off things.

Keeley poured herself another mug of coffee, entered Camilla Featherstonehaugh's details into her iPhone, and dialled the mobile number, as Camilla had advised her.

'Camilla Featherstonehaugh,' came the autocratic, Anglo voice in her ear.

'Camilla? It's Keeley Considine here.'

'Who?'

'Keeley Considine. We met at Ophelia Gallagher's birthday party yesterday.'

'Oh, yes, of course. The journalist.'

'Turned literary agent,' Keeley reminded her politely.

'That's right. Yes. You had some kind of insider info on Ophelia's book.'

Keeley smiled, and launched her Exocet. 'It's not Ophelia's book. She didn't write it.'

'What?'

'The book was written by Paloma Gallagher, Hugo Gallagher's deceased ex-wife.'

'*What?*'

And Keeley filled Camilla in on the story behind the story, of how *Catgirl and the Pleasure Palace of Adventure* had come to be written.

'You mean it was written for that extraordinary-looking girl – the one in the bandana? Hugo Gallagher's daughter?'

'Yes.'

'But how on earth did Ophelia think she could get away with it?'

'It just must never have crossed her mind that Cat knew the story by heart. Or that there was a tape recording in existence.'

There was a pause on the other end of the line as Camilla digested this information. 'Well, my goodness. I daresay people have got away with stupider scams. You say the girl can paint?'

'Yes. I own one of her paintings.'

'Could you send me an image?'

Could she? Keeley guessed she could take a photograph of Cat's painting and email it as a JPEG. 'Sure.'

'Do you have a photograph of the girl?'

Keeley wanted to laugh. She'd known this question would come.

'No. But I can get one, no problem.'

'This is *very* exciting news! I mean – I'm gutted about Ophelia of course. But every cloud and all that. The concomitant publicity could be huge. Really fucking huge. Oh, I am so sorry. Pardon my French.'

'No worries, and couldn't it just?' Keeley smiled, catlike. This was the response she had been banking on. She'd hit pay dirt already, and she hadn't even registered her agency yet. How green was her valley!

'Can you bring the girl to London? I'd like to schedule a meeting.'

'No problem.' There *was* a problem, actually. Cat's fear of flying. She'd told her about that the day they'd driven to Oaf's – Ophelia's party. But pah! That was a ha'penny place problem. Since the ash-cloud business, everyone was taking the ferry these days. Keeley could drive Cat to London.

'Would next week suit?' asked Camilla.

Keeley almost laughed out loud. It would appear that Camilla had already written off her dawdle in the Dordogne, and got her priorities right.

'I'll run it by Cat. She's working on a project right now.'

'What kind of a project?' Camilla's voice was so urgent that Keeley had to hold the phone away from her ear. She wasn't about to tell Camilla that Cat was working on refurbishing a house.

'A series of landscapes,' she said.

'Are there other Catgirl stories, do you know?'

'Yes.' Cat had made reference to stories that took place not just in King Frederick the Great's Sans Souci, which was where *Catgirl and the Pleasure Palace of Adventure* was set, but in Ancient Egypt and the era of the Celtic Twilight and on the Planet Zog and Atlantis. During the year that Cat had spent in and out of hospital, Paloma had worked harder as a storyteller than Scheherazade, in order to keep her daughter's spirits up. 'Didn't Ophelia tell you?'

'No. She said she was working on ideas for a series of stories, but she had nothing concrete to show me.'

And that, Keeley deduced, was because Paloma had written only one of the stories down. The rest were in Cat's head, or on her Walkman. Cat was the only person who had access to them.

'I'll have them transcribed onto a Word document for you, Camilla. Compatibility mode?'

'Super!' said Camilla.

'And I look forward to doing business with you,' said Keeley, smoothly. 'I'll go hunt Cat down now, and get back to you directly.'

'Absolutely! Talk soon, Keeley. Oh – and you might fire off an email to me, so that I have a record of your address.'

345

'I'll do that right away. Goodbye, Camilla.'

'Goodbye!'

Keeley set down her phone, and eased herself into a satisfying stretch. She wondered when the story behind the true identity of the author of *Catgirl and the Pleasure Palace of Adventure* would hit the newspapers, and decided that really Leo should be the first to know. She'd phone him presently. But first she needed to talk to Cat. Hitting speed-dial, she waited and waited again for Cat to pick up. But the phone still rang on endlessly.

Bugger, thought Keeley. She would just have to get her ass down to the big house on the beach. No hardship really, since the weather was fine, and she could do with the exercise. She donned her walking boots, slid her phone into her bag, and set off.

But when she got there, there was no sign of life. She rang the front doorbell and knocked on the kitchen window and tapped on the sliding glass doors that led onto the deck, but all in vain. Finally, she gave up, and set off back to the village. She was thirsty now, and could murder a bottle of Ballygowan. It was lucky for her that she chose Ryan's over O'Toole's, for there, in the corner shop, was Finn. In his wire basket was a baguette, a punnet of strawberries and a bottle of *prosecco*.

'Hello, Finn! Celebrating something?'

'Um. No. It's for my ma. She needs cheering up.'

'Poor Río,' said Mrs Ryan lugubriously, from behind the counter.

'Poor Río,' agreed Padraig Whelan, counting out change from his purse for the Sweet'N Lo he'd just slid into his Bag for Life.

'Yeah. I thought a glass or two of fizz might help,' Finn told Keeley, handing over his Laser card. 'I'll get that for you.'

346

'The water? Thanks. I was hoping I might run into you, actually,' Keeley told him. 'I'm looking for Cat.'

'Oh, yeah?'

'Yes. I've just come from your house, and there's no sign of her there. Do you know where she might be?'

Finn frowned at her, and Keeley realised that he was reluctant to answer any questions in front of Mrs Ryan.

'Hang on two secs,' he said, entering his number in the chip and pin. 'There we go. Thanks, Mrs Ryan. Good day to you.'

'Good day to you, young Finn. Be sure to send your mother my love, and my condolences.'

'Tell her I'll drop her in a copy of *Oprah* magazine,' said Padraig.

'Will do.' And Finn left the shop, followed by Keeley.

'Sorry about that,' he said. 'It's best not to say anything in front of Mrs Ryan. Or Padraig, for that matter. They're all ears, and there's a story doing the rounds of Cat gate-crashing some party and making a scene.'

'Oh! You're talking about Ophelia Gallagher's birthday party. I was actually there.'

'You were? What happened?'

Keeley explained.

'So Cat is that famous painter's daughter?' asked a surprised Finn.

'Yes. Didn't you know?'

He shook his head, bemused. 'I hadn't a clue. She hardly ever talked about her family, or her past.'

'But you're in a relationship with her, right?'

Finn looked a bit dubious. '*Was* in a relationship, by the look of things.'

'Was?'

'She's gone.'

'What?'

'Cat's gone. She went off on some mysterious jaunt – I guess it was to that party – and then came back in the middle of the night, packed up all her things and left.'

'So she's not living with you any more?'

'Doesn't look like it. She turned up in Lissamore out of the blue, and now she's disappeared back into it.'

'And you've no idea where she might be?'

'No.'

'She didn't leave a note or anything?'

'Just a Post-It saying goodbye.'

'But aren't you worried about her?'

Finn shrugged. 'Not really, to be honest. Cat's well able to take care of herself. She's the most streetwise chick I ever met.' He frowned, considering. 'Maybe she's gone to Galway. She mentioned something about having a brother there.'

Warning bells were starting to go off in Keeley's head. 'Where was she living, Finn, before she moved in with you?'

'On a houseboat. But she won't be going back there.'

'What makes you say that?'

'It was torched.'

'Oh, shit!' Keeley felt a sudden flash of pure panic. 'I have to track her down, somehow.'

'Why?'

And Keeley quickly filled Finn in on the putative book deal she had lined up for her client.

'Well, all I can do is keep an eye out, and let you know. Have you a phone number for her?'

'Yes. But she's not picking up.'

'Text her.'

'Good idea. Look, here's my card.' Keeley produced a business card from her bag. 'Phone me at once, will you, if you hear from her. Or ask her to phone me. Tell her it's urgent.'

'Will do.'

'Thanks, Finn. How's your dad, by the way? I saw him at Adair's funeral, but didn't get a chance to talk to him.'

'He's gone back to LA. Left for the airport this morning.' Finn looked at his watch. 'I'd better get my ass on down to me ma's. I promised to do lunch for her. Bye, Keeley. Good luck.'

'Goodbye, Finn.'

And Finn strode off down the village street, swinging his carrier bag, leaving Keeley standing outside the corner shop feeling . . . well . . . cornered. Cornered and antsy.

What was she to do now? Who would know Cat's whereabouts? Moving across to the sea wall, Keeley sat down on it and sent Cat a text saying **Pls fone. Urgent.** before accessing her contacts. Ophelia Gallagher. Would she know? Unlikely. But her husband might. And then Keeley cursed herself for not having entered the landline number of the Crooked House in her phone. All she had was Ophelia Gallagher's mobile number, and she had an inkling that Ophelia would not be picking up her phone to anyone today – especially not to members of the press.

Stupid Keeley! She thought and thought, gazing unseeingly at the boats bobbing exuberantly in the marina, exercising her brain like the clappers. Hugo's gallery, the Demeter in Dublin. His agent there would know the number. But it was bound to be ex-directory, and there was no way they'd give it out. She'd just have to go there, to the Crooked House, and pay him a visit in person.

The sound of a cork popping made her look up. On the balcony of her apartment, Río Kinsella was cracking open her bottle of *prosecco*. Keeley watched through her mirrored sunglasses as she poured herself a glass, then set the bottle on the table, and sat down on a canvas director's chair. She had never seen anyone look so forlorn: Río must be gutted by the loss of her husband. Poor woman, to have been bereaved so tragically so soon after her wedding! But Keeley didn't have time to dwell on Río's plight. She needed to find that Gallagher girl, and she needed to find her fast.

Rising from the sea wall, Keeley tucked her phone back in her bag, then sprinted at the double back home to where her trusty green Ka was waiting for her.

If she'd waited just a moment longer, a familiar voice might have kept her there, by the marina.

'Good doing business with you,' Cat said, spitting on the palm of her right hand, and shaking on it.

As Keeley rounded the bend on the driveway that led to the Crooked House, she spotted to her right, like flotsam on the lakeshore, the weathered remains of a small dinghy. *Catkin* was the name painted on the stern, in letters rendered almost illegible by time and tide. She guessed that Cat would have spent countless hours sailing on and swimming in that lake as a small girl, since there wasn't much else in the environs of the Crooked House to keep a child occupied. No wonder she had inhabited a world of the imagination. No wonder she had felt the need to make that world concrete in paintings, since she could not tell stories in words. And how lucky Cat had been to have a mother who understood, and who had helped bring all those places to life for her: the pleasure palace; the submarine world of the coral reef; the Planet Zog.

Keeley pulled up alongside the steps that led to the front door and killed the engine. It was perfectly silent here in the grounds of the Crooked House. A dead midday heat had descended, and Keeley was glad that she'd exchanged her walking boots for flipflops, and her jeans for a light cotton frock. She slid out of the driver's seat and climbed the steps.

No one answered the door on her first ring, nor on her second. She decided to go round the back, to the kitchen door she'd seen Cat enter the house by, on the evening of Ophelia's party.

In the stableyard, no trace remained of that event: the marquee had been dismantled and taken away, no jolly balloons or birthday banners or bunting were fluttering here now that Ophelia had nothing to celebrate: no birthday, no book deal, no new-found fame and fortune as an author. And yet, and yet . . . there was cause for celebration still. Soon Ophelia would be celebrating the birth of her baby, and that was something that she, Keeley, would never be able to celebrate, since Keeley would never be able to conceive a baby. Keeley Considine had become a career girl not through choice, but by design, because she had had no alternative.

The kitchen door was partially open. Through it, Keeley could see Hugo sitting at the table, eating a banana. There was something so incongruous about seeing a major artist eating a banana that Keeley stopped in her tracks.

Then, from beyond the door that opened on to the hallway, came the sound of the phone ringing – the so-called 'polite' tone of a real old-fashioned telephone. It rang twice, and then the answering machine kicked in. After Ophelia's recorded message had played, and the beep sounded, Keeley heard Cat's voice say: 'Da. Dada . . . I just called to say I love you. I'll be in touch some time. Good luck with the work.' And then the long beep sounded that told Keeley the incoming message had been saved. Phew! At least the girl was still alive!

Keeley saw Hugo smile. Then he tossed his banana skin into the sink, reached for a bottle, and poured himself a glass of red wine.

Cautiously, she tapped on the door.

'Come in, whoever you are,' said Hugo.

Keeley stepped into the kitchen.

'Oh – hello,' said Hugo. 'It's Keeley something, ain't it?'

'That's right. Keeley Considine.'

'Come and join me in a glass of wine, Keeley.'

It was more of a command than an invitation, and Keeley thought it prudent to obey.

'Thank you,' she said, taking a seat opposite him at the table. 'How is Ophelia?'

'Ophelia is dying of mortification, that's how she is. She's taken to her bed, and there she will in all likelihood stay until our baby is born. It's a bloody bore. It means I have to cook for myself, and the only thing I'm any good at is scrambled eggs. My cholesterol levels will go into orbit. But then, if I pop my clogs from heart failure and clogged arteries – no pun intended – I guess that's good news for anyone who owns one of my paintings. They'll double in value. What brings you here, Keeley Considine? Are you hot on the heels of another scoop?'

'No. I'm actually here to ask about Cat.'

'My daughter, Caitlín?'

'Yes. Do you know where she is?'

'Why do you want to know?'

'I'm setting up as a literary agent. I'd like to represent her.'

Hugo laughed. 'That's rich! Why would a literary agent want to represent someone who has problems with reading and writing? You do know my girl's dyslexic, don't you?'

'Yes, I do know that. But I would like to be able to represent her as custodian of the stories that your late wife wrote for her. And I'd like Cat to illustrate them.'

Hugo set down his glass and leaned forward, eyes aglitter. 'Now you're talking!' he said. 'I always maintained that Cat

352

should have illustrated that book, not that Jasper prat. But of course I understand now why Ophelia baulked at the idea. Poor, misguided Ophelia! I don't think she'll ever live down the shame.'

'So, can you help me, Hugo? Do you know where Cat is?'

'Haven't a clue. She comes and she goes. She's her own woman, is Cat.'

'You really have no idea?'

Hugo spread his hands and shrugged. 'Search me. You could try her brother, Raoul. She's in touch with him more frequently than she is with me.'

'Do you have a number for Raoul?'

'Yeah. Somewhere.'

Shambling to his feet, Hugo left the room. Keeley sat with her hands in her lap, wanting to jiggle her foot with impatience. Instead, she took a swig of wine, and was impressed to find that it was a *very* potable Bordeaux. A glance at the label told her it was from the Dordogne, where – were it not for her – Camilla Featherstonehaugh should currently be holidaying. Keeley gulped. The editor had postponed her vacation on account of her, and now it looked like Keeley wasn't keeping her side of the bargain, which had, after all, been to hunt Cat down and get back to Camilla 'directly'. She took another swig of wine, and mentally prayed that Hugo would hurry up.

Looking around the kitchen, Keeley saw that it was in a state. If Hugo's studio – or wherever he'd gone to, to locate Raoul's phone number – was in a similar condition, Keeley could be waiting here all day. Dishes were piled unwashed in the sink, laundry was tumbling out of the machine, a battalion of wine bottles was standing sentry by the door. Keeley suddenly felt very, very sorry for Ophelia Gallagher, lying hugely pregnant and humiliated upstairs. She trusted that Hugo would get enough of an advance for his new

353

paintings to fork out for some hired help once the baby arrived.

Finally he was back, a leather-bound address book in his hand. It looked ancient and wore a patina of dust, and Keeley saw as he sat back down at the table and started to leaf through it, that the pages were covered not just in names, addresses and phone numbers, but in doodles and scribbled drawings. What a collectible artifact! Hugo Gallagher's address book was probably worth as much as one of his paintings, and would doubtless fetch thousands at auction after his death. How unsettling it must be to be an artist and to know that anyone who owned one of your works was on tenterhooks waiting for you to kick the bucket, just so they could cash in.

'Here you are.' Hugo found the number and dictated it to Keeley, who entered it in her phone.

'Thanks so much,' she said. 'I really appreciate your help. And should Cat happen to be in touch with you any time soon, will you please ask her to contact me as a matter of urgency?'

Hugo gave her a lazy smile. 'My daughter doesn't really do "urgency". A deplorable trait she inherits from me. Will you have another glass of wine, Ms Considine, before you depart?'

'No, thanks, Hugo. I'm driving.'

'Well, good luck, then,' he said, watching Keeley rise to her feet. 'I hope you and my little girl make shedloads of dosh. I'm glad she's got someone looking out for her.'

'Thanks. Here's to the beginning of a mutually beneficial relationship.' Keeley raised her glass, took a last gulp of wine, then set it down. 'Goodbye, Hugo. And have a lovely baby.'

'A baby. Sweet Jesus. What untold tribulations have I brought down upon my own head?'

And as Keeley made for the kitchen door, Hugo drained the remains of the wine into his glass, and lunged for the corkscrew.

Halfway down the serpentine driveway, Keeley pulled over and dialled the number Hugo had given her for Raoul. Cat's brother sounded guarded when Keeley told him who she was, and why she was looking for his half-sister. 'You say you have Cat's number?' he said.

'Yes.'

'Well, all I can suggest to you is that you keep on trying it. I'm sorry I can't be more helpful. I'll tell her you called, and I'll pass on your message.'

'Tell her she can call me any time, day or night,' said Keeley, knowing that she was sounding desperate, and not caring.

'Will do,' said Raoul, and ended the call.

Fuck. Keeley slumped over the steering wheel, wanting to bang her head off it. She was feeling very hot and bothered now, and the wine hadn't helped. Opening the passenger door, she emerged on to the driveway, closed her eyes and flung her head back, drawing in greedy gulps of air. And when she opened her eyes, there, above her in the arms of a great tree was something that looked like a heron's nest. And then Keeley realised that she was standing under the broad-branched cypress that housed Cat's childhood treehouse.

She had to see it. Setting her foot on the first rung of the rope ladder, she tested it to make sure it would withstand her weight. Then she climbed cautiously, one rung at a time until she emerged on to a platform constructed of timber planks. The house itself had been woven from willow branches: Keeley was reminded of Yeats' cabin on Inisfree, 'of clay and wattles made'. A weathered, handpainted sign read 'Cat Gallagher. Private. Keep Out on Pain of Death.' Stooping, Keeley insinuated herself through the low doorway and – since the roof was too low to permit her to stand – hunkered down on the floor.

So this had been Cat's bolthole, her lair, her little den! Looking around, Keeley pictured the girl lying here, listening to her mother's stories of Catgirl's magical escapades, or drawing in sketchbooks. The treehouse was furnished with a low table and three chairs. There were two moth-eaten beanbags and a cupboard on the other side of the small space, and on the wall were childish drawings in clip-art frames.

Keeley took a closer look. Catgirl, riding on the back of a pig. Catgirl, swinging from the tail of a kite. Catgirl, swimming with turtles. Catgirl, clinging on to the neck of a giraffe. There was a framed photograph, too, of Cat Gallagher cocooned in a duvet, gazing up at the face of a woman whom Keeley recognised as Paloma. There was something so poignant about the photograph that Keeley felt a lump come to her throat. She should not be here. She was an intruder. She should have heeded the sign that had warned her to keep out on pain of death. This was Cat's private space, and Keeley had no right to come snooping. But the journalist in her, the investigative instinct, won over, and she found herself moving over to the cupboard and opening the door.

Inside were books. *Dr Seuss' ABC. Annie Apple's Adventure. Bouncy Ben's Birthday. Clever Cat and the Clown. My ABC Board Book.* There was an old exercise book too, and Keeley felt a bubble of excitement rise. Could this be one of Paloma's Catgirl stories? Cat had told her that her mother had written them down in old school exercise books. But when Keeley opened the book, she saw that the pages were covered in letters penned in alphabetical order by a childish hand.

Oh, God! The lump in Keeley's throat grew larger. She saw in her mind's eye Cat laboriously tracing the letters, her hand guided perhaps by Paloma, and wondered what age the child had been when she realised that she was never going to be able to write without difficulty, or read any of the books that were piled on the shelves of the cupboard, books that Paloma must have read aloud to her daughter. Keeley did some mental arithmetic. You wouldn't construct such a treehouse for a child who was much younger than seven or eight years old. Cat had clearly still been struggling to master the alphabet then. She, Keeley, had been reading on her own from the age of six. All the classics. *The Secret Garden. One Thousand and One Nights. Swallows and Amazons.* The *Just So Stories.*

All these books were present and correct here in Cat's library, and all of them were warped and damp, some of them with rotting covers, most of them with well-cracked spines. Keeley reached for the volume of Kipling stories, the ones that she too had loved as a child, and the book fell open at the story of the 'Cat that Walked by Himself'.

'But the wildest of all the animals was the Cat,' read Keeley, sitting back on her heels. 'He walked by himself, and all places were alike to him.'

Except someone had taken a pen and crossed out the words 'He' and 'himself', and substituted 'She' and 'herself'. Keeley ran her eyes over the text. All the pronouns 'he' or 'his' or 'himself' had been changed, so that the animal in the story became a she-cat, not a tom. 'I am not a friend and I am not a servant,' she read. 'I am the Cat who walks by herself, and I wish to come into your Cave.'

The Cat who walks by herself. Cat was that, all right.

It looked as though hunting her down might prove to be as challenging as the great white tiger hunts of legend. And some small interior voice was warning Keeley that Cat Gallagher might not like the idea of anyone hunting her down. Why, oh, why was life never simple?

Laying the volume of *Just So Stories* back on the shelf next to a Taschen volume of Rousseau reproductions, Keeley shut the cupboard door, feeling like the stable boy whose horse had already bolted. Then she climbed back down the rope ladder to where her car was waiting for her, and headed wearily for Lissamore and home, and a very large gin and tonic.

Chapter Twenty-Five

Río and Fleur were watching a vintage movie on DVD. It was *Gone With the Wind*, and it was about the fifth time they had watched it together. They took it in turns to watch their favourite movies, either in Río's eyrie, or in Fleur's bijou apartment over the shop. Fleur's favourite film was *Stella Dallas* because she so identified with the heroine as played by Barbara Stanwyck, and Río's favourite was *Gone With the Wind* because she so identified with Scarlett O'Hara, who had worked her fingers to the bone cultivating the land at Tara. Right now on Fleur's plasma screen there was footage of a calendar with the pages being plucked off one by one, and scattered to the four winds to denote the passage of time.

'That's what it feels like, sometimes, time passing, doesn't it?' remarked Río. 'Days flying by, with nothing to distinguish one from the other.'

'Dooley Wilson got it in one,' said Fleur.

'Dooley Wilson?'

'The song in *Casablanca*. "As Time Goes By". Moonlight and love songs . . .'

'Never out of date . . .'

Fleur and Río looked at each other and smiled.

'I'm well past my best before date, that's for sure,' observed Río.

'Nonsense, darling!' protested Fleur. 'There's lots of life in us old dogs yet!' She puckered her forehead thoughtfully (no botox for our Fleur! thought Río) 'But it really must be awful, mustn't it, to be an artist's muse, like that Ophelia Gallagher. Then, at our age, you really would be past your sell by date.'

Their attention was diverted from the screen by the small snorts of vexation being made by Marguerite, who was sitting beside her mother on the chaise longue perusing *Hello!* magazine, and trying to pick up pictures of shoes from the pages.

'Look at Marguerite!' said Río. 'She's fairly come on in leaps and bounds in the past few months.'

'Yes,' concurred Fleur, allowing herself a smug smile. 'Isn't her hand–eye coordination extraordinary?'

'I remember Finn at that age,' said Río. 'Except it was pictures of guns or fish he'd be trying to pick up from pages, not pictures of shoes.'

'How's his dive venture going?'

'It's looking good. They've negotiated another ten grand downwards. And he tells me that Shane has officially signed up now, as a shareholder.'

'Will Finn and Izzy live over there, on the island?'

'Yes. The accommodation's pretty basic, but you know Izzy. She'll make it work.'

'Oh! Aren't you blessed, Río? To think that you believed once upon a time that he'd end up on the other side of the world. And now he's just a hop, skip and a jump across a causeway.'

'Yes. I am blessed.' Río laughed as she watched Marguerite try and help herself to a pair of Jimmy Choos. 'And so are you. Look at your clever daughter! She's clearly inherited her mother's expensive tastes. She's dead set on those Jimmy Choos – won't even touch the sensible Clarks ones. It's very distracting, you know, having a baby in the room. You should put her away. I'd much rather watch her than Scarlett.'

'She's an upstager, all right.' Fleur dropped a kiss on her baby's downy head. 'Best thing I ever made.'

'I broke the mould when I made Finn. Literally – since he's one of a kind. Remember the day you picked me up from hospital, after I'd had my tubes tied? You came with an antique silver-handled walking cane so that I could waddle my way through the car park. You always were a class act, Fleur.'

'Thank you, *chérie!*'

'And I'm so glad you had a baby girl! It's lovely to have a baby in our lives again, at our advanced age.'

'Maybe Finn will present you with a granddaughter. Are he and Izzy an item again, Río?'

'Well, he seems to spend more time in the Bentley than in Coral Mansion, so yeah – it seems they are. He never tells me anything.'

But Río had done a little espionage. Just last night she had checked out Finn's Facebook profile. It had told her that he was 'in a relationship', and a browse through his latest pictures was testimony to this. An album entitled 'New Beginnings' displayed photographs of Finn and Izzy hand in hand, gazing at a sunset over Inishclare island; Finn and Izzy wielding lump hammers, laughing as they demolished a wall; Finn and Izzy sporting scuba-dive T-shirts – hers featuring a silkscreen print of kissing angelfish, his emblazoned with the legend 'Eat More Plankton'.

'Whatever happened to that Gallagher girl, I wonder?' asked Fleur.

'I don't know,' admitted Río. 'I never even got to meet her. It seems strange, since we lived so close, and had so much in common, and loved the same boy. Maybe we'll meet up some time, somewhere. I'd like to think we will. She's a real visionary – her paintings remind me of Rousseau.'

'She stopped me in the street once, and asked if she could exhibit in my shop.'

'Oh? What did you tell her?'

'I said that yours were the only paintings I ever put on display.'

'How loyal of you! You're a real pal, Fleur.'

'I sold another watercolour for you today, by the way. That's two so far this week.'

'Excellent! Well done, Clever Clogs – and it's not even high season.'

The summer was well over, and the tourist head count was down. Lissamore was seguing into autumn, and starting to look out its winter woollies. The green patchwork quilt that was draped over the environs of the village in the summer months had morphed, chameleon-like, into shades of auburn and russet and gold. And this morning there had even been a tracing of frost on the dunes, when Río had gone for her swim.

'I'll go get the cash for you while I think of it,' said Fleur. 'And another bottle of wine. We've at least another hour before Scarlett wakes up to her big mistake.'

Fleur pressed the pause button, and rose to her feet. When she opened the door of the den, the sweet aroma of baking came wafting in from the kitchen.

'What have you got in the oven?' called Río.

'Madeleines,' said Fleur, throwing a smile over her shoulder.

Of course! Fleur's madeleines were baked to her mother's recipe, and were the most heavenly little cakes Río had ever tasted. Some famous author – Proust, wasn't it? – had said that the smell of madeleines took him straight back to the past. Yes, it must have been Proust, because that's what his novel was called. *Remembrance of Things Past.*

Río didn't care much for remembering things – of the recent past, at any rate. Nothing much of note had happened, anyway, since Adair's death. She'd got on with life, and she guessed that that was as much as a recently widowed body was able for. She'd got out of bed in the mornings and showered and watered her plants, and she'd done a fair bit of painting, and tended her orchard, and swum in the bay below Coral Mansion on all but the most bloody-minded of days.

She had been right about Shane. Now that he was a married man, Río no longer had access all areas. She emailed from time to time, but because she could not be sure that Elena didn't have access to his email account, she could no longer be as open and spontaneous as she had been heretofore. She called him on Skype occasionally, but she never knew if Elena was somewhere in the background, listening. And once, when she called his mobile number, Elena had picked up and said: 'Shane Byrne's phone. Elena speaking,' and Río had garbled 'Wrong number', and dropped the phone. She felt as if she had lost a soul mate. Her lover, her friend, her very own Rhett Butler.

Beside her, Marguerite was growing fretful, clearly pissed off that she couldn't have the Louboutins she was trying to pluck from the pages of *Hello!*

'*Tais toi*, Marguerite,' said Río, echoing what Fleur sometimes said to her daughter. 'Let's see what's on the next page.'

The next page featured Catherine Zeta-Jones at home with Michael Douglas. Catherine Zeta-Jones was a good friend of Elena's, Río knew. She pictured them all cosying up together in their mansions, that Hollywood elite, having barbecues by the pool or informal suppers in their de luxe theatre rooms. Talking shop, talking Rodeo Drive, talking carats, talking surgery. What on earth had made Shane think that she, Río, would *ever* be able for that lifestyle? But of course, he'd known Río wasn't able for it, which was why he had bought Coral Mansion for her. He had bought the equivalent of a Hollywood mansion, right here in Lissamore, because Lissamore was home, and home was where Río's heart was. And she'd turned her back on him, just as stupid Scarlett had turned her back on Rhett.

Fleur came back into the room, bearing a bottle of wine and a plate of madeleines on a tray.

'Are you reading about Catherine Zeta-Jones?' she asked, setting the tray down on the coffee table.

'Yes. It's splendidly mindless stuff, isn't it? No wonder you're so addicted to glossy mags.'

'Take it home with you,' said Fleur. 'Someone else might as well get a go of it before it ends up in the recycling bin.'

'What a chum you are, Fleur,' said Río, smiling up at her. 'I'd be lost without you, you know.'

'And I'd be lost without you,' returned Fleur, refilling Río's glass. 'That's what friends are all about, after all. Helping each other find a way through thick and through thin. *Santé*, darling! Chin up, and down the hatch.'

And Fleur pressed 'Resume', and Scarlett O'Hara was back on the screen, shaking her fist at her fate writ high in the heavens.

Two hours later, Río was wending her way homeward down the village main street. She waved at Mrs Murphy, who was doing neighbourhood watch from her upstairs window, she threw a stick for the postmistress's Airedale, she thanked Padraig Whelan for the *Kitchen Garden* magazine he'd put through her letterbox, and she stopped for a brief chat with Seamus Moynihan, who had recently sold Finn a RIB.

'Second boat I've sold in as many months,' he told her.

'I saw *The Minx* was up for sale. She's gone now, is she?'

'Gone a while back. I'll miss her. She was a nifty boat, that *Minx*. A lovely little blue-water cruiser.'

In Ryan's, Río helped herself to a pint of milk and a tin of cocoa. She fancied hot chocolate before she went to bed this evening. Oh – and a copy of *Hello!* She'd forgotten the back issue Fleur had offered her, and she badly wanted brain candy to help her set sail to the land of Nod tonight. She'd had awful trouble sleeping since Adair's funeral. Correction. She'd had awful trouble sleeping since her wedding day, and now she thought of it, Scarlett O'Hara had been plagued by nightmares as well.

As she waited for Mrs Ryan to finish serving old Mr Moriarty, who always paid for his groceries by cheque, Río started to leaf through the glossy pages of *Hello!* Featured in this week's issue were celebrity uni-name couples. Brangelina, TomKat, Garfleck. Río found herself thinking that if Finn and Izzy got hitched they'd be known as 'Fizzy'. Very appropriate for a couple setting up a dive centre. Absently wondering if Katie Holmes had had surgery, she turned the page to find Elena Sweetman smiling up at her.

'Our Baby Joy!' trumpeted the headline. 'Hollywood A-listers Elena Sweetman and Shane Byrne are looking forward to the arrival of their first baby next spring . . .' read Río.

And then she put her wallet back in her bag, returned the magazine to the shelf, bade farewell to Mrs Ryan, and left the shop.

Down on the shore by Coral Mansion, the beach was littered with razor shells. She must ask Finn what had happened, to wash so many of them up from the depths of the Atlantic.

A stiff breeze had got up, making Río wish that she'd wrapped herself up warmer. In her orchard, some apples and pears were still waiting to be picked. There was still time to prune the roses and cut back the raspberry canes, and next month she'd plant bulbs that would flower in the spring, and blueberries that would ripen in the summer.

In her mind's eye, she pictured herself and Fleur and Dervla picnicking there again during the lengthening evenings. By then the grass would have grown over the track that she'd had laid down for Adair's tractor – already weeds were pushing their way through the hardcore, reclaiming it. And she would plant new apple trees next week, to replace the ones that had had to be cut down. It was all good. The dead wood would soon be all gone, and come April, spring would be strutting her stuff, flaunting her blossoms on the trees, and Marguerite would be toddling around, grabbing fistfuls of the daisies that were her namesake, and Río would be feeling whole again, and Finn would have a half-brother, or a half-sister.

As Río made her way up to the highest terrace, she became aware of a regular thumping noise, the sound of a branch hitting something, a sound she was familiar with. By the entrance gates to Coral Mansion, the 'For Sale' sign was up again.

Parked outside was a Land Rover, and a rangy, dark-haired man was leaning against the bonnet, taking a picture of the gate, which was covered in undercoat. Finn had never got around to finishing the paintwork.

'Are you thinking of buying?'

The man lowered his Nikon, and smiled down at her. 'No. I wouldn't want a house like this, even if I could afford it. I'm more the half-doored cottage type, myself.'

'With hens, and a pile of turf against the gable wall?'

366

'Yes. And a marmalade cat.'

Río smiled back at him. 'Why are you taking a picture of the gate, then?'

'I'm a photographer. It's interesting – the shape of the scrollwork and the tree branch against the late evening sun.'

Río squinted up at the gate, shielding her eyes with a hand. 'You're right,' she said. 'There's a kind of fretworky vibe going on, isn't there?'

'That's just what I thought. Who used to live here?'

'Lots of people,' Río told him. 'You wouldn't think to look at it that such a modern house could be haunted. But there are lots of ghosts banging about in there.'

The man raised an amused eyebrow. 'Sounds intriguing,' he said. 'Might you tell me about them over a drink in O'Toole's?'

Río hesitated, listening to the clamourous ghosts calling to her from the grounds of the house that was once known as Coral Cottage, hearing the voices of family and friends and kindred spirits: her mother, her sister, her son; the men she had loved, the men she had lost. Then she turned back to the tall dark stranger and gave him a level look.

'I might,' she said.

Keeley was in her Dublin office, working late, listlessly going through her slush pile. The slush pile was full of wannabes. Wannabe Marian Keyes and Cathy Kellys and Sheila O'Flanagans, wannabe Stig Larsons and John Connellys. There was not a single voice calling out to her from that pile that said 'Choose me! I'm different! I'm a notice box, and I'm very, very good!'

Relations with Camilla Featherstonehaugh had cooled since Keeley had not been able to produce Cat from the hat. She had felt like a complete tool when she'd finally had to 'fess up to the fact that her protégé had gone AWOL, and the wondrous *Catgirl* series with her. Keeley had tried and tried to contact Cat on her mobile phone, but without success. It was as if the girl had been a chimera, a figment of Keeley's imagination, a *pooka*.

Casting aside a typescript aptly entitled *These Foolish Things*, Keeley reached for her phone and pressed speeddial for Cat. This she had done on a random basis, every few days or so before she had moved into her smart new premises and got bogged down by business, never really expecting the girl to pick up. But, hey . . . what was this? There was something new about the ringtone. Aha! Catgirl was on the move, somewhere foreign, by the sound of it.

'Hello.'

Keeley nearly dropped the phone.

'Hello?' she bellowed.

'Wrong number,' said Cat.

'No! No, Cat! Don't put down the phone! It's me! It's Keeley!'

'Who?'

'Keeley Considine!'

'Oh. Hello.'

'Cat – where the fuck are you? I've been trying to get hold of you for weeks! Oh – thank God I've finally reached you!'

'What's up?'

'Listen up. I've fantastic news. I've set up an extraordinary deal for you, with a major publishing house in the UK. World rights to the Catgirl books, with illustrations by you!'

'Oh, yeah. Raoul mentioned something about that.'

'He did? So why didn't you get on to me right away?'

'Why would I want to do that?'

'Because this is *huge*, Cat! This deal has the potential to make you a very rich woman indeed!'

'Like a millionaire?'

'Yes!'

'Well thanks very much for the offer, Keeley, but no thanks. I'm perfectly happy as I am.'

Keeley laughed. 'Don't tease, Cat. I'm absolutely serious.'

'So am I. The stories aren't for sale.'

'What?'

'They're my stories. They're mine, and nobody else's. My mama made them for me, and nobody else should ever have laid eyes on them.'

'But Cat . . . don't you see the potential? We're talking a global phenomenom here – translation into countless languages! Movie rights! Audio books in Klingon! You could be as big as J.K. Rowling!'

'Who's he?'

Was this girl for real? 'Cat – listen to me. Please listen.'

'No,' said Cat. 'No. I'd rather not listen. Goodbye, Keeley.'

And there came the sound of what might have been a splash, and a fizzy noise, and then silence.

'Cat? Cat! *Cat!*'

Keeley pressed 'End Call' and then 'Redial' with frantic fingers. Nothing happened. She pressed 'Redial' again, and again, and again. Still nothing. Electric with panic, Keeley scrolled through her contacts, fingers going like Road Runner, until she found Raoul's number.

'I'm sorry to bother you, Raoul,' she gibbered. 'It's Keeley Considine here—'

'Sorry. Who?'

'Keeley Considine – the literary agent who wishes to represent your sister Caitlín.'

'Oh, yes. I told her you'd phoned. Did you get in touch with her yet?'

'Yes. We've just spoken, but I think her phone's on the blink, and I can't reconnect with her.'

'What did she say?'

'She said she was perfectly happy, and that she didn't want to do a deal. Can you believe it?' Keeley managed a shaky laugh.

'Yes, I can. She *is* perfectly happy. I think you should leave her alone now, Keeley.'

'What? You can't be serious! Have you any idea how much this deal could be worth? We're talking megabucks here! We're talking millions!'

'That's not what it's all about, Keeley. It's about the work, ain't it? It's about getting a fair price for what you think your work is worth, and some things simply aren't for sale.'

'Good God, Raoul – I can't believe you're saying this! Don't you see that this could set your sister up for life?'

'She's well set up where she is. She's already told you that she's perfectly happy. I'd leave her alone now. Goodbye, Keeley.'

'But Raoul—'

'Goodbye.'

And Raoul put the phone down.

What! What the *fuck* were the Gallaghers up to? They were mad. Stark, staring fucking mad – all three of them. They were certifiably insane . . . they needed their thick fucking heads read.

Keeley was so infuriated that she sent her new iPhone skidding across the coffee table. It landed on the slush pile, not the floor, thank goodness. Marching into the little kitchen that adjoined her office, she poured an indecent amount of wine into a large goblet, then returned to the sitting room, wishing she smoked, or that the wineglass had been a cheap one. Then she could have smashed it instead of setting it carefully down by her cream suede upholstered armchair.

She needed something – *anything* to do, to stop her mind

careering around that fucking Gallagher girl who had messed around with her life with such insouciance, with such fucking *aplomb*! Grabbing the jiffy bag at the top of the slush pile, Keeley ripped it open with such force that the contents spilled all over her maple wood floor. 'An Ordinary Girl' she read on the title page of the typescript. Pah. Never mind the title, she told herself, hunkering down and gathering pages together. Feel the width.

And as she boxed the A4 sheets into shape (about 100,000 words, she calculated – just right), she saw the photograph. Wow! Bella was just that – a stunningly beautiful girl. *Bellissima*. She had golden skin, a mane of glossy hair, a tip-tilted nose, a crooked smile, and eyes that could melt a man at forty paces. 'An Ordinary Girl', Keeley read again. 'A Novel by Bella Blake'. Bella Blake was a name to conjure with. It had the ring of bestsellerdom about it. Keeley wondered was it a real name, or a pseudonym.

Stapled to the photograph was a resumé. 'Bella Blake was educated at Kylemore Abbey International Boarding School, in the wild west of Ireland,' she read. Kylemore Abbey School. Keeley wondered was this Bella a contemporary of that Gallagher girl? It would serve Cat right if she was, she decided childishly – and if she, Keeley, was responsible for discovering her and turning her into a big star in the literary firmament. Ha! Cat would rue the day she turned down representation by Keeley Considine.

'Bella holds a BA mod in history and psychology from University College, Dublin,' continued the resumé, 'and a certificate in fluency in the Japanese language from Keio University, Tokyo. She has trained and certified as a Game Ranger in KwaZulu-Natal in South Africa, and is also a scuba-dive master. She is currently employed as a scuba-dive tourist guide in AQWA – Western Australia's largest marine

371

life aquarium – where she gets to swim every day with nurse sharks, loggerhead turtles and manta rays. She has dreamed of becoming a published author since the age of fifteen, when she had her first piece of journalism published in the Irish *Evening Herald*. It was a glowing review of *Harry Potter and the Half Blood Prince*.'

Well, at least *she* knows who J.K. Rowling is, thought Keeley darkly, unlike that clueless Cat Gallagher. But can she write? This Bella Blake may be a PR person's dream, but even the dogs on the street know that you don't judge a book by its cover. Or, in this instance, by its author's biog and mugshot.

Keeley curled up in her armchair and took a sip of wine. Then she set her glass down, and started reading. 'The little old lady on the balcony could not believe what she had just seen happen on the street below her . . .' she began.

Several hours later she had reached 'The End', wishing it wasn't midnight. It was too late now to phone Camilla Featherstonehaugh. She would have to do it first thing in the morning. And then she would phone her brand new client in Western Australia and congratulate her. Because Keeley knew that by this time next year, beautiful, talented Bella Blake would be a household name.

Cat chucked her Nokia into the tide, rueing the day she had let Keeley Considine have her number. Now she'd have to fork out for a new pay-as-you-go.

At least she'd earned a few bob today, to cover the cost of replacing the phone. An elderly couple on the beach had admired her painting. It had been an acrylic of Catgirl at the helm of *The Minx*, and she'd let them have it for a hundred euro. She was glad she was able to mark her paintings down to a fairer price, now that she'd realised her dream of buying her own boat. She didn't feel quite so manipulative.

Manipulative! Now there was a word to conjure with. Had she allowed Keeley to persuade her that selling her mother's stories was a good idea she, Cat, would have become a manipulated creature. Raoul had told her that she'd have been the puppet of a big conglomerate, a product to push, a walking, talking mannequin. She'd have had to go to stuff like press launches and publishing lunches and gala this and celebrity that and be on her best behaviour, and Cat would *hate* that. Imagine having to smile at people you didn't even like! Imagine having to have your photograph taken with them! It was true, what the Masai and the native Americans said, that every time you have your photograph taken, a piece of your soul is stolen. No wonder the Western world had become such an arid, soulless place. People were taking pictures all over the place – she'd seen people taking pictures of their *food* in the local taverna! And imagine, just *imagine* having to wear proper clothes! High heels and sucky-in Spanx and underwired bras and tight belts and fitted this and tailored that. Ew!

Today Cat was wearing baggy cotton trousers, a matelot-striped jumper, espadrilles and trademark bandana. She looked like a cartoon cat burglar, she realised as she packed her paintbox away, slung her backpack over her shoulder, and hit the road that would take her to the top of the hill. Except Cat never stole anything. Cat earned her keep, just like the cat in the Rudyard Kipling story, the cat who had become her role model when she had been a little girl, when her mother had read her stories. Images came into her head now, of Catgirl swinging out of a kite, Catgirl sliding down a giraffe's neck, Catgirl cantering on the pig's back. That's where she was right now, she thought, fingering the two fifty euro notes tucked in the pocket of her trousers. Maybe they could afford to eat out tonight.

She reached the end of the road, and turned left on to a sandy pathway, at the end of which was a whitewashed house. High on a ladder, a beautiful dark-skinned boy was painting the window frames on the upper story in a vibrant Aegean blue, similar to the shade of acrylic paint she'd used earlier, for the sky in her picture. That mile high, bright blue Greek sky she'd dreamed about so often.

'Hello there,' said the boy, looking down at her as she dumped her backpack by the front door and blew him a kiss. 'How are you?'

How was she? *Who* was she? 'I am the Cat who walks by herself,' she said. 'And I wish to come into your house.'

'That's nice,' said Andreas, with a smile, pushing a wing of dark hair away from his face. 'Be my guest.'

And so Cat did just that.

THE END

Acknowledgements

If I allowed myself to be effusive, I would be a veritable geyser of praise for the following: my editor Kate Bradley and all the team at Avon HarperCollins: Sammia Rafique, Caroline Ridding, Helen Bolton, Rhian McCauley and Charlotte Wheeler. In Ireland, I would be lost without the support of Claire Power and Moira Reilly. I would like to thank Shay Healy for permission to quote from his Eurovision classic 'What's Another Year', and Brendan Kennelly for permission to quote from his epic poem *The Man Made of Rain*. Thanks also to Patricia McGettrick for Cat's eyes; to Teresa O'Reilly for being such a brilliant wedding planner, and to Sarah Webb for her seafaring savvy. Thanks to my agent – Charlotte Robertson – for her insight, and to Sue Leonard for her journalistic nous. Special thanks must go to those gals with whom I walk and talk the most and whom I am blessed to call my friends: Cathy Kelly, Marian Keyes, Fiona O'Brien and Hilary Reynolds.

Now here comes the really fulsome bit. There are two people in my life whom I worship, and of whom I am not worthy. These are my husband, Malcolm, and my daughter, Clara. Namaste.

Read on for
A Reader's Guide to Lissamore

A Reader's Guide to Lissamore

You wouldn't want to be in a hurry to get to Lissamore. The motorways that spew traffic out of Galway city will take you nowhere near it. These main arteries skirt the mountainous boundaries of Coolnamara, beyond which the small village nestles, leaving you to dawdle along the secondary roads that wind westward through some of the most mesmerising landscape you'll ever lay eyes on.

To the north, the mountain range rears: heather-clad in summer, in winter dusted with a layer of frosting-sugar snow; to the south, a patchwork quilt of pasture and bogland lies between you and the horizon; to the west can be caught the occasional tantalising glimmer of sea; to the east, behind you, the road leads back to industrial estates and identikit housing developments. For centuries the highway ahead led to an inhospitable domain with its own Brehon laws, ruled over by fierce clansmen and pirates. Today there is still a sense, as you travel westward, that you are entering a realm apart; a realm where the sands of time have shifted slightly, and life goes by at an easier pace. Take a deep breath of ozone rich air, feel the muscles in your shoulders start to unknot, and shift down a gear as you follow the twisting trail through Coolnamara.

As you approach Lissamore, you'll see on your left a dry stone wall bordering an estuary that broadens out into Coolnamara Bay. Beyond the sea wall the foreshore is submerged at high tide: peer over and you might spy an otter playing in the shallows with her cubs, or a heron frozen mid-arabesque, poised for a strike. At low tide cormorants perch on barnacled boulders so that the breeze may fan their outstretched wings. Further out to sea an occasional seal can be spotted snoozing on a sun-warmed rock. The bay is bejewelled with islands boasting circlets of golden beaches. On a calm day, waves lap at these beaches like kittens; in storm force gales, they stalk the shore like tigers. Most of the islands are uninhabited – although one stalwart Lissamore local has been known to take a shortcut in a currach to and from his cottage on Inishclare in all weather, even after an evening spent downing pints of Guinness in O'Toole's.

A little further on, on the outskirts of the village, a modern apartment building rears its ugly head. This is where showbiz entrepreneur Corban O'Hara once owned a penthouse: ignore it – it's the sole architectural eyesore in Lissamore, built at a time when a handful of short-sighted developers had more money than sense. Several of the luxury apartments are still for sale: you could snap one up now for half the original asking price.

In the heart of the village, the main street is flanked on one side by a terrace of pretty two-storey nineteenth century houses, washed in shades of pink and blue and primrose. They're the type of houses that epitomise the estate agents' cliché *'oozing with charm'*, and tourists frequently piss the residents off by posing on the doorsteps for photographs. Halfway along this terrace, if you look up, you will see a balcony that in summer is riotous with clashing hues of fuchsia and geranium, and dripping with purple wisteria: this is the eyrie occupied by Río Kinsella.

On the other side of the street brightly painted fishing

boats bob in the shelter of the harbour, where nets and lobster pots are stacked next to serpent-like coils of thick rope. The harbour is overlooked by O'Toole's, a bar and seafood restaurant where, in the evenings, privileged diners get to feast on the day's catch: crab claws or prawn tails, lemon sole or sea bass, or – it they're really lucky – lobster Fra Diavolo (some prefer it *au naturel* with melted butter). Upstairs, the restaurant with its big picture windows is awash with light that comes bouncing off the sea; downstairs, the bar with its smaller casements and centuries-old red brick floor, is cosier. The solid mahogany countertop wears a patina of age; framed marine charts and glass cases containing stuffed fish adorn the walls, and a fire burns in the hearth on all but the sunniest days.

Further along the main street, where the road branches left on to the quay, you will come upon a shop with a sign bearing the legend 'Fleurissima', in Art Deco font. This is the boutique that belongs to Fleur O'Farrell (née de Sainte Euverte). Drop in and have a look around: Fleur always welcomes browsers, and if you fall in love with one of the costlier items on her dress rails, she may invite you to relax with a glass of complimentary Perrier Jouet and a copy of French *Vogue* while she cocoons your purchase in tissue paper spritzed with a little lavender.

Outside, around the corner from the shop and on a level with her duplex, is Fleur's deck. It's not the most private of suntraps, but that doesn't worry the proprietress of Fleurissima. It means she can lean over the rail and have a natter with whoever happens to be passing by on the quay. Fleur's a sociable creature, and more often than not on a summer's evening you might see her entertaining friends there, holding court with baby Marguerite on her hip, fingers entwined around the stem of a champagne flute.

Back on the main street, past one or two more pubs and opposite the post office, you'll find Ryan's corner shop. Mrs Ryan caters for all tastes: her stock includes baked beans, Sunny Delight and Jammy Dodgers as well as finest Manuka honey, Chateau-bottled Chablis and virgin cold-pressed olive oil. Scented candles can be located on a shelf next to cans of fly spray; cedarwood body brushes snuggle up to floor mops, and on the book carousel, Booker prize-winners rub shoulder with Mills & Boon bodice-rippers. Over by the counter there's an array of tourist information: attractions include a famine village constructed especially for *The O'Hara Affair* – a major motion picture that was filmed in the environs some years ago. Feel free to ignore the tourist info – you'd be better off asking the barman in O'Toole's for advice on where to go and what to do. And if it's gossip you're after – you'll find more of that particular commodity in this unassuming-looking corner shop than in all the copies of *OK!* and *Hello!* ranked on the magazine shelves.

On the outskirts of the village further to the west, leafy boreens wind their way here and there, seemingly directionless. But each will lead you to a random beauty spot, the most pleasing of which is so off the beaten track that you could skinny dip or sunbathe nude, weather permitting. If you look up you'll see the once resplendent Villa Felicity, but there'll be no one there to look back at you from its shuttered windows. The only person you might happen upon is Río. If she's not swimming or soaking up rays on the old slipway, she'll be combing the shallows for mussels, or gathering barrow-loads of nutrient-rich seaweed to keep her fruit trees thriving in the winter months. Introduce yourself, and ask if you might take a photograph of her orchard to put up on your Facebook page, alongside the pictures you took earlier in Lissamore of the mountainy man leaning on the windowsill of O'Toole's nursing his pint, the donkeys that came to greet you as you passed through their field, the heron rising skyward from the shore, and the clouds settling over the mountains like a Slumberdown quilt.

Tell Río I sent you. Tell her I said hello.

For images of Lissamore and its environs, please go to www.lissamore.com.

Want to find out how it all started?

Turn the page to read an extract from Kate Thompson's first
Lissamore novel, *The Kinsella Sisters*.

Prologue
Summer 2001

'Hey, you! What do you think you're doing?'

It was a girl's voice, brittle as cut crystal. Río, daydreaming amongst sea pinks, wondered if the words were directed at her. Lazily, she turned over onto her tummy, pushed a strand of hair back from her face, and leaned her chin on her forearms. From her vantage point atop the low cliff she had a clear view of the shore, picture-postcard pretty today, with lacy wavelets fringing the sand. Below, on the old slipway that fronted Coral Cottage, a girl of around twelve years old stood, arms ramrod stiff, hands clenched into fists.

'You!' said the girl again. 'Didn't you hear me? I asked what you were doing.'

The boy squatting on the sandstone glanced up, took in the blonde curls, the belly top, the day-glo-pink pedal-pushers, the strappy sandals, then resumed his scrutiny of the rock pool that had been formed by the receding tide. 'I'm looking for crabs,' he told her.

'Smartarse. I didn't mean that. I meant – what are you doing on my land?'

'Your land, is it?' murmured the boy. 'I don't think so, Barbie-girl.'

'You may not think so, but I *know* so. That's my daddy's slipway, and you're trespassing. And don't call me Barbie-girl, farm-boy.'

Río smiled, and reached for her sunglasses. Bogtrotter versus city slicker made for the best spectator sport.

'Shut up your yapping, will you? There's a donkey up in the field beyond trying to feed her newborn. You'll put the frighteners on the pair of them.'

Río saw the girl's mouth open, then shut again. 'A donkey? You mean there's a donkey with a baby?'

'Yip.' The boy rose to his feet. 'I'll show you, if you like.'

The girl looked uncertain. 'I'm not supposed to go beyond the slipway.'

'Why's that?'

'I've got new sandals on. I might get them dirty.'

The boy shrugged. 'Take 'em off.'

'Take my shoes *off*?'

'They're not nailed to your feet, are they?'

From the field beyond came a melancholy bray.

'What's that?' asked the girl.

'That's Dorcas.'

'Dorcas is the mother donkey?'

'Yip.'

'What's her baby called?'

'She doesn't have a name yet.'

'What age is she?'

'A week.'

'A week! Cute!'

'She's cute, all right,' said the boy, moving away from the slipway.

The girl gave a covert glance over her shoulder, then reached down, unfastened her sandals and stepped down from the slipway onto the sand.

'My name's Isabella,' she said, as she caught up with him. 'What's yours?'

'Finn. Do you want some liquorice?'

'He*llo*? Don't you know the rule about not taking sweets from strangers?'

'Liquorice isn't really a sweet. It's a kind of plant. Have you clapped eyes on a donkey before?'

'Yes, of course. On the telly. What's that stuff?'

'That's spraint.'

'What's spraint?'

'Otter poo.'

'Ew!'

Finn laughed. 'Wait till you see donkey poo.'

The children's voices receded as they moved further down the beach. Río was just about to call out to Finn, to warn him to mind Isabella's feet on the cattle grid, when new voices made her turn and look to her left.

Two men were strolling along the embankment that flanked the shoreline. One sported a shooting stick, the other had a leather folder tucked under his arm. Both were muttering into mobile phones, and both wore unweathered Barbours and pristine green wellies. City boys playing at being country squires, Río decided.

The men clambered down the embankment, then meandered along the sand until they came to a standstill directly below Río's eyrie.

'Get your people to call mine,' barked one man into his Nokia, and: 'I'll get my people to call yours,' barked the other into his, and then both men snapped their phones shut and slid them into their pockets.

As Isabella and Finn disappeared round the headland, Río heard Dorcas greet them with an enthusiastic bray. One of the men looked up, then raised a hand to shade his eyes from the sun. Leaning as he was on his shooting stick, he looked like a male model from one of the naffer Sunday supplements.

'What's that bloody racket, James?' he asked.

'A donkey. You'd better get used to it,' said the man with the folder. 'Noise pollution in the country is as rampant as it is in the city, only different. You'll be waking up to the sound of sheep baaing all over the place.'

'And birdsong. Felicity's having a statue of some Indian goodess shipped in from Nepal, so she can greet the dawn every morning from her yoga pavilion.'

Yay! Río realised she was in for some top-quality eavesdropping. Yoga pavilions! Indian goddesses! What kind of half-wits were these?

'Did Felicity mention that she wants me to relocate the pavilion further up the garden,' asked the man called James, 'in order to maximise the view?'

Sunday Supplement Man swivelled round to survey the bay, then nodded. 'She's right. Imagine starting the day with that vista spread out in front of you.'

'She'll be like stout Cortez.'

'I beg your pardon?'

'Stout Cortez. Upon his peak in Darien. It's Keats, you know.'

'Oh, yes.'

Río smiled. Something about the man's demeanous told her he was bluffing, and that he didn't have a clue about stout Cortez or Keats.

'You'll be able to moor your pleasure craft there,' observed James, indicating a buoy that bobbed some fifty yards out to sea. 'That's where the previous owners used to moor their row boat, according to the agent.'

'I'll need a rigid inflatable to take me out. I assume there'll be space in the garage for an RIB as well as the Cherokee?'

390

'Of course. And space for the garden tractor too. I was mindful of all that when I drew up the dimensions. But while you're in residence you'll be able to leave your RIB on the foreshore below the gate.' James indicated the five-bar gate that opened onto the foreshore. It was the gate into the old orchard that adjoined the property, the orchard where Río had often picnicked as a child because it was a designated right of way onto the beach.

'That's commonage, yeah?'

'Strictly speaking, yes.' James opened his folder, and drew out an A6 sheet. 'But if you plant a lawn – see here, where it's marked on the plan – that stretch of foreshore could easily be incorporated into the garden.'

'Could be dodgy. People can be very territorial.'

James shrugged. 'Only someone with local knowledge will know it's an established right of way, Adair. And I don't imagine many locals go strolling here, away from the beaten track.'

I do! thought Río indignantly. *I* go strolling here! And not only that, but I go skinny-dipping here too. And picnicking. And once upon a time I even managed some alfresco lovemaking here. Try planting a lawn on that foreshore, *Adair*, and I'll tether Dorcas there and have her crap all over it!

'I don't want to make any enemies, James,' said Adair. 'It's going to look bad enough, pulling down the cottage and putting up a structure ten times its size.'

'I shouldn't worry too much about that. The cottage would be sure to have a demolition order slapped on it within the next year or so in any case – if you hadn't had the nous to snap it up first. Derelict buildings are anathema to the boys in Health and Safety.'

'And anathema to every developer worth the name.' Spreading an expansive arm that took in the foreshore, the embankment and the cottage that Río knew lay nestled in the tangle of ancient trees beyond, Adair – looking more like Sunday Supplement Man then ever – sighed with contentment and said: 'This will be our bucolic retreat, far from the maddening crowd. Our very own Withering Heights. There's a literary reference for you!'

If Río hand't felt so pissed off, she might have sniggered.

'Have you dreamed up a new name?' James asked, with alacrity. '"Coral Cottage" will be a serious misnomer once you've increased the square footage.'

'How about "Coral Castle"?' suggested Adair, with a laugh.

'That may be more accurate,' agreed James. 'But it's hardly the most diplomatic of choices, if you want to keep the locals on your side.'

'You're right. As I said, I don't want to make any enemies.'

Río bit down hard on her lip in an effort to stop herself shouting out the retort that sprang instantly to mind. But she was hungry for more insider knowledge and had no wish to alert these city gents to her presence – not just yet, anyway.

'I've done a fair amount of tweaking since we last spoke.'

'Good man, James!'

'Allow me to show you the redrafts.' James spread a sheaf of plans over a flat rock, and both men hunkered down to study the drawings. 'As I said, I've changed the aspect of the yoga pavilion. It'll mean less privacy, but by angling it a fraction more to the east it will catch the morning sun full on, and . . .'

And on. And on. And *on* the architect went. Several more minutes of prime eavesdropping went by, during which time Río learned the following: the house was to have underfloor heating. It was also to have a vast feature fireplace in the sitting room, floor-to-ceiling triple-glazed windows throughout, and state-of-the art white goods in the catering kitchen. It was to have two family bathrooms, three en suite bathrooms, a downstairs shower room, and a hot tub on the deck. It was to have an entertainment suite, a games room and a bar, as well as a home gym and a home spa and a home office so that Adair could keep in touch with his business associates in Dublin and London and New York. It was to have a guest suite with *more* en suite bathrooms, where Felicity's friends could take up residence when they came down from Dublin for house parties. It was to have a swimming pool – a swimming pool, fifty yards from the sea! – and, of course, it was to have a walk-in wardrobe-cum-dressing room in Felicity's suite, where, Río presumed, the lady of the house could stash her Ralph Lauren casuals. It was – in James's words – 'a home with a kick'.

A home with a *kick*? Whatever happened to a home with a heart? Or was home in Celtic Tiger Ireland no longer where the heart was? Was it more imperative to construct a great big kick-arse des res that announced to the world your great big kick-arse status?

'Felicity can start compiling her invitation list,' was Adair's final observation, as the two men got up to go. 'She's planning some serious parties. She's asked Louis if Boyzone might be available for the house-warming.'

Boyzone! What planet were these people living on? Río rose stiffly to her feet and followed their progress from behind the dark lenses of her sunglasses. Their voices came back to her intermittently on the breeze as they trudged along the sand. They were talking money now. They were talking millions.

'Adair?' A woman wearing a butterscotch suede shirtwaister and matching loafers was making her way with difficulty along the overgrown path that flanked Coral Cottage. Her hair was swishy and stripy with highlights, her tan looked airbrushed, and her accent was a grown-up version of Isabella's. '*Adair!*' she called again. 'Where's Izzy got to?'

'I thought she was with you?' said Adair.

'No, no! I thought she was with *you*. Where on earth *is* she?'

'Maybe she's exploring.'

'Well, I hope she's not. I told her if she set foot on the beach that she was *not* to go beyond the slipway. Izzy? *Isabella!*' The woman's eyes scanned the shoreline, and then her hands flew to her neck and clasped at the pearls that encircled it. 'Ohmigod. There are her sandals.'

'Where?'

'There, on the slipway. See? But *where is Isabella?*'

The tableau the three of them struck looked so much like something out of a Greek tragedy that Río felt like a *deus ex machina* as she stepped forward to the edge of the cliff.

In Loving Memory
of

Anthony Tony Salvin

11.8.1969 - 14.3.2011

Mass offered at

The Roman Catholic Church of St. Thomas More
Hartlepool

Thursday 17th March 2011 at 1.00 pm

Service conducted by Father H. McCann, Parish Priest
Funeral Director - Gerald Martin

HYMN

Colours of day dawn into the mind,
the sun has come up, the night is behind.
Go down in the city, into the street,
and let's give the message to the people we meet.

So light up the fire and let the flame burn,
open the door, let Jesus return.
Take seeds of his Spirit, let the fruit grow,
tell the people of Jesus, let his love show.

Open your eyes, look into the sky,
the darkness has come, the sun came to die.
The evening draws on, the sun disappears,
but Jesus is living, and his Spirit is near.

HYMN

All things bright and beautiful
all creatures great and small,
all things wise and wonderful,
the Lord God made them all.

Each little flow'r that opens,
each little bird that sings,
he made their glowing colours,
he made their tiny wings.

The purple-headed mountain,
the river running by,
the sunset and the morning,
that brightens up the sky.

He gave us eyes to see them,
and lips that we might tell
how great is God almighty,
who has made all things well.

HYMN

Morning has broken like the first morning,
blackbird has spoken like the first bird.
Praise for the singing! Praise for the morning!
Praise for them springing fresh from the Word!

Sweet the rain's new fall sunlit from heaven,
like the first dew-fall on the first grass.
Praise for the sweetness of the wet garden,
sprung in completeness where his feet pass.

Mine is the sunlight! Mine is the morning
born of the one light Eden saw play!
Praise with elation, Praise every morning,
God's re-creation of the new day!

He Is Gone

You can shed tears that he is gone
or you can smile because he has lived.

You can close your eyes and pray that he'll come back
or you can open your eyes and see all he's left.

Your heart can be empty because you can't see him
or you can be full of the love you shared.

You can turn your back on tomorrow and live yesterday
or you can be happy for tomorrow because of yesterday.

You can remember him and only that he's gone
or you can cherish his memory and let it live on.

You can cry and close your mind, be empty and turn your back
or you can do what he'd want:
smile, open your eyes, love and go on.

Dignity
CARING FUNERAL
SERVICES

Mason & Gerald Martin Funeral Directors
& Memorial Consultants
129 Park Road, Hartlepool, TS26 9HT Tel: (01429) 862 021